Exiting the Bluegrass Turnpike

RABBIT HOUSE PRESS
Versailles, KY 40383

Published in the United States by Rabbit House Press,
January 2025. Printed in the United States of America.

For inquiries about author appearances and/or volume orders contact:
Emily Wilhoit or Kristin Minter at rabbithousepress@gmail.com

ISBN: 979-8-9907833-8-6 (Paperback)

For additional information on Benjamin Rue Silliman, go to
benjaminsillimanliterary.com

Edited by: Erin Chandler
Interior and cover design: Brooke Lee

Exiting the Bluegrass Turnpike

Benjamin Rue Silliman

RABBIT
HOUSE
PRESS

rabbithousepress.com

Dedication

For Kentucky, the technicolor of my life

For Fred Mills, the "Emcee of the Kentucky Theatre"

For my loving husband, Frank, my 'forever man'

For Pop, you made me who I am, and I dearly miss you

And for my dear, sweet "mezzanine love," your love is always with me

A Warning to Readers

Exiting the Bluegrass Turnpike is written as a fiction, but part of the story is based on a horrific actual event experienced by the author when he was 17 years old, described in detail by the protagonist, Zackary Kingdon in the book. The story contains a chapter that depicts an incident involving rape by two men in June, 1981. In addition, another character explains a painful and horrifying incident where she was a victim of sexual assault by her boyfriend. And there is a chapter where the protagonist contemplates and attempts to carry out suicide. This warning is presented here at the beginning of the book to warn and protect any reader who may be triggered or negatively affected by content depicting these horrific events. There are resources provided below to assist you if you need help. You are not alone in this world and resources are available for you.

- National Sexual Assault Hotline: Call 800.656.HOPE (4673) to be routed to a local sexual assault service provider in your area.

- RAINN (Rape, Abuse or Incest National Network). Free, confidential, 24/7 help is available at 1.800-656.4673 or visit online. rainn.org to chat with a support specialist.

- The Trevor Project's confidential phone support for LGBTQIA youth is available 24/7 at 866.488.7386.

- National Domestic Violence Hotline: 1.800.787.7233 or www.thehotline.org. The hotline provides 24/7 confidential, one-on-one support to each caller, offering assistance and information about next steps. Bilingual advocates are on hand.

- National Sexual Violence Resource Center at www.nsvrc.org/survivors. NSVRC offers information, support and advocacy for survivors of sexual violence. Find resources for healing, prevention, education and awareness in your area or online.

- National Suicide Prevention Lifeline: Call 1.800.273.8255. You may also text 988, and resources are at www.988Lifeline.org, a national mental health hotline.

Chapter One

August 1981

The distant chug of the Norfolk Southern railroad moved cargo through Lexington as the humming of the central air conditioning timed out. Zackary woke from a deep sleep. It was a quiet, warm, early August morning, too early for the birds to start chirping but a car engine was running somewhere in the distance. The seventeen-year-old stayed nestled under his thin blue quilt with tiny yellow daffodil patterns on the edge. His father kept the house at a freezing fifty-five degrees at night, causing him to pull the covering up to his neck. The revving of the engine grew louder, causing Zack's eyes to crack open. As he glanced across the pitch-dark room, headlight beams appeared, rolled onto his closet door, then the ceiling, and stopped. It was three in the morning. The car sounded like it was in the driveway below his second-floor bedroom. Lights flickered as the revving became louder. A slight scent of lingering car exhaust hit his nose. Zack fully opened his eyes. His heart beat quickened. Within seconds, sweat formed on his forehead. He sat up, breathing rapidly, overwhelmed with fear.

The phone rang earlier, waking Zack up sometime after midnight. He thought it was his mother, drunk calling from California. He picked up the phone extension in his room and heard his father say, "Hello?" but there was no reply from the other end. The caller hung up. Zack put the receiver down and fell back asleep.

Now, hearing the sounds outside, consumed with fear, Zackary pulled the blanket off and slowly climbed onto the floor in his pajamas. Keeping his head down, he crawled to the large window overlooking the vast front yard and peered over the sill to make out a red sedan below with its headlights on the brightest setting. He dropped to the floor, remembering on the drive home from his job, a red sedan had been following him. *Is this the same car? Did I lock all the doors to the house? Should I call the police? Should I wake up Pop? What do they want?* By this time, Zack's pajamas were saturated with sweat. He carefully crawled back into bed and wrapped himself up in the sheets and blanket, pulling them over his head. The revving of the car was becoming louder. He began to shake, and tears rolled down his face. It was three-thirty-six in the morning.

"Why won't they fucking leave me alone?" he whispered aloud. The car engine suddenly shut off, but the beams continued to shine on Zack's bedroom ceiling. The central air came back on, and Zack tried breathing deeply under the covers as fear enveloped him even more. Suddenly, the headlights switched off, and darkness overtook the bedroom. He leaned up in bed to see if the car was still in the driveway. He could not make out the person but saw a glowing orange dot. They were smoking a cigarette. Zack lay back down in bed, shivering, he stared at the dark ceiling, tears continuing to fall down his face, heart still pounding.

"Zack, honey, wake up. Son, son. Wake up," his father shook him. Zack opened his eyes and realized he had crawled into his father's bed sometime earlier in the morning. The sunlight in his dad's bedroom reflected sharply off the canary yellow paint on the walls and he covered his eyes with his hands. "Son, what is it?" His dad asked hugging him tightly. Zack had not slept in the same bed with his father in years. When he was twelve, and his mother had moved out, her sudden abandonment made Zack sleep next to his father regularly. Looking up, he saw Pop with a concerned look, staring into his eyes.

"Papa…" Zack strained to say, continuing to hold onto his father.

"Son, what happened? Are you alright?" Zack allowed his father to hold him as he began to cry and shake. Pop put his hand on Zack's forehead to see if he had a temperature. "Honey, why are you crying?" As Zack began to calm down, Pop wiped the tears off his face, tightly pulling him in for a hug. "Are you sick? Tell me why you're crying." Zack could only look at his father in a state of shock, then fix his eyes on the plush carpet of his dad's bedroom.

"I don't know, Pop… Can we talk later about me not working at the ice cream store anymore? I need to work hard next year on my grades."

"There's got to be something else going on. We can talk about it. Now go down and make some coffee while I get cleaned up."

"Yes, sir," Zack replied, kissing his father. His father kissed him back.

Walking across the hall to his bedroom, Zack peered out his window to see if the car was still there. It was gone. *Did I dream everything?*

Chapter Two

Downstairs in the kitchen, a lime green robe over his pajamas, Zack quickly stepped outside to the driveway to pick up his father's newspaper. Walking halfway down, he noticed a cluster of cigarette butts near the street. *One of them was here. Or maybe both...* When Zack reentered the kitchen, Pop was pouring coffee, which, as usual, he lightened with milk.

"Daddy, don't sip until I take your sugar reading."

David Kingdon, a balding fifty-seven-year-old, might have been six feet two, but it did little to obscure his weight, which was over 320 pounds. He suffered from high blood pressure, had already had open-heart surgery, and required daily insulin shots, which Zackary administered. Daily, he dressed in a uniform of khaki pants, an oxford shirt, a tie, and black wingtip shoes. He and Zackary had nearly identical facial features, including their noses, thick brows, and gentle lips. However, the elder Kingdon had blue eyes, while Zackary's were dark hazel, the same color as his mother's.

Pop had diabetes, and Zack had to inject his father with insulin each day in the morning. Zack used a device to prick his father's finger to take his blood sugar reading. He placed a slim stick in a device that measured his levels. He put an alcohol-soaked gauze on his dad's finger. Zack recorded the reading in a logbook and dutifully wrote the daily date, time, and reading. "Okay, you can drink your coffee now," he told his father. Zack had pulled the medicine out of the icebox, and after removing the plastic tip covering the needle, he filled the syringe with insulin. He then tapped it to move any air bubbles to the top and shot a quick squirt. With an alcohol cotton ball, Zack rubbed a spot on his father's exposed upper right arm.

"Here we go." Zack pinched the area and inserted the needle while Pop read his *Lexington Herald*. After pulling it out, Zack took a small gauze pad and taped it to the injection spot with a Band-Aid. Getting up, he kissed his father on his head, knowing he was in a lot of daily pain. "Are you okay?" he sweetly asked while placing the syringe in a medical waste container by the icebox. Pop smiled and reached over and patted Zack on his arm.

Zack poured himself some black coffee, prepared a bowl of Life cereal with milk, and sat down. Pop put a toothpick in his mouth glancing over at Zack and moved from the paper's front page to the business section. When he quit smoking in 1977, after his open-heart surgery, he substituted his cigarette fixation with toothpicks and sugar-free Trident. He didn't have breakfast at home and usually ate on his way to work at Tommy's, a local diner where his business brethren hung out. As a result, he was often hungry—and cranky—while sitting at the kitchen table first thing in the morning.

"Goddamn Reagan, these tax cuts better work. At least he's better than that sorry-assed son-of-a-bitch Carter," Pop barked. Zack quietly ate his cereal. "So why do you want to quit the ice cream store?" Zack was timid and afraid to answer. "Goddammit, son, I don't have all morning. Sit up in your chair. What is it?"

"I've decided I need to work on my grades in school, Pop. I'm thinking I may want to try out for a play. I need to concentrate on improving my record after last spring." Zack said this all to his bowl of cereal.

"Look at your daddy when you talk to me," he said gruffly. "I wish you wanted to try out for football, but we won't get that, will we?"

Zack continued avoiding his father's gaze. "Pop, I am trying to do things to improve my transcript. I am never going to be a football player like Cameron."

"Football is how you become a man. Look at your brother; he applied himself. What happened? The Blue Devils won the state championship. But you, you never applied yourself or tried. And you were terrible at basketball years ago. You don't seem to be good at anything. I don't know what to goddamn do with you."

This was an exceptionally touchy subject, having had to spend an enormous amount of time on school. As a young child, Zack suffered from several learning challenges. He couldn't pronounce certain words in elementary school, but Pop made sure he saw a specialist in the school system. Zack's mild impediment remained, but his overall speech patterns improved. After repeating the third grade from his inability to read, Pop picked Zackary up from school three times a week and drove him to Mrs. Bailey, a specialist, who helped him with reading comprehension. While his dad did what he could, he berated him for what he perceived as his "deficits."

Zack began tearing up at the table. "Don't say that to me, Pop. I'm having a hard time right now. I've probably got a better shot at getting my grades up than becoming some football hero."

Pop shrugged, reached over, and took Zack by the wrist. Zack put his spoon down and placed his hand over his father's.

"Son, your daddy loves you. I want you to do well and be happy." He sighed and peered up at the ceiling before returning to Zack. "All right, you can quit the job. But I don't want you moping around here all day. I'll give you an allowance of twenty-five dollars a week if you do the yard work. How's that sound?"

"Thank you," Zack muttered. "I appreciate it."

Pop paused a moment before asking, "How do you feel? You seem a little pale."

"I'm okay, I guess."

Pop stared at him. "Son, you don't eat enough. You're not finishing your cereal." Zack avoided eye contact. "Try to cheer up. School's about to start." He stopped talking, repositioned his toothpick and with a deep exhale stared at Zack, "your mother's leaving did a number on you. You're crying all the time, that is not normal. I'm going to call the doctor."

Zack was too tired to argue and watched Pop labor to stand, pick up the phone, and call the family internist for an appointment. After a minute's exchange, he hung up. "Son, run upstairs and get ready. Dr. Burkhardt can see you at ten o-clock. I'll take you with me to Tommy's first." He then made a call to his office to move his appointments.

Walking upstairs, with last night's terror still clawing at him, Zack had a difficult time breathing but was comforted by his father's efforts to protect him. A few minutes later, Zack was cleaned up, and the two were out the door and off to Tommy's for breakfast. Zack managed to splash on some Eau Sauvage cologne to compete with his daddy's Old Spice. As they walked to the car, he noticed his father inspecting him.

"Those pants are slightly wrinkled at the bottom, son."

"Should I change?" Zack asked, glancing down.

"No, but it looks sloppy. Your shoes haven't been shined properly either." And once he settled his weight behind the steering wheel, he added, "That cologne smells awful," and then backed into the street.

Zack's father, a developer, contractor, and co-owner of a lighting and supply concern in Lexington, had made his first fortune on hundreds of small starter homes in south Lexington. "Son, I'm sometimes afraid you believe money grows on trees. You think you're special. You have to work hard for everything you have in life!"

Zack nodded his head in agreement, "I know."

Pop continued in his usual grumpy and determinative way, "this is how it is. I want you to observe these men at Tommy's. They all work hard to build their businesses. I rely a lot on them to do contract work for me. That's what life is all about, son: Building working relationships. So, stop walking around sulking and feeling sorry for yourself and open yourself up to some possibilities."

Zack began noticeably grimacing, and his father looked at him, realizing he was being somewhat moody.

"Don't disrespect your daddy, son."

"Yes, sir."

Tommy's was a diner off Nicholasville Road where construction workers, plumbers, drywall proprietors, and painters dined. Pop had taken Zackary to Tommy's on many Saturday mornings throughout his childhood. Once inside, Zack encountered the usual cigarette smoke filling the air and the walls covered in fake wood paneling with black 'burnt' lines separating each 'plank.' A jukebox and a pinball machine were at the far end of the restaurant. Johnny Cash cycled in and out of the speakers along with a regular supply of the Eagles, Paul McCartney and Wings, and Buddy Holly. As the two Kingdons sat at the table, the waitress brought some coffee.

"Here's a men-ya, Dave," the waitress said, smiling.

"Darling, you may give the boy some coffee," Pop instructed before ordering his usual. "Two poached eggs, cooked over easy, so they aren't like bouncing balls, sausage, wheat toast with grape jelly, and grits." He then added, "And whatever the boy's having."

The waitress took Zack's order of pancakes and a small orange juice. The pancakes, called "griddle cakes" at Tommy's, were, to his pleasure, often overcooked and slightly crunchy from being cooked in butter. "Sweetheart, you're good-lookin' just like your daddy!" she cooed sweetly, winking at Zack.

He beamed back, "thank you, ma'am."

Zack noticed how many men at the table had serious demeanors while Marlboros dangled from a few of their mouths. A few, like Pop, had heavy, dark circles under their eyes. One of Pop's associates, Bert Chandler, asked Zack how old he was and what year he was going into at Henry Clay. Zack let them know he was going to be a senior. Another one asked, "Zack, does your daddy give you a hard time a lot?" which caused a round of loud laughter.

Zack replied shyly, "no, sir, he's usually nice to me."

Then, the conversation came around to President Reagan and the recently passed tax cuts. "I read the entire Kentucky congressional delegation voted for it. Now we can write off the cost of new equipment more aggressively, which'll be a good thing."

Pop jumped in, "I like it too, but it'll do nothing to get inflation under wraps. It'll cause demand for new equipment to rise, and then the prices will rise."

Another man crushed his cigarette on a finished plate. "Dave's right. The taxes we'll save is good in the short run, but Reagan has a bear to deal with inflation and interest rates, which are killin' us."

The man to his right chimed in. "Reagan wants to do something, but I don't know if he knows what he's doing. Carter was destroyin' us all. It's too early to tell."

Mr. Chandler snickered, "you know, Carter talked like us, looked like us, but he wasn't a thing like us. I don't know if that 'movie star' will be any better, but he sounds like he might know what the hell he's doing!" Zack listened and took in all the opinions.

When their food arrived, Zack put the usual minimal syrup on his cakes, and a man sitting to his left asked him what he wanted to do with his life. The younger Kingdon was chewing his first bite and replied, "excuse me, sir," before clearing his throat and continuing, "I think I'm going to become an accountant."

The table seemed to approve. "Oh, yeah, that's a good job. You'd be workin' inside all day," someone replied. Another man nodded and suggested that Zack should get his "CPA," and then Pop announced to the men, "I have big plans for this one if he'll do what I tell him. He never played football, so he's got to do something productive with his life."

Zack wondered what football had to do with his being productive. To Dave Kingdon, a man's worth was his ability to play contact sports, a form of self-legitimacy. Zack disliked his dad's scornful manner in public.

One drywaller told Pop, "Kids don't do what their parents tell 'em, but it's part of being a kid, right, Zack?"

The boy felt he had been put on the spot, "yes, sir, but I try to mind my pop," he quietly replied, glancing over at his father.

"He's a good boy, but he's got a lot of growing up to do," Pop said, smiling at Zack before he dove into his eggs.

Eventually, the talk moved to Kentucky football, and a free-for-all ensued about the upcoming season. "Fran

Curci's got ta get this team to stand up. Dammit, they have to strengthen their defense. It was shit last season!" Instantly, the discussion became lively. God forbid anyone mentioned Bear Bryant and the upcoming University of Alabama game. Finishing his breakfast, he watched Pop slather his toast with grape jelly. Discreetly shaking his head in an attempt to get his father to avoid the extra sugar, he only got a stern glare in response.

Dave Kingdon could talk for hours with these "wise men" of business. One handed the Louisville newspaper to Zack, who opened the business section and began reading. Then, he began to feel like he was being watched. He took his eyes off the *Courier Journal*, glancing to the right. Sitting at a small table adjacent to the wall all by himself was a young man staring at him. Zack suddenly froze, quickly looking away. He then slowly peered back over. *It's him.* The guy was still staring back, waving coyly with a few fingers. Zack's heart suddenly began beating fast. He was scared to death. Suddenly, he heard a chair screech. The guy got up and walked directly toward Zack but then turned and proceeded to the front to pay. When the cashier said, "Thank you, honey," he turned around and stopped, staring back. Zack was having difficulty breathing. A crude grin crept onto the man's lips before he winked at Zack and raised one eyebrow. Then he walked out the door.

Petrified, Zack stared down at the floor. He recalled the cruelty the man had inflicted on him earlier that summer. And he was probably in the car in his driveway the night before. Trying to hold it together, Zack breathed deeply, but with all the cigarette smoke floating around him, it was difficult. It was nearing nine-thirty, and Pop told Zack to get ready for the doctor's office and said goodbye to the men at the table. Two of them shook Zack's hand as he was leaving. Once he stepped outside, Zack gasped for air. Abject fear raced through his mind. *Is he following me?* Then everything went black.

Suddenly, seeing his father's face, Zack heard, "Son! Son! He's coming around!" He realized he was lying on the ground with his father cradling his head. "Son, breathe. Are you dizzy? You fell, and I grabbed you."

A small crowd had gathered around him. "Dave, he did appear mighty pale at the table. He might be dehydrated," one man suggested. A waitress handed Zack a plastic tumbler of water, which he sipped. Pop and another man helped him slowly up to his feet. "What's going on with you, son?"

Once safely to his feet, Zack became embarrassed, noticing everyone staring at him. "Pop, I don't remember anything. I'm sorry." Zack's father helped him walk to the car and get inside.

Driving to Dr. Burkhardt's nearby office, Pop asked, "What happened, son?" Moving his toothpick back and forth, he added, "I'm getting concerned about you."

Zack feared what had happened to him earlier in the summer was overtaking his mind and his body. Once in his office, the doctor gave Zack a physical examination and asked him several questions while looking into his eyes, throat, and ears. The doctor asked what he thought was bothering him. "I don't know. I'm unsure, sir," Zack replied sheepishly. "And I don't remember fainting."

The doctor concluded Zack might have anxiety, which can be a symptom of depression brought on by the abrupt abandonment of his mother. "God damn that woman," Pop barked.

The doctor told them that perhaps Zack should see a therapist. "Hell, no. I did that with his mother, and now she's a crazy goddamned mess!"

The doctor pushed no further and prescribed a light sedative. For the remainder of the day, Zack was to avoid sun and heat, get in bed and rest. Drink lots of fluids.

Chapter Three

When Zack came home from swimming at the Lexington Country Club, he was feeling better. After showering and dressing for dinner, he heard the television turn on downstairs. It was nearing four-thirty. Given his low sugar levels, Pop had to sit down to dinner no later than five each night. Zack quickly walked down the steps in a yellow polo shirt, khaki pants, and Top-Siders with no socks.

"Those goddamn moccasins are unacceptable! Where are your socks? Go put on some dress shoes with socks. What are you, a hobo?" Pop admonished. Zack frowned and slowly started back up the stairs. "I don't have all goddamn day," Pop barked. Halfway up the staircase, Zack stopped, glared at his father, then turned and slowly stepped up one step at a time while his father was about to erupt. Toothpick wedged in his mouth flipping up and down, he added, "Hurry the hell up, goddamn it, and stop being a smart-ass!"

As large as Pop had become since his divorce finalized in 1980, he had been even heavier years earlier. Zack saw how his daddy indulged in rich food, desserts, ice cream, any kind of pie, pecan sandies (pronounced 'pee-con'), marshmallow pinwheel cookies, Brach's candies, including chocolate-covered raisins, peanuts, and sugar-covered gumdrops. He'd heard that his Pop's desire for fatty food and desserts began when he was a young boy growing up in Danville, Kentucky, during the Depression. Food was his release. Since his separation years ago from Zack's mother, Virginia, Pop fixated on food, causing his health to further decline.

A few minutes later, Zack and Pop were in the Cadillac Fleetwood on their way to dinner. It was hot outside, but the air conditioner was blasting in the car. Pop had one of his Yma Sumac mambo tapes playing.

"Where are we going?" Zack asked.

"Morrison's," was his father's reply.

Zack knew to keep conversation to a minimum when his father was hungry, holding off requests for money or permission to do something. When Zack was younger, he had learned how to be diplomatic with his father, and Rule Number One was not to not speak until Pop had finished his dinner. He thought about when he was six, he would climb into the car with his daddy, and they would drive to go pick up Sunday dinner at Kentucky Fried Chicken. It was the late sixties, and for most families, Sundays were considered the "Day of the Lord" in Lexington, but to Zack's mother, Virginia, it was the day the stove was cool. Dave would drive each Sunday to Kentucky Fried Chicken on Romney Road, where he would order a bucket of chicken with all the fixings, biscuits, mashed potatoes, and white gravy. Ever since Zack could remember, Sundays at four o'clock meant climbing up in the Cadillac with Pop and going to pick up a bucket for "din din." It was one of the few occasions on which Zack felt close to his father as a small boy and it became their Sunday ritual. Pop referred to little Zack as "daddy's little helper," as he placed the hot bucket of chicken in between his little legs to make sure it was held secure for the drive home. The bucket was often piping hot, hurting his legs, making him squirm. On one drive, Zack would imitate his father's driving by turning the round bucket, left, then right, pretending it was a steering wheel. Pop yelled, "Stop playing! Hold the chicken tight, goddammit! Don't spill the bucket!" Zack remembered becoming scared and starting to cry when his father yelled at him. Pop then gently pulled his "little helper" up next to him, reaching down and kissing the boy's head.

The two got into silly conversations on those Sunday drives. Once, Zack asked his father about the images on the side of the bucket, which suggested reasons for getting a bucket, including parties, dinner guests, and "mom's day off," as depicted by a woman with a coat, waving to her family as she was walking away. Zack asked his dad when his mommy had a day off. "Your momma doesn't want a day off, son. She is happy the way things are. And she should be." He remembered replying he would like to have a day off. Pop would get annoyed, "goddammit, son, you get a day off every day. Someday you will know how hard it is to make the money to buy you that chicken." Dave Kingdon ranted on about how "woman's lib" was ruining America. At age six, Zack listened to his father pontificate about how during the Depression his own mother had to work twelve-hour shifts as a waitress at the Townhouse in Danville after his father died and still barely kept a roof over his and his brother's heads. "Son, my momma had no choice. She worked so hard to take care of your Uncle George and me, and we also worked several jobs to help out."

Pulling into the Morrison's parking lot, Zackary Kingdon put his index fingers in his ears. He hated the sound of his father spitting each time he got out of the car. Pop rolled his eyes at the silent protest. Zack wasn't keen on dining at

Morrison's Cafeteria. The food tended to be mediocre and oily. Inside, once they were getting their meal, Pop told Zack to put more vegetables onto his tray, complaining he needed vegetables as a growing boy. Going through the cafeteria line, they loaded up, each selecting a meat entrée, then a bunch of small side dishes served in small bowls.

At the table, Pop began eating his roast beef, along with creamed spinach, corn and squash, with coconut cream pie for dessert. Zackary picked up baked chicken and mashed potatoes. The two ate quietly. Pop pointed out that his son was not eating all the meat, accusing him of wasting food. Zack had listened to his father scold him since he could remember so he took it in stride.

"Son, you need to get a green vegetable in you every day. Where's your green vegetable?"

"Sorry, sir. I'll eat one tomorrow." Zack wanted to be left alone, to eat in peace. Pop asked about the ice cream job. "I took a letter in and gave notice earlier today," he told him. "I have to take my uniform in."

"Son, I think your abruptly quitting makes you and me look bad," Pop said. "I helped get you this job, then you up and quit with no notice. That's classless, and my name is attached to it. Why, you have no idea how the world works."

Zack stared at the worn carpet below him with its outdated design of commingling bananas, pears, coconuts, and something that appeared to be a papaya. "And I suppose you are going to teach me, Pop?"

"You know, son, nobody gives a damn about what you have to say about anything," Dave Kingdon attacked his son. "You can't play sports worth a damn, your yard work is mediocre at best, you're terrible in school, and I can see why you are so bitter."

Zack stared at the half-eaten food on his plate, put

down his fork and knife, and began, "Well, I'm so sorry to disappoint you, but…"

"You do," his father interrupted, "in every way. I care for you, but you are an abysmal disappointment to this family and me. You never put your best foot forward. You are not driven to be anything." Dave usually eased up after he'd had dinner and began to enjoy dessert, but not tonight. Over coconut crème pie, he continued dropping his bombs, "I don't know what's going to become of you, but right now it's not looking good."

On the way home in the car, Zack wanted to stay quiet, but had made plans with his best friend Matt and so had to at least let him know they were going to see a movie later, the one with a comic English actor playing a rich, alcoholic man-child.

"So you are going to see a movie about a drunk?" He snapped. "Like your mother, a goddamn drunk!"

"Are you saying you don't want me to go?" Zack asked in frustration.

"Do whatever you want." Pop moved his toothpick from the left side of his mouth to the right, glaring at him. "But don't be out late."

Chapter Four

A few days later, Zack was on his way to pick up Matt and head downtown to take him to dinner for his birthday. When Matt got into the car, Zack had a Billy Joel cassette playing. Like most of their rides, the two boys turned the music up loud and sang along, holding pretend microphones in their fists. They let loose till they got to their destination. Columbia Steak House was an established Lexington watering hole and restaurant decorated with horse racing memorabilia, as many patrons were regulars at the Red Mile, a local harness racing track. The dark walls were covered with pictures of Triple Crown winners, including three recent winners from the past decade. Sitting down with menus and no parents, the boys felt like adults. But it wasn't a place just known for its environment, Columbia cooked its world-class meat in butter, making it easy to cut even without a steak knife. When the waiter came to the table, the boys ordered. Zack put on a deep voice to fool the waiter into serving them alcohol. Moments later, to their delight, a Merlot was uncorked and poured into two glasses. Zack laughingly toasted to Matt's eighteenth birthday and his "becoming a man."

Zack and Matt Adler had been close friends since the day they met in 1976 sitting next to each other in science class at Morton. Matthew was originally from Lima, Ohio, and moved to Lexington that summer. He also came from a broken home and the two spent a lot of time together when Zack's parents separated that year, building ship models, flipping through comic books, going to the movies, listening to music, and riding bicycles all over town. Matt was Zack's escape. A talented artist, Matt was also probably the brightest student in school. When Zack needed help with his homework, his friend tutored him in every subject, from geometry to diagramming sentences. The two loved each other like brothers and were extremely loyal to one another. In ninth grade, when Zack began dating his girlfriend, Amy, he always made time for Matt. He refused to be the kind of person who dropped his other friends when he started seeing a girl. However, during junior year, Matt met a senior named Colleen, who quickly became his first love. After that point, the two friends rarely saw each other and Zack felt replaced, but still relished the opportunities to spend time together.

Relaxing into the deep red booths, after their discussion of the usual subjects subsided, they both got quiet. Matt looked at him seriously. "Zack, you haven't been the same since you… you know, revealed to me that you were gay last winter and broke up with Amy."

Zack panicked a little at the subject being brought up in public, "I haven't told anyone else, even Amy. It has to stay that way."

"Okay, but you still seem so sad," Matt replied.

"I don't know, man," Zack stared into the distance for a moment before looking Matt in the eye again. "I miss her. I loved her, but it got so weird. I can't believe she was seeing that guy in Cincinnati."

A salad arrived at the table, which the two shared.

"C'mon, Zack, you broke up with her because you're gay, not because of some guy. Don't you think the breakup has been hard for her?"

Zack with a mouthful of salad, nodded his head, "I feel terrible about it. We were together for three years. I heard she wasted no time moving on."

"Okay, if you say so," Matt replied with a confused expression, and then he proceeded to talk about how he and Colleen had grown so much closer, spending nearly every day together. "After my shift at the record store ends, we have resorted to fucking in the back room," he admitted with a gleeful grin. "I even have a sleeping bag I keep in my trunk."

Zack did not look up. He became uncomfortable when Matt got into detail about what he was doing with Colleen. He sensed Matt was perturbed that he wasn't excited to hear all of his sexual encounters, particularly when Matt bragged about his self-pronounced superior skills at oral sex.

"You don't like Colleen, do you?" Matt abruptly asked.

"No, I do, she's sweet," Zack replied, caught off guard.

"Well, Colleen doesn't think you like her."

Zack stopped eating and exhaled, "I just don't know her that well. I'm rarely around her. She seems wonderful. I… I guess I miss seeing you, that's all."

Matt continued chewing his salad, but would not let up on Zack, "are you jealous of Colleen and me?"

Zack sipped his wine. "No. Of course not."

The conversation became tense as if Matt had an agenda. "You're awfully quiet, Zacky."

"What are you getting at, Matthew? I'm going through a lot right now. I just don't give it up like you do. Why are you giving me shit?"

Matt sat up straight, staring at Zack.

"Don't curse. It doesn't sound authentic coming from you."

"It's only been a few weeks since I got back from California," Zack explained, "and I'm still processing that trip… seeing my mother. I miss her. She's gone, like forever. When she left for the West Coast in March without any notice, I was devastated. You know I was. Even if I didn't see her much in the last six years, I always knew she was a few minutes away. But just leaving like that, without barely saying goodbye, really messed me up. That's when I really started screwing up with school. Amy listened to all my concerns, but she seemed distant and not too interested. That's when I found out she was secretly seeing that guy, Rick from Cincinnati."

"Zack, okay, if we're gonna pretend the gay thing had nothing to do with it, you still didn't try that hard to make things work," Matt continued. "Women need to get fucked. You didn't fuck her and give her a chance!" Zack hated Matt's degrading way of referring to women by claiming he was an expert on a woman's sexual needs. Infuriated, Zack shot back, accusing Matt of being in a "sexual apprenticeship" when his "virgin permit" had not yet expired. He pointed out Matt had under six months of sexual activity with Colleen, while acting like a Casanova.

"Zack, calm down," Matt pleaded. "You can't put all the blame on Amy. Sounds like you're getting your cake."

"Stop talking to me like that," his face was red with anger. "I don't like what you are implying. I feel bad I never told Amy about me, but I'm afraid she'll tell people. This is a very private thing."

Things got quiet. The steaks arrived, with the sound of the butter still sizzling on top, along with two huge baked potatoes. "How is your dad, by the way?" Matt asked, changing the subject.

"The usual stuff, 'You're an awful kid, you'll never amount to anything, you're so unimpressive,' but he did want me to tell you 'Happy birthday,' and dinner's on him."

"Zacky," Matt said, cutting into his filet mignon, "your father is a great man, please tell him thank you. I know he talks rough with you, but God knows you still love him."

"Pop adores you. There were so many times you saved me in school and we both appreciate that. But he considers me a failure, unlike my brother and sister. I'm a write-off, a loser to him."

Matt swallowed the first bite of his loaded potato, "you're an amazing guy. You don't believe him, do you?"

"I don't know," Zackary said. "It's hard to hear it every day. He'll even berate me when I'm giving him insulin. You know I'm so careful not to hurt him, right? But… 'You're the worst kid ever!'" Zack said, imitating his pop. "One time, I held the needle, staring at him, and said, 'You want to go there now? I can leave all these air bubbles in the syringe.'" The two boys laughed before Zack turned serious. "San Francisco visiting Mommy was awful. She was drinking and let loose about how my father was 'miserable in bed' and 'could not get it up.' I mean some really cruel stuff a son should never have to hear. She enjoyed carving him up too much. Then she would go into her bedroom with this man she called her 'husband' and scream while he was apparently getting it on with her. I was in the next room. It's all so sickening."

"Wow," Matt shook his head. "That is rough."

"Then this horrible man she married hit her in front of me," Zack said, visibly emotional.

"And threatened me. I haven't told Pop that part."

"Don't. Your dad would erupt." Matt paused and took a sip of wine, he wanted to de-escalate the situation. After the plates were carted away, the boys ordered dessert. Over a candle-less chocolate silk pie, Zack sang "Happy Birthday" under his breath, making his friend laugh. They drank coffee and engaged in some Henry Clay gossip. "Do you know Gwen Farris?" Matt asked.

"Yeah, she's lovely," Zack said. "I interviewed her for an article I wrote for the yearbook last spring."

"I heard she was in a bad car accident this summer," Matt informed his friend. "She only had a few minor injuries, but her car was totaled. It's a miracle she's alive, and I think she's been really shaken up."

"Oh God, that's horrible! She's okay?"

Matt nodded. "Yeah, but Gwen was a real bitch to me. Once she called me a 'radical' in a student council meeting."

"Well, you are," Zack laughed. "You put yourself out there like a goofball, Ralph Nader, hippie type."

"Maybe so, but I have a conscience. By the way, though, I do feel bad for Gwen."

Zack took a long sip of coffee, nodding, "I do too. Maybe I'll send her a card."

After paying the check with Pop's cash, they got into Zack's Toyota and drove to find a perch to continue drinking. Matt took the wheel since Zack felt slightly woozy. He went behind the Eastland Shopping Center and parked in a lot on a hill that overlooked New Circle Road. The landing had a view of the Continental Inn, and Lexington's very first McDonald's. The two sat in the car and drank a bottle of wine Matt purchased earlier at a liquor store. After his first cup, Matt was emboldened to bring the subject up again, "So… like I said at dinner, Colleen and I get the feeling you're jealous of us."

"I don't know what you mean," Zack replied.

Matt turned in the driver's seat, facing Zack, "Colleen knows you're gay."

There was dead silence, except for the cars driving by in the distance. "I told you not to tell anyone… even Colleen."

"She thinks you have a crush on me. I've sorta thought

so, too, for a long time. Do you?" Zack felt flush and refused to look at his friend. They sat there in silence. "Zacky, talk to me." Matt reached over, putting a hand on his arm.

Afraid to speak, Zackary began crying and covered his face, "I, um…"

Matt put his arms around Zack, hugging him tightly. "Come on… Hey, I love you. Come on," he said, not letting go.

Zack cried for several minutes before he could speak. "You… You have no idea what I have been going through. I hurt so much inside. Just leave it alone, Matthew," he mumbled through his tears.

"Look at me, Zack. Are you in love with me?"

Zack kept his head down, gently nodding.

"How long have you felt this way?"

"I don't know. I did for a while, I guess."

"Have you ever slept with a guy?" Zack stared ahead, not responding. "There's nothing to be ashamed of." Matt carefully asked, "But you're attracted to me?"

Zack turned and stared gently at his friend. "I am," he quietly replied. Zack thought of all the times the two were naked in front of each other, and the sight turned him on.

"You know, I don't see us happening. I mean, you know how I feel, Zacky, but I don't love you *that way*. . . You understand, right?" Zack again turned his eyes away, clearly uncomfortable. "But if I were into guys, I would definitely want to be with you." The car became very quiet.

"Matt, if any of this gets out at Henry Clay, dear God. You can't tell anyone else, especially Amy." His tears started up again. "I don't know what I'm going to do. My family can't find out."

"When are you going to get with a guy?"

"That's not the point," Zack replied with frustration. "And who knows?"

"I know this, you're sweet, quite cute. Any guy would be lucky to have you in their life. You're always so sad."

Chapter Five

Pop knocked on Zack's door at six-fifty-nine in the morning. "Son, time to get up. Be sure to wear a good shirt, khakis, and dress shoes. We're going to Tommy's. And after, we're getting you some dress clothes for school." Zack could smell his Old Spice through the door. He followed his father's custom of rising early, bathing, shaving, and getting properly dressed every morning, including on Sundays. This was one of Dave Kingdon's many Depression-era philosophies on how to live a successful life. He believed enough was never enough, meaning you could never work hard enough, play ball well enough, or manicure a lawn beautifully enough. Pop reminded Zack he was a perpetual deficit.

The boy did have a talent for getting out of bed and being fully ready to go, all within fifteen minutes. With a military-short haircut, it was manageable. This morning, though, it took nearly twice that amount of time. He spent an extra ten minutes masturbating in the shower thinking of Matt.

After breakfast at Tommy's, Zack and his father went to Leonard Cox & Co. on Main Street, one of Zack's favorite stores. This was the premiere haberdashery in downtown Lexington. Many students from Zack's high school bought most of their apparel there. Dave had an appointment at the store with his college friend, Horace Willis, the head sales manager, who always took care of dressing Zack and his older brother over the years. On the drive downtown from Tommy's, Pop told Zack Mr. Willis had dressed all the men of consequence in Lexington. Walking into Leonard Cox, the odor of fresh fabrics was as tantalizing as freshly baked bread emerged from the ovens at a Magee's bakery.

"Dave, how you doing?" Mr. Willis said as the Kingdons entered. He then shook Zack's hand and remarked with his smoking-rasped, Kentucky accent, "You've gotten so tall! I still remember when you were in a stroller."

"Horace, let's get this boy some outfits for his last year in high school."

Minutes later, Zack was trying on pants in a dressing room. For the past few months, he had avoided staring at his reflection from the shame he'd been harboring, but here, he glanced at himself in the mirror. Suddenly, his breathing stopped, and he felt his stomach drop. Nothing had been the same after that night back in June. Coming out of the dressing room, he saw Pop and Mr. Willis in deep conversation.

"Goddamn it, Horace, I'm not a Rockefeller," Pop said loudly.

"Davy, you're wearing wingtip shoes on a Saturday," Mr. Willis barked back. "Who ya think you're fooling?" The two men chuckled and continued to speak about various people they both knew. Mr. Willis re-measured Zack and loaded the boy up with more pants and shirts and ties to match. "Dave, you have such a nice son. Zack's almost grown up," Mr. Willis lamented as Zack stood forward, staring at the tailor's three-way mirror.

"Horace, that boy had better grow up. He drives his daddy crazy, but after his goddamn momma ran out on us, I guess I should be happy he's still in one piece."

Zack went back into the dressing room. The next pair of pants he tried on had a blend of soft worsted wool with fine stitching in the seams. Wearing a pair of thick wool pants in August in Kentucky was strange, but fall was coming, and it was time to return to school. Zack took great pride in his appearance and was already a semi-muscular kid. Since his birthday last September, he lost his baby fat and grew a full inch in height. After running two years on the track team, his legs had become well-defined. He stepped out of the dressing room, Mr. Willis examined him and said aloud, "Now that's a nice-looking young man! Up on the stand."

Pop beamed widely, muttering how he could not believe how nice Zack looked in the various pants and sports coats. While Mr. Willis made his measurements, Zack could see his father's face in the mirror, and his pride bolstered him. Putting on freshly pressed wool trousers and finely buffed oxfords gave him some confidence, but the well-chosen outfit felt like camouflage for the shame he felt inside. He flashed back to the night he had nearly been asphyxiated from the pillow covering his face. As beautiful as the clothes were and as hard as Zack tried to push down those images and feelings, he couldn't look at himself in the mirror. Seeing one of the men who had brutalized him at Tommy's had taken over his entire consciousness. He thought about what would have happened had he not been able to get air into his lungs when they were both on top of him. Then came the difficult breathing, feeling the frightening impact of that night. His father was so gentle and caring for Zack at that moment, completely unaware of the horrible things that had happened to him. *If I had died back in June*, he thought to himself, *what would have happened to Pop?* Glancing again at his father in the mirror, Zack felt like he was shrinking, and an impenetrable fear took over. Suddenly tears fell down his pale face.

Mr. Willis looked up, "Zack, are you okay, son?"

Sobbing, Zack covered his face with his hands. Pop and the man quickly helped him down, guiding him to a chair. "Son, are you all right? Why are you crying?" Zack kept his hands over his face as his father held his head. The intensity of his tears and his shivering made his father hug him tightly. Mr. Willis rushed to get Zack a cup of water, then returned.

"I'm so sorry, Daddy," Zack muttered. Wiping his tears with his father's handkerchief, Zack took the cup and began to sip from it.

"He fainted recently. Take slow, deep breaths," Pop instructed. "Breathe through your nose, son."

"Pop, I'm so sorry," Zack cried.

"Son, it's okay. Take it easy. Drink the water."

Zack realized that that horrible incident would not slip quietly away like some bad dream. He could not compartmentalize it in his mind, and the memories began manifesting in his daily life. He no longer had control over his feelings. Zack slowly got up and told his daddy and Mr. Willis he felt better. He wiped his tears and said to Mr. Willis, "I'm so embarrassed, sir. Thank you for the water."

"Oh, I'm just glad you're feeling better," Mr. Willis replied.

Zack handed the man the water cup and returned to the measurement stand. All was still. Mr. Willis completed the measurements for the pants and had Zack try on a navy sport coat, followed by a herringbone coat, tailoring them both to fit his body but with some additional room to grow. Still sniffling from the tears, Zack returned to the changing room. He could hear what the two men were saying. "Horace, the boy, has been traumatized by his mother's abandonment. I know that's what it is. He cries all the time. I fear it is a lot worse than I thought."

Emerging from the dressing room, he handed the pants to Mr. Willis, who tagged each garment for alterations. After the purchases were rung up and paid for, Dave was given alteration tickets for multiple items which needing tailoring and could be picked up in ten days. Mr. Willis then brought them the bags of shirts and ties.

"Son, you have an amazing father," Mr. Willis said. "Dave Kingdon is one of Lexington's finest. I hope you feel better. And have a great senior year at Henry Clay."

Zack shook Mr. Willis's hand, "thank you so much, sir. I appreciate all of your help today. It was a real pleasure to see you again."

Pop shook his friend's hand, "Horace, I can see why you think I'm 'Lexington's finest' after what I goddamn spent here today!" Both men laughed loudly as Zack and his dad left the store.

Walking along the brick sidewalks of downtown Lexington, heading to the parking garage, Pop put his hand on the back of Zack's head. Zack remembered how his daddy had always done that when he was a young boy. He knew his father was there for him, and he would never leave him, unlike his mother. Once in the car, he hugged his father, kissing him on the cheek.

Chapter Six

A few days later, Zack reached over and turned off the alarm at six-twenty-eight in the morning, two minutes before it was set to go off. The bright sun filled up his bedroom, but it was still unnaturally cold from the night's air conditioning. Today was the first day of Zack's senior year. Usually, he would be excited, but this time, he just felt apprehension, largely from the idea of facing everyone. It would also be the first time he'd see Amy after their breakup in early June. They hadn't spoken once since then. Zack knew he had not handled it well, not calling her after he ended things. One of his male co-workers at the ice cream store bluntly counseled Zack after the breakup, "when a guy's done with a girl, that's it, break it off and never go back to the scene of the crime." It was advice he'd found unusually cruel sounding, but that's exactly what he'd done. Today, Zack would see Amy in yearbook class during sixth period.

Zack got out of bed, showered, and put on the outfit he had set out the night before. He wore a white polo shirt over his cotton tee, navy dress pants, black belt, navy cotton socks, and black Bass Weejuns. He wanted to look good but didn't want to stand out. It was supposed to get up to ninety-eight degrees during the day, but like his father, the school kept the air conditioning near-freezing. He splashed on Eau Sauvage cologne and glanced in the mirror long enough to neatly comb his thick, light brown hair, grooming the cowlick on his forehead.

Henry Clay started at eight-thirty in the morning, and everyone had to report to homeroom on the first day. One item on Zack's agenda was to get a locker anywhere but "Green" hall, where he'd been stuck the last two years. Henry Clay had four main halls painted in bright colors, green, blue, orange, and yellow. Green Hall was legendary as being the spot for the children of old Lexington money to congregate. Many came from the Lexington School, a prominent academy, with students from coal or horse farm money or whose parents were prominent physicians or lawyers. Some of these "greenies" were quite nice, but the majority was not. "Perhaps they are just unhappy?" Zack once remarked to Matt. Zack wanted to maneuver through the day without running into people he knew and avoid Green Hall as much as he could, but he had one class in that corridor. He was feeling extremely self-conscience about people staring at him.

After homeroom, Zack maneuvered through Green Hall to his first period, running into Morris Alden, the grandson of a Louisville cigarette magnate who was actually nice. "Kingdon, you seem different, skinnier." The two had attended tennis camp at the Lexington Country Club several years ago and were still friendly, even though they had no classes together. Zack always thought Morris was cute. He was standing next to Beth Campion, the daughter of the Campion Pharmacy chain family. As Zack passed by, she glared at him, rolled her eyes, then looked away. Several others did not notice Zack or glanced at him arrogantly, then turned away. He did not come from an old money family. Suddenly, Emma Jean Rossner appeared, standing in front of Zack. *When it rains*, Zack thought.

"My God, it's Zackary, come in for a hug," she warmly said, her arms extended, and then an embrace, pressing her huge breasts into him.

"Hello, Emma Jean, how are you?" Emma Jean was a beautiful, well-kept student whose outfits were stunning. She wore a gorgeous Lilly Pulitzer bright yellow and green shirtdress.

"Zackary, it came to my attention that you and Amy are not together anymore. What happened?" she asked, staring him up and down.

"Uh, it's a long story, but, yeah, we broke up." The daughter of a wealthy Paris Pike horse family, Emma Jean had a reputation of "engaging" with a variety of Green Hall boys. Many girls resented her because she had a habit of speaking in a highly sexualized manner. Some people accused her of doing that on purpose just to give boys erections. She and Zack had sat next to each other in Algebra II last year, and he liked her. The warning bell rang.

"You call me, Zackary. I would love to go out sometime."

He waved goodbye and made his way to Mr. Pillsbury's room for "Twentieth Century Novelists." In a colloquium format, this first-period class was quite small, with about twelve students. The reading list was long for a twelve-week course, about a novel a week. The first books assigned were *The Great Gatsby* and *All the King's Men*. Zack made a note to go to Wallace's Bookstore to purchase discounted copies of Cliffs Notes for each assigned. When the bell rang, Zack exited and walked to his accounting class, keeping his head down and avoiding eye contact. Then, as he turned to walk forward, he noticed standing at the end of the hall near the stairwell was Gwen Farris with two other girls. She had a nice figure, beautiful auburn hair pulled back in a ponytail with a grosgrain ribbon, brown eyes, and a sweet, lightly tanned face. Her smile was contagious. She, too, came from the Lexington School but exuded warmth and had been especially genuine and nice to Zack last year. *She has such a lovely, calm, gentle manner, he thought.* Gwen made eye contact with Zackary and began beaming as he walked closer. The news of her accident made his heart sink. She could have easily lost her life, he thought. Zack felt so bad that she had been suffering from her experience after Matt told him the news, he followed through and wrote her a card the next day.

As he approached, Zack stopped and said hello to both of the girls, Rebecca and Anna, then turned to Gwen, reaching out his hand, which she took, and gently said, "Gwen, hello! I am so sorry about what happened to you. I've been thinking about you. You look amazing, and I'm so glad to see you. I do hope you are doing better."

"Thank you, Zack. I received your lovely card." Her eyes began to well up. "That was so sweet of you."

After releasing his hand, Zack then started up the steps and turned, saying, "See you…" with a huge smile. The two girls also had huge grins on their faces. He thought it was so nice to see Gwen. During the interview last year, he remembered how the two had laughed about so many things. Deep inside, it troubled him that she had suffered, and he felt good she seemed to be doing better, causing him to smile widely as he walked to his next class. *She's wonderful,* he thought. *I want to get to know her better.*

Zack made it to his accounting class on time. Ms. Watson walked in, closing the door. She had been his typewriting teacher for the past two years. The students' desks faced the front of the room, and Ms. Watson was behind them. She began walking to the front. During the two years of this class, Zack was the only male. Ms. Watson was kind to him, and he considered her his favorite teacher.

"Good morning, honey. How are you?" she asked Zack. The entire room turned around.

"Doing well, thank you, ma'am," Zack replied, smiling.

A few minutes later, after distributing textbooks, Ms. Watson gave a brief lecture on the reasons for properly recording accounting transactions in business. This was right up Zack's alley, he wanted to consider majoring in accounting in college.

After the bell rang, Zack moved on to third period, psychology. Walking into the classroom, he saw Gwen talking to her friend Rebecca. She looked up and waved to Zack, immediately pointing to a seat in the back row next to her. He took the seat, so Gwen sat to his left, Rebecca to Gwen's left, and to the right was Keith, a student who had been in a few of his classes but whom Zack never really knew. Gwen was laughing hard about something. She had a distinct laugh worthy of patenting, causing Zack to laugh. He turned to Keith and introduced himself. The two shook hands.

"I remember you from chemistry last year," Keith said.

"I remember you, too. Nice to officially meet."

Mr. Hendrix closed the door. He was new to Henry Clay and had a rather unkempt beard. Gwen whispered to Zack that Mr. Hendrix's eyes seemed like Igor's from *Young Frankenstein*. Zack barely contained a snort. The teacher approached the lectern and semi-dementedly looked left and right, raised his right hand high in the air, and then loudly muttered, "good morning" while surveying the classroom. Gwen and Rebecca would not stop laughing. Gwen whispered that Mr. Hendrix sounded like he was testifying out loud at a religious cult. He then took roll, calling out students' complete names exaggeratedly, only causing more laughter from everyone. When he got to Zack, he announced it like a member of the royal family was entering the room, "Zackary *Benjamin* Kingdon," emphasizing the consonants. "Here," Zack replied. Once the roll was completed, Mr. Hendrix gave a long, thorough, and highly unusual definition of psychology. His goal clearly was to educate through entertaining, and the entire class was in hysterics. Zack had not laughed that hard in years. Keith was so overwhelmed by the teacher's antics that he was gasping for air.

When things had calmed down and the bell rang, Gwen put her hand on Zack's arm and whispered, "I heard about you and Amy. I'm really sorry."

"Thanks. Yeah, it hasn't been easy." Somehow, Zack felt comfortable enough with Gwen to add, "That and other things…"

"I guess we both haven't had the best summer," she said. "Maybe we could get together and talk sometime?"

Gwen asked for Zackary's phone number. He wrote it down on a sheet of paper and handed it to her. As they moved into the crowded hallway, she turned to him, "hey, thanks for being so sweet to me earlier today, and for the card."

"Oh, sure," he smiled. "I meant it. You look great! Well, have a good day," he said, heading up the stairs to trigonometry.

Later, Zack sat in his car in the parking lot and ate his lunch. While he'd had a few pleasant encounters with fellow students that morning, he still felt extremely self-conscious. He walked through the halls with his confidence shattered, feeling like he didn't belong. That June night had taken away something from him, and he was sure others had noticed. Seeing students laughing, happy, and excited to see each other felt strange to him. For some reason, though, he felt good going up to Gwen Farris and enjoying the laughter and their talk during third period. Glancing at her, Zack could tell she was suffering, but she appeared to be making efforts to move forward. He wished he could.

Zack had finally gotten a new locker assignment, away from Green Hall. Before fifth period, he decided to go and find its location on the second level. On his way to computer science class, he ran into Matt.

"Why didn't you come to lunch?" his friend asked.

"I sat in my car. I didn't want to deal with Amy."

"She's in my calculus and physics classes and sat with the group at lunch. She's looking amazing, by the way. I am really happy she's dating Rick from Cincinnati."

With an immediate suspicious reaction, Zack replied, "Why are you so happy for Amy? She began seeing that guy behind my back."

"She has a right to move on with her life, Zack… " Matt said. Before Zack could respond, the class began, and he was glad for the interruption. Once it was over, he left quickly to avoid any more sparring.

In sixth period, yearbook production, the class was loudly socializing. Zack sat down and waved at a few of his fellow classmates. He did not see Amy. There were several new additions to the yearbook staff, mostly sophomores, Lexington School arrivals, all hardcore preppies. Then Amy walked into the room with Todd Adams, the new editor. She sat down on the other side of the room. As Zack gazed around the room, he noticed some of his classmates from last year whispering and eyeing him. He decided to open up his trig book. Mr. Pillsbury, who suffered from Tourette's, emerged from his back office cursing up and down, "Fucking cocksuckers!" While he was an especially temperamental man, Mr. Pillsbury, in Zack's estimation, was one of the best English teachers at Henry Clay.

Zack worked on his trig homework and kept his head down, avoiding eye contact with Amy. But then, a couple of minutes before the dismissal bell rang, she sat down in an adjacent chair, startling him.

"Hey, Zacky," she said.

"Oh, hi, how are you?"

"I'm doing great!" she enthusiastically replied. "Never better!"

"Well, good," he said calmly.

The two made small talk at first. Zack asked about Amy's family, then told her he quit working at the ice cream store. But the whole time he was talking, Amy barely looked at him. "So, what's going on with you?" he asked.

"Well, as you may know, I am with Rick now. We're doing great, everything's great!" Zack listened, awkwardly pressing his lips, noticing she mentioned 'great' twice. The dismissal bell rang. "Okay, take care," Amy said, quickly getting up and returning to her desk.

Zack put his belongings into his book bag and headed for his car in the parking lot. *I am so glad to get away from her, he thought.*

Chapter Seven

Groggy after a restless night, Zack woke the next morning. His brief encounter with Amy left him very unsettled. Dragging himself to school, he arrived just as the bell rang. Taking his seat in third period, Gwen smiled at him. When the bell rang at the end of class, Gwen turned and spoke to Zack. "Hey, how are you?" she asked with a huge grin as he placed his notebook in his bookbag.

"I'm doing okay."

Maintaining her lovely glow, Gwen said, "Good. It's so nice to see you."

"It's really nice to see you, Gwen," Zack looked back. "Thanks."

The two stood up and slowly moved into the hallway. "You know, I'm glad you came up to me yesterday," she said as the two stood in the hall.

Nodding, he told her he was happy to see her too. Zack confessed he had been wanting to get to know her for a while because he knew she was a nice person. She laughed, making an awkward face, "You, too. Goodness, Zack. Well, thank you. You're a nice guy. It meant a lot yesterday." She went into her purse, opened a small spiral notepad, and handed her telephone number to him and the two discussed finding a date and time to meet after school.

Zack knew Matt would be in the cafeteria or the art studio during lunch so he walked towards the studio first, hearing music blaring. Once there, he saw Matt standing and painting alone. Inside the empty art studio, flecks of paint covered the walls, but there was thick paper on the concrete floors to protect from spills. Matt reached over and turned down a large boom box blasting the Talking Heads. "I saw Amy yesterday in yearbook," Zack began.

Matt interrupted him, "I have to tell you something. I was with the gang at the lunch table yesterday in the cafeteria, and your name came up. One of the girls, I can't remember who, mentioned they thought you were gay. Amy heard this and got really upset. She asked me what I knew. I felt cornered, so I said you had those thoughts. Amy said she thought you might be, then claimed you betrayed her. I feel so bad for the girl."

"You feel bad for Amy because I'm gay? I 'betrayed her'?" Zack angrily replied, his hand over his mouth. "You all were talking about me? I asked you not to say anything. You told everyone at the table and confirmed it. Matt, they'll just tell more people."

Looking up from his paintbrush, Matt backpedaled, "Zack, I don't mean to upset you more, but people have already suspected it. You have nothing to be ashamed of. It's who you are, man."

"What do you mean they 'suspected it'? I wish I never told you," Zack looked down. "Oh my God. Amy now knows, these people know now. Why did you all do this to me?"

Matt put his paintbrush back down, walked over and

put his arm around Zack, "hey, hey, come on." Matt hugged him. "I should have told you about this. Fuck me."

"No wonder she seemed so strange when I saw her yesterday," Zack released the hug abruptly, wiped his face with his handkerchief, walked over and closely examined one of Matt's paintings. "You take such care in your work, Matt. You think of every detail in each stroke before you place the tiny brush on the canvas. You seem so willing to protect Amy's feelings, but not mine. You don't seem to be aware of those details." Zack vowed to himself never to tell Matt anything private again.

Matt muttered, "It's not a big deal. People don't care."

"Yeah, right. 'People don't care.' Are you kidding? Jesus, Matt. At best, everyone will probably stop talking to me, and at worst, I'll probably get beaten up on a regular basis. I can't believe you did this to me!"

"People will not find out," Matt picked up his brush, staring angrily at Zack. "Stop overreacting!"

Later, in yearbook class, Zack was working on his homework but could see Amy coming over out of the corner of his eye. Zack was terrified to face her.

"Hey, can we talk after class?" she said. "I need to ask you something."

Zack reluctantly nodded.

After the final bell rang, Amy suggested they speak somewhere outside. The two walked in silence out to the Blue Devils Stadium behind the parking lot and climbed up a few steps to a spot with an expansive view of the football field Zack's brother, Cameron, had played. It was a clear, sunny, warm afternoon. Once seated, Zack looked at Amy.

"So, Matt told me you're gay. When did you know?" she asked bluntly.

With hurt eyes, he shifted his gaze away, "I don't know." Tears formed in his eyes, and shame crept over his body.

"Zack, when did you know this about yourself?" Amy pressed.

"I don't know, Amy," he said trying to shrug off the question, visibly uncomfortable, staring out at the field.

"I knew something was up with you. I thought it was your mom moving away, but there was something else. I knew it," Amy determinedly said.

Zack pressed his lips, turned, and looked directly at her, "I didn't know what to say. Matt confronted me last December. He asked me if I was gay. I told him I was attracted to guys. I didn't know how to tell you. I've felt this for a long time and…"

"Yeah," she interrupted, "and you did not bother telling me. Zack, you weren't interested in me this whole time. This was in my head all summer! Last year, I lay naked in front of you. You wouldn't touch me. I knew something was up then. Just for the record, Rick and I are going steady. He does touch me and is good in bed."

Zack sat stoically, "Amy, please don't say I wasn't interested in you. I never wanted to hurt you, but this is who I am. I'm so sorry. I should have told you."

"Yeah. I bet you're sorry," She stood up, angrily picked up her canvas bag, and walked back down the stadium steps, turning to glare at Zack once before disappearing. "I'm the one who's sorry. I wish you'd told me three years ago so I wouldn't have wasted my time with you."

Devastated, Zack stared out onto the field where the football players now practiced.

Chapter Eight

David Kingdon took his toothpick and pushed it firmly between his lower teeth, putting the newspaper down. His son was in the process of giving him insulin when he said, "Son, I would like to see you finish your cereal, you've got to stay healthy. And look at me when I'm speaking. I'm in poor health. I've got a whole battalion of doctors telling me my prognosis is poor. I have to lose a hundred and twenty pounds, my diabetes is worse, I can't feel my feet sometimes, and my ulcer burst last year." Soberly, he added, "I think you know what I'm saying. I want to make sure you're taken care of if something happens. Son, face it, this is not a question of 'if' but 'when.' I know you are having a difficult time, but you have to pull yourself together and become a man. My daddy died when I was nine. It was the worst thing to ever happen to me. I come home from work early to be here for you… and I am here for you, but I want you to be prepared. You have to grow up and stop crying all the time."

Zack's was suddenly terrified, shaking with fear, his face covered in tears.

"Come on," his dad reached over and took his hand, "I didn't want to upset you, but you're always crying like a spigot about something. You're a good boy, I love you. Go wash your face and get ready for school. Do your job. Work hard in school and get the yard cut when you get home. It's going to rain tomorrow."

Zack couldn't stop crying. He took his cereal bowl, washed it in the sink, and ran down the hall to the powder room, closing the door. After washing his face and composing himself, he walked back into the kitchen. Approaching his father, he hugged him tightly and kissed him on the cheek. "Don't leave me, Pop."

In third period that day, Gwen smiled at Zack as he made his way to a desk. He smiled back. The sight of Gwen brought Zack a joyful feeling. Her beautiful face and hair, her pure goodness made him feel warm. "Good morning, hon," Gwen said.

"Hey, you look so lovely."

"Oh, thank you," Gwen smiled. "You always look so nice."

After the class settled down, Mr. Hendrix began his lecture on Abraham Maslow. As he went through the American psychologist's theory on the "hierarchy of needs," Zack found the lecture relatable. Mr. Hendrix's descriptions and examples were quite humorous, and made the students laugh. He described self-actualization as if it was the achievement of an orgasm. The class roared at that. As everyone was convulsing, Zack's thoughts were suddenly interrupted by flashback visuals of the horrible abuse he sustained back in June. He quickly stared at the floor, panicking, trying to clear his head. Gwen whispered, asking if he was okay. He nodded. After class, they walked into the hall, where Gwen gently put her hand on Zack's back. "Hey, you seemed upset earlier."

He shook his head, "Oh, it was nothing," knowing his mind and body were regurgitating the pain.

"So, Zack, wanna go to Joe Bologna's for something to eat

after school? Maybe next Friday before Labor Day weekend?"

Zack immediately accepted but asked, "Is this going to cause problems with you and your boyfriend?"

"Don't worry about Ed. He'll be at wrestling practice." She stood there smiling, "you and I have a lot to talk about. You've been the best part of returning to school. So, thank you for that."

"You, too," Zack replied jovially before heading to trigonometry. "And thanks! You have a nice weekend!"

At the end of the day, Zack had an appointment with the guidance counselor. "Sit," Mr. Evans bluntly directed Zack. His office had posters of various colleges and universities on the walls. He admonished Zack about his junior-year grades. "You're not like your brother. He could play football and baseball, was president of Key Club, took honors courses, and got straight As."

"I know, sir," Zack turned red. "I was considering applying to Indiana, Miami University of Ohio, and the University of Kentucky. Do you think I have a chance?"

"Honestly," he shook his head, "no, I don't, not to IU or Miami. UK has to take you, though. It's the law. I have your ACT scores. You scored a fifteen. What the hell? Most of my stupidest athletes score higher than a fifteen."

Zack was momentarily silent, deeply offended for himself and the athletes. "Sir, you know I have some learning challenges. I can't read fast. Those passages on the ACT are so long…"

Mr. Evans interrupted, "well, that makes my point. I greatly doubt you're college material. But I would retake the ACT." He handed Zack the test application. "So, we're done here."

Zack stood and reached out to shake Mr. Evan's hand, saying, "Thank you," but the man ignored him.

Chapter Nine

The Friday prior to Labor Day, Zack opened his locker. Sitting at the bottom of it was a note, which apparently had been shoved through the vent. It said, *Zack, Fuck you, you disgusting faggot. Fuck off if you know what's best for you, you disgusting parasite.* It was not signed and Zackary did not recognize the handwriting. He cautiously looked around to see if anyone was watching. Since Amy had confronted him about being gay, he'd noticed how students either glared at him, quickly looked away, or said "hello" rather quickly. He pushed the note deep down into his book bag.

At the end of sixth period, after the final bell rang, Zack waited for Gwen in the hall like they had planned. She appeared wearing a navy-blue Lacoste alligator shirt, a white skirt, and Tretorn sneakers, carrying her canvas L.L. Bean tote. With a huge grin on her face, she hugged him, "Ready? I am!"

During the drive to Joe Bologna's, Gwen opened up about her auto accident back in June. Coming home from her job at a florist in Chevy Chase, she was sitting at a traffic light when a drunk driver struck her at high speed. Her car was totaled, but Gwen miraculously suffered minor trauma to her neck, back, and spine and didn't have any long-term physical effects. She was really suffering, though, from severe mental stress from the accident, experiencing nightmares and anxiety. On impact, she believed she was going to die and had been too terrified to drive ever since. After Zack parked in the lot across from the restaurant, he turned to her, "I am so sorry. Thank God you are okay. That must have been horrible."

Gwen quietly responded, "I guess. I don't like to talk about it much."

Zack quickly got out of the car and walked over and opened the passenger door for her. As the two began walking to the corner of Maxwell Street, Gwen reached down, took Zack's hand, and asked, "you don't mind if I do this?"

"No, of course not," Zack replied, smiling, realizing crossing the heavy traffic intersection seemed to frighten her. Her tiny hand felt nice in his.

After entering the restaurant, the two were seated in a corner booth. Joe Bologna's was a local institution, serving Chicago-style, one-inch-thick pizza. All eras of University of Kentucky football and basketball pictures adorned the walls of the restaurant. They ordered breadsticks covered in melted garlic butter and a large mushroom and sausage pie. After Zack got his Coke and Gwen her Tab, he learned she was an only child and that her father was an ophthalmologist and her mother a part-time librarian at the University of Kentucky.

"My parents are wonderful. I'm lucky I have such a great relationship with them. I told my mom about you. She wants to meet you."

The breadsticks arrived. "Gwen," Zack began, "does Ed know you and I are becoming friends?"

She stared at him while chewing on a breadstick. "Well, Ed's a difficult situation." She wiped her fingers with a napkin. "Where do I begin? We've been dating for over a year. He's not good with my parents. To be honest, he's not good with me."

"How so?"

"Well, he's sort of a mean guy. Do you know him?"

Zack nodded his head, finishing his first breadstick, "I do. He and I went to school since first grade at Cassidy. What do you mean he's a 'mean guy'? He hasn't hurt you, has he?"

There was a long pause as Gwen stared down at the plastic red-and-white picnic table covering. "This has to stay between us," she said. "Rebecca knows, though. Ed's giving me a lot of grief because I won't have sex with him. I'm not ready. It makes him so angry."

"That's terrible he's pressuring you," Zack said, feeling a blush of anger. "May I ask, if you… I mean, have you ever… um, maybe this is too personal a question?"

She laughed, "I am fine with answering. You are such a gentleman, by the way. No, I have not. I may be one of the few girls at Henry Clay who is a senior and a virgin, but I'm just not ready. And I'm not ashamed to say it. More specifically, I will not lose my virginity to Ed Sims. He's not the right guy."

"I totally understand. Um, you know, I am a virgin, too."

"No way!" Gwen's jaw suddenly dropped. "You were with Amy. Really, you guys never?"

Zack shook his head, "we didn't. But since we are keeping things confidential, Amy and I got naked together once, but that's it."

Gwen immediately asked the waiter for refills, then turned her attention back to the table, "Zackary Kingdon, I learned something new about you. Can I ask you a delicate question?" He agreed to answer whatever she asked. "I am going to be honest with you. I think you are so cute. I mean, you are a good-looking guy. A lot of girls think so. You could date any girl…"

"Oh, now that is simply not true," Zack interrupted, blushing. "Gwen, thank you. You are really sweet. And I think you are a beautiful girl. And I am not just saying all this, we're friends."

Gwen began laughing as she turned red, "Zack, Amy's a beautiful girl. I know it's sensitive, but can you tell me what happened?"

Zack explained, "She and I were drifting. It's difficult to describe." Squirming a little, he told her how Amy began dating another guy behind his back.

"Did Amy not want sex?" Gwen gently asked. "Or did you not want to? Maybe we shouldn't go there?"

Zack paused, then answered, "I didn't want to. I didn't want to have sex with her."

"I didn't mean to upset you."

"It's okay," Tears quickly formed in his eyes.

"Let's talk about something else," she said quickly. "I think I did upset you. I'm so sorry."

Zack began having a difficult time breathing, his lips were quivered, "I loved her, but Gwen, I'm gay."

Gwen looked shocked as tears began falling from Zack's eyes. She immediately jumped up and came around to the other side of the booth and sat next to Zack, wrapping her arms around him.

"It's all right, Zack," she comforted him. "Honey, I understand. Come here, it's all right, thank you for telling me. I didn't know."

Zack hugged her back and managed through tears, "it's so awful. She hates me now. And she's told people. I got this awful note in my locker today."

"I'm so sorry, Zackary," Gwen said, in tears herself now.

"You are such a good person. Listen, I want you to know you have someone who cares about you. I am your friend." She held him tight as the waiter brought over napkins.

"I'm so scared people will find out but thank you for being so sweet," he said finally, quietly. "I've been crying a lot lately. I just lose it."

"My friend," she smiled, "you can cry all you want. On the first day of school, when you came up to me, you were so warm and made me feel so appreciated. You didn't have to do that, but you did. My gosh, where have you been all my life?"

Wiping his eyes and blowing his nose, Zack asked, "So you don't hate me because I am gay?"

She took his hands and squeezed, "I think you're wonderful. I am so happy you told me. You seem so tormented. It's our secret, Zackary. You know, I would never hurt you, ever. You are a sweet guy. I can't imagine going through what you are going through, but I am here for you."

Zack smiled ear to ear. A few moments later, the two were sipping their sodas through straws, smiling, laughing, and holding hands. Gwen placed her head on Zack's shoulder, wrapping her arms around him once again.

Chapter Ten

Labor Day came and went. At his locker before first period, Zackary Kingdon glanced over and noticed Joe, a classmate he'd known since third grade, staring at him. He was in Boy Scouts with Zack ten years earlier, a fun kid. Now he stared at Zack and then back at his locker. Zack shut his locker and approached Joe, greeting him warmly with an extended hand. He looked at Zack flatly, refusing to shake his hand.

"How've you been?" Zack asked.

Joe slammed his locker and said, "Kingdon, I would appreciate it if you wouldn't talk to me."

"Why? What's wrong?"

Joe shook his head, "I heard you fuck guys. You make me fucking sick, man. So no longer interact or talk to me. I'm not a faggot. Do you understand?"

Zack stood stunned, unable to respond. Joe turned and walked away. Frantically searching his mind, Zack thought, *Oh my God, people do know.* He felt sucker punched and his forehead began to perspire walking to Novelists class. Sitting down, Zack was completely terrified that other students would find out he was gay.

This deep secret had the risk of traveling like wildfire through school. Zack tried to pull himself together, but suddenly felt sick to his stomach.

After accounting class, he cut across the main foyer past the school's theater on his way to Psychology. He saw a flyer posted, *Try outs for "You're a Good Man, Charlie Brown," a musical. Monday, September 28 at 3:30 PM in Lassiter Theatre.* He took one of the flyers. Being cast in a play could be a healthy distraction, he thought. In that moment, Zack decided to step up and audition. He made his way down the steps by Mr. Hendrix's classroom and saw Rebecca in the corner hugging Gwen, who was crying. Rebecca peered over at him and shook her head, signaling for him to keep walking. His heart sank. Zack walked into the classroom and sat next to Keith. Rebecca followed and whispered something to Mr. Hendrix, who nodded and then exited. Zack became concerned. The bell rang and Gwen and Rebecca still had not arrived. About fifteen minutes later, the two girls entered the room, quietly taking their seats. He turned to Gwen, who quickly glanced at him, appearing distressed. It bothered him to see Gwen hurting.

Zack tried to give Gwen her privacy by staring ahead and focusing on the lecture. A few minutes later, he noticed she was staring down, covering her face and crying. Zack quickly reached into his right pocket and handed Gwen a fresh handkerchief. Pop taught Zack to have two handkerchiefs at all times, "One for yourself, and one to offer someone else in need." Gwen took it and began to wipe her eyes with her left hand. He reached over and gently touched her right hand. Appearing surprised, Gwen uncovered her face to turn and look at him. He took her hand, pulling it slowly below the desk to hold it, whispering, "It'll be okay. I've got you."

Gwen glanced back and nodded, muttering, "Thank you." His heart racing, Zack wanted his friend to know he was there for her. He clasped his fingers between hers, holding it securely. He could feel her start to relax and she mustered up a gentle smile. He smiled back. The two held hands for the remainder of class.

When the bell rang and the class was jumping up, Gwen and Zack were still in the same seated position with their fingers interlocked, "Are you okay?"

"I'm so much better now," she said. "Thank you."

The two finally released hands. Rebecca and Keith jumped in and the four made small talk. Gwen gave Zack back his handkerchief. Walking into the hall, Rebecca made sure Gwen was fine before she and Keith headed to their next class. Gwen and Zack remained together, facing each other.

"Thank you," she squeezed his shoulder. "That was so kind of you. It made me feel much better."

Zack handed the handkerchief with his initials, ZBK, back to her, "here, just in case."

"Thank you," she replied.

While he was taught to ask a woman if she needed a handkerchief or if she needed any assistance, Pop instructed Zackary that a gentleman never asks a woman the cause of her tears. She would reveal the reason if she wished. "Gwen, are you going to be all right? Do you want me to walk you wherever you are going?"

"No, but that is so nice of you," she tilted her head. "It was great spending time with you at Joe Bologna's."

"You mean the Joe Bologna's Summit?" he replied.

She laughed. "Oh, it was a 'summit,' all right!"

Zack showed Gwen the audition flyer for the school musical, telling her he might audition. She nodded enthusiastically, "I think it's wonderful! I'll come with you to the audition if you want." Gwen unexpectedly leaned over and kissed Zack on the cheek. "You are an amazing guy. Thank you for making me feel better!"

"Listen, call me if you need to talk or anything," he said. "Have a good rest of your day."

"I will now," Gwen said walking down the hall before turning back with a wave. "Thanks to you."

Chapter Eleven

In late September, Zack had already taken a few exams, submitted a paper in Novelists, and was performing well academically, including trig. He and Gwen had spent more time out of the public eye, enjoying their moments together and speaking on the telephone often. However, daily life at Henry Clay had become more difficult for Zack. Three more notes maligning him were shoved into his locker. One said how sick it was for a guy to "suck cock" and to "get fucked up the ass," while another note made a direct threat, "Watch your back, faggot!" The hateful words were starting to lodge deep inside his psyche, and he felt anxious each time he opened his locker, feeling he was being watched.

Walking the halls, Zack noticed people whispering and glaring, particularly boys, while some students he knew turned away. It was all too clear he wasn't paranoid, so he kept his head down, avoiding crowded areas of the hall. It was exceptionally lonely. The feeling he did not belong grew even stronger. Seeing Gwen was the good part of each day.

Trying to stay positive, Zack preoccupied himself with thoughts about upcoming auditions for the school musical and pondered singing, "New York, New York." He drove to

Don Wilson Music and bought the sheet music. He sung it some years ago when he'd been in chorus in junior high. Between choral training and lung-strengthening years of running track, Zack was able to push out and hold a note. At the forefront of his mind, though, was the upcoming weekend. It was his birthday, but Gwen already had a date, as did Matt, and Pop was going to a UK football game with Pat Daniels, his new "woman of interest." She was a psychiatric nurse at the mental institution where Zack's mother had been hospitalized years earlier. It was going to be his first birthday all by himself. Zack planned on doing some yard work and then working on his audition piece in the basement. He was actually looking forward to the solitude.

Gwen had given Zack a card with a picture of Clark Gable on the front. Inside, she had written, *Dear Zackary, I know this is not a traditional birthday card, but it is one of my favorites. Now I want to give it to you. In the month I have gotten to know you, I don't feel the same about anything. I look forward to seeing you at school every day. Thank you for being so kind to me. I want you to have a happy birthday. We will find time to go out and celebrate soon! Always your friend, Gwyneth.*

Later at home, Pop wasn't back yet so Zack went to the basement and listened to his audition piece on the stereo. He tried to talk through the song a few times. Some of the lyrics, like "vagabond shoes," needed sharpening, as Zack realized it was not a shoe brand. He spent a few minutes warming up his voice. After another glance over the lyrics, Zack started singing. When he got to the line "these little town blues are melting away," which Minnelli and Sinatra both belted, Zack felt he practically nailed the delivery, loud, clear, and impactful. At the end, he could hold the 'York' in "New York" for nearly ten seconds. *This is the song,*

Zack thought, knowing he had to prepare. Still no sign of Pop. The phone suddenly rang, Zack picked up the basement extension.

"Hello?"

A male caller asked, "Is this Zack Kingdon?"

"Yes, this is he," Zack responded.

"What is it like choking on a dick, fucking faggot? You make me want to fucking puke, faggot!" The caller hung up. Zack slowly and gently placed the phone back on the receiver. Standing in place, he was literally stunned.

The sound of his father's Cadillac pulling into the driveway startled him. A few minutes later, Pop sat in the drawing room watching the news. Zack walked in and hugged and kissed his father.

Hugging Zack back, he asked, "How's my boy?"

"I'm good. Pop, I am going to audition for a part in the fall play."

"Well, that's a perfect waste of time, Son."

"I remember you saying last month you were fine with me being in a play?"

"What are you getting out of doing this nonsense?" Pop's toothpick began moving. "Not a goddamn thing!"

Zack became angry and sharply began, "Well, you ought to know—"

"Watch that goddamned mouth now! The disrespect you show your daddy!"

Zack sat angrily with his arms crossed, "I'm not saying anything else."

"Well, we're all grateful for that. You never have anything interesting to say anyway. All you do is walk around here complaining you're not-happy-with this, not-happy-with that!" Pop repositioned his toothpick.

Zack realized it was after five o'clock, and his father wasn't at the dinner table. *No wonder he was extra mean*, he thought.

"Take the scowl off your face and go up and wash up and change for dinner. We're going to the Cape Cod."

On the drive to Chevy Chase, Pop played Henry Mancini's, "Days of Wine and Roses" tape. As was often the case, he was driving with one index finger, usually his right, so he could move his toothpick around with his left finger.

"Son, you continue to amaze me how you can't do anything right. I asked you to trim the hedges, they aren't flat and equidistant. Oh, no, you cut a sort of incline. It looks goddamned awful! You know, what's worth doing is worth doing right."

"Pop, you seem to think so little of me," Zack muttered.

"Son, I remember when you were a Cub Scout, I had to put tacks into the bottom of the wooden toy car in the Pinewood Derby race back when you were about eight years old. These tacks helped weigh down the car, making it go faster. You won because your daddy showed you how to win. Well, you're a slow learner. I had to get you Mrs. Bailey, that reading specialist. You couldn't pronounce anything worth a damn, so I sent you to the speech pathologist. Your goddamn momma was never around. Your brother and sister are doing well in life, but you? You're a real winner! We all have our fingers crossed. I wouldn't put money on your 'Derby horse.'"

Zack kept staring out the window, trying to cast his thoughts away from listening to his father's litany of disappointments. At the restaurant, Pop ordered a salad, fried clams, fried Boston scrod, lots of hush puppies, extra tartar sauce, and a baked potato with butter and sour cream. Zack ordered a salad, with olive oil on the side, baked fish, no butter on it, with a baked potato, the butter on the side. Pop got annoyed at all Zack's "on the side" requests.

"The boy eats his food plain," Pop said to the waitress, laughing. "He doesn't know how to live life, I tell you." She turned to another table.

"Why do you give me such a hard time?"

"Oh, son, you act like such a baby. You are thin-skinned, lazy, and quite unimpressive, in my view. You should be grateful to your daddy for pointing all of this out!"

Zack's birthday was the next day, and Pop seemed to passively pursue détente by asking what he would be doing to celebrate.

"No plans. I have yard work and some homework, then I have to prepare for my audition on Monday." The salads arrived.

"Son, that's pathetic! It's your eighteenth birthday. Why are you not going out with your friends? I told you I have a football game tomorrow, dinner afterward at the Campbell House with Pat Daniels, the woman I introduced you to."

"So you're going out with that woman who downed fifteen beers at dinner?"

"You watch your goddamned mouth, Pat's a nice lady, quite refined. She likes to have a few beers after a long day's work, so lay off her."

Zack knew he caught his father's weak spot, "Oh, does she? Did I hear you say 'refined' or did you mean 'pickled'?"

"Stop it, son, that is no way to speak of a lady."

"You introduced her to me, and she burped."

"Goddamn it, have some respect. Your mother is the true drunk."

"Pop, Mommy has problems. Pat Daniels has an agenda, to marry you and get your money."

"Son, did it ever occur to you that your daddy is a nice-looking man?"

"Then why are you with her? She looks like one of the women in the drunk-driving tank at the county jail who..."

"That is enough! I mean it. Eat, and no more talking!" Pop had steam coming out of his ears.

Chapter Twelve

Waking up to the sweet smell of smell of bacon and eggs, Zack put on his robe and went downstairs to the kitchen. It was only six-fifteen in the morning and Pop had made a full breakfast, including pancakes. "Happy birthday, son!" Barely awake, he hugged his father who was hovering over the stove. "Sit down and get your cakes," Pop ordered. After first gauging his father's blood and injecting his insulin, the two sat and enjoyed breakfast. Before they finished, his father handed him a card. *To Zackary Benjamin, my last son. Happy birthday. Love, Pop.* The sentiment touched Zack and he was grateful for the hefty sum of cash inside. His father could be mean, but could also be generous.

Zack was cutting the grass later in the afternoon when he saw his father getting in the car about to head out. He stopped the mower and walked over to the Cadillac. "Pop, do you have your inhaler? It's getting hot. Do you have your nitroglycerin pills?" His father nodded. Zack reached in and kissed his father, "Okay, I love you."

"Son, please go do something fun."

"As soon as I get done, I'm going running. I'll be fine. Have a nice time," Zack said, smiling and waving. As his father pulled out of the driveway, Zack stared at the perfectly blue, cloudless fall sky and continued to mow the yard. He enjoyed the beautiful flowers he had planted, but many were already dying from the late summer heat. He thought about the large six-bedroom house he grew up in on Lakewood, which his father designed and built. Upon a recommendation to start a hobby by his cardiologist in order to relax, Pop began growing flowers, which became his passion. He installed a greenhouse in the basement where he cultivated orchids and African violets. When Virginia convinced him to move to their smaller Lakeshore home in 1976, Pop had to give up his treasured greenhouse, all in compromise for his wife. Six weeks after they moved into the new residence, Virginia Kingdon moved out.

A nice yard meant the world to Zack's father, even at the Lakeshore residence. It was his statement to the neighborhood, presenting lush, beautifully maintained flora for each season as if he had entered a year-round "Southern Living" contest. Pop delegated all the yard duties due to his ailing back and knees, his weakening heart, and his inability to handle the intense summer heat. Whenever Zack planted seeds or live flowers Pop picked up at Hillenmeyer Nursery, his father would sit in a lawn chair and yell at him while he worked. While the yard made his daddy feel good, the work was a way for Zackary to constantly keep busy and prevent thinking.

Later, after he had gone for a long run, Gwen phoned Zack as he was drying off from a shower and wished him a happy birthday. The two were spending the next day together. "Gwen, I want to introduce you to some of my special friends tomorrow. I certainly want them to meet you."

"Oh my gosh, who are these 'friends'?" She asked curiously. "Do I know them from school?"

"Oh, no," Zack said, giggling. "You haven't met them, but special people get to meet my special friends, you'll see."

Around nine in the evening, after rehearsing his audition piece in the basement, Zack went up to his bedroom and began searching for something on his desk. He suddenly noticed a car pulling into the driveway. Immediately frightened, he ran downstairs to lock the kitchen door. *Is it them?* Zack believed it might be the two men who hurt him. Terrified, he turned off the lights in the kitchen and hallway and scurried into the drawing room, which was pitch dark. His heart pounding. Zack peeped around and saw it was Matt at the kitchen door.

Beyond relieved, he turned the lights back on, opened the door and heard, "Happy birthday, Zacky! What's with the locked-up house?" Zack embraced Matt with a warm hug.

"You're a man today, Zacky!" Matt continued, not letting go of his friend. "Let's go to Max & Erma's. I want to take you out for some dessert for your birthday!"

Zack could tell Matt had been drinking. "Hey, are you okay, Matt?"

He finally released Zack from the hug and the smell of alcohol was more apparent. "Colleen's in the car. She's driving. We want to do this for you."

Zack was about to climb into bed and wasn't in the mood to go out, he wanted the day to end but acquiesced. He was wearing sweatpants, so quickly ran upstairs and made himself presentable. *It would have been nice if they had invited me out earlier.*

Walking to the car, Zack got in the back seat. Colleen leaned over from the front and kissed him, "Happy birthday, Zack!" She was one of the most beautiful young women ever. She graduated from Henry Clay last spring and was at Transylvania University majoring in theater arts. At the stoplights on the way to the restaurant, Matt engaged in deep kissing with Colleen, he liked showing off in front of Zack that he had a girlfriend. Zack was well aware Matt knew it turned him on. He wished Matt was kissing him.

Once inside the establishment, loud with rock music and a football game on the television, Zack noticed Matt did not stop at the host area to be seated but kept walking. Matt suddenly put his hands over Zack's eyes.

"Whoa, what are you doing, man?" Zack asked.

"Hold Colleen's hand, she'll guide you."

Colleen and Matt led Zack through the restaurant and then suddenly stopped. He heard laughter. Matt pulled his hands away from Zack's eyes.

"SURPRISE!!"

Zack had to do a double take, feeling slightly disoriented. He was suddenly standing in front of a large table of people. Initially, he had a big involuntary grin on his face from the surprise, but when he looked at the table, his smile quickly dissipated. It was full of Matt's friends, who, as far as he knew, all hated him. He knew they thought of him as part of an elite crowd. They were the same group of gossipy girls whom Zack suspected were telling students he was gay. Sitting down, to his right was Amy, speaking to the person beside her and ignoring him. *What is going on?* The confusion going through his mind was overwhelming.

"How does it feel to be eighteen?" someone yelled. Zack couldn't tell who asked. He faked a grin and began sweating. To make things worse, it was clear the entire table had been drinking for a while. The restaurant had old-fashioned dial telephones at each table, and the one at theirs began ringing after the group yelled "surprise" and hadn't stopped. Zack surveyed the members around the table, no one was looking or speaking to him. A few appetizers were sitting in the middle of the table, but empty, dirty plates were evidence they had finished dinner. Multiple mugs of beer completed the tablescape. Amy did not once make eye contact with him. Inside he was panicking, knowing the people around the table despised him, and he overheard one girl tell Amy she had wasted her time being with such an "idiot" for three years. Zack began feeling more nervous and felt he was unraveling. *Why did Matt bring me here?*

Amy turned and glanced at him, "Zack, what's wrong? You don't look well."

"I'm fine, I wasn't expecting this."

Matt came behind Zack while a cake with eighteen candles was placed in front of him. "See, Zacky, these people care about you." The table began singing "Happy Birthday," but Zack, not smiling and staring at his lap, felt like he was about to faint. He was trying so hard not to cry, but then tears erupted.

"What the fuck, man!" Matt yelled. "Why are you crying?"

Zack put his face in his hands and was sobbing and shaking.

"Guys, he's having a hard time," Colleen yelled across the table.

"Let's get him out of here."

Zack felt Matt's hand helping him up, "come on, I got you." Colleen helped Zack out of the restaurant while Matt pulled up the car. Colleen hugged Zack tightly, "Oh my God, what has happened to you, Zack? Honey, we love you. I had a feeling this wasn't a good idea." As Matt's Mazda pulled up, they helped Zack into the car. Sitting between the two, he continued wailing. Colleen held him.

"What is your problem, man?" Matt said in angry frustration. "We tried to do something nice for you. FUCK!"

Colleen gently tried to calm Matt down, "Hey, honey, he's hurting. He's in pain. This was not a good idea."

After parking in the driveway of his house, Zack slowly

got out of the car. The two assisted him through the kitchen door. Colleen hugged Zack, who would not stop crying. "I am so sorry," he muttered. Matt helped Zack up the stairs to his bedroom, sat him on the edge of the bed, took off his sneakers, and helped remove his shirt and undershirt, then his pants.

"Zack, what the fuck, man. I cannot believe you did this." Matt pulled back the sheets and blankets, letting his friend climb into bed. Matt grabbed Zack and hugged him tightly. "Come here, what's wrong? I've never seen you like this."

"I'm sorry, Matt," Zack said through tears. He could tell Matt was furious with but still bent over and hugged him again. Matt headed back downstairs and out the front door. Zack fell into a troubled sleep.

Chapter Thirteen

It was nearing seven-thirty when Zack opened his eyes. He could smell coffee brewing downstairs. He felt stiff as he sat up, realizing his body had reacted with deep pain the night before. Lying back down, he thought about what happened, feeling humiliated. *Why did Matt do this to me?* But maybe even more than that, he was scared of how out of control he'd been. After rousing himself, Zack walked into the kitchen and saw Pop reading the *Courier Journal* at the table. He quietly came up behind and hugged and kissed him.

"How's my boy?" Pop asked.

Zack had visions of when he was about five years old in the Lakewood house. He would wake up early on Sundays and make his way downstairs in his pajamas. The smell of coffee let him know his daddy was awake before he saw him. It was so quiet. After tiptoeing up to the closed double doors that led into the breakfast room and kitchen, Zack would gently push open one door. His father would be sitting at the head of the table, with his back to Zack, reading the newspaper. "Do I hear a little squirrel behind me?" Pop gently said. Zack remembered slowly walking up beside his father, who reached down with his large hand and rubbed Zack's hair. Pop then would pick up his giggling son and put him on his lap. Zack would kiss his daddy, then wrap his arms around his father and place his head on his shoulder as Pop engulfed in him a warm embrace. "How's my boy?" he would ask. "I'm good, Daddy," he'd reply quietly.

"So, how did you end up spending your birthday?" Pop asked.

"I went for a long run, got some takeout, and prepared for my audition," Zack said, pouring himself some coffee, not mentioning the faux "surprise" party. The kitchen door was open, and the cool fall air made its way inside through the screen door.

"Your momma never called to wish her youngest 'happy birthday.' No card, though?"

Zack gently nodded, replying, "Nothing."

Pop turned the page on the paper, "she's a goddamned sorry-assed son of a bitch!"

Later in the morning, Zack drove over to Gwen's home on Adair Road in one of the wealthiest enclaves in Lexington. The homes there were beautiful and regal, Tudor-style dwellings, similar to ones in Beverly Hills or Lake Forest. Gwen's home was especially grand with its manicured bushes and weeping willow tree in the expansive front yard. Right at noon, he rang the doorbell. Zack Kingdon wore a crisply ironed blue oxford dress shirt with grey flannel slacks and black penny loafers. The door opened and it was Gwen's mother.

"Zackary? Welcome," she had Gwen's sweet face, eyes, and lips. "Come in. I'm Jenny Farris. We are so pleased to meet you. Gwen has spoken so fondly about you."

"Oh, thank you, ma'am. The pleasure is mine."

Mrs. Farris invited Zack into the living room, "Gwen will be down shortly. Do you go by Zackary or Zack?"

"Oh, Zack is fine, ma'am. Thank you."

She laughed, "you don't have to call me 'ma'am,' but it's sweet. Can I offer you something to drink?"

"I'm fine, thank you." He examined the massive bookshelf that went from the floor to the ceiling in the living room, fully stocked with hundreds of books. Upon a quick eyeing of the selections directly across from the couch he was sitting, he could see Walt Whitman's *Leaves of Grass*, which was also on his father's bookshelf, and *In Cold Blood*, the Capote title he was starting to read for Mr. Pillsbury's class. Zack heard footsteps on the marble in the entrance hall as the two were talking. It was Gwen. As she entered the room, Zackary stood up.

"Oh, you don't have to stand for me," she said while Mrs. Farris smiled brightly. "You are so sweet, isn't he, Mother?" Gwen wore a stylish khaki shirtdress, a navy canvas belt, and navy espadrilles, most likely Pappagallo. Gwen's hair was pulled back and wrapped up with a thick ribbon, highlighting her gorgeous face. "Mom, Zack is trying out for a play at school tomorrow," Gwen offered.

"That's wonderful. What is the play?" she asked.

"*You're a Good Man, Charlie Brown*. It's a musical."

"How fun. Gwen's father could not be here today, but we would like to have you over for dinner, and we would like to come see you in the play."

"Oh, thank you. If I get cast. I may not make the cut," Zack replied, but Gwen cut him off…

"You'll get cast. He's been practicing for the audition."

Minutes later, Zack and Gwen were in the Toyota driving to Frisch's Big Boy for lunch.

"You have a sweet mother."

"Oh my God," Gwen beamed. "She adored you. I could tell."

Once at the restaurant, when their orders were taken,

Zack told Gwen about his disastrous night at Max & Erma's. "Matt must have thought he was being kind to me, and I lost it."

She listened thoughtfully and asked, "why is Matt such good friends with these girls?"

"I don't know, and it bothers me. None of them are nice. I've known some of them since seventh grade. Over the years, they became more antisocial. They think I'm stupid, calling me 'elitist' because of how I dress. Matt thinks they're so cool. They all smoke pot and do other drugs, ludes, I suppose. I mean, I do know for sure that they despise me."

Gwen shook her head, "they seem to hate everyone. A group of them caused a major disruption to a student government meeting."

The hamburgers arrived and Zack's burger was plain, with lettuce and tomato on the side. He ate the vegetables separately, not liking to mix food. The real treat at Big Boy was the crinkled fries. The two began eating their lunch, but Gwen put her burger down and stared at Zack, "I feel terrible this happened to you, and on your birthday. Just know that I am your friend, always."

Zack reached over and briefly squeezed Gwen's hand, "thank you."

When they finished lunch and walked to the car, Gwen told Zack that she had gone out with Ed and his friends the night before. "He can be sweet, but his wrestling friends are rough. I mean, some of these guys could crush you if they get you in a headlock." She looked down. "They glare at me because I don't 'put out' for Ed. He gets rough and impatient when we're alone in his car. He told me he wanted to put his fingers inside me."

Zack reached over and touched her arm, "hey, you tell him you don't want to, right?"

"I do. I've told him 'No' so many times, and then he screams at me. I do not feel it with him, and he is so aggressive. He knows it too."

"Don't do anything you don't want. That's his problem. I'm worried he might force you to do something you don't want. He's definitely not respecting you or your feelings. I wouldn't want anyone to harm you."

"Zack, you're so much better looking than Ed."

"Where did that come from?" Zack was surprised by her compliment, but he didn't mind. "I don't like hearing he does this to you. You don't deserve to be treated badly by anyone, ever!"

"Wow, you really do care about me?"

"I do. You're an amazing friend."

Zack opened the passenger door for Gwen. Getting in, she asked, "you must be curious about what it's like to be with a guy?"

He walked around and got behind the wheel. "Well, like you, I guess when I'm ready… and I meet the right person." Deep down, he was afraid of being with a man. Starting the engine, Zack paused before adding, "I'm, well… afraid." A bead of sweat ran down his brow. "Gwen, to be honest, I think I've been attracted to guys for a while. But I was too scared to admit it to myself. Being gay, well, you're considered a pariah, and especially in a place like Henry Clay." As he drove, Zack told Gwen about the notes he received in his locker and the phone call on Friday.

"Oh my God and you were all alone at home when this creep called? That would upset me too."

"Now that people have found out about me, I'm afraid. I just get harassed, phone calls, notes, calling me a 'faggot.' Terrible thoughts go through my mind. Regular life is hard enough… and I have to do things for my father. I'm trying to stay focused and mind my own business. But it hurts!

All of this hurts. People seem so matter of fact about their hatred. It confuses me. Do they hate me specifically or hate me because I'm gay?" He turned to her, "don't let Ed ever hurt you. Gwen, if he forces himself on you, run away. I never want to see you get hurt. You're wonderful."

Zack pulled the car over at Gwen's insistence. Gwen then reached into her purse and pulled out a wrapped box, "this is for you. Happy birthday."

"Oh, you didn't need to," Zack replied, smiling. "This is so sweet of you." Unwrapping the present, he discovered a black belt with a gold horseshoe buckle was inside.

"I noticed you wear black belts and black Weejuns."

"Oh, I love it. Gwen, this is so nice. Thank you," touched by her kindness, Zack reached down, took her left hand, and brought it to his lips, kissing it. "You really are so kind to me."

Gwen began discussing senior picture day, which was the following week. "What are you wearing?" She asked. "I want a picture. I know you will be the best-looking boy photographed there."

"Oh, right, Gwen, I'm sure," Zack said sarcastically, laughing, realizing he had a fan. "You're so silly. I want a picture of you, too. You're so beautiful." At that moment, with the smile on her face, Gwen had not looked better to Zack. She seemed so happy in the moment. Deep inside, Zack was starting to have feelings for Gwen, which was confusing. She was so kind, caring, and respectful of him, and she was his one friend who respected his orientation. He and she were both hurting inside and had found each other. He cared for his new friend and, at that moment, realized he loved her.

Zack resumed driving, taking Gwen over to his childhood street so he could introduce her to some special friends. Driving down Lakewood and seeing his old home brought back troubling memories that reminded Zack of unhappy and lonely years growing up in an empty house.

"What a beautiful home," Gwen remarked, gazing at the large structure his father had built. Zack parked, and the two got out, he grabbed a bag of apples from the back seat.

"What's this for?"

"You'll see."

The two walked towards a fence. It was the Engel Farm, which had several horses running freely around the pasture. Zack admired the picturesque open hillside, which was a perfect playground for these beautiful creatures. The smell of freshly dropped hay blended with notes of cut grass. He peered over the black wooden fence, climbed up on the bottom rung, and started making smooching noises. Within seconds, three horses appeared and began slowly walking towards them. "Come here, sweetheart. It's so good to see you," Zack said, smiling widely at the animals, revealing his dimples. "Here you go, baby," he gently held out an apple to one of the horses. Gwen stayed back, afraid the horse would bite. "Oh, no. They're sweet," Zack explained. "Give 'em apples and they'll let you pet them." Two horses crowded around, and then the third horse made its way up. Zack carefully stroked the horses on their muzzles, which were extremely soft. One horse had a beautiful, brown head mixed with white blaze, while the other two were all black. When he gave them apples, they ate them, making a dripping mess when they chewed. Zack held out an apple and had Gwen put her hand below his. The horse took the apple and chewed it vigorously. "See, the babies love the apples." Gwen was fascinated, watching and listening to how lovingly Zack talked to the horses. "Aren't you gorgeous? You know it, don't you, sweetheart?"

The three horses kept eating apples, then one by one, backed away to resume grazing. Standing in the background at a slight distance was a grey mule. "Isn't he sweet? Come on, baby, come over here, sweetie. Come see your Zacky," he called out. The mule stood reluctant and still, eventually walking forward after Zack made smooching sounds. He explained to Gwen that when he was a little boy, he would bring the horses and mules apples, which made his mother angry. "Once, she was going to make a pie with some Granny Smiths and was furious with me." The two laughed as Zack fed the mule.

"This sweet creature reminds me of you," Gwen said, "hovering in the background, not trying to stand out, minding his own business."

He turned and looked at Gwen, who had a beaming smile on her face. As the two pet the mule, Zack placed the side of his head on the mule's head while it was chewing, gently hugging the animal. "The horses are fiercely independent," he said quietly, "feisty, unpredictable, but truly God's finest creatures. I love them. And when I was much younger, around six or seven years old, I used to think only the horses loved me. I would come home from school, and my mother wasn't there. An empty house can play with your mind. I'd get scared and come over and play with my friends across the street. I've been doing it for years now."

Gwen put her arm around Zack's and leaned against him, "how could anyone be anything but sweet to you?"

As the mule had a third apple, Zack said goodbye to his gentle four-legged friend, and he and Gwen began walking back to the car.

"That was wonderful," she gushed. "Thank you for introducing me to your 'special' friends. I have never seen you light up like that. It was beautiful."

Zack opened the passenger door for Gwen and ran around and climbed in, "they're my friends, and so are you. You are always happy to see me, which means a lot."

"You'll always have me," she replied, taking his hand.

Zack knew he needed to tell someone what happened to him in June. Gwen was now his closest friend and confidant. He believed he could trust her.

Chapter Fourteen

"I sure wish you were interested in things that mattered, like football," Pop proclaimed while reading his paper and shaking his head. Zack had a bowl of oatmeal in front of him and the sheet music he was studying intently for the musical audition that afternoon. As he ate his breakfast, he saw his father in his peripheral vision doing his usual inspection, staring at him, making sure his hair was perfectly combed, and he hadn't misbuttoned his shirt.

"That play is worthless!" He'd finished his food and was fully charged. "You waste everyone's time with all this goddamn bullshit!" Zack silently stood up from the breakfast table and quietly washed his dishes in the sink. "Make sure you clean that goddamn bowl properly! Oatmeal sticks."

Zack fumbled through his book bag, walked over and kissed Pop goodbye on his forehead, "I love you, Daddy." Walking out the back door to the car, tears formed in his eyes. He quickly shook his head and tried to steer his mind to the school play. He badly needed some distraction in his life.

Later at school, as Zackary made his way towards Ms. Watson's class, he spotted Gwen in the distance, standing at her usual post at the bottom of the steps.

"You look amazing, Zacky!" She exclaimed. "What do you think, ladies?"

Michelle and Rebecca offered a positive appraisal, "Amazing. Classy! Such a nice horseshoe belt! Is that new?"

"Oh, thanks. Yes, it is actually," he said, smiling at Gwen, who had on a beautiful outfit. He leaned in and whispered, "so you're calling me 'Zacky' now."

Gwen blushed, "do you not like me calling you that?"

"Of course you can, darling," he whispered back, laughing. "See you all later." Zack turned, held his warm gaze, and walked up the steps. He turned and noticed three classmates staring up at him, he waved. Walking to class, Zack could not get out of his mind how much he appreciated Gwen. Her kindness was like a rare salve, offsetting many of the horrible feelings he was grappling with.

While working in their group in third period, Keith asked Zack if he wanted to get together on Saturday, possibly a movie. He agreed, pleased someone had reached out to him and they exchanged telephone numbers. Zack figured he needed a new male friend.

Gwen whispered in Zack's ear, "I know you will do great today!"

"You think so?" He whispered back.

She turned her head towards him, placing her elbows on her desk and resting her head on her hands. "I really do." The two stared at each other and began laughing. When the bell rang, Keith and Rebecca wished Zack good luck on the audition. Gwen and Zack walked into the hall. She asked how he was doing.

"Good, I guess," he said. "Thank you again for the lovely belt."

Gwen stared at the horseshoe at the center of it, "you wear it well. And it's extra luck for the audition! Not that you need it. And thank you for yesterday, seeing the horses. I will always remember that afternoon. So, listen, I'll meet you after sixth period. I'm not missing your audition for anything." Gwen gave him a quick hug, and Zack climbed the stairs to his math class. He'd found a note earlier in his locker but didn't open it in an attempt to avoid getting upset. Staying calm and collected also included avoiding Matt, so he decided to eat lunch alone in his car. But later, after fifth period, Zack ran into Matt, who wished him luck but kept asking Zack why he "ruined" his surprise party on Saturday. Zack did not want to engage and steered away from a potential confrontation.

As they approached Mr. Pillsbury's classroom, Matt placed his hands on Zack's shoulders. "Good luck! I have faith in you. Call me tonight and let me know how it turns out."

"Thank you, Matthew." Despite being hurt and embarrassed by the Max & Erma's incident, Zack appreciated his friend's seemingly heartfelt support. He then entered yearbook class and sat down, opening his sheet music to study the lyrics. It was nearing three-thirty when Gwen and Zack met and walked toward the Lassiter Theatre entrance. He printed his name on the sign-in sheet, along with the song he planned to audition with and the parts he wanted to be considered for. Walking into the theater, Zack felt relief seeing that most of the people in the audience were girls. He and Gwen sat down. She waved at several of her friends and members of student government. Ms. Avon came walking out from behind the curtain. Zack was a background player in the play she directed, "She Stoops to Conquer," and had her for Speech as a sophomore.

"Good afternoon. For those of you who do not know me, I am Ms. Carol Avon. Welcome to the audition. I will ask those auditioning to hand your sheet music to our pianist, Christi, then walk and stand here where the 'x' is marked."

She called up the first person. A slim boy walked over and handed his sheet music to Christi with a flourish. He sang, "The Way We Were." Zack tried to restrain his judgment on his music choice, as he was auditioning with a song originated by Liza Minnelli. The audition continued and Zack realized the majority of the audience had come just to watch and not actually audition. Zack witnessed two other boys' dreadful auditions, provoking sparse, timid applause from the audience. After three girls vied for the two female roles, Ms. Avon announced, "Zackary," smiling at him.

Gwen squeezed his hand. Zack rose, walked over and handed his sheet music to Christi who asked, "do you want me to hold the last verse?"

"Yes, ma'am, thank you." Zack walked and stood at the "x" as the music for "New York, New York" began. The crowd seemed to recognize the song and lit up immediately.

Zack began to sing calmly in his baritone voice, "Start spreading the news. I'm leaving today. I wanna be a part of it, New York, New York!" The audience seemed quite receptive. He saw Gwen smiling. Once he was at the challenging place in the song, he leaned his head back and glanced at the ceiling while clutching his fists, then belted, *"Those little town blues… are melting away… I'll make a brand-new start of it in old New York."* With his arms out in front, he brought it home, *"If I can make it there, I'll make it anywhere! Come on, come through, New York, New York!"* Zack held the last "York" note for more than twelve seconds. The audience roared. They kept clapping as Zack took a bow and Christi kept on playing like Zack was exiting a nightclub act. Gwen was laughing hysterically and screaming. Zack felt such a jolt. Ms. Avon came over and quietly whispered to Zack, "Amazing."

When he returned to his seat, Gwen wrapped her arms around him, "Unbelievable! You were great," she whispered. A few more students auditioned, each quite good. Inside, Zack felt so relieved. As it approached four-forty-five, Ms. Avon thanked all the students for auditioning.

"I am going to announce the cast now," she said. Eventually, he heard, "For Snoopy, Zackary Kingdon. Rehearsals begin Wednesday, but we are having an organization meeting tomorrow afternoon in the theater at three-thirty. Thank you, everyone!"

Zack was ecstatic. He'd gotten the part he wanted. As the crowd stood up, he and Gwen hugged. "Thank you so much for being here for me today, Gwen. I couldn't have done this without you!"

As they released, Gwen had a tear in her eye, "I'm so proud of you. You needed this!"

Rebecca had arrived late and had been sitting further up in the back, watching. "Zack, you were amazing!" She hugged him. "Congratulations. You'll be great."

As they began to leave, Zack took Gwen's hand in his and slowly walked her up a few steps before pausing to face her, "this meant so much to me." The two embraced, and he turned and walked back down to meet the other cast members.

Later that afternoon, after getting into his car, Zack quickly glanced at himself in the rearview mirror. He could not have been more satisfied at that moment. Smiling triumphantly, he rolled down the window, deeply breathing in the cool Kentucky air as he drove home.

88

Chapter Fifteen

Searching for a fresh pencil in his locker, paper shreds from the edges of the notes inserted accumulated at the bottom like snow. Zack discovered another note containing a vividly crude drawing of a figure penetrating a person bent over. He crumbled it and threw it away, retrieved his morning class books and slammed the door closed. In third period, as Mr. Hendrix was writing on the board, Zack whispered in Gwen's ear, "hey, can we meet after school today? I need to tell you something." Looking a little nervous, she turned, nodding.

After school, Zack met Gwen outside of yearbook class. She was waiting with her coat on. The two walked outside and got into the car. Stopping briefly to get some snacks and drinks, they reached Jacobson Park and parked near the lake. Zack sat a few moments before turning to face Gwen, "you know how I used to work at the ice cream parlor? An incident happened in June, right after I broke up with Amy. It's not easy to talk about. In fact, I haven't told anyone, but I… I just think I can trust you."

"Of course, you can," she said, taking his hand. "I'm here for you. Tell me whatever you want."

Zack took a deep breath and began his story, "two guys had been coming into the store almost nightly and requesting I wait on them. They were both incredibly handsome, staring and flirting with me while I worked, which made me feel awkward. They seemed like they were six or seven years older. Then one night, after my shift ended, as I walked to my car, they sat in a car next to mine, blinking their headlights at me. One guy said my name, which he knew from my name tag. He introduced himself as Tom, and the other guy's name was Mark. I said I had to get going and he said, 'You sure are handsome.' The whole thing made me nervous, but also excited because they found me attractive. The guy then asked me to come over to his place to 'relax and get to know him better.' Gwen, my heart was racing. I thought they were gorgeous and couldn't believe they liked me. Tom gave me his telephone number on a napkin. I gave him my number, which I shouldn't have, and called Tom the next day. He gave me his address. I was so excited. This was the first time I had ever gone over to another gay man's home."

Gwen looked at Zack warmly with no judgment in her eyes. "That night," he continued. "I snuck out after I put Pop to bed. When I got to Tom's home off Ashland Avenue, he brought me out to the back porch, it was all lit with picnic table candles. He said all kinds of complimentary things to me. I sat down on a porch swing. He had an amazing, muscular body, wearing tight jean shorts and a sleeveless tee shirt. It turned me on. His friend Mark hadn't gotten there yet. I remember hearing thunder way off in the distance and it was extremely humid. Tom handed me a Coke and sat next to me on the porch swing. He was smoking. I was about to ask him how long he'd lived in this house when he leaned over and began to kiss me aggressively. This was the first time I'd kissed another male. I had never experienced kissing someone with cigarette taste in their mouth and it was unpleasant. There were no gentle touching or romantic gestures. I remember he looked into my eyes and said, 'You are a gorgeous creature. I am going to devour you.' Then he invited me inside. We went down the hallway of his darkly lit house into a small bedroom and he asked me to take off my clothes. I was so nervous but slowly undressed. After I did, he began to move his hands down, feeling my rear." Zack stopped, feeling overwhelmed and nervous, revealing such private details to Gwen.

He slowly continued, "Tom put my penis in his mouth and pleasured me… it was the most sensational feeling. Then he turned me around, got on his knees, and began kissing and doing things orally to me. I started to get dizzy and told him I needed to sit down. I began to catch my breath, but my heart was pumping fast like a racehorse. Then I sat on the edge of the bed and he told me, 'I can't wait to stick my dick up there!' He meant my butt. I did not like what he was saying, I am terribly afraid of the idea of anyone, excuse me for saying, 'fucking me.' I told him I didn't want to and he said, 'Sure you will.' I said, 'Someday, maybe, but I am not ready for that. This is my first time, ever. I don't want to.' And he said, 'Sure, baby, whatever works for you.' Then he jumped up and directly positioned himself in front of me. I was still sitting on the edge of the bed. I stared at his penis. He let me touch it. He wanted me to put it in my mouth, but Gwen, I was afraid to, but I didn't want to make him feel bad. I'd never done that before, and I told him."

Gwen nodded, "I understand what you're saying, and feeling."

Zack looked at her, then continued, "suddenly, there was a knock at the back screen door, interrupting the moment.

The other guy, Mark, had arrived." Zack paused, tears falling down his face.

"What is it, honey? They hurt you?" she quietly asked.

He slowly nodded, "they did. It was awful." He took a deep breath and explained how he felt like a captured animal. "Tom shoved this nasty-smelling stuff in a vial up to my nose, which I refused. It smelled like the glue I used to build my model ships." Zack recounted how he briefly stood up while Mark kissed him and touched his body, then forcefully pushed him onto the single-sized bed. "I tried to sit back up, but he hit me on my chest, then pushed me back, causing me to hit my head against the wall. It really hurt, and I felt dizzy." He recalled how the two men refused to listen to his plea that he did not want to get 'penetrated.' "Then Mark said, 'I want to fuck your beautiful butt.'"

Gwen squeezed Zack's hands as she began to tear up, pressing her lips together tightly.

"I pled with them that I was not ready for that. While I was on the edge of the bed, they stood over me, then turned and looked at each other. Mark nodded and grabbed me under my arms, while Tom grabbed my legs, turning me over and onto my stomach. I was so terrified and started to fight to get up. I screamed 'No' over and over, staring into sheets with my head pushed up into a corner of the wall. I was completely panicking. I kept yelling for them to stop."

Zack began panicking again as he told Gwen, "the guy, Mark, took several minutes trying to insert himself into me. It was the most excruciating pain ever. I don't know how to describe it. It went on for several minutes. He eventually pushed himself inside me. I screamed in agony. I tried to get up, but Tom pushed his knees into my shoulder blades, holding down my arms. I kept yelling for Mark to stop, but he wouldn't stop."

The worst part, Zack explained, was when Tom hit him for yelling. "He took two pillows and covered my head, pressing down so hard, preventing me from breathing. He was asphyxiating me. Gwen, he was trying to kill me. I… I cried for my life, begging, fighting, gasping desperately for air. I was suffocating and he would not let up, pushing the pillows down. He pressed his knee further into my back, pushing air out of my lungs as I was fighting for air. I knew it was going to end for me. I didn't know what else to do. I wasn't raised religiously, but I asked God for help. I said, 'Please help me… Please save me.' I was beginning to black out. Then, there was a sudden break between the sheets and pillows, and I was able to capture a gasp of air. As I took it in, I thought about my father, how I kissed him good night, telling him I loved him, how I had crept out late that night, and he may never see me ever again. He didn't know where I was." Zack explained how he felt he was getting what he deserved, "'fucked in the ass' because I'm told on a daily basis by my father and others that I am a 'nothing,' 'worthless,' 'a loser,' with no value to my life."

Zack told Gwen that Mark raped him for over thirty minutes, removing himself at one point, then inserting fingers with sharp fingernails, then reinserting his penis again. "He then pulled out. The pain was still killing me. Tom bent down and whispered, 'My turn.' They turned me on my back, pulling my legs up with my knees up. Gwen, I did not put up a fight. I breathed, lying emotionless, enormously grateful for the available air. The air was life." Zack explained how Tom inserted himself and raped him for several minutes. "I was like a motionless zombie," he said.

"After it was over, I was completely spent, mentally and physically. My rectum was in throbbing pain. Tom said, 'See, getting fucked is the best thing ever.' He watched me wipe myself off with a towel while he smoked another cigarette. They hugged me, trying to kiss me, and I went along so I could just escape the house. I quickly got my clothes back on. Once I felt grass below my feet, I knew I would live, I was freed. I got into my car, locked the doors, started the engine, and began driving. I was so sore in my neck and my shoulder and my chest and back and legs. My entire ass was burning in pain." The recounting of the trauma was overwhelming, Zack put his head on the steering wheel. "It was over… but I know it will never really be over."

"When I drove off, I started to gag and immediately pulled over and threw up. I was sick to my stomach, Gwen. I threw up again later when I was showering. I went to bed shaking, so terrified. When I woke up the next morning, my father knocked at the door. He needed his medicine. I felt sore all over. My body had been through this relentless fight. I had strained every muscle in my body during the attack. My skin didn't feel right. Lying in bed, I felt damp in my pajama pants. At first, I thought I had somehow soiled myself. I pulled the sheets back, and it smelled like chlorine. Then I saw blood, which had seeped from my rear. I quickly jumped out of bed, pulling my pajama bottoms down. I started to panic but was being really quiet. I was so afraid they had hurt me physically, you know, inside my rectum. I threw away my sheets and mattress cover. Finally, I maneuvered over to my dresser mirror, and I viewed, up close, bruise marks on the back of my neck and shoulders where Tom nearly asphyxiated me with his knee. Going to the bathroom was so excruciatingly painful for about six days."

Gwen held his hand and rubbed his arm. It hurt her to hear the pain he had gone through. Tears streamed down her face, but she remained strong for him because she knew how hard this horror was to recount.

"That day, I went to work," he continued, spent. "I was so scared, humiliated, ashamed. I wore a long-sleeved shirt to hide my bruises. But, Gwen, I couldn't live with the pain. It was killing me inside. That night, I took a box cutter from the store. I was going to cut my wrist in the bathroom. I was at such a point of unhappiness inside… I was about to kill myself. As I put the blade to my wrist, I suddenly thought, who's going to give my daddy his medicine? How could I leave him? I love him so much. It would kill him. I'm all he has. So, I decided to stay. It's been so hard walking through my life with this," Zack broke down in sobs. Gwen was crying too, and she held her friend closely. They sat in the car crying for several minutes.

"I'm here, Zack," Gwen whispered. "No one's going to hurt you, sweetheart. I'm here for you." It was starting to get dark. "You're safe here with me," she muttered.

"I thought we were all going to have fun," Zack said through his tears. "I had no idea they would do this to me. I honestly did not know. I didn't know."

Gwen firmly held onto Zack as he cried uncontrollably, "how could you have known, Zack? How could you have known?"

He got out of the car sick to his stomach, walked over to the water and vomited. After he spit up, Zack could barely see his face in the reflection of the water as the sun had fully set and the sky darkened. He felt the experience had been displayed on one of the notes that fell out of his locker that morning.

96

Chapter Sixteen

Rehearsals were intense for the next month. Ms. Avon screamed and cursed at most of the cast, stomping her foot, waving her cigarette like a prop. As a result, Zack came prepared, working for hours at night and on weekends on his three numbers in the basement out of Pop's earshot. Even so, Ms. Avon brutally jumped on him a few times. Still, Zack loved playing Snoopy.

The last Sunday in October, Zack took Gwen to see "Casablanca" at the Kentucky Theatre in the afternoon, which neither had seen. As a second-run house, the tickets at the Kentucky were $1.75 and the theater had recently been renovated. It was a glorious palace with gorgeous, restored marble walls and mirrors throughout the lobby. The Kentucky Theatre was also about to celebrate its sixtieth anniversary. After he and Gwen bought popcorn and sodas, then descended the long aisles in the massive near-thousand-seat theater, the two took their seats halfway down. They talked about Gwen's relationship with Ed.

"He's getting forceful with me," she said. "I'm really becoming more afraid of him."

"Gwen, it's not my place," Zack started, "but it's obvious he is becoming more aggressive. How much longer are you going to stay with this terrible guy? You deserve so much better."

"I feel so safe when I'm with you, thank you," she said, chewing on a small handful of popcorn. "He tried to touch me down there again and when I pushed him off me, he called me a 'bitch.'"

Zack nearly choked on his sip of soda, "oh, honey, I'm so sorry. That's a cruel thing to say." Gwen stopped partaking in the popcorn and became quiet. "It's not my place to tell you what to do, but I have this fear he's becoming more aggressive because you're refusing his advances."

She kept staring ahead, "Zacky, he's strong. I fear Ed's gonna cross the line…" Gwen pressed her lips tight, then said, "at one time I wanted to have sex with him, you know. I think he's attractive, but not when he's like this."

"Hon," Zack said, rubbing Gwen's arm, "I think it got worse because I resisted them. My point is, as you resist, Ed's been pushing harder. I think he's becoming dangerous." She nodded.

"I'm here for you. I care about you."

Suddenly, the large curtains covering the screen began to open and the house lights slowly dimmed. Zack took Gwen's hand and kissed it. She reached over and kissed him on the cheek. During the movie, the two held hands and snuggled.

After the film ended, Zack saw Fred Mills, the theater manager, in the lobby greeting people. Having gone there so many times over the years, Zack waved to him. Mr. Mills saw him and waved. "Hello, how are you both doing?" he asked.

"Fine, sir," Zack replied. "What an amazing movie. I had never seen it."

"We usually get big crowds for this one. I always try to

sneak in to listen when Sam sings, 'As Time Goes By.'" Then he added, "I hope to see you here more."

They shook hands. Zack and Gwen proceeded through the lobby, out to the street, and finally to the parking lot.

"Clearly, he likes you, Zackary," Gwen offered.

"Yeah, he's a nice man. He always says 'hello' to me. I remember him from when I was a little kid."

I wonder if Fred would hire me at the Kentucky? Zack thought. *I would love to work there.*

Chapter Seventeen

It was the Saturday before a week of "You're a Good Man, Charlie Brown" performances. On this cool November morning, Zack arrived at Gwen's house at eleven to pick her up and go to the library. Dr. Farris opened the door and enthusiastically invited him inside. Firmly shaking his hand, he addressed her father, "good morning, Dr. Farris. How are you, sir?" Gwen came down the stairs, and Zack's smile widened, "hey, don't you look amazing!"

She warmly embraced Zack wearing a light brown dress and a navy-blue cardigan with a white blouse underneath, gentle yellow flowers imprinted all over. Zack helped her put on a thick wool coat, picked up her tote bag full of books and headed to the car. After opening the door for Gwen, he climbed into the driver's seat and drove to Frisch's Big Boy for lunch.

"You know, my parents think the world of you," she said. "We have whole dinner conversations about what a 'nice boy' Zack is."

"No way! That's sweet," Zack laughed, quickly looking at her. "Sound like there's a 'but'...?"

"No. Not at all. My parents adore you, but they dislike Ed. When he picks me up, he honks the horn."

"Are you kidding me? If one of my sister's boyfriends ever did that, my pop wouldn't have allowed her out the door."

Driving down Richmond Road toward the library, Zack took in the sky above. There were several clouds, filtering a translucent yellow and pink light which gently colored the leaves in the semi-barren trees. The deliciousness of fall in Kentucky overwhelmed Zack's senses. Arriving at the Gratz Park Library, the two walked in and found a space at a table they could each spread out their schoolwork. Zack went to the card catalog and searched the location of a couple of books for his term paper on Truman Capote.

After working a few hours, Zack suggested they take a break. He helped her on with her coat, then walked to the door. Gwen carried a container of brownies. Once outside, the two came to the Gratz Park Fountain in the park adjacent to the library. They sat on a cold concrete bench staring at the water. It had become much chillier, and the skies were more overcast. Zack noticed the park was beautiful, with a variety of colors. Fall was turning the leaves. Some still clung to branches, while others surrendered and lay scattered on the ground. Gwen opened the foil wrapping and handed Zack a brownie, "Zack, I have something serious I need to tell you."

"Okay, what is it?" he said, eating the dessert.

"Zacky, do you promise not to get mad?"

He quickly became pensive, "okay, I promise."

She paused, looked away, and then looked back at him, "Zack, I can't believe I am saying this. I… I love you."

Without even hesitating, he replied, "Well, I love you, too."

Gwen took Zack's left hand, then clarified, "no, I mean I am falling in love with you… and, please, let me finish this… I know you're gay, you were honest with me from the beginning, but I still feel so much in my heart for you. You are the sweetest, handsomest guy I have ever met. I don't want anything to change what's between us, but Ed's not you. I mean, I can talk to you about anything."

"Yes, you can," Zack replied, becoming emotional.

"You get me, Zackary," she put her other hand on Zack's face as he teared up, stunned by Gwen's overture.

"I care about you, Gwen, but… but I can't… you know, I can't be that kind of a man for you. I wish… I wish so badly I could, but… I don't want to lose or hurt you," he said through tears, deeply touched by Gwen's honesty.

"Honey," she said, "you will never lose me. There are no boys like you. You make me so happy. I know this may sound funny, but… can I kiss you?"

Zack paused for a moment, "sure." The two kissed each other on the lips, then hugged. Both were now crying. Zack felt confusion, happiness, and a sense of trust, ultimately resulting in a smile. "Gwen, I couldn't be there for Amy, so I don't want to hurt you."

Still holding his hand, Gwen beamed. "I know. I don't expect you to be my boyfriend or my lover. As you said, God made you this way. But we can still love each other as something much greater than friends." Zack was confused but Gwen continued, "I see our love as maybe falling somewhere 'in-between' friendship and romance. It's almost as if it's located in the middle of a relationship, with friendship on the lower level… and romance on the upper level, you know? We fall in that in-between special place. I see what we have as being much more than friends, or I hope it can be. It's sort of like 'mezzanine love.'"

He thought, *what Gwen is saying is that we are in a place where clearly both our hearts and heads agree.*

"I'm not Amy, Zack. I understand," Gwen finished.

The two leaned forward, turning their heads towards each other for a few minutes, smiling as they each ate brownies and took in the fall coolness. He thought more about what Gwen had proposed. "These are so good," Zack timidly commented about the dessert.

"You enjoy your treats," she said, smiling.

He reached over and held Gwen's cool hand, smiling at her. She pointed to her upper lip, indicating Zack had powdered sugar on his face. They laughed quietly. While their relationship was developing, Zack was nervous she might still have expectations in the future. But for now, it was comforting to know someone loved him and had his back.

"I love you, Zack," she said again.

Chewing his last bite, Zack giggled, trying to speak. Finally, he said, "Mezzanine love. Okay, I definitely feel it." He reached over and with powdered sugar on his lips, gave her a very long kiss. "Gwen, honestly, I fell for you back in August."

She put her hands over her face, ecstatically saying, "I knew you felt it. I knew you loved me with the way you looked at me." Zack wrapped his arm around her as they embraced on the cold bench and kissed again.

After letting the moment sink in, the two walked back into the library, holding hands. While he was working on his paper an hour later, Gwen reached over and gently touched his arm. Zack put his pen down and held her hand, gazing and gently smiling at her. The two stared into each other's eyes, grateful for their love. Gwen continued gazing at Zack across the table. She had a glow on her face as the late afternoon sunlight briefly beamed through the window, lighting her up and making her auburn hair shine. She appeared to be happy. He felt an intense love for her, so unexpected. He believed Gwen helped him feel again, that he was valued, and her gesture in the park had so touched him. By unexpectedly revealing her beautiful heart to him, showing she cared about him, similar to how Zack bravely walked up to her on the first day of school, Zack decided to move forward, not be afraid, and accept Gwen's love.

Chapter Eighteen

Zack took his father's sugar level reading. After writing down the numbers, he took an alcohol gauze and rubbed his father's arm and then injected the insulin. "You know I'm bringing Pat to the show tonight," his father announced. Zack quickly looked up.

"Unfair, you're telling me after the needle was inserted," he said, making a face.

"Don't do that," Pop complained.

He put the Band-Aid on and gently smiled, "that's fine. I'm glad you're coming." He kissed his father, then walked over and poured milk over his Wheaties. Pop went through the paper, stopped and glanced over at Zack eating his breakfast, holding his gaze.

"You seem happy, son. What's going on?"

Zack didn't realize he had a warm glow, "I'm fine. I'm good, Pop."

Pop reached across the table and placed his hand over Zack's, "You're a good boy. Your daddy's proud of you."

Zack opened a mouth full of Wheaties.

"Oh, goddamn you, you ruin everything," his father protested.

Zack laughed, giggling like a little boy, settling back into a calm and serene place. A few minutes later, after packing his lunch, Zack went over and put his bag down, then wrapped his arms around his father.

Later at school, walking to his locker, Zack heard someone yell, "FAGGOT," then shoved him from behind hard into the wall. He fell flat on his stomach. Two boys helped Zack up and he saw a group of guys walking away, laughing. At his locker, Joe smirked, "I hope you didn't mess up your hair, 'King-woman.'" Zack kept moving forward.

After third period, Gwen caught up with him, "Can I ask you a favor, Zack? You know my parents and I are flying up to visit Bryn Mawr this weekend? We have a subscription to the Philharmonic, and we can't go Sunday afternoon. If I give you the tickets, will you go?"

"I don't know who to ask to go with me," he said. "I guess I could go by myself. Yeah, I'll do that. Tell them thank you for me."

Gwen asked if he would be willing to go somewhere and kiss, "I love kissing you. You're not trying to grab my breasts or reach into my pants."

Zack giggled. "I don't want to cause problems."

"I understand, but you're not leaving today without kissing me."

"All right, a quick one," he looked around, then kissed Gwen. "How's that?"

She nodded. Zack put his hand on her cheek, "love you."

As he walked up the stairs, Gwen yelled, "Break a leg, Snoopy!"

As he walked into the Lassiter Theatre, Zack felt centered, secure, and prepared. The dress rehearsal went well the night before. With his father attending the opening performance, it meant a lot to show him he was worthy, that he could do something well, and that he'd done this completely on his own, no tutors or other assistance. Zack understood his father had no confidence in him. Tonight, however, he would not believe he was marginal.

Nearing seven o'clock, moments before the premiere of the show, the cast quietly concentrated, and each began to fall into character. Ms. Avon summoned the house lights to dim, and everyone took their places. After the "Schroeder" number, Zack performed his first solo called "Snoopy." This was his moment. Happily, Zack heard his father laughing in the back of the theater, particularly during the number when he danced and sang, "I feel every now and then I gotta bite someone," with some intense percussion playing. After the number, he climbed up and lay on top of the doghouse, staring straight up. He felt a sense of calmness, as it was the first time since that terrible night in June that he felt alive again, and he silently thanked God for the feeling.

The second to the last song of the evening was "Suppertime," where Zack sang and danced with a flat-brim hat and cane. Pop could be heard in the back of the theatre laughing out of control. This meant the world to Zack. At the end of the song, raucous applause seemed to go on and on. As the last notes were sung, the lights dimmed, and the audience erupted again. As each cast member took bows, Zack glanced up to the upper level of the theater. His father and Mrs. Daniels had already left, but he was pleased people were there for him, including Keith and Rebecca. Eventually, Zack made his way to the parking lot and drove home.

Zack entered the kitchen and made a cup of vanilla ice cream and walked upstairs. Pop was in bed watching television and Zack noticed him grimacing, "Where's my ice cream?"

"You want some?" He dutifully retreated to the kitchen and brought up a small bowl, hoping the dessert would cause his father to be kind. Taking his seat on the floor next to his dad's bed, the two were quiet for the next few minutes, watching television and eating ice cream.

After they finished dessert, Pop put his hand on Zack's head and ran his fingers through his hair, "You did really well, son. Pat and I enjoyed the show."

Zack put his bowl on the table and gave his father a big squeeze. "Thank you, Daddy," he said with a kiss. This was more than validation to Zack, it was acknowledgment that he mattered. Carrying the empty bowls to the kitchen, Zack stopped halfway down the stairs, set the bowls down, covered his mouth, and cried. He was overwhelmed with relief. After washing the dishes and returning upstairs, Zack tucked his father in and kissed him goodnight. He got into his own bed at ten o'clock, turned off the light and stared at the ceiling, "Thank you, God, for being there with me tonight," he said out loud. *Thank you for everything you do for me.* He turned to his side and was fast asleep within a minute.

The next morning, after first period, Zack ran into Gwen, Rebecca, and Michelle at the bottom of the stairwell on his way to accounting class. "Good morning, ladies!" he cheerfully said.

"How are you doing?" Rebecca asked.

"Tired, but the play gives me a lot of satisfaction."

Gwen stood, smiling, and immediately hugged Zack tightly, not letting him go, causing him to blush and laugh. "Ladies, can you please convince Gwen to release me?" he laughed.

Michelle, who apparently had not been privy to the

gossip wagon, gleefully said, "Oh, you both make such an adorable couple." Gwen's and Zack's eyes widened.

Gwen gently released Zackary, looking at him, "sounds good, doesn't it, honey?" she said.

Zack, recuperating from laughing, replied, "It does, 'honey.'"

"Zack, you were amazing in the play!" Rebecca enthused.

"Thanks. I'm so glad you liked it," he replied, climbing the stairway to his next class.

In third period, Gwen reached over and took Zack's left hand, clutching it down between the desks. His love for her at that moment was unlike any feeling he had ever experienced. His heart beat so fast his breathing became rapid. He peered over at her as she stared ahead. *Nobody has ever loved me like this girl. She offered me her heart. I love her more than anyone*, he thought. While Zack had cared for Amy, he realized that with Gwen, this was the first time in his life he had ever felt a deep affection for a person. His heartbeat was different as his breathing became freer. The feeling was inoculating him from the pain he carried. *It feels so good to feel good.* Zack also knew in the back of his head that his feelings for Gwen were incompatible with his orientation, but he could not deny the here and now.

On Thursday afternoon, nearing five-ten, Zack was awakened from a brief nap by his father's knock on the door. It was time to have dinner, which Pop had cooked. The two had barely spoken when Zack reached for a second chicken breast. "Son, use a goddamn fork," Pop chastened. He laughed at his father for grumpily saying "goddamn" in each sentence. During dinner, Pop informed Zack that his brother, Cam, and new wife Alice were coming home for Christmas. He added that his sister Emily was also coming. Zack knew Cam disliked him. For the past several years when visiting, Cam hardly looked at Zack or acknowledged his presence. Emily was also cold, distant, and judgmental. This was enough to send Zack into a deep depression.

For the second and final night of the show's performance, Gwen, her parents, Matt, and Colleen were all in the audience. Ten minutes to seven, cast members quietly concentrated and fell into their characters, one last time. Zack took his place behind the curtain backdrop thinking of positive memories to clear his head. He thought of his affection toward the horses and the mule he fed apples. The house lights dimmed, and Snoopy came alive. During the show, the applause from the audience made Zack feel like the entire house was filled. The clapping invigorated his spirit. He imagined Gwen was staring at him as he lie on the top of his doghouse, 'sleeping' during the "Peter Rabbit" number.

When Zackary delivered his lines for the start of "Happiness," he was aware this was the final moment of one of his life's most meaningful and enjoyable experiences. It was hard for him to hold back tears, but he managed, distracted by the canine howling he had to perform at the end. The audience roared when the song ended, and the house lights dropped. When Zack took a solo bow at the curtain call, full smile across his face, the screams made him feel like a rock star.

Chapter Nineteen

Fixing his tie in the foyer mirror, Zack had on a suit for the Lexington Philharmonic's fall concert. It was cold and dreary outside so Zack decided to wear his navy dress coat over his suit. Before leaving, he walked back upstairs to say goodbye to his father who was enjoying his usual full day of NFL games on television and finishing a tray of Long John Silver's Zack picked up earlier. Pop told Zack a few college applications had arrived in Saturday's mail and were on his desk in the drawing room. "Don't get your hopes up for those schools," Pop declared. "You won't get into any of 'em. Your ACTs were embarrassing. I made sure you went to the best high school in town, but you are too lazy, stupid, and unwilling to apply yourself."

Zack entered Symphony Hall at Transylvania University and was directed to the center of the orchestra section. The Farris's had terrific seats with a full view of the stage. A large crowd filling the grand auditorium. Glancing at the program, Zack remembered when his mother brought him to the Lollipop Concert at Transy when he was a young boy to hear "Peter and the Wolf." As the auditorium filled up, many seats surrounding him became occupied.

He could see the musicians warming up their instruments.

Minutes later, the lights dimmed, and the curtain rose with a thunderous applause. As the orchestra played George Gershwin's "Rhapsody in Blue," the music began subtly and slowly, requiring the clarinet initially, but eventually erupting into a full-bodied score. Zackary took in the sounds and enjoyed the acoustics, feeling so adult sitting in the audience with the cultured citizens of Lexington. While he was a long way from being well-rounded, Zack was at a place in life where he was interested and willing to learn and experience things outside of his comfort zone.

The second half of the concert was devoted to Leonard Bernstein selections, including compositions from *West Side Story*, which caused him to get slightly emotional. When the philharmonic played "One Hand, One Heart," it made him think of the memorable moment the previous Saturday when Gwen proclaimed her love on the park bench. *I do love her, more each day,* Zack thought.

After the concert, Zack went down to the reception in the lower level of the auditorium, up for the free food. The crowd was massive, and the line to the desserts and coffee was long. Zack accepted a champagne from one of the servers and took a few crackers. A few minutes later, musicians filed into the room to applause, which became louder when the conductor entered. Amidst the din, Zack surveyed the room, smiling, taking in the experience. All of a sudden, one of the musicians, an attractive man in a tuxedo, began walking towards him. Zack noticed he appeared to be staring right at him. *God, he's so gorgeous!* Zack thought. As the musician got closer, Zack's heart almost popped out of his chest and he threw back the remainder of his champagne.

"Hello, I saw you in the audience. My name is Jeremiah, Jeremiah Pruett." The man was over six feet tall and thin, with a beautiful, chiseled face and dark brown eyes, perfect teeth, and lovely, thick brown hair.

"My name is Zackary, Zackary Kingdon. It's such a pleasure."

Jeremiah had a striking smile. "You're adorable. You look like a Zackary."

"I do? How so?"

"It's a strong male name," Jeremiah noted. "You seem like a strong male."

Zack could not take the embarrassed grin off his face. "Okay, I believe you," he replied. They stared at each other, admiring. Zack noticed Jeremiah had thick eyebrows like him, great skin, and lips he could get lost in. The silence between the two was getting awkward.

"So, what instrument do you play?"

"Violin. I'm first chair."

Zack nodded, realizing the chair business was a big deal in the music world.

"Shall I get you another champagne, Zack?"

"Oh, no, I snuck this one. I should have a Coke." Jeremiah put his hand on Zack's wrist and whispered, "I shall get you one. Stay right here, cutie."

Zack, overwhelmed, replied, "I'm not going anywhere."

Jeremiah soon returned with a glass of red wine and handed Zack a Coke on ice. They clinked glasses. Jeremiah explained he was graduating from the University of Kentucky with a degree in music in December, "I am working part-time for the music department, and right after Christmas, I'll travel to New York and briefly Europe to study for two months with a consortium of musicians." Zack was fascinated, nodding as Jeremiah revealed he was twenty-two and had big ambitions. "I hope to someday permanently move there and play in the New York Philharmonic. The competition is insanely intense. I'll be on the road, traveling, playing, and studying with some great musicians. I don't see myself getting involved with anyone at this point in my life, but I do like to have fun, particularly with really handsome men."

Zack maintained a shy smirk, not knowing what to say to Jeremiah's overt come-on line.

"So, Zackary, what do you do?"

With a bashful grin, he said, "I go to high school. I'm a senior at Henry Clay."

"So, you're eighteen?" Jeremiah asked.

"Yes, as of September," Zack smiled. He began telling Jeremiah how much he loved music and going to plays. He also told him he was in a production at school.

"I find you so cute, Zackary," Jeremiah said again. "You really are quite handsome."

A nearby table opened up as the crowd began to thin out, and the two sat down. "Oh, I appreciate it. You are… um… really nice-looking yourself."

"So, are you out at school?" Jeremiah asked.

"Me? Oh, no, but some students found out."

Jeremiah's warm face immediately went to a serious look as he began to nod, "have you been harassed?"

Nodding, Zack pressed his lips tightly and glanced away. Jeremiah reached over and took his hand, Zack initially resisted, but he let him hold it. "I'm so sorry. I hope it isn't serious."

Zack squeezed his hand back, trying to smile through a pained face, "it is, but I keep moving forward."

"I know what it's like," Jeremiah said. "Horrible. I was abused in school. I was beaten up, harassed, scared. It gets better when you graduate. I promise you. Now, you seem like you need a hug, may I?"

Zack felt self-conscious, but as he gazed at the next table, he saw two men kissing not even two feet away from them. He stood for a hug. With a tight embrace, Jeremiah whispered in his ear that he would never hurt him and was sorry about what he was going through. Zackary thanked him for understanding, it had been terribly difficult and Jeremiah's charisma and kindness enveloped Zack. The two continued to speak about Lexington, horses, movies, and fun things they each enjoyed doing. Jeremiah hated sports altogether.

"Oh, I am a huge UK basketball fan," Zack explained. "I admit it. I used to 'play' basketball by sitting on a bench in junior high school. I played once, but when I got the ball, I panicked and shot it into the opponent's hoop. The coach immediately blacklisted me."

Jeremiah was in stitches, shaking his head. The two laughed, and enjoyed gazing into each other's eyes. Zack told Jeremiah he ran track and field and was a strong runner. "I still run two or three times a week," Zack said. He noticed how Jeremiah looked him up and down.

"Oh, my imagination is going wild hearing of you running track," Jeremiah said. "I can tell underneath this nice suit that you must have an amazing body."

Zack shyly stared down, smiling, after sipping his Coke. "Oh, who knows," he replied awkwardly, giggling.

"I would love to know," Jeremiah coyly replied.

Oh my God, this man is going to make me hard in my suit! What will I do then?

Jeremiah asked Zack if he wanted another drink, as a server was nearby. "Oh, none for me, thank you," Zack replied. "In fact, I probably need to get home. I have school tomorrow."

Jeremiah smiled, "can I at least escort you to your car?"

"Sure," Zack agreed and told him that he was parked near Gratz Park. He wondered if it was too far, but Jeremiah said it wasn't and in turn asked for a ride to his car on North

Broadway. As they made their way out, Jeremiah touched on various topics, and Zack retrieved his overcoat from the coat check. The cold, early evening air refreshed them both as they walking down the steps from the auditorium entrance to the parked car. Jeremiah told Zack funny things about being a musician and Zack was impressed at what a sunny disposition he had. It was comforting.

"I bet you were cute," Jeremiah offered on Zack playing Snoopy. "I can see you being really good at it."

"It was one of the most incredible moments in my life," he confessed. "Playing a cute little dog, singing, and dancing. I really got into it and loved it. It helped me cope with a lot."

Jeremiah stopped and kissed Zack on his cheek, "you have such a beautiful face. I can't take my eyes off you."

After coming upon Zack's parked Toyota, the two got inside. Zack let the car warm up. Jeremiah asked if it would be alright if he kissed him. Zack was hesitant. "Just a kiss, Zackary," he said. "You have such sweet lips." Jeremiah leaned over from the passenger seat, then wrapped an arm around Zack and locked lips with him. It was the first time Zack had kissed a kind, gentle man. The kiss was substantial and lasted for about a minute, but it was almost chaste. As Jeremiah released, Zack pulled him back, and the two engaged in a deeper kiss. Zack was getting all charged up and could not control his erection. After a few minutes of intense kissing, he emerged and once he caught his breath, the two laughed.

"Whew, that was fun, Zackary," Jeremiah said. "We should get together soon. I really want to get to know you better. Would you be up for a movie next weekend?"

"Sure. I would like that." The two kissed again, then released and Zack drove the few blocks to Jeremiah's car.

"Call me on Friday," the musician gave him a card with

his number on it. "We can figure out an afternoon movie on Saturday. How's that sound?"

"Sounds perfect. It has been such a pleasure, or I meant to say the pleasure has been mine," Zack reached out his hand to shake. Jeremiah leaned in and gave him another doozy of a kiss, pushing in a half inch of tongue. As he got out of the car, Zack got a glimpse of Jeremiah's beautiful butt before he put his tuxedo jacket back on.

"Bye, cute Zackary. Get home safe," he said, then blew him a kiss.

Oh, dear God!

It was almost eight o'clock when Zack parked in the driveway and noticed snowflakes melting on his windshield. He sat in the car feeling so excited about meeting Jeremiah Pruett. After walking inside, Zack peeked out the kitchen window. He saw snow coming down in the cone of light shining into their backyard from the neighbor's garage. It was starting to stick a little.

Chapter Twenty

The following week was the beginning of the second trimester. Zack was taking a course in economics during first period. He left the initial class invigorated by what he'd learned. After school, Zack and Gwen met up and went to Wheeler's Pharmacy. They shared French fries at the fountain counter, and each had a milkshake. She talked about Bryn Mawr, the beautiful campus, the distinct keystone buildings, and her excitement about applying, "and they have an excellent premed program!"

Zack listened, thinking how his dear friend would probably be leaving Lexington. However, in the back of his mind, he could not contain his excitement about meeting Jeremiah Pruett the previous weekend. He was reluctant to tell Gwen about him, unsure how she would react to his meeting a guy.

"Did you enjoy the concert?" She asked. "We hated missing this one. Mom loves the Gershwin selections."

"It was fantastic. Thank your parents again for the tickets." Putting one of the remaining fries in his mouth, Zack smiled at Gwen and told her he was happy she was so into her preferred college. "I am going to miss you. It will be difficult when you go away."

"I have to get in first."

He then looked at Gwen's face, reaching in and gently kissing her, gripping her hand, "you will. Nobody's more talented than you."

On Saturday at one-twenty in the afternoon, Zack followed the directions to Jeremiah's apartment complex near Tates Creek Road. His apartment was on the first floor. Classical could be heard through the door. Jeremiah opened it wide, looking amazing in a lovely Shetland navy sweater and tight blue jeans. He hugged Zack and gave him a long kiss.

"I've missed your beautiful face. Come on in, let me take your coat." Zack had on nicely pressed khaki pants, a blue oxford shirt with a grey cable knit sweater, along with blucher moccasins. "Don't you look nice," he added.

A warm glow covered Zack's face as he followed his host into an open kitchen and was given a glass of white wine. "So, Jeremiah, how did you know I was gay?"

"Zackary, a nice, young, handsome man sitting alone at a concert," his eyebrows whirled up and down, "I took a chance and looked for you after, and here you are." Jeremiah smiled widely. They discussed the violinist's passion for music and New York City. Jeremiah played like he was interested in Zack's desire to become an accountant. "Oh, we need good businesspeople, especially really cute ones like you," he said, reaching up and combing his fingers through Zack's hair.

"Ah, that silly cowlick," Zack muttered. When they sat down on the couch, Zack noticed the apartment was somewhat tiny but functional. In the corner, which is where Jeremiah practiced his violin, there was a sheet music tripod, a chair, and an overhead light. On the floor next to the tripod was a neat stack of sheet music. He had a framed poster of Carnegie Hall, along with another picture of musical notes.

Zack felt comfortable sitting with his new friend. The two had some crackers and sipped on white wine. Jeremiah was kind and respectful, telling him about his life, his dreams, and gently revealing his desires. Zack found him sophisticated, and they bonded nicely, laughing and talking endlessly. Then Jeremiah asked Zack if he would mind if they made out. Zack paused, then said, "Okay."

The two began gently kissing at first. Then kissing became more intense for several minutes. Jeremiah kept a hand on the side of Zack's face. "My God, Zackary, you are such a gorgeous young man," he whispered. Zack's heart beat fast, his erection out of control. "Do you mind me asking if you have been with another guy before?"

Zack shook his head, "no." They resumed kissing.

"Boy, you can kiss so well," Jeremiah said, coming up for air.

"Oh, so do you," Zack quietly blurted, taking a deep breath.

After a few more minutes of passionate kissing, Jeremiah pulled Zack closer to him, wrapping his arms around him. Eventually, Jeremiah moved from sitting to lying on his back on the couch, pulling Zack on top of him. Zack's leg lie between Jeremiah's and he could feel Jeremiah's erection pushing against him. Jeremiah stuck out his tongue and Zack gently kissed it, then licked back. Jeremiah ran his fingers through Zack's thick hair, then asked if it would be all right if they got into his bed. "You don't have to remove any of your clothes. Do whatever you are comfortable with."

Zack paused before replying. "Um, I would like to do that, but can we stay on the couch today?"

"Of course," Jeremiah said quickly. "I… I hope I wasn't being too forward."

"No, not at all," Zack said, then stared at the floor.

"Are you upset?" Jeremiah asked.

Zack turned his head away from Jeremiah, feeling intense embarrassment and self-consciousness.

"I'm sorry," his host squeezed his hand. "I shouldn't have said that."

Zack squeezed his hand back, then turned and looked at him with tears falling down his face. "It's not you. You're being so kind. I need to take this slowly. I actually wasn't completely honest with you, but I… well, I got with these two guys last summer. It was my first time… and they really hurt me, so I get frightened." Zack broke down in tears, still holding Jeremiah's hand.

Jeremiah put his head on Zack's shoulder, "I'm so sorry. Bless your heart." Zack turned and the two embraced as he cried. Jeremiah whispered in his ear, "I promise I would never harm you. I'd be gentle and show you kindness and respect. You sweet man, you didn't deserve that."

"Thank you. I do believe you, I… I get so afraid. I'm so sorry for all this!"

Jeremiah kissed Zack again on the cheek, "please know, Zackary, you are dear, so sweet."

Zack slowly turned and looked at him directly in the face, then reached forward for a kiss. Jeremiah wiped Zack's tears with a tissue then the two continued kissing. "I can tell you're reluctant to go into the bedroom. No pressure, I fully understand. Would you instead want to cuddle here with me on the couch? I can get some pillows and a quilt."

"That would be nice."

Jeremiah briefly went into the bedroom. Returning to the living area, Jeremiah had the couch comfortably set up with sheets, a quilt, and two pillows from his bed. He slowly removed his sweater and shirt, with an undershirt, revealing a nice muscular build. He kept his jeans on. Zack smiled as Jeremiah walked over and helped him remove his sweater and shirt, keeping on his undershirt. He folded Zack's garments neatly on an adjacent chair next to the couch. Zack kept his khakis on. Jeremiah lay down sideways on the couch. "Come lie with me, sweetheart. Let's take a nap together." Zack felt comfortable lying clothed with his new friend, who was tender and compassionate. "You are such a beautiful man," Jeremiah said.

Zack climbed onto the couch, cuddling up against his friend, leaning against his chest, "thank you for being so sweet to me." Arms wrapped, they fell asleep facing each other.

Over an hour later, Zack felt Jeremiah kissing his forehead, "hey there, sleepyhead. Did you rest all right?"

Zack opened his eyes, "I feel like I haven't slept this well in years, gosh."

"Let's lie here together," Jeremiah played with his hair. "Zack, I adore getting to know you. You do something to me. Maybe it's your youth, your innocence, but you don't come across as, well, transactional like a lot of gay men."

"Well, you know, this is my first, first official time, with a man. I hope it's fine cuddling with me?"

He gave Zack a long look, "you are . . . you are wonderful to be with," he emphatically replied.

Zack realized, as overwhelmed as he was, he had an effect on Jeremiah.

"I am so excited to be leaving for New York, but I really want to see you while I'm still here in Lexington, stay in touch while I am gone, and see you when I return home."

Zack moved out of his nook, said, "That would be wonderful," and kissed him. As he laid his head back on Jeremiah's chest, he could hear his heartbeat. Zack began to feel comfortable with his new friend. He moved up until they both had their heads on the same pillow.

"You are so at peace when you sleep," Jeremiah said softly. "I can tell you are lovely. I can also tell you are in a lot of pain. We don't know each other that well yet, but I hope we will become great friends."

Zack smiled warmly as Jeremiah kissed his nose. "I would like that so much. Thank you." He felt that this man, whose arms were wrapped around him, was genuine and kind and appeared to have a loving heart. Time would tell. For today, he thought, their kissing and cuddling was one of the most romantic experiences of his life. After the two were dressed, takeout Chinese food arrived. Together, they set the table and organized dinner. Bach's "Air is on the G String" was playing, along with a suite of other music. The meal was delicious, and Jeremiah talked more about his devotion to music. "I think it is tremendous you have this talent and work so hard at it," Zack said. "I can tell you sacrifice to develop yourself. It's so impressive. I think being in New York, wow, I can't imagine how exciting it must be."

"I will be practicing and rehearsing for long hours, so getting out into the city will be challenging, but it's the greatest place in the world. The noise, the energy, the art, the people." Jeremiah asked Zack if he wanted the last egg roll, and he shook his head. Then he brought up a tough topic, "You know, Zack, many men in New York are dying. Gay men. Public health officials have called it GRID, but it's like a disease killing gay men. It's really scary. When I've been in New York, I like to go to some bathhouses. I'm kind of afraid now, though."

Zack reached over and took his hand, "that sounds really scary. I wouldn't want anything to happen to you."

"Thank you, honey. You are so kind and sweet. I want to come home and see you."

Zack fanned himself, "you… you flatter me. I'll be here." Squeezing Jeremiah's hand, he continued, "I want you to do well up in New York. I am so impressed." "I need to get back and see you," Jeremiah gently kissed Zack. He stood up and changed the record. "This is 'Introduction and Tarantella, Op. 43' by Pablo de Sarasate, one of the pieces we will be performing in New York. Listen for the violin? I am learning these chords, practicing for hours."

Jeremiah put the focus on Zack, "what do you want in your life? Where do you want to go?"

Zack was self-conscious, "I hope to get into a university somewhere. I want to study accounting. I'm taking it now in school, and I hear it's much harder in college, but I really want to try to become a CPA."

Jeremiah leaned in, "I'm so glad you're not a musician. I could never go out with another male musician. It never works out. I think what you want to do is great. You know, if I ever move to New York, for good, there's always a demand for CPAs up there, I imagine."

Zack giggled, blushing, "Oh, wow. Listen, my father doesn't believe in me, and I doubt that could ever happen."

"I'm sure he loves you but probably doesn't know what's best for you. You can figure this out for yourself. You must decide your destiny. It's not your parent's decision. My father hated that I became a musician when I was young. Too bad, I worked for hours, seven days a week, practicing. That is the way you develop your talent, have talent. Now, I'm one of the Philharmonic's youngest first chairs. As I graduate from UK, I have been invited, along with this consortium of graduates across the country, to study, rehearse, and perform together. I may end up going to Juilliard for graduate school. My mother is my biggest supporter. I thank God for her."

Jeremiah's tenacity and willingness to compete so hard to be the best made an impression on Zack. *He even has a beautiful soul,* Zack thought. As the two were cleaning dinner plates, Jeremiah reached into the soapy water, taking Zack's hand, "so, my sweet Zackary. Would you like to sleep over tonight? Nothing sexual unless you want to."

Zack looked up at him, smiling, "I wish I could, but I

must get home to my father. He needs me. I have to give him his insulin in the early morning."

Jeremiah dried his hands, then wrapped his arm around Zack, kissing his hair, "okay. We might need to plan this in advance sometime. I love the warmth of your body against mine."

As Zack wiped his hands dry, he turned and kissed him again, and tearing up he said, "today has meant so much to me. So much, you have no idea." They hugged for several minutes.

After Zack put his coat on, the two began another intense make-out session. "Whew, I may have to take my coat off," Zack said.

"Fine with me!" They both laughed.

"Thank you so much for this wonderful day and for being so kind and understanding."

"Call me when you get home?" Jeremiah asked.

Zack nodded. The two briefly discussed getting together the following Saturday. After one last tight embrace and kiss, Zack walked out to his car in the darkness. Jeremiah poked his head out of his door, "amazing butt, kid!"

Zack turned around, blew him back a kiss and waved goodbye.

Chapter Twenty-One

On the Monday of Thanksgiving week, Zack walked up to his locker and saw a couple of students staring at a piece of paper taped to it. When he got closer, they walked away and he discovered it was a drawing of a figure with his mouth open and what appeared to be a penis shoved in it with the words "COCKSUCKER'S LOCKER IS HERE." Zack ripped it down without looking around, but he knew people were looking at him. After opening the door, he found three more notes shoved in. He quickly hung up his coat, got a notebook, then slammed it shut. His face was red with anger. The constant barrage of notes was beginning to get to him. As he walked down the hall he heard a guy yell, "FAGGOT!"

When sitting down in psychology class, Gwen turned towards him. She whispered, "Hey, are you all right?"

Zack quickly told her, "Gwen, you once offered that I could move my locker in with you. I'd like to today, if possible."

She looked concerned look, "what's wrong?"

He stared at her, "I need to. Is that okay with you?" She nodded yes. "I'll move my things in during lunch. It's my books and a coat."

Gwen wrote the combination down and handed it to him. Zack was still hot with anger, staring forward as class began. *Why do people care if I'm gay? What did I ever do to them?* During class, he put his left hand down and Gwen reached and clasped it. Zack looked down with a sad face.

In the hallway after class, Zack hugged Gwen and she asked, "what's happened, honey? You seem upset."

"I don't want to talk about it," he shook his head. "Listen, I ordered some flowers to arrive tomorrow for your mother to thank her for those letters of recommendation she is writing for me. I'm dropping the Indiana and Miami applications in the mail as soon as I get the sealed letters of recommendation from Mr. Evans. I have an appointment with him today after trig."

Gwen opened her bag and pulled out the two sealed envelopes containing her mother's recommendations. "Oh, wow. She wasted no time. I really appreciate her doing this. It means a lot to me."

Gwen put her hand on Zack's face, "you look upset. You'll tell me when you want. I'm here for you."

Zack, looking around, reached back and kissed her, "you just saying that is a real help to me."

After trig class, Zack picked up his recommendation letters from his guidance counselor. He walked over and cleaned out his locker with several more notes shoved inside. Down the hallway at Gwen's locker, he put a few belongings in, and his eyes welled up. With limited time for lunch before going to fifth period, Zack sat in his car and ate alone. Afterward, walking back into the building for his next class, he ran into Matt.

"You know, you and I never do anything anymore," Zack said. "We should hang out when you have time."

"Zacky," Matt replied with a grin, "I was thinking the

same thing. But if I'm not working, studying, or going to school, I'm trying to find time to fuck Colleen."

Zack put up his hand, "Matt, please stop saying 'fuck.' She probably wouldn't be too happy if she heard you saying it. She's such a nice person."

"Zackary, you are such a prude," Matt laughed. "I don't speak like that around her, only you. So, then I say 'fuck' and 'pussy.'"

As they walked into class and sat down, Zack whispered to Matt, "when you love a person, and I know you do feel it with Colleen, I believe you have to think, speak, and dream the kindest thoughts about that person. For you, Colleen's a treasure. I would never imagine speaking that way about someone I truly cared about and loved."

Matt whispered back, "you are an incurable romantic, Zacky. I can't wait until you have a boyfriend, and you say, 'He shot his load in my mouth' and 'I fucked his hot ass.'"

Opening his notebook, Zack glared back. Hearing Matt's voice made him miss when the two flew kites together, went for long bike rides, read comic books, had sleepovers, went to the country club, played tennis, swam, and went to the movies. At this moment, Zack realized his childhood was over. He blankly watched the teacher writing on the board and wished everything could be innocent again.

After school, Zack drove to the library at Gratz Park to do some research for his economics paper on tax policy. He started by searching for two volumes upstairs in the stacks. While walking along the dimly lit bookshelves, Zack noticed a young man staring at him at the other end of the aisle. He was tall, thin, and nicely built, with black hair, thick sideburns, and a mustache. He was wearing black sunglasses. No one else was around. He could hear the guy quietly moving up and down the aisles. Zack finally located the books he was looking for. As he reached for them, he saw the young man looking through the shelf, smiling directly at him. Zack didn't think anything of it. Flipping through the pages of one book, Zack sat down on a stepladder. It was incredibly quiet in the library, but suddenly, he heard a soft sexual moaning. Zack looked around and thought it was his imagination. He resumed reading when he heard, "Ooooh, yeah. Ooooohhh uuuhhh." Zack was shocked and looked through the bookshelves to see where the noise was coming from. He thought to himself, is someone up here having sex in the stacks? He heard more moaning, but this time it was closer and louder. Zack became nervous, but also found it exciting. Noticing movement in the adjacent aisle, Zack stood up and pushed the books aside on the shelf to his left and the same man was looking directly at him with a big grin on his face. It shocked Zack at first, but then he realized the man was following him.

"Hey," the man said.

"Hello. Do I know you?" Zack asked.

"Not yet," he replied devilishly and raised his left eyebrow twice. There was still nobody around but Zack and the man. "I haven't seen you here before, what's your name?"

"Um, Zack."

The man then began gesturing with his eyes for Zack to look down at the lower bookshelf.

"What are you referring to?" Zack stupidly asked.

"Second shelf, move the books and look," the man directed.

Zack got on his right knee and pulled out a batch of books with both his hands, gently placing them on the floor. As he stared through the shelf to the other side, he could see the man stroking his flaccid penis.

"Oooohhh, come around and suck it," he summoned.

Zack's eyebrows instantly went up. He wasn't about to do anything sexual in a library, but he was surprisingly turned on watching the show. Sweat beads formed on his forehead, "no thank you. Have a nice day."

As Zack quickly walked away, he heard from a distance, "come back, I didn't get your phone number."

Zack turned to look for a few seconds and then headed back to his table, his heart beating fast. The sexual tension was real and immediate, but he was afraid to act on something in a public place or with a stranger.

Back home, Pop asked, "Son, I want the Christmas tree up on Friday." He believed in putting the tree up early in the season.

"Pop, can Gwen help me decorate the tree?" Zack asked, relieved to be at his house. "I would like you to meet her."

"Of course."

Zack worked on his homework, and around eight o'clock, he jogged up and down Lakeshore Drive. After arriving home, Zack took a shower and broke down in tears thinking about his mother, whom he dearly missed. *She will be alone for Thanksgiving.* He dried off, brushed his teeth, and put on a fresh pair of pajamas. In his father's bedroom, Zack sat on the edge of the bed, then got up and lie down in bed up against his father, who put his hand on his wet hair. "Son, I put the checks for the college applications on the kitchen table."

"Thank you, Daddy."

Chapter Twenty-Two

Thanksgiving morning, in his suit and tie, along with an overcoat, Zack went out to warm up the Fleetwood. The overnight rain had stopped. Pop came out with his hat and suit, covered by a camel coat. Zack moved over, and Pop drove the car. He wanted to be on the road by eight-thirty in the morning, Uncle George had made reservations for dinner at eleven for the Old Crow Inn's first serving. His uncle was a diabetic, too, so they had to eat early.

Through rolling hills, they drove past late autumn foliage, going down the highway and crossing the bridge at the Kentucky River, then winding down a long mountain and crossing the bridge at Herrington Lake. When Zackary was a child, he enjoyed when Pop drove him to Danville once a month to visit his aunt and uncle. On the way back home, they used to stop at a surplus store that sold souvenirs and ice cream, his dad always indulged. Turning to watch two ducks fly low over the waters, Zack smiled at the memory.

Grey sky broke as clouds attempted to cover the sun. Cool dampness and obscured light accentuated the dark, rain-soaked bark of the trees. After pulling into his uncle's driveway, Pop and Zack walked in the kitchen door. The

Danville Kingdons had an inviting home, with warm wooden floors throughout. Aunt Norma greeted them with hugs, kisses, and her signature huge smile.

"How are you all? Zack, come on in, honey." He hugged and kissed her before walking into the den behind Pop where Uncle George sat in his large chair, one long arm arched over the back of his head in a comfortable position.

"There's Zack!" Uncle George announced. "How are you doing?"

He reached down to embrace his uncle, "I'm fine, sir. So good to see you." Zack hugged his cousin, Ann and shook hands with her husband, Kenny. The television was on with images of the Macy's parade.

"Zack, can I get you a ginger ale?" his aunt asked.

"Oh, no, ma'am, thank you," he replied. Zack sat close to the massive fireplace, burning brightly. The den was full of Kentucky Derby pictures, horse figures, and horseshoes, all carefully arranged by his aunt. A papier-mâché turkey sat on the dining room table that he had been fascinated with since he was a little boy. Ann asked about how his senior year was going. Uncle George inquired what he was going to do for college. "Most likely UK, sir. I sent applications to Miami of Ohio and Indiana University, those are long shots, but I applied. I most likely will study accounting."

Pop jumped in, "Son, speak up so your uncle can hear you."

"I heard him fine, Davy." Turning back to Zack, he added, "Good. Accounting, then maybe law school."

"George, we don't need another goddamn lawyer," Pop said, interrupting a little too loudly. "He needs to become a CPA, but I seriously doubt he's capable of doing even that."

Zack was embarrassed by his father, but his Uncle

George came to his rescue, "Davy, was I talking to you?"

He looked at his cousin Ann with wide eyes and a funny look.

She laughed, whispering, "I know, goodness, do I know."

Uncle George quietly told his younger brother that his son should study what he wants, "you know, Davy, he needs to go somewhere away, where he can get those thoughts of his momma out of his head. He's a nice boy. Zack is capable of doing anything. You've done a good job with him."

"Maybe I have, maybe I haven't. Boy won't stop crying all the time and he messed up in school last year."

"Davy, as I recall, you cried a lot when Daddy passed away," George said. "It's hard on a boy to lose a parent one way or another. Virginia was a fine woman, but it's terrible what she did to you, and abandoning Zack."

A few minutes later, Aunt Norma walked into the den and asked Zack to talk in the living room, "Honey, are you sure I can't get you a ginger ale?"

"Okay, ma'am. That would be nice." After pouring the soda into a glass, the two entered the living room with its thick, creamy yellow carpeting. It was a large, cozy room with tall ceilings, bright yellow and white flower-patterned wallpaper and dark wood furniture pieces, which pulled in the sunlight. He and Aunt Norma sat on the couch. She had coasters with different Derby-winning horses on the coffee table, similar to those at his house. Zack carefully placed his beverage on "Secretariat." He handed Aunt Norma an envelope with his senior portrait.

"Look at you! Oh, this is wonderful. I will frame it. You are such a handsome boy!" Zack grinned. "How have you been, honey? I think about you all the time," Norma said sweetly, holding his hand.

"I'm alright, I guess. I was busy with the play, and I mailed two of my college applications."

"Honey, have you given any thought about attending Centre College, living here in Danville? I think it would do you good."

Ann walked into the living room. "Mother, I think Daddy is ready to go."

"Zack, why don't we go for a spin after we eat, just the two of us, and keep talking?" Zack nodded eagerly.

Pop and Uncle George each drove Fleetwood Cadillacs, and as the family made their way to their cars, Zack noticed how his Uncle George and father looked quite a bit alike. Both were tall, broad, and heavy with similar faces and they each carried themselves proudly. However, they were different in many ways, as well. Uncle George enjoyed life. He never left his hometown after returning a war hero from World War II and UK law school, unlike his younger brother. During the war, he saved the lives of several POWs, including a man who called George every year to thank him, and remind him that his large family would not have happened if Seargent Kingdon and his troops had not rescued him from the Germans. His uncle was someone who definitely led by example, Zack thought.

The Old Crow Inn was a large and stately mansion constructed in 1780 entirely of stone with four columns in the front. Norma and George walked into the dining room like local royalty and knew practically everyone eating there. There was a stone fireplace burning nearby, and the colonial design with wooden beams and wooden floors bolstered the historical theme of the holiday. Since Danville was in a dry county, Aunt Norma brought a bottle of bourbon and poured herself and George a drink at the table before dinner. Zack sat with his aunt to his left and Ann to his right. Daddy, Uncle George, and Kenny sat on the other end. Pop and George always had a long and animated conversation going. Norma spoke to the waiter and got George some rolls and butter. Not long after, a salad appeared.

Like every year, Zack was extremely happy spending Thanksgiving in Danville. He was struck by how normal, kind, and affectionate this particular Kingdon household was. Ann would have been a great sister. And Uncle George was a man set in his ways like Pop, but he had a genuine kindness and humanity to him. Having Norma as his wife, truly one of the most loving individuals ever, probably helped him stay that way. Zack could see similarities between her and Gwen. When Zack's mother had her mental breakdowns and hospitalizations and eventually moved out, Aunt Norma often came to Lexington and dropped in for a visit. He was quite young when all this began, but Norma regularly greeted him when he arrived home from school. She'd taken an active role in Zack's life.

Pop and Uncle George were talking about President Reagan, and it didn't sound to Zack like they were in agreement. Zack admired how his uncle had a heart. Pop became agitated with his big brother's Democratic views. He recognized how Uncle George's sharp mind poked holes in David's arguments. He also managed to do it without cursing. As a result, Pop watched his "G-Ds" around Norma, who never spoke ill of anyone and disapproved of coarse language. The turkey finally arrived with cornbread stuffing, gravy boats, mashed potatoes, green beans with ham hocks, creamed corn, cranberry sauce, and more yeast rolls. Knowing his predilections, Aunt Norma made sure Zack's plate did not have any gravy or cranberry sauce. She also begged her "Georgie" not to eat too much fatty dark meat. Before digging in, they all held hands while Uncle George gave the blessing.

Later, when dessert showed up, Zack had vanilla ice cream and a little apple pie. He saw that his father and uncle each ordered slices of pecan and pumpkin pie. Aunt Norma informed the table she had picked up several pies herself at the bakery and reserved three of them for Zack and his dad. As Zack was having some coffee, he overheard Pop and Uncle George quietly talking about Virginia. While it had been years since his mother was present for Thanksgiving, for some reason, her absence at this holiday hurt him so much. He immediately thought about his mother's amazing holiday dinners when he was six. She cooked the meal herself and had always created a memorable Thanksgiving for everyone. Norma reached over and gently placed her hand on his arm, "Honey, how's your dessert?"

"Fine, ma'am," Zack replied. "Thank you."

"We'll take a drive in a little while," she said, patting his arm. He turned and looked at his aunt smiling warmly, and thought, *I want to be like her. She finds the sunshine in everything and in everyone.*

After the dinner, Norma told Zack she was ready to drive around town. Once in the car, he marveled at the many gorgeous homes, particularly the antebellum red-brick house used in the 1957 film, *Raintree County*. After driving to a few other sites, including his father's childhood home, she parked the car near the Dr. Ephraim McDowell House on 2nd Street to have a real conversation. Zack enthusiastically regaled her with tales of playing Snoopy in "You're a Good Man, Charlie Brown", making her laugh.

Eventually, the two made their way back home, walking inside to see all the Kingdon men watching football. As it neared four o'clock and started to get dark, Pop was ready to head home. Zack hugged all his relatives and saved his last goodbye for Norma, who embraced him tightly, "You call me if you ever need to talk, honey."

"Thank you so much," he kissed his aunt, breaking

into a huge smile. As Zack and Pop made their way to the car carrying pies, he asked his father if he wanted him to drive.

"Son, you're not old enough for this drive with all these winding roads. Let me do it."

On the ride back, crossing the bridge at Herrington Lake, it was practically pitch dark. Hearing the purring noise on the tires, Pop began questioning Zack about college, "Son, I don't know where you'll get in. You might as well go to UK." The toothpick was relatively steady. "I am afraid you won't be able to handle college. UK'll be brutal. You're not capable or mature. Your grades from junior year are embarrassing, and you have little to show for yourself."

You're terrible, you have terrible grades, you aren't worth shit, you have nothing to show for yourself, you're just awful, was the message coming in loud and clear. Further in the drive by the time they were nearing Nicholasville, driving by the Dish Barn, the conversation had gotten rather combative.

"Zack, your teachers all think you're a terrible student. You never wanted to participate in sports," Pop lobbed.

Zack had heard this record playing over and over. "Oh, here we go again. First, I ran track one year in junior high and one year at Henry Clay, but I 'never participated in sports.' But I lettered in basketball at Morton, sitting on the bench the entire season. Pop, I was a lead in a play. I received a pretty good report card. I am trying my best. So you're wrong," Zack angrily responded.

Pop wouldn't let up, "being in a play is not getting you anywhere. Son, you have a mediocre record, because you are mediocre. I got you tutors, got you help with your motor skills, but you're too limited to go far in life. I am not even sure you can do accounting."

To Zack, those were fighting words, "Pop, stop shitting on everything I try to do! I'm never good enough to you."

Pop's toothpick began to gyrate, "watch that goddamn mouth, boy! You'll be pickin' up your teeth in Winchester!"

Zack, realizing he took a risk, apologized, "Sorry."

Pop yelled back, "SORRY, SIR!"

"Sorry, sir," Zack turned red. Neither muttered another word for the rest of the drive.

Later that night, as it approached ten o'clock, Pop lie in bed watching a football game in overtime. Zack sat down on the edge in his pajamas. He could feel his father rubbing his back. Zack turned and kissed him good night, "why are you so tough on me, Daddy?"

"Son, I need to toughen you up," he said. "You don't understand how hard the world can be, how cruel it can be."

"Oh, I think I have an idea," Zack gently interrupted.

Pop just sat up and kissed him again on the cheek. Zack knew it was his father's way of letting him know he was sorry for his harsh words.

Chapter Twenty-Three

"I think you're the only person I know who orders his pancakes well done," Gwen teased. She and Zack were on the drive back from breakfast.

Zack was relaxed and happy whenever he was with Gwen. She helped him feel like himself again. "Bob Evans doesn't get them right, I'm telling you. I'll take you to Tommy's one day and you'll understand… and thank me for expanding your horizons."

Arriving home, the two found Pop in the drawing room watching television. "Pop, I would like to introduce you to Miss Gwen Farris."

David Kingdon rose from his lounge chair. "Well, hello, Gwen. It is nice to meet you. Welcome."

"It is such a pleasure to meet you, sir," she said. "Thank you for having me over. Zack tells me such nice things. I am so taken how the two of you resemble each other."

They continued small talk, with Gwen expressing her appreciation for the Christmas tree in the drawing room that Zack had already started decorating earlier in the morning. Then the two of them retreated to decorate the second tree in the living room. Zack turned on some music while they finished stringing the lights.

"Why are you putting up the decorations so early?" Gwen asked.

"Oh, Daddy wants it done now," he said. "When I was a child, my mother was usually in the hospital this time of year. It was an 'all hands on deck' endeavor. I mean, he had to take care of Emily and me, buy all the gifts, dragging me everywhere with him. It was a sad time for everyone, but when it came to Christmas, he did what he could to make it wonderful for us. He's really good that way." Winding a strand through some firm branches, Zack added, "I think he likes to see the lights. It distracts him from those painful memories around the holidays."

"You care about him so much," she held his hand. "I enjoy hearing you speak so kindly of him."

Zack rolled his eyes, bending down to gently unwrap more ornaments, "Oh, God, yes! He also drives me crazy, makes me so mad sometimes, but I dearly love him. Underneath it all, he is a kind soul and a tremendous man. He never left me as a child." Zack began to tear up.

Gwen hugged him, "you've been through a lot. He's your 'lighthouse,' Zack."

He nodded. The two then stared at each other, and he reached in and kissed her, "you're an amazing friend."

After finishing the tree, Zack went in and checked on his father, who wanted his lunch. Zack prepared him turkey sandwiches on Magee's Bakery yeast rolls with Durkee sauce, a kosher dill pickle, and a glass of milk. Gwen looked at the leftover Thanksgiving pies, "my goodness, you all have some serious desserts."

"Let me get him settled, and I'll fix us something in a moment," Zack replied, taking Pop his lunch.

Pop's tray table was already set up and he instructed, "now I want a piece of apple pie and pumpkin pie."

"Okay, now, Pop, you can get one, but not both."

"I'm not asking!" Pop yelled. As Zack returned to the kitchen, Gwen was covering her mouth laughing from overhearing the exchange.

"Your dad's funny," she stared as Zack cut two slices of pie she thought could fit on one plate.

"Oh, no," Zack said mock serious. "The apple has to be heated. There's a whole routine. And, of course, he wants a scoop of vanilla with it."

Zack got out the Roman Meal bread and made them turkey sandwiches and milk. Enjoying the moment, he reached over and took Gwen's hand, "if I'm thankful for anything this Thanksgiving, it's meeting you. I am so blessed to know you." Gwen teared up, nodding.

"Son… Son… Son… I need my pie." The two broke down in laughter. "Son," he yelled again.

"I heard you the first time, Pop. I'm coming." Zack got up and heated the pie. Taking the metal scooper, he ran it under hot water, put a large dollop of ice cream on the plate next to the heated apple pie, then grabbed a dessert fork. Looking over at Gwen, he said, "Be right back." After caring for Pop, Zack and Gwen shared a slice of apple pie.

Later in the afternoon, after all the decorations were up, Pop came out and did his inspection, "Oh, this is great," Pop glowed. "You all did such a tremendous job."

"Daddy, would it be alright if Gwen and I go up to my room to listen to music?"

Pop, staring at the decorated room, nodded his head. Zack may have been eighteen, but he wanted to show his father respect, and Gwen respect, by keeping the bedroom door open. Once upstairs, the two lay on the bed together, wrapped in each other's arms, gently kissing. Gwen then sat up on the edge of the bed. "I like that I can kiss you," she said, putting her hands on his chest. "God, you may be as confused about your feelings as I am, but the fact you can feel anything after all the terrible things you have shared with me is tremendous." Gwen began to stare out Zack's window.

"What is it? You're all quiet," Zack asked.

Gwen smiled and looked back at Zack. "I wish I could find a man in my life who would be sweet to me like you are." He leaned up. "Zackary, you have redeemed my faith in men. Ed's harshness and cruelty overshadow his wonderful qualities, and he has some. But one of the reasons I love you as I do is because you do show yourself. You show me your heart. It really matters that you never lose that. It's simply beautiful to see." Gwen was in tears.

"Come here. Come here," Zack said, sitting up and holding Gwen. "You are the finest person I have ever met. You're a beautiful girl, and I am so much better and happier since I met you." He gently kissed her, combing her long, flowing hair with his hand. The two hugged and kissed on the bed for several minutes.

Gwen muttered, "Zack, you're gay. You're attracted to guys. It's the way you are."

"Gwen, that's physical," he kissed her hard. "Maybe I can feel this way with a man, too, but I dearly love you. Don't underestimate how much your friendship has meant to me. Why are we kissing? We love each other."

The two continued making out on the bed. A few minutes later, Gwen revealed that Ed saw Zack's jacket hanging in her locker. "What did he say?"

"Do you really want me to tell you?" He nodded. "Well, he called you 'f'ing queer' and he demanded I quit hanging out with you. I told him no damn man's going to tell me what to do!"

Zack immediately tried to backpedal, "Gwen, I can get another locker. I'm sorry. I didn't want to cause problems."

She put her hand over his mouth, "S-h-h. You didn't. I want you there. I want you to share the locker with me. I don't care if it bothers him." Zack sensed something was brewing, and it would get ugly between Gwen and Ed and eventually Ed and himself. "Ed tried to feel me up two nights ago. I always pushed his hand back, and he would pull back, but this time he refused to stop." Tears fell down her face.

"Oh, Gwen, no. Oh, honey, I am sorry. Dear God!" She was overcome with tears. Zack wrapped his arms around her and began crying.

"He… felt me, he inserted his finger. I begged him not to, but he wouldn't stop. It really hurt and he wouldn't stop. Zacky, you warned me. You told he would hurt me. You were right."

Zack took some tissues and wiped her tears, "God, I wish I was wrong. You sweet thing. He's such a fucking asshole, man."

She told Zack she would call him Sunday night and break up with him on the phone. "I told my parents everything and I'm going to tell him I did. He can never come near me again. My mother is beside herself." The two laid their heads back down on the bed, "see, I can tell you things, even the most painful, and you cry more than me, Zack."

"Gwen, nothing hurts me more than to know you're hurting like I did. It kills me inside, because I know… I know the fear and pain and loneliness, and I don't want you to." Zack was overcome with grief. The two cried for several minutes. He pushed his head against hers. Zack gently kissed her, tasting her tears.

Gwen clutched his hands, "I guess I'm blessed I met you. You make me feel so safe and loved."

"Gwen, I'm so glad you told me," he kissed her hard. "I'm glad you told your parents. This is terrible and I'm here for you."

She whispered in his ear, "Honey, I am afraid Ed is going to come for you. You have to be careful. Ed thinks you put things into my head. He doesn't know about our talks or how I feel about you or that we kiss, but he knows how fond I am of you. He says 'faggot' and 'cocksucker,' horrible things about you. I never wanted to tell you."

"I know he could take me, he's massive. I'm scrawny compared to him, but I'll be fine. Ed Sims can't hurt me."

"Hon, he can. He's dangerous. Please be careful."

Zack kissed her, "I don't want him ever coming near you again!" The two held each other.

Later, after Gwen had left and he was getting ready for bed, Zack sat at his desk and called Jeremiah to confirm their date. He was still a little rattled from what she had shared with him, but it didn't extinguish his feeling when he thought about this wonderful new man he'd met. "I am so looking forward to seeing you tomorrow," Zack said.

"I can't get you off my mind," Jeremiah said over the phone wire. "Can I ask you something?"

Zack put his elbow on his desk, "sure."

"I want you to feel safe being with me. I hope I am not too forward here, but how can I put this? I would like to do more than kiss you on the couch tomorrow. But you tell me if that's all right. I would never hurt you or try to force you to do anything you are uncomfortable with."

Zack held the phone, smiling, touched, and quite turned on but still reluctant to go forward. "Let me sleep on it, okay? I do want to, believe me. Let me sleep on it. Thank you for telling me this so kindly."

"Zackary, I really care for you. I promise you I will show you nothing but love."

"That's sweet. Thank you," the two said good night and Zack sat at his desk, feeling a sense of euphoric elation.

Chapter Twenty-Four

Zack and Jeremiah stood, enveloped in a deep kiss, as the musician slowly closed his apartment door. He took Zack's coat and hung it up, "I've missed you," Jeremiah said, walking briefly into the kitchen.

"Oh, God, me too," Zack replied.

Jeremiah handed Zackary a glass of water, steering him to the couch as he sat down on his stool to finish practicing the piece he was working on, "I hope you don't mind me taking a few minutes to finish the last part of this composition?"

Zack smirked, "Are you kidding? I would love to hear you play."

Jeremiah took a dark cloth and placed it on his shoulder at his neck, quietly picked up his violin and bow, and positioned the instrument. "This is a piece by Schumann." He then closed his eyes and deftly played a slow-paced portion of the arrangement. The control over the instrument demonstrated that Jeremiah had much more than just skill but real talent. The dexterity of his fingers on the strings, his subtle, but nuanced movements of the bow, procured a soothing, slow sound that steadily, but eventually built into a robust melody. Jeremiah knew the composition, kept his eyes closed throughout, the control he seemed to master while quickly breathing and then exhaling, and his rapid, bodily gyrations—all with simultaneous coordination of his efforts was spectacular to watch. The lilting notes at one point created a lovely melody, causing Zack to smile. Jeremiah not only played the music but allowed it to flow through his soul. About twenty minutes later, he put the instrument down, exhaling deeply, as Zack clapped.

"Gosh, you are impressive. I could never do that."

"Ah, but you could, Zackary. You have so much untapped talent, I can tell." After putting his violin back in its case, Jeremiah stood up, sat next to Zack on the couch, sipped his water, and kissed him. He put his hand on Zack's upper leg, which excited him, and wrapped his arms around Zack, who leaned his head against his chest. "I need to take a shower," Jeremiah said. "Would like to join me?"

Zack sat silent, then muttered, "I would, but I need to do this slowly."

"You're safe with me," Jeremiah promised, gently touching Zack's face.

The two kissed, and Jeremiah took Zack by his right hand and led him into the bedroom, where the two began undressing. Zack looked away from Jeremiah, shy, as he removed his jeans and shirt, placing them carefully on the chair next to the bed. "Such cute boxers."

Zack snickered and turned around. Jeremiah was completely unclothed, standing across the room. He was immensely attracted to the man's naked body.

"Are you okay?" Jeremiah asked.

Smiling, Zack replied, "you're really, um, gorgeous."

Jeremiah walked towards Zack, "I will only be loving to you."

Still in his underwear, Zack stretched up and kissed

Jeremiah, who was nearly a foot taller. "I'll be okay," he said. "I get a bit scared. I need to hold your hand through this. It makes me feel safe."

"If it gets too much for you, tell me at any point."

Zack removed his undershirt, "I want to be with you." Then he pulled down his boxers, standing completely naked and shivering. Jeremiah led Zack to sit on the bed, holding each other. Zack reached up and kissed Jeremiah passionately. Removing his lips, Zack muttered, "I do. I want to make love with you, too." Jeremiah beamed.

The two stood up and walked into the bathroom, where Jeremiah turned on the shower. They stepped inside and embraced under the hot spray, kissing. Jeremiah took the soap and gently washed Zack's body. He eventually moved the soap down to his pubic region, then moved to his thighs, avoiding touching his penis. Getting down on his knees, he continued soaping up the back of Zack's thick upper legs, slowly putting the bar up into his butt. Zack moaned as Jeremiah kissed around his thigh. The sensation was new to him. "I adore your butt." When he reached and took Zack's erect penis in his hand, Zack sharply yanked himself back, "Oh, I'm not hurting you, am I?"

"No. No, I'm fine. I'm a bit sensitive…" Zack replied, noticing it must have been a defense mechanism from the rape.

"Can I put it in my mouth?"

"Yes." At the feeling of his warm mouth, Zack began shaking, pushing against the tile for support, and moaned as he experienced inexplicable pleasure. For the next few minutes, Zack felt Jeremiah use his fingers underneath his testicles in the taint region, gently pressing a fist upward against Zackary's prostate. He slowly used his mouth on Zack's penis, causing him to close his eyes, feeling the water hitting his back, and taking in such a sensational and blissful moment. Zack held Jeremiah's head with one hand, balancing him, and his hand with the other. As Jeremiah stood back up, the two kissed. Zack took the bar and soaped Jeremiah's body, slowly washing his chest and belly, then felt his penis, slowly stroking it. Turning him around, Zack washed his back, his butt, and then his legs. Zack had never seen a more beautiful ass in his life.

After rinsing and turning the shower off, Jeremiah began to dry Zackary off with a towel, going slowly, "you have such a beautiful body."

"Thank you, you do too," Zack replied. The two played with and touched each other's bodies, then walked into the bedroom. Jeremiah turned classical music on his radio. As fading afternoon sunlight shone through the bedroom window blinds, for the next hour, Jeremiah took his time, kissing and loving Zackary's body with his hands and tongue, causing him to gyrate and moan at times. Asking for Jeremiah's hand as the musician pleasured him, Zack clutched it throughout to feel safe. He could tell Jeremiah understood how to please a man, feeling the warmth of his soft tongue move slowly around the back of his knees, and his nipples, then licking his belly, leading to and focusing on the tender, sensitive nerve endings in his anus and penis. Zack clenched his teeth, moaning, tearing up, feeling overwhelming, intense pleasure, tightly gripping Jeremiah's hand. He spent a great deal of time putting his face and tongue on Zack's butt, blowing his breath on it, then licking, sending Zack into a blissful trance. He found the experience with Jeremiah so sensational. The man was a fully committed lover. They then hugged and passionately kissed.

"I enjoy seeing you get so into it. It's beautiful," Jeremiah commented.

"I think I'm going to come soon," Zack said, as the two kissed.

Jeremiah looked into his eyes. "Zackary, would you want to be inside me? I would love to feel you penetrate me."

"Sure, but are you sure? I've never done this before."

"I have longed for your doing this to me. I'll teach you."

"Okay." Jeremiah turned over and got on his knees. He handed Zack some lubricant. "I don't want to hurt you."

"I'll guide you. Start by gently inserting a finger," Jeremiah replied, positioning himself on all fours on the edge of the bed, while Zack stood on the floor behind him.

Clutching his partner's fingers, Zack found Jeremiah's anus, tenderly rubbing it, then gently inserted a finger. He removed it and slowly began pushing the head of his penis on the area for a few minutes, afraid he was hurting him. Jeremiah instructed him to push a bit harder, eventually moving himself inside all the way. The warmth and the pressure inside felt so amazing. Jeremiah moaned loudly.

"Is this okay?"

"Oh, it's fine." As he moved his pelvis back and forth, Jeremiah begged Zack, "Push hard… thrust as hard as you can. Push your hips and butt-forward really hard."

Zack was afraid, concerned he would hurt him. He put one leg up on the bed, giving him more leverage, then began stepping up his pace. After several minutes, Zack was saturated with sweat. Jeremiah motioned for him to stop.

"Let me get on my back. Oh, you are so good!" Jeremiah shifted his position, lying down on his back with his legs in the air.

Zack, out of breath, muttered, "Are you sure I'm not hurting you?"

"I'm fine, you feel fucking amazing!" Jeremiah sat up and kissed Zack.

Lying on the corner of the bed, Zack put on fresh lubricant, then pushed and held Jeremiah's long, thick legs up to his shoulder, as he slowly reinserted himself. As he began thrusting, he looked at Jeremiah's gorgeous face, seeming to be experiencing a delirium. Zack resumed tightly, clutching his hand. "Are you all right?" Zack asked.

"You are the best. Keep going. Please don't stop." Jeremiah then leaned up and pulled Zack slowly down towards him, reaching up and kissing him. The thrusts became more aggressive, and the two men were soon covered in sweat. Jeremiah reached up, put his hand on Zack's pubic hair, then gently and slowly rubbed his belly. The feeling of his hand on Zack's stomach happened as he was building an orgasm. Jeremiah yelled, "Shoot inside me! Breathe through your nose when you come and hold it!"

"I'm… I'm… going to…" Zack yelled, Jeremiah squeezing his left hand.

"Keep going, hold your breath!" Zack then ejaculated, experiencing one of the most intense releases, ever. Jeremiah simultaneously yelled as he came all over his stomach. Zack's face was red as he gently pulled out. Jeremiah reached for some paper towels adjacent to the bed. Zack sat on the edge of the bed and helped clean Jeremiah.

Zack softly said, "I think that might have been the most wonderful experience I've ever had."

Jeremiah smiled back, "you are so beautiful right now, Zackary. All sweaty, gentle, and loving. I believe you became a man just now."

"I suppose I did. I'm so glad it was with you!"

The two kissed, exhausted from their passionate release. They got up, embraced, and walked into the bathroom and the shower. As Jeremiah washed him, Zack began to feel something warm in his heart for this man. He thought about how slow and gentle Jeremiah was with his tongue, his kisses, and his touches, making it so romantic. *He makes love to me the way he plays a musical instrument,* he thought. As Zack washed Jeremiah, feeling his body, studying him, he suddenly became emotional.

"Zackary, what is it?"

Tears had unexpectedly started, "this has been so overwhelming, so wonderful. I'm sorry. I don't know how to handle your compassion."

"Ohhh," he said, exhaling. "Honey, you are such a dear person. This was a really important release for you. I enjoy pleasuring you and being with you."

Zack kept crying, wiping his tears, "thank you for being so caring and making me feel safe and wonderful. It means so much. I'm sorry… I get emotional."

Jeremiah kissed Zack again, putting his hands on his face, "Sweetheart… let's dry off, get in bed and take a nap, then order dinner. We can cuddle together." As they dried off, Zack began laughing. "What's so funny?"

"Apparently, there are nerve endings in my butt I never knew I had."

"Zackary, I loved making love to you. I was imagining what it would be like to experience your naked body. You give me such pleasure. I feel different with you. What about you, Zackary, that causes me to want to hug and kiss you all the time?"

"Goodness, I don't quite know," Zack said with his sweet Kentucky accent, breathing heavily.

After drying off, the naked men walked back into the bedroom. Jeremiah retrieved some fresh sheets, and the two put them on the mattress. Once the bed was set up, Jeremiah got under the quilt and sheets. Zack joined him, pressing up against his body. Putting his head against his chest, listening to Jeremiah's heart, Zackary immediately fell asleep.

About an hour later, Zack woke up with Jeremiah's arms wrapped around him, still asleep. Zack noticed his breathing was different, calm, feeling, without hesitation, a state of blissfulness. Jeremiah helped him feel he mattered as a young man but also had physical and emotional needs. *That was the best orgasm of my life,* he thought. Suddenly, he felt Jeremiah's hands squeezing him tight and his lips kissing his neck. The two pressed their foreheads together, smiling and laughing.

After ordering and having dinner, they talked while listening to classical albums. Jeremiah spent the next hour or so describing each musical piece's nuances and distinguishing refinements, having Zack listen closely. "Zackary, you can spend your life studying music and never fully understand all the brilliance and artistry behind these classical composers. But it is so enjoyable to hear or notice a subtle chord or a sound you have never experienced before, the instruments or combination thereof, it makes life worth living. My ears have been trained to allow sound to enter my mind incrementally. As a musician, I can listen to a piece hundreds of times and find it a new experience each time. Zackary, it's the subtleties that make the piece so great. It's the subtleties that make you so irresistible." Zack did not understand quite what he meant.

The two then enjoyed some ice cream, "do you think you'll ever be able to live in Lexington after your travels?" Zack asked.

Jeremiah leaned in, "I'm keeping this apartment, so I expect to return in late February or early March. I am funded through then with the grant, which begins in January. It could get extended, then I would travel to who knows where. I have a hiatus for ten days in March so I can see you then. I have every intention of keeping Kentucky my home."

"Jeremiah, so listen, while I look forward to seeing you next weekend, my pop's going to Cincinnati on the seventeenth and returning the twentieth. I was thinking…"

"Yes, come stay with me!" Jeremiah said, reaching in to kiss Zack's lips. "I want to sleep overnight with you so badly."

"I would really like that too." The two made out as their ice cream melted.

Approaching eight in the evening, Zack had to begin making his way home. The two held hands when Jeremiah asked, "Zackary, without getting too descriptive, um, when I was pleasuring you earlier in bed, I've never experienced a feeling like that before with another man. I felt like I was literally making love to your body, and I realized how much I'm infatuated with it. I've never experienced that with anyone else. It was so special."

"What a beautiful thing to say," Zack passionately kissed the musician as tears ran down his face. His heart raced, "this is all so overwhelming. Oh, I have something for you." He handed Jeremiah an envelope with his senior portrait, "this is for you."

"Oh my gosh, you are so cute! Oh, Zackary, thank you. Look at you in your sports coat and tie. I can't get over this. Gosh, you are so handsome."

Zack blushed and he giggled, "oh, you say that to all the guys!"

Jeremiah pulled back. "Do you see any other pictures here? No, you don't. But I will buy a frame for this."

"I'm glad it makes you happy," Zack laughed, pleased his picture had such an effect. As he put on his coat, Jeremiah said he wanted him to call each night before bed and say good night.

Zack began to well up, "you know, I don't do well with people leaving me. And I really care about you."

"Roaming around is a big part of the life of a musician… lots of traveling. So, let's enjoy, experience, and explore this wonderful feeling between us before I leave, and keep it going. Gosh, now there's a reason to return to Kentucky!"

Lying in his bed later that night, Zack felt so calm. In his mind, he was no longer a virgin. The experience made him realize he had fallen hard for Jeremiah Pruett.

Chapter Twenty-Five

The next day, after Zack put up the Christmas lights on the house, he took Gwen for lunch at Jerry's Restaurant. After she ordered, she turned to him with a smile on her face, took his hand and kept staring into his eyes. "What is it?" Zack asked.

"You, you seem different," she said. "Happier than usual."

Zack's eyebrows quickly rose. He was reluctant to tell Gwen about Jeremiah, unsure of how she would react. She and he had become very close after the talk of her "mezzanine love" for him earlier that month and he didn't want to disturb this friendship that was more than friendship, but he also felt wrong keeping Jeremiah a secret from her. As Gwen began drinking her Tab, Zack cleared his throat. "So, I need to tell you something."

"Sure, what?" she said, still smiling.

"Um, you remember when you gave me tickets to the Philharmonic? Well, I met… I met a guy at the reception afterward."

Gwen's smile slightly flattened, "Oh, wow."

"Yeah, I mean, he's a musician, um… he's really nice.

He's graduating from UK next month. We've actually gone out twice. His name is Jeremiah. I would have told you, but I wasn't sure how things would develop between him and me."

Gwen's smile evaporated completely. She looked down at her Tab, "well, good." The table was awkwardly quiet.

"Gwen, you aren't upset, are you?"

"No, why would I be?" she forced a smile. "I understand. Tell me more about him. What did you all do together on your dates?"

Zack became uncomfortable and looked down, "we spent time getting to know each other. He's really kind, extremely smart. He's going to New York after Christmas for two months."

"That's exciting," she said quietly. "I'm sure he must be good-looking."

"He is," Zack said, smiling and feeling awkward. Then, to his relief, there was the distraction of their food arriving.

As Gwen bit into her grilled cheese sandwich, she softly added, "well, I hope he's nice to you."

"He is… he's been really kind."

Nodding, Gwen kept eating while the sounds of other diners' silverware clanked against their plates seemed to get louder to Zack. He began fidgeting with his club sandwich and Gwen wiped her hands on her napkin and then carefully sipped her Tab. "So have you two… you know… had sex?"

Zack paused and took on a more serious expression, "yeah, we have." He remembered how awkward he'd felt when Matt talked about having sex with Colleen. It made him ill at ease deep inside, since Zack had feelings for him.

Gwen nodded, smiling, but appeared somewhat uneasy, "was it nice?" she quietly asked.

"You know," Zack looked up. "I consider it my first time. He was tremendously gentle. This is hard for me to talk about. I actually got emotional at first, and I was pretty scared. But he made me feel safe. It was quite lovely."

"I'm glad for you," she replied, not completely convincingly. "Did you go to his dorm room?"

Zack shook his head, "no, he has an apartment. Gwen, is this making you uncomfortable?"

"No," she lied. "I know you and I are not that way with each other. But it's hard for me. You know I care about you a lot and love you."

"I feel the same way, too," Zack replied quickly, interrupting her. "You know that."

Gwen reached over and put her hand on his, "are you falling for him?"

"I think so," Zack teared up, nodding. "It's moving so fast."

Gwen clutched Zack's hand, "please be careful. You're so vulnerable right now, Zack."

"I'm trying," he said. "But he's been so good to me."

"I get it, but you said he's leaving," she reminded him. "I don't want to see you get hurt."

"He's leaving, but he's coming back in March."

Gwen gazed out the window at the parking lot, "I'm not surprised this happened. You're pretty cute, and you deserve to be happy. Did he say he loved you?"

Zack shook his head. "No. But he did say he was 'falling for me,' though."

"Are you falling for him?" she asked.

Zack ate two fries before answering. "Gwen, I have so many emotions running through me right now. I'm so confused. But the time he and I spent together has been, well, wonderful... I've just felt things, emotionally, physically, that I didn't even know I could."

"I can see that," Gwen nodded, keeping a serious face. "Listen, keep it all in perspective. That's why I've never gone all the way. I want to hold out for someone special."

Zack smiled widely, "when that happens, he'll be the luckiest guy. You're so beautiful and incredible."

Gwen just looked at him, "if I had not given you those Philharmonic tickets, you would have never met Jeremiah."

"I guess it was fate, huh?" Zack couldn't read her expression. "Gwen, this doesn't affect how I feel about you. I'm not going anywhere. I dearly care about you."

She sipped her Tab, then slightly smiled, "I know. I love you, too."

Once in the car, Zack turned the conversation to Gwen. "How are you holding up?" he asked, referring to her being violated by Ed Sims.

"I have the strangest feelings at times. I feel completely fine, then horrible thoughts go through my head… and I find myself crying. I'm so thankful for my parents and for you."

Zack explained how difficult it was to go back to school and face people after his assault. "It's as if your rhythm is out of sync with everyone else. For me, I felt so different, as if I was a shell of myself, I still do on many days. When someone overpowers you, they take everything from you. It's hard to describe, Gwen. I vividly remember the pain. It was so horrifying. And what Ed did, terrified you, and it kills me inside to know you suffered." The two hugged. "Gwen, I adore you so much. You have been the one who's saved me this year, giving me such happiness, knowing someone understands me, that I'm not a freak, but I'm hurting. I FUCKING HATE HIM for hurting you! He better not come near you!"

Gwen kissed Zack on the cheek, "hey, calm down. Ed could snap you in half. You're not violent."

"I don't care what he does to me. I care what he does to you. He will never touch you again, God as my witness!"

Later, at Jacobson Park, Gwen looked out at the reservoir as the sun shone through the barren trees, casting pink and yellow on the water, "I don't know when I will ever be able to let a man touch me after what Ed did."

Zack took her hand, "you will when you are ready when you're with the right guy, hon."

Gwen looked at Zack, "can I ask you something? I feel strange asking this now that you've got a boyfriend. Feel free to say 'no,' okay?

"Of course," he replied.

"I… I really would like to touch a man's body someday. Just look at it, touch it. I have been too afraid to ever ask Ed… you gently caress his knee, and he wants to rip off his clothes and, well, fuck. It would help me feel more comfortable if I could see what a man's body is like."

Zack nodded, "I understand."

After a moment, Gwen asked, "Zack, would you ever consider taking off your clothes for me sometime? It would be nothing sexual, just let me see and touch your body. If this bothers you, say no."

"I would gladly do that for you," Zack squeezed her hand.

They both laughed, and then their lips met, kissing deeply. Zack put his hand up to Gwen's face, and when he slowly pulled away, he stared at her, smiling, "you're such a beautiful girl." She kissed him again.

That night, Zack was in his pajamas, reading his economics book in bed, when the phone rang. He answered and it was Gwen in tears.

"Zack, he told me 'go fuck yourself' when I said I didn't want to see him anymore. He then told me our relationship 'isn't over' for him. Zacky, I'm scared. My mother's afraid he might try to hurt me."

"Gwen, I'm so sorry, darling," he sat up, ready to console. "I know you're upset. Please try to calm down.

You did the right thing. Do you want me to pick you up in the morning?"

"Oh, you are the sweetest guy I've ever known."

"So, listen, I'm here for you," Zack said. "I will do my best to prevent him from getting anywhere near you if I can. I'll be your human shield."

After they hung up, Zack walked across the hall to check on his father. Sitting on the bed, Pop was watching an NFL game. "Son, the lights look great on the Christmas trees. You did such a nice job. I feel so much more relaxed now that it's all done." Zack bent over and kissed his father. "Can you get me a piece of pie?"

"Pop, I thought we talked about this. You're supposed to…"

"Get me the goddamn pie," he snapped. "And a glass of milk!"

After fulfilling his dad's wishes, Zack called Jeremiah. "Zackary, you have been on my mind all day. Today, I practiced for nearly nine hours total and took a break midday to go to UK to take a swim for an hour and I was thinking of you the entire time. I'm looking at your picture right now. I can't wait to see you on Saturday."

"I wish you were with me, too. I have room in my bed," he said, laughing quietly.

Jeremiah spoke of how lonely it is rehearsing and practicing daily for hours. He said their meeting was quite a lift for him. "Zackary, I will dream my arms are around you in bed tonight. Yesterday was amazing."

The two hung up and Zack finished reading his chapter and turned off the light. His thoughts turned to Gwen. "God, please protect her," he prayed aloud. "She needs your blessing. And please protect my mother."

Chapter Twenty-Six

It was a cloudy morning when Zack knocked on the Farrises' door. Gwen's mom greeted him with a concerned look and started right in with no pleasantries. "Zackary, please be safe and be aware of your surroundings for the next few days," she warned. Gwen came down the steps and hugged Zack.

"I am watching out for her. Rebecca will be with her as well," Zack assured Jenny, helping Gwen with her coat. "It'll be okay. Let's get going."

Gwen then hugged her mother, who kissed Zack sweetly on the cheek. "Take care of yourselves," Mrs. Farris said.

On the way to Henry Clay, when they came to a stop at a red light, Gwen reached over and kissed Zack, pressing her lips hard against his. He could tell she was frightened, "you'll be fine. I'm here for you." She nodded but didn't seem convinced. Driving onto campus, Zack felt a sense of doom build with the realization that Ed Sims was most likely coming for him. After they parked, Gwen began crying. "Honey, don't . . ." he said, reaching over to her. "Do you want to hold my hand when we walk in?"

"Yeah, I would… I'm scared."

"I hate seeing you hurting like this," he said. "Let's do this. I'll walk you to your first period." Zack got out of the car and helped Gwen from the passenger seat. She took his hand, and they entered the building. He looked over at her and smiled. "It's gonna be fine, hon."

Walking through Green Hall, a few students looked at Gwen and Zack holding hands. As they turned the corner, Zack could see Colonel Jacobs, his junior year history teacher, standing outside his classroom door, which was directly across from their locker. "Good morning, Colonel," Zack said. The man nodded, holding a usual stern grimace during hall watch duty. Gwen opened the locker. Zack helped take off her coat. Rebecca walked up and greeted them. As she and Gwen talked, Rebecca suddenly looked concerned, "Zack, turn around," she said. As he did, Ed Sims was standing there with three of his wrestling buddies.

Gwen turned and immediately froze. "Zack, be careful."

Zackary turned and stood in front of Gwen, shielding her. He thought he could be diplomatic. "Hey, man. What's up?" Zack asked.

"Why is a faggot like you hanging around my girlfriend? Take your fucking faggot self and never go near her again!" A crowd began to form.

Zack remained calm, putting Gwen's tote bag down. His heart raced fast, "Ed, you need to stay away from Gwen. She wants you to leave her alone. I don't want any problems."

Ed tried to reach around and grab Gwen's arm. When Zack pushed his arm away, he yelled, "Don't touch her!" Ed began punching him in the face, making him fall back against the lockers. He punched him again three more times, then put both hands on Zack's neck, choking him and pushing him against the wall. Panicking and with his face turning blood red, Zack used his arms and hands, trying to push him off. Zack was aware students were watching and some were screaming. Colonel Jacobs tried to pull Ed off him. When Ed finally released the chokehold, Zack fell to the floor on his knees, covering his head. He then felt hard kicks up against both sides of his torso, the blows hitting his ribs and his shoulders.

"FUCKING QUEER!" The boy spat.

He could hear Gwen screaming as one of the sidekicks was pulled off him. Zack suddenly felt a strong kick to his lower back, falling forward. As he tried to lift himself up, one guy jumped on top of Zack, pushing him flat onto the floor, squeezing him tight in the embrace, he took his arm and pushed against his neck so hard he could not breathe. "Fags go down forever," he yelled.

As he was asphyxiating, Zack flashed back to fighting for breath when Tom was sitting on top of him, suffocating him with a pillow. "I can't breathe..." Zack could barely mutter, unable to get air. The guy would not release him but eventually let go when someone pulled him off. Zack began fighting for breath, coughing furiously with his face on the floor. Gwen kneeled down and, with the help of some other students, slowly turned him over onto his back. Gwen held his head, putting her sweater underneath it. "Are you all right? Zack?" she cried.

He couldn't move, could barely hear, blood ran out of his nose. He was unable to breathe, tears rolled down his face, mixing with the blood. There was intense commotion in Zack's peripheral vision, feet moving nearby, people asking Gwen if he would be okay.

As Ed was pulled away by two teachers, he bent down and spit on Zack's face. "FUCKING FAGGOT!"

Gwen wiped his face, and Mr. Passmore, the assistant principal, appeared with a first aid kit. He told Gwen to go to class. "NO. I will not leave him. He's hurt," she replied.

"Young lady," he warned.

"Look, I love this boy. I'm not leaving him!" said Gwen sternly.

The Colonel knelt down, "Son, we've got to get you up to the nurse's station." Looking at Mr. Passmore, the Colonel continued, "he's the Kingdon boy." The bell rang, and the hall cleared as the teachers told everyone to move along. Zack could not speak. He could taste blood in his mouth and was so weak he couldn't move.

Gwen wiped his face, "you're hurt… they hurt you… God, I feel awful, Zack." She reached down and kissed his forehead.

The school nurse arrived and bent down, "Zackary, can you hear me? I think he's in a mild shock. His eyes are moving, but his pupils are dilated. He has a cut on the right side of his head. His neck appears to have sustained some trauma." School personnel tried to get Zack to sit up a few minutes later. His body was sore, but, with assistance, he gradually stood up.

Once up in the nurse's station, Zack could hear Pop in the hallway. He came into the small room to check on Zack. "Oh, God, son. They did a number on you."

Mr. Hunt came in and asked Zack how he was feeling. "Not good, sir," he muttered. The principal asked Zack's father to come into his office. They were in what seemed to be a twenty-minute discussion. Gwen refused to leave. Once they emerged, they came back into the room. Zack's father wanted swift action against the four boys who harmed Zackary. He told Mr. Hunt how grateful he was to Colonel Jacobs for breaking up the fight. Pop asked Zack how he was feeling. "I'm really sore, sir," he answered.

Mr. Hunt began asking more questions about the attack. Zack tried to answer. Gwen briefly left to get some of his belongings from their locker.

"Zack, we are going to send you home. But before you

go, is there anything more you want to tell us? Maybe about some of the comments, the boys shouted?" Mr. Hunt asked.

Zack froze, turning red, looking down, as if all eyes were on him, "no, no. I don't think so." His father looked angry. Mr. Hunt's question had Zack concerned.

Pop approached Zack, took his hands and helped him up, "Son, put on your shirt. I'm going to get you looked at by Dr. Burkhardt."

Gwen returned with Zack's coat and book bag, "I'll call you." Zack reached his hand out, and she briefly took it. After putting on his coat, Mr. Passmore escorted Zack and his father to the Cadillac.

"Son, give me your car keys. I'll have one of my construction men come over and drive it home later today."

Zack's left knee was injured in the fight, which left him limping slightly. After getting into the Fleetwood and driving to Dr. Burkhardt, Pop seemed quiet and distant for much of the ride. The doctor thoroughly examined Zack and found no head injuries other than neck trauma, but he sent him to get X-rayed, which revealed no internal issues. Pop was relieved as Zack was only issued a neck brace.

Sitting with his father, Pop reached over and patted Zack on his right leg, "after you're checked out, let's get lunch and pick up your medication at the pharmacy. Then we'll get you home and put you in bed. It's all going to be all right."

He sat in the booth with Zack, waiting for the prescription and drinking a milkshake. Pop stared but then looked away, seeming lost in serious thought. "You're going to have a black eye from this, son. Goddammit." Zack had some difficulty eating, as his jaw was sore. After finishing lunch and retrieving the prescription, once they arrived home, Pop helped Zack as he went upstairs. "Son, I want you to take a hot shower, get into your pajamas, and get into bed."

A few minutes later, with the sun still shining, Zack was

dutifully in bed in his pajamas. Pop came in and helped him put on his neck brace, then sat down with an ice pack. "Honey, why did this happen to you? Why did that boy call you those names?"

Zack looked away, over at the window. He began crying, "I don't know." There was a long pause, which terrified Zack. *He knows.*

"Son, you're in a lot of pain. You're going to need to stay home for a few days. I'll work from here. I don't want to leave you alone. I'm worried about you." Pop took his handkerchief and handed it to Zack, who wiped his eyes.

"I'm so sorry. I didn't want this to happen, sir. Ed was coming for Gwen," Zack cried.

Pop helped Zack situate his pillows so his head would be more elevated and instructed him to sleep on his back. "I'm glad you were there for her, but you got caught up in a melee. Your ribs and your side muscles are going to be too sore for you to sleep on your sides for a few days." Pop tucked his son in, then kissed him on the forehead, "take this pill, then drink this glass of water, all of it. Later on, you can get into my bed and watch TV. For now, I want you to sleep. These pills will knock you out. You need lots of rest."

After Pop went back downstairs to the drawing room to work at his desk, Zack began crying hard, terrified by what had happened. The turbulent thoughts of being attacked again swirled through his mind until the medication took over. All went black.

As if no time had passed, Zack heard Pop open the door and turn on the bed lamp. His clock said five-thirty-seven. He had slept for nearly five hours.

"Son, how are you feeling? Gwen's downstairs and brought you some treats. Are you up for seeing her?"

Zack lit up, "Yeah."

"I'm going to finish cooking dinner. I roasted a chicken and made you some mashed potatoes and asparagus and carrots." Pop helped Zack into the washroom, "she's a sweet girl, Zack." Once he helped Zack back into bed, Pop handed him a glass of water and then went downstairs.

Moments later, Gwen came in with a basket of cupcakes and cookies.

"You didn't need to do that."

She pulled up Zack's desk chair. "Oh my God," she said, seeing Zack in the neck brace. "Does this hurt? I am so worried about you." Gwen reached over and kissed Zack.

"It's not too bad to wear."

"You're starting to look bruised. I wanted to tell you that Mr. Hunt suspended Ed and the others. I heard the Colonel is throwing the book at them. He's recommending they be transferred to Lafayette or Tates Creek High School."

Zack sipped his water and liked what he was hearing.

Gwen reached over and held his hand, and the two stared at each other, "Zacky, I'm so sorry. I feel responsible for this."

Zack squeezed her hand, shaking his head, "it's not your fault, Gwen. I don't want that fucking asshole, sorry, touching you or bothering you ever again. At least he didn't hurt you today. I'll be fine, but he cannot go near you after what he did to you."

She teared up, "you have no idea how much you taking me to school, being there to protect me, meant to me. It kills me you were hurt but I know you love me." She moved over and sat next to Zack on the bed.

"Oh, gosh, I do, honey," he replied.

"Your father and I spoke downstairs. He said the nicest things about you, Zacky." She lay down against him, and they held hands. She then rang her mother from his phone to come and pick her up. Gwen reached back over and snuggled up against Zack on the bed.

"Gwen, if you take this basket downstairs, Pop will eat everything. He's like the Cookie Monster. It'll just disappear."

"Oh, he had his eyes on those cupcakes!" It hurt, but Zack laughed.

"Do you remember earlier in the fall when I came into Hendrix's class late, all upset?" she asked. "You handed me your handkerchief, then held my hand." Zack nodded. "I'll never forget that." Gwen sat up on the bed, turned, and looked at him. "That day, Ed told me in the hall that I was 'not worth fucking anyway' because I wouldn't allow him to touch me the weekend before. Honey, I am so thankful I met you. I always felt safe knowing you were there. I will never forget your being there for me today." She leaned in and kissed him.

He smiled, holding her hand, "Ed is an awful person. I'll always be here for you."

Gwen looked out the window and saw her mom pull into the driveway. She kissed Zack, "you're my prince," then made her way downstairs.

Zack sat alone with the thought of being rejected by his father for being gay. It was his biggest fear. Pop was the last branch left on his family tree.

Chapter Twenty-Seven

Zack's physical wounds slowly began healing. However, the pain from the incident was still deep within. He knew the assault by Ed Sims and the wrestlers was as much an attack on his being gay as a response to his trying to protect Gwen. When Matt came over to see Zack after school the next day, he was shocked, hardly recognizing him with the bruises to his face and neck, let alone the discoloring to the rib cage, entire butt, and lower legs he couldn't see.

"Motherfuckers! Did they hurt your gonads?"

"No, Matthew, but they called me 'faggot' a few times."

Matt sat down and gently hugged Zack.

After school the next few days, Gwen got a ride with Rebecca to visit Zack. She brought him handouts, assignments from his teachers, and treats, snuggling up to him in bed as they worked on homework together. Gwen brought sunshine back to life, she loved *him* for *him*. He also talked to Jeremiah on the phone every night, which also nourished him. But his entire body continued to ache over the week, and only towards the end did his black eye and swelling slowly begin to heal.

When he returned to school on Friday, after missing four days, Zack walked into the building with a fast stride and continued quickly through the hall, receiving long stares. But many students, including ones he didn't know, were unusually kind to him. Ms. Watson, Zack's accounting teacher, was elated to see him and horrified by his bruised face. In psychology, Mr. Hendrix exuded real concern. Zack held Gwen's hand in class, which helped him feel calm and less self-aware. He had so many thoughts racing through his head. Months of glares, hostile expressions, and people who just looked away made him feel like a freak. Inside, he'd felt hurt and diminished, and now that he had marks on his body, he wanted all of them to see the black eye and bruises on his face and neck. He wanted them to feel uncomfortable when they looked at him. Anger had replaced his tears. Zack walked the halls looking directly at everyone. Gwen and Zack became even closer after the attack. At their locker, he kissed her, not hiding anything, "I don't care what people think anymore, Gwen. You're my friend."

The following weekend, Zack drove over and spent the afternoon with Jeremiah, who was mortified seeing all the bruises in person. The two lay on the couch, hugging and gently kissing. While they did not make love, they got into the bed after disrobing, and Jeremiah saw all the hateful evidence on Zack's naked body. Lying there, holding each other, Jeremiah whispered in Zack's ear, "I care so much for you. I feel so bad you're in pain, Zackary."

Zack looked back at Jeremiah's face, nodding, then leaned in for a long kiss. "Thank you." He knew his time with Jeremiah was fading, which made him deeply sad. *When he leaves for New York, my heart is going to break. I don't think I can handle it.* As it neared four o'clock, Zack dressed and stood at Jeremiah's door. "I'm going to miss you," he said through intensifying tears. "I don't want you to leave. Being with you, our time together, I don't want it to end. It hurts so much knowing you won't be here."

Jeremiah pulled Zack back to the couch and sat him down. He got on his knees and hugged him tightly, "I'll miss you, too. You have meant more to me than any man I've ever met. Maybe we've only known each other a month, but I can honestly say I am so grateful to have you in my life."

"All this I'm experiencing with you overwhelms me," Zack said. "The lovemaking, lying together in bed, kissing. It's all new to me, and I cherish it, but it scares me, too." Jeremiah helped Zack get up, put his coat on, and walked him to his car.

Zack slowly got behind the steering wheel, Jeremiah kneeled down, put one hand through Zack's hair, and said, "this pain you're feeling for me is real. *This pain is love.* No man has ever cried for me like you have. I'm here for you. I promise. Even if I'm in New York or an ocean is between us, I am thinking of you, Zackary, because you are in my heart, you beautiful man!" Zack slowed down his tears and wiped his face. Jeremiah then added, "I love you, sweetheart. I do. There's nobody like you. I've never said this to another man, but I mean it. Please call me before bed." He reached in and pressed his lips tightly, placing his hand on Zack's face. "Get home safe, I love you. Call me later." Zack was speechless.

Driving home in the dark, Zack was stunned and delighted that Jeremiah had admitted his affection for him. As he pulled into the driveway, he saw Mrs. Daniels's car. After walking into the drawing room, he heard, "where were you all day?" Pop had some suspicion in his voice. Zack offered a quick excuse about the yearbook. Mrs. Daniels looked up and glared at him. Pop continued, "are you sure that's all you did? Go wash up. Put on a jacket. We're all going to the Campbell House."

On the drive to dinner and while seated at the booth in the dining room, Pop was unusually hostile towards Zack at points, then would ignore him altogether. Zack got the feeling he and Mrs. Daniels had been talking about him. During dinner, Zack noticed Mrs. Daniels eyeing him up and down. She reminded him of his sister Emily, who constantly scrutinized him, similarly looking him over in a cold, judgmental manner. On the way home, Pop began yelling at Zack while glancing at him in the rearview mirror, "you may think you don't have to do any chores because you're bruised up, but you found time to go out and have fun doing who-knows-what today." Looking out the window as the dark suburban scenery passed, Zack did not respond. Mrs. Daniels whispered something in Pop's ear. *Who the fuck is this woman to tell my father anything about me?* he thought. It became clear to Zack that she was putting negative, possibly antigay, thoughts into his father's head. Pop was on edge with him the entire evening.

Once home, Mrs. Daniels got into her car and left, and Zack went upstairs to his room. About an hour later, he walked downstairs to get an apple and heard a football game in the drawing room. "Get in here!" Pop yelled. "Is there something you're not telling me about that fight? Pat and I were talking…"

"Pop, it's none of her business," Zack snapped.

"DON'T YOU EVER TELL ME WHAT IS OR ISN'T MY BUSINESS! DO YOU UNDERSTAND ME, YOUNG MAN?" Zack stood there unresponsive. "DO YOU?"

"I do, I'm sorry, sir," Zack meekly replied.

"Pat thinks you're not telling me what happened."

Zack looked down, staring at his apple, "Sir, with all due respect, Pat wasn't there, so how could she know?"

"YOU DID NOT EVEN THROW ONE PUNCH! Mr. Hunt said you were called all kinds of things…"

Zack interrupted his father. "Pop, Mr. Hunt wasn't there either. It was all wrestlers… against me. They BEAT ME ALL OVER! AND YOU WANT ME TO TELL YOU WHAT?"

"There is a reason these boys went after you, son. They said you were…"

"WHAT, Pop? WHAT? That I'm a 'faggot'? People call each other names all the time," Zack said with tears falling down his face, slightly shaking.

Pop paused, then resumed arguing. Zack left the room and walked upstairs. He did not go in and say good night to his father that night.

Chapter Twenty-Eight

Over the next few days, there was palpable tension between Zack and his father. One day, when Zack arrived home from school, he noticed two coffee cups in the sink, one with lipstick. There was also a full ashtray on the kitchen table. Zack heard the television on in the drawing room and walked in.

"Pop, hi. Who was here today?"

"Your momma. She called me yesterday. She left Lee in California, was driving through today, and wanted to see me. She's moving up to live with your grandparents."

"Why didn't she wait for me to come home? I want to see her. She came over without seeing me?" he said angrily.

"Son, your mother is a broken and worn-down woman. She didn't want you to see her right now. She's in bad shape, that's why I didn't tell you she was coming. I offered to let her stay with us, but she refused."

"So, she doesn't stay to see me?" Zack said, sitting down.

"She said she'll see you once she gets all settled in with your grandparents." Despite all of his father's bluster and despite all of her hostility towards him, Zackary knew Pop still deeply loved her and worried when she was hurting.

On Thursday morning, the Cadillac warmed up as Zackary placed his father's suitcase into the trunk for his trip to Cincinnati. He packed his insulin travel kit with his other medications. Pop walked to the car and handed Zack a large amount of cash. "Now, I left the hotel telephone number on the kitchen table. You have work to do in the yard. I want you to cheer up and have a nice weekend." He pulled Zack in for a hug, "I love you, son."

Zack hugged him back, reaching over to give his father a kiss on the check, "me too. Have a nice time. Drive safely." Zack watched him pull out of the driveway and waved. He then went inside, finished his cereal, changed into jeans, and drove to school.

After third period, Zack and Gwen briefly spoke, holding hands, "I guess you're excited about your sleepover with Jeremiah?"

Zack smiled, "I am. I can breathe when I'm with this man. He's great!" She pulled her hand away. "What's wrong?" he asked.

"You seem so happy," she said, head down. "I guess he's your first love."

"I don't know, it's too early, but he is a tremendous guy, and I really care about him. Besides, I consider you my first real love."

Gwen looked confused, "you were with Amy first."

He took Gwen's hand and kissed it, "yeah, but I never felt with her like I do with you. I don't know how to describe it, and I know you and I are more than 'great friends,' but, honestly, Gwen, I've never met anyone as loving as you. During my prayers, I thanked God for leading me to you. You're a gift." She leaned in and passionately kissed him. The two hugged tightly, and Zack went up the stairs to trig class.

After trig, Zack met Matt in the art studio. He was venting about college, "all these elitist fuckers with their early decision applications yelling, 'I'm applying to Vandy,' 'I'm applying to Yale,' 'I'm applying to Harvard,' FUCK YOU! I could puke."

Zack giggled while trying to chew his peanut butter sandwich, "now, Matthew, don't be bitter."

Matt painted, reaching close to the canvas, squinting his right eye, trying to perfect a stroke, "doesn't it make you sick that these phony people get everything they want? I have to work so hard in my life."

Zack put his sandwich down, stood up, then walked behind Matt, wrapping his arms around him, "hey, man. Come on, stop it. Let it go. They still have to get in." Zack found Matt's pettiness about Henry Clay elites a bit tiring. He released his friend, sat down, and reached over and poured Matt some more tea.

As Matt simmered down, he began staring at Zack, "what's with you, man? You look different, even with your fading bruises. You're glowing, Zackary. You got fucked, didn't you?"

Zack's mouth was full of sandwich as he blushed heavily, putting his hand over his mouth, "no. No. You're so silly."

Matt looked suspicious, chomping on Cheetos, "you seem so centered, calm. The past few weeks, you were so fucking mad after the attack, and I don't blame you. But look at you, I've never seen you like this. You seem so happy. Did you?"

Zack looked at Matt, rolling his eyes, "did I what?"

"Did you get a big ole dick shoved up your ass? You're too confident acting, Zack. It's not like you. You know, research suggests people who get fucked regularly are confident."

Zack rolled his eyes, shook his head, then laughed, "research suggests you need to shut up!"

"Hmmm, Zacky, I'm not quite convinced. I'll have to get you fucked up with a doobie when I come over later. You'll tell me then."

Zack sipped some tea, "nothing has happened. I upchuck after I smoke that shit."

Matt pulled his brush away from the canvas, laughing with orange lips, "no cursing!"

Matt's questioning made Zack nervous, but he invited him over after school anyway. Zack said he was making chocolate chip cookies for him, his favorite. The two began packing up to go to fifth period. Eagerly, Zack knew tomorrow would be the last day of school prior to the two-week Christmas break… and his weekend with Jeremiah.

"This shit is awful," Zack remarked coughing. He handed the joint back to Matt.

"You're such a lightweight, Zackary," he laughed.

The two sat on a couch on the patio, wrapped up in a quilt, chuckling about the fun times they've had together. Matt complained about Reagan, accusing Zack of being too naïve about "big business" with his interest in accounting, "you're a Republican, just like your dad!"

"I am not! Just because I take pride in my appearance."

"Zack, you do dress nicely, always have. I admire how you carry yourself. And unlike the Green Hall snobs, you're still the same ole Zackary. Although still resistant to smoking pot." Matt suddenly laughed sadistically, "I forgot to tell you, Colleen's mad at me. She was recently giving me head, and I shot my load into her mouth. She went ballistic! But it felt so fucking good!"

Quickly turning his head, Zack said, "whoa, that is not cool."

Matt kept laughing, "she made me promise to warn her from now on, but it was the most amazing feeling, Zack." He took another toke on the joint.

Zack stood up disgusted, ready to go back inside, "that's not funny, Matthew. You know she's Catholic." He began to fold the blanket, turned off by how cruel and disrespectful his friend, who was laughing uncontrollably, had become.

"Zacky," Matt reached a hand out, "hey, I immediately kissed her afterward!"

Benjamin Rue Silliman

Chapter Twenty-Nine

The next afternoon, Zack arrived home from school, showered, and put a few changes of clothes in his book bag, along with his toothbrush. Jeremiah told him to pack his trunks so they could go swimming at UK on Saturday. Zack also brought a Christmas card. In it, he wrote: *Jeremiah, you have shown me your heart, which has changed me forever. Thank you for being gentle and kind. I am forever blessed to have met you. I will miss you during your exciting travels and look forward to your return! Merry Christmas! With sincere gratitude, warmth, love, and deep appreciation, Zackary.* Zack smiled, realizing his friend would be off to New York in over a week. Shaking his head, he took off out the door.

Hours later, Zack was in Jeremiah's bed, engaged in a deep kiss. He finally felt brave enough to try to pleasure Jeremiah orally, like he had done to him, finding the experience awkward at first. Zack enjoyed showing his affection as much or more than receiving, going slowly, breathing through his nose, trying to emulate his amazing lover's techniques. He had never experienced giving oral sex and found it an insatiable turn-on. Jeremiah recently told Zack, "You learn to show love to a person by gently kissing and tasting their body." That afternoon, Zack gratefully understood what he meant, finally comfortable taking Jeremiah's penis into his mouth. He watched his partner go into a joyful trance, moaning and clenching his teeth. He worked to make Jeremiah feel he cared for him, as had been lovingly done for him. The two tightly clutched hands throughout.

Zack eventually consummated the enjoyment by standing up on the edge of the bed, holding Jeremiah's legs to enter him. He leaned forward, staring into his beautiful brown eyes, feeling the delightful warmth being inside him. Several minutes later, as Zack was building up to an explosive orgasm, Jeremiah was touching himself and came, suddenly screaming, "Oh my God, I love you, Zackary!" Responding to the pleasure and these words, Zack immediately ejaculated, moaning loudly, his body tensing up as he thrust himself forward, tightly clinching his butt, breathing through the nose. He climbed back onto the bed, and Jeremiah kissed him. It was the most passionate exchange in his life.

"Zackary, you will be the first man to sleep overnight in this bed with me," Jeremiah confessed. "I love being here with you, your gentle manner, and beautiful smile."

Zack's smile reflected what he felt in his heart, "thank you. No man has been kinder to me. I cannot wait to sleep alongside you tonight." Zack glanced over to the shelf and saw his framed picture.

"I can't take my eyes off it," Jeremiah said.

Zack smiled, turning red, "you're a sweetheart."

Jeremiah suggested that after he and Zack shower, they get dressed, go to dinner, and then dance downtown at the Bar.

"I'm a little nervous dancing in public."

"You're with me, cutie. I so badly want to be seen with you and I love to dance."

Zack exhaled, "for you, I'll try anything."

During dinner at the Merrick Inn, Zack reached under the table and held Jeremiah's hand, saying, "thank you for such an amazing afternoon."

Jeremiah smiled back, "oh, honey, you, you are a man to keep. The pleasure was mine, trust me!" The two smiled warmly at each other. "So, tell me more about Gwen," Jeremiah asked, enjoying his dinner. Zack had a picture of her and showed Jeremiah. "What a beautiful girl. So, she's your closest friend?"

Zack nodded, "Gwen is the greatest girl I've ever met in my life, and I've only known her since August, but I adore her. She's so cool about me being gay. So sweet to me."

Jeremiah continued sipping his wine, "have you slept with her?"

Zack threw a more serious look at his date, "no."

Jeremiah laughed. "Zack, there's nothing wrong with that. I am not judging you. It wouldn't bother me if you did. I've been with a girl. My friend Annette, who was a violinist in the Music Department."

Zack leaned in, "really?"

"Annette knows I'm gay. She is one of my closest friends. It's been over a year. We traveled and played together during the summers. She graduated in May and is now playing in the St. Louis Symphony."

Zack had a confused look, "did you like doing things with her? I think it's great if you were turned on."

"She was great in bed," he told Zack. "We did quite a bit sexually. I mean, it's not like being with a guy, but we were traveling, and we stayed together and slept in the same room and bed. It was great fun. I actually became better in bed with men from pleasuring her."

Zack was keenly interested and put down his knife and fork, "how so? I hope I'm not getting too personal."

"No, not at all. Well, you know how you seem like you're in a delirium when I slowly orally pleasure your butt. I got good at it from going down on her."

"Were you in love with her?"

Jeremiah shook his head, "no, but I care about her and love her as a great friend. She was kind to me and passionate, and we slept together so well in bed. I don't like to sleep alone. Unlike a lot of guys I've been with, Annette's so giving, so into it. Look, I'm not bisexual, Zack. I'm gay. We had wonderful times. Women understand the emotional part of lovemaking, which makes it satisfying. I never met a guy who did, until I met you." Zack blushed and smiled. "I've never had a real boyfriend. I dated a few guys for a week or two, but nothing worked out. The two I dated, for short periods, didn't treat me well. I'll admit they were quite handsome, but they weren't that nice. They wanted me to pleasure them, but neither would kiss me or do the wonderful things you do to me, Zackary. You get so into it you allow yourself to feel and get emotional. I asked you to call me each night because I want to believe what I feel for you is real. It's hearing your sweet voice every night. You're such a nice person. I'm not good with relationships because no one I met ever wanted to commit. Once they squirt, they get up, put their pants on, and leave. No man ever fell asleep with me afterward, except you. You let me hold you when we briefly sleep together. I feel like we have a real connection."

Zack kept smiling, sipping his wine, "you mean so much to me, too. I'm going to really miss you while you're gone."

"I don't want to think about it. Let's go to the bar, dance, then go home and make love again, or go to sleep, no pressure. How's that sound?"

Zack nodded, "it sounds great."

Later at the Bar, the two danced for several hours. Zack could not believe how sexy-looking Jeremiah was on the dance floor, loving the disco music and dancing around all the beautiful men, many of whom stared at him. Zack relished how Jeremiah would kiss him while they danced, making him feel free and jolting his heart. As the two were leaving, Zack ran into Fred Mills from the Kentucky Theatre, who reached in and kissed him, wishing him and Jeremiah a merry Christmas. As they were all talking, Jeremiah referred to Zack as his "boyfriend." The warmth Zack felt in his heart was overwhelming. Later at the apartment, they jumped into bed and made love again. Lying in Jeremiah's arms after, Zackary heard him say, "you know how to show me your feelings unlike anyone else ever has." At that moment, Zack realized he did, in fact, love this man. He dozed off in Jeremiah's arms, feeling safe and loved.

The next morning, Zack felt Jeremiah's warmth press up against him. Opening his eyes, he felt a kiss on his forehead. "It's nearly ten-fifteen," Jeremiah said. "How did you sleep?"

Zack muttered while cuddling him, "Terrific. I never sleep late like this." That entire weekend, Zack slept deeply, feeling Jeremiah's loving soul. When Sunday morning arrived, Zack had to leave early to get home. Once dressed, Zack agreed to return on Tuesday for the official "goodbye." Jeremiah was leaving for Paris, Kentucky, to spend Christmas with his family before heading to New York. Zack handed Jeremiah his Christmas card at the door.

"Zackary, thank you. This has been an incredible few days. I'll never forget it. Call me later," the two held a deep, sustained kiss.

"Thank you for the best weekend of my life," Zack said, before quickly turning and going to his car, holding back the tears, desperately trying to avoid breaking down in front of his man. Once he was on the road, he sobbed. Zack felt a maelstrom of emotions inside his heart. He felt dearly cherished, exhilarated by their passionate expressions, but also afraid and sad Jeremiah would be leaving Kentucky. As Zack wiped his tears, he thought Jeremiah Pruett was an escape from the world he lived, allowing him to experience love, warmth, and kindness safely and freely from another man, as he began to develop into a man himself. It was all new and overwhelming.

After putting his tired father to bed that night, Zack called Jeremiah to say good night. "Zackary, I wish you could come with me. It bothers me that I will be under such intense pressure and not have you with me. I need your sweetness. You have a way of making me feel so secure."

Zack smiled hugely, "you're nice to say that."

"You have a man's body, Zackary," he continued. "Whew, when we're together, you're no 'kid.' You certainly make love like a man!"

"Thank you, you're a sweetheart."

"I'm not going to have you in my arms for a while," Jeremiah started, "and I hate to bring this up, but I hope you will understand my request."

Zack paused, "what?"

"Look, I have to be honest with you. While I'm in New York… I'll go to the baths… and have sex with other men. It has nothing to do with how I feel for you. It's merely a release, nothing more. I wouldn't care if you did the same while I'm gone." Zack couldn't find the words to respond. "Say something. Did I offend you?"

Zack became very upset, "um, I'm confused. You need to go and take 'baths' with other men to get fucked?"

Jeremiah exploded in laughter, "no, no. I go to the bathhouses in New York. They're men's sex clubs. Everyone is naked. I need to get off with someone."

"Oh, but I thought we were an item," Zack said innocently. "You said you loved me."

"Oh, honey, I do," Jeremiah implored honestly. "That would not change. I'm a man who is under intense pressure. It calms me down. I hope this doesn't upset you that I need an open relationship. You have your needs, too."

"Well, that's why God gave us a right hand" was all Zack could come up with. Jeremiah laughed, but Zack did not know how to react or navigate forward. "Jeremiah, you're the only man I want."

"Zackary, Zackary, I-LOVE-YOU, only you!" he announced. "This is not meant to hurt you. If I could pack you in my suitcase, I would be so happy, but I can't, honey. Call me tomorrow night. I can't wait to be with you before I leave. Zackary, nobody, nobody can replace you."

"I love you, too." After hanging up. Zack suddenly stared out his bedroom window, unsure how to digest the news. *So, this is what an open relationship is? What if he meets a man and leaves me for him?*

Chapter Thirty

While Jeremiah was constantly on his mind, along with all the complications being romantically involved with him, Zack had to help his father get ready for house guests. It was Christmas vacation, so he also made sure to carve out time with Gwen. On Monday, four days before Christmas, Zack went to Gwen's home, and they baked cookies with holiday music playing in the background.

"Tell me about your weekend," she asked.

Zack told her a few details about what he and Jeremiah did, and happily, she didn't seem to mind. She even laughed hysterically when Zack went so far as to explain how a gay man's anus functioned like a woman's clitoris. Once they collected themselves, Zack looked at Gwen. "Can I tell you something?" She nodded. "Jeremiah told me he loved me."

With her eyebrows rising, Gwen put her hand over her mouth, "oh, honey, this is getting serious. Do you love him?"

Zack looked directly at her, then nodded, "I do. I do. He's been wonderful to me." A tear fell down his face. Gwen wiped his tears with her paisley apron, then pulled Zack in for a hug. "It scares me so much," he said.

Gwen squeezed him tight, "please be careful, hon." Pulling away from the embrace, Zack covered his face, crying. Gwen leaned against him.

"Jeremiah has helped me feel good after everything that happened in June… and that my feelings matter. And he's leaving on Sunday."

"Sweetheart, take a deep breath," she held him out with her arms stretched. "You're swimming in your emotions."

Blowing his nose, rolling cookie dough, he said, "there's a kicker, though. The other night on the phone, he told me he wants to have sex with other men while he's in New York. He said he needs to 'release,' that he is under such intense pressure."

Gwen pulled a batch of cookies out of the oven, "what does he expect you to do?"

Zack looked down. "He told me we have an 'open' relationship. It's so confusing, Gwen. I guess it's different with gay men. He said he loves me but wants other guys to 'fuck him'?" Zack began cutting cookie dough. "Jeremiah told me he had a romance with a girl while he was touring. He said she knew he was gay, and from what he said, he was into her."

Gwen stopped placing the dough balls on the cookie sheet, "you're kidding, he's bisexual?"

Zack shook his head, "no, he says he's not, but they 'did quite a bit' in bed, and he actually got better at oral sex with men by going down on her." Gwen smiled and resumed scooping dough with her spatula. "He asked if we had slept together." Gwen stopped again, a surprised look on her face, seeming caught up in thought. "You're all quiet. What are you thinking?" he asked.

She then turned and looked at Zack, "oh my gosh, would you ever want to?"

"What?" he replied with a serious look. She reached over and gently kissed Zack.

"Would you ever want to make love to me?" she asked coyly.

After a long look, he replied smiling, "yeah, I would. I'd like to make love to you, Gwen."

Gwen dropped the spoon on the counter, "wow, you are full of surprises today. Oh my God, you have to know I think about you constantly. I know it's crazy. I also know you think about Jeremiah all the time."

With a semi-smile, "yes, I do think of him, but I think of you, too." He took her hand, "I'm gay, Gwen, but it doesn't mean I don't have feelings for you. I mean, we kiss each other. I never felt this way for another girl. I mean, I've never known anyone like you. I would enjoy making love to you if you wanted to."

Gwen put a hand over her mouth, then deeply exhaled, "I have so daydreamed about you being my first." She wiped her hands on her apron, then hugged Zack. The two kissed passionately.

"I think you're beautiful. We love each other… more than friends," Zack said. Gwen walked behind him, wrapped her arms around his back, and pressed tightly against him.

They pulled the last batch of sugar cookies from the oven a few minutes later. While washing dirty mixing bowls and cookie sheets, Gwen told Zack her parents were working during the days most of the following week and were going to Shakertown on Saturday with some friends. As Gwen dried her hands and stared at Zack, he came in for another kiss.

"Are we doing something we shouldn't?" she asked.

"Listen, let me get naked first. We already discussed this. You can touch me. Do whatever you feel comfortable with. Then you can decide if you are ready to take your clothes off, I will be nothing but gentle with you. Gwen, I want to be honest, I don't know anything about pleasing a woman below the belly button, but if you want… I will try. I believe the best way to experience a person is, well, when you love them. And I know we both love each other."

She kissed Zack hard, "oh, I do love you, honey."

Zack noticed the time and realized he had to get home for dinner with his father. As she walked Zack to his car, Gwen handed him a tin of the cookies they'd made. He took Gwen in his arms before getting into the car, "you make me happy. You know, after I say goodbye to Jeremiah, I will be a mess."

Gwen kissed him, "I'm here for you. You are not alone this Christmas!"

On Wednesday morning, around eleven-thirty, Zack knocked on Jeremiah's door, hearing symphony music playing behind it. Jeremiah was in a towel when he opened up and pulled Zack into the apartment. The two embraced and kissed, "come on, let's shower." While under the water sprays, Jeremiah did things to Zack that sent him into orbit. The two moved to the bed, and Zack clutched Jeremiah's hand tightly throughout. Knowing it would be their last time together for a long while, Zack wanted to show Jeremiah how much affection he had for him, making their time together extremely memorable.

Later, after an emotional and physical release, the two were back in the shower, embracing and kissing deeply. "I'm going to miss everything about you," Jeremiah whispered. He took the soap and washed Zack's back end, causing him to moan. "I'm especially going to miss your butt. I wish I could take it with me." After rinsing and turning off the shower, the two dried off. Zack had about thirty minutes before he had to leave. There were several packed suitcases strewn about. Jeremiah was relatively quiet. As Zack got dressed, he began to feel emotional, but he fought back tears. Jeremiah summoned Zack to sit next to him on the couch.

"Your card was beautiful," he said. "You're beautiful. I promise I will write you. Zackary, honey, you're crying. You're so sweet. Nobody's ever cried over me. Come here."

Tears fell down Zack's cheek as he turned and hugged Jeremiah, "I don't want you to leave me. It hurts too much. I know you have to go, but it's killing me. You mean so much to me."

Zack was crying like a little boy when Jeremiah took his face in his hands, "Zackary, always know you are such a beautiful man. You have an amazing heart… I pray what we have never ends." A few minutes later, Zack had on his coat and Jeremiah took his hands, "look at me, sweetheart. I want you to know, Zackary, I consider us so close, so intimate. I see us together. Wait for me. What we have here, together, is so worth it."

Zack's crying worsened as he pulled his hands and hugged Jeremiah, "I love you. I have to go. I will think of you every day. Please write me, I have to hear from you." Zack reached in, and the two kissed for nearly two minutes. When Zack released, he hugged him one more time, saying, "You do well!" Zack opened the door and stepped out of the apartment into some drizzle.

"Zackary, I sent you something in the mail! Merry Christmas. I love you!"

Zack waved, then went to his car. It was raining harder now. He couldn't bring himself to drive away and sat behind the steering wheel, sobbing, as water drops pummeled the windshield.

Chapter Thirty-One

Around nine the next morning on Christmas Eve, the phone rang, and Zack answered. "Hello?"

"Put Pop on," Cameron said, without even greeting Zack. Zack called downstairs to his father and Pop answered. He hung up his phone.

A few minutes later, Pop yelled upstairs, "your brother'll be here around four o'clock."

He initially did not reply, feeling apprehensive about this pending arrival, but then walked halfway down the steps, "Pop, I need to tell you something about Cameron."

"What, son?" his father looked up from bottom of the stairs.

"Last Christmas, Cam came in drunk," Zack explained, "and I was sleeping on the couch downstairs. He startled me and I woke up, then he called me a 'f-ing faggot.' Alice had to get in front of him… he lunged at me. It really scared me. He hates my guts."

Pop stood stoically, taking his hand and moving his toothpick around, pressing his lips, deep in thought, "why don't you sleep in my bed with me, son? I didn't know he did that. Did he hit you?"

"No sir, but he seemed like he was about to. It scared me."

Repositioning his toothpick, Pop said, "I don't know why you and your brother don't get along."

After Emily arrived that afternoon, Zack went downstairs to greet his sister, but as she closed the drawing room doors, muttered, "Oh, I need to speak with Pop alone." She didn't even say 'hello.' Zack's brother and sister rarely spoke to him and never asked how he was doing. A beautiful Smith graduate, working in Washington, D.C., she possessed long, thick blonde hair and blue eyes. Growing up, Emily and Cam were hardly ever kind to Zack, considering him stupid because he had learning challenges as a child. His siblings treated him as if he was the write-off in the family, absorbing Pop's denigration of him in front of everyone. In grade school, Zack firmly remembered being constantly called 'retard' by Cam, who was more than a decade older. For his part, Zack considered them the interlopers, ruining his holiday each year.

Before Zack fully understood who he was, his two siblings whispered comments, accusing him of being gay for years. Aside from their general nastiness, the other big problem with the holidays was Zack being kicked out of his bedroom. Cam and Alice took control, always keeping the door closed. He felt he was experiencing high school in his own home, just waiting to be called 'faggot.' While Emily and Pop had their impromptu conference, Zack changed his clothes and went into the front yard, raking any residual leaves that had fallen. There weren't many and it was freezing cold, but he was glad for once to have chores to keep him outside.

While working in the lawn, Pat Daniels pulled into the driveway. "Wonderful," he said sarcastically and kept fussing with the rake for another half hour before entering the house. In the kitchen, Pat was engaged in a lively conversation with

Emily. Zack said hello to Mrs. Daniels, who ignored him from the kitchen table. His sister did not even look up, still not having hugged or even really said hello to him. Zack walked into the drawing-room, where Pop was watched television on the edge of his chair. He squeezed his hand affectionately, "how are you?" Zack asked.

"Good, son. Did you invite Gwen to join us tonight?"

"I did, she's coming over later."

"Looks like your sister may be getting a promotion. Be sure to congratulate her." Zack stared at the television, not saying anything.

He went upstairs and called Gwen, who was happy to hear his voice. "What is it? You seem down. Are you upset about Jeremiah?"

He sighed, "yeah, but I also wanted to hear a kind voice. Shall I pick you up around eight?"

"Yes, that's great," Gwen said before offering, "listen, my mother wants you to know you can come here and spend Christmas with us if it gets too uncomfortable."

"That's nice of her," he said. "I look forward to seeing her and your dad later on."

Zack took out his gifts for Pop and brought them downstairs to place under the living room Christmas tree. He didn't get his brother or sister anything. The previous year, Emily gave him the book *How to Win Friends and Influence People*, which was meant as an insult. Through the front window, Zack saw the postman. He opened the front door and retrieved the mail, wishing the carrier a "Merry Christmas." There was a letter from Indiana University and one from Miami University. Zack stood outside and opened both, each containing rejections. *I knew these two colleges were long shots, but I desperately wanted to get out of this place, have my own life, and meet new people. That's not likely to happen now,* he thought glumly. He noticed there were several holiday cards. One card was addressed to Mr. Zackary Benjamin Kingdon. The return was "JAP" in the top left corner of the envelope. Zack immediately opened it.

My dearest Zackary,

I feel such an emptiness in my heart as I prepare to leave for New York City. You give me every reason to want to cancel this trip and be with you! You want me to succeed and dearly care about my love of music and my goals. Zackary, you are a beautiful person, but also an extraordinarily kind young man. Your heart is so pure. I appreciate your sharing of yourself with me. These past weeks, the time we have spent together, have been some of the best moments of my life. I miss you and look forward to seeing you and spending time with you in 1982! I also can't wait to kiss you and make love to you—the man I have fallen in love with. Merry Christmas!
Love, Jeremiah Abbott Pruett

Any disappointment from the two rejection letters slipped immediately as Zack's heart filled with joy upon reading Jeremiah's letter. Tears formed in his eyes. *This beautiful man adores me. It's official, it's in writing, and I love him back!* He thought about all the lovemaking he had experienced with Jeremiah. Zack walked back inside the house and up to his bedroom. He took Jeremiah's letter and placed it in his book bag, which was sitting on the floor next to his desk. From the bag, he pulled a book Matt had given him as a gift, The *Joy of Gay Sex,* which explained, with graphic drawings, the details of sexual acts between two males. Zack was touched by Matt's gift and turned on by the pictures. Secretly, he still wished he and Matt performed some of the acts together in the illustrations. He pulled open the bottom dresser drawer and hid the book in the pajamas, which also wrapped up some gay magazines. Zack lay down on his bed, closing his eyes. It was dark outside. He woke from a deep sleep when he heard a loud voice. Zack sat straight up, listening. It was Cameron, who always talked very loudly. Zack walked down the steps and into the kitchen a few minutes later. Cameron Kingdon, an investment banker, was a Vanderbilt, then Wharton MBA graduate, residing in Raleigh, North Carolina.

"Son, go get your brother's bags and take them up to his room!"

Wearing her usual tight-fitting hot pants, Alice muttered, "here's the keys. It's a Mercedes, be careful."

Feeling like the hired help, he turned around and walked out the door. *Take the bags up to 'his room'?* Not one person said hello to him. Holiday after holiday, Zack quietly existed in the background. While he pulled the seven suitcases out of the trunk, Cam poked his head out of the kitchen door, "oh and be careful with the gifts. Two of them are breakable. And Pop says to bring more beer from the garage for Pat."

Zack was fuming inside. After several trips up the stairs, he walked downstairs to the dining room and returned the keys to Alice, who ignored him. He then retrieved a case of beer from the garage and loaded more in the icebox. Stepping into the drawing room, he noticed Pat Daniels was laughing and had her hand on Cam's knee. Zack began imagining how the electrical charge went through the head of the female monster in the movie *The Bride of Frankenstein* when he watched it as a child on "Thriller 18", the late-night show. *The corpse came alive*, he thought. Zack turned and went into the living room, fetched a William Faulkner book he never finished in his Novelists class, sat down and began reading. The laughter coming from the drawing room made him feel like more of an outcast, Cam spewed his usual "me, me, me" bullshit. His home had been taken over by people who hated him.

"Zack, Zack, where is he?" Cam yelled. Zack put his thumb into his book as his brother came around the corner. "Zack, Pat needs another beer," his brother ordered. Zack reluctantly walked into the kitchen, got the beer, then walked into the drawing room. Cam grabbed the beer out of his hand, handing it to Mrs. Daniels.

"Oh, thank you, darling," she enthusiastically said to Cam as if he had retrieved her beverage. She continued to refuse to look at Zack. He asked if anyone wanted anything, but there was no response. Pop shook his head. He then walked to the kitchen, muttering to himself, "Zack, keep it civil."

Pop had asked Mrs. Dupree, his housekeeper, to prepare the holiday dinner. She cooked an amazing pot roast and delicious yeast rolls from scratch. Zack set the table in the dining room using the rose China and crystal water goblets. Mrs. Dupree helped him make sure each setting was perfect. Cam yelled to get Pat another beer, which he did, and then went in and assisted Mrs. Dupree with the hot food. She asked Zack who was the beer drinker. "Pat Daniels, the lady in there."

"Lord mercy, she's got a drinking problem if you ask me. Keep that between us." Zack nodded his head. Organizing the many desserts, Mrs. Dupree said, "go let your daddy know it's dinnertime! I have to get home. I'll be over tomorrow with the turkey."

"Yes, ma'am. Thank you for all your help! Merry Christmas." Zack gave Mrs. Dupree a hug, then walked in and told his father dinner was ready.

The family and Mrs. Daniels strolled into the dining room. As everyone sat down, Cam was holding hands with Pat, who laughed and said, "I always heard you were the favorite son, and I sure can see why." Zack poured white wine. "I prefer my beer. Tell him, please," she said to Cameron.

"Zack, Pat prefers beer."

After he poured Alice's wine, Zack looked up and smiled at Mrs. Daniels, quietly saying, "yes, ma'am." He walked to the icebox and retrieved a Budweiser, then walked and placed the can of beer on the table.

"Wait," Cam blurted, "have enough class to open Mrs. Daniels's beer can, Zack. A fine lady never opens a bottle, or snaps open a can."

This was a settled *faux pas* in the Kingdon home, when Zack first got Mrs. Daniels a beer in October, he served it in a glass, knowing you never serve a beverage in a can or bottle. She refused to drink it, demanding it be served in a can.

Zack began to reach for the can, saying, "excuse me, ma'am," and then opened it.

"Okay, son, sit down and eat your dinner," Pop said in an annoyed tone.

As he took his seat, Zack looked across the table and saw Mrs. Daniels finish the beer within seconds, holding her mouth over the opening of the can like it was a tit, slurping loudly, her body shaking, while everyone couldn't help but stare. As Zack began to eat his pot roast, enjoying his first bites, Cam said, "Zack, Pat needs another beer. Get it for her, now!" Zack put on an unreadable poker face, never revealing his frustration. He quietly put his knife and fork down, wiped his mouth, got up, and went into the kitchen, returning with another beer. Standing over Mrs. Daniels, Zack opened the beer and placed it on the table. The table was getting boisterous, seeming to irritate Pop. As Zack sat down, Pat was crudely sucking on her beer can. As he resumed dinner, Cam said, "Zack, Mrs. Daniels needs another beer." Pop yelled, "SHUT UP, goddammit! Let the boy eat his supper!" Zack did not look up. A few minutes later, sitting adjacent to his father, Zack whispered, "are you okay, Daddy?" His father nodded. During the meal, Cam continued bragging about himself. Emily did the same. Loads of laughter filled the room, but not from Zack. He quietly ate his dinner, thinking about Jeremiah's sweet card and imminent departure. Then he began thinking of Gwen and his admiration for her. He was looking forward to spending time with her later. Suddenly, Cam abruptly stood up from the table, glaring at Zack. He went into the kitchen and brought Pat another beer. Zack noticed his father was especially quiet as Pat Daniels consumed beer after beer, slurping loudly when downing each can. There were four empty cans sitting on the sparkling white linen tablecloth.

Once everyone finished eating, Zack cleared the plates. He brought in the desserts and placed them on the table. He decided to hold off and have his when he brought Gwen over. "Would anyone like coffee?" he asked.

"Pat would like another beer," Cam muttered.

"Mrs. Daniels, would you like coffee?" Zack asked. She did not answer. He had heard Cam mutter 'gimp' under his breath while pouring the coffee, something he called Zack when he was a child. After pouring coffee for the few takers, Zack returned to the kitchen and resumed cleaning up while the family enjoyed dessert. He gently hand-washed the China. Mrs. Dupree taught him that you never place fine China in the dishwasher.

Cam entered the kitchen and stood next to Zack at the sink, "you don't like us here, do you? Well, I'm here to tell you that you don't impress anyone, faggot!" Cam said, practically spitting bile on him.

As he strutted away Zack muttered, "go fuck yourself!"

Cam turned around and pushed Zack back, causing him to drop a China plate he was washing. It shattered on the floor. Cam got up in Zack's face, shoving him back against the counter. Alice came into the kitchen and yelled, "Cam, STOP!"

Pop entered the kitchen, came up behind Cam, and with one arm, pulled him back, pushing him against the icebox. "DON'T YOU EVER TOUCH MY BOY, EVER!"

Cameron yelled, "he's a fucking disrespectful faggot! He's a dumb fuck, always will be!" Zack stood by, shaken.

Pop took Cam by his shirt collar, "leave my boy alone, or I will throw you out of this house! He's your brother. What's your goddamn problem?"

Zack bent down and picked up the pieces of the shattered plate, then continued washing dishes.

Cam continued, "see, he's like a girl washing dishes. I'm a man. I don't wash dishes! Faggot!" Alice told her husband to shut up.

Zack, fuming inside, did not look at Cam. As he collected the shards, his hands shook, tears in his eyes. Pop gently gripped Zack's arm, "are you all right, son?" Zack looked, reluctantly nodded, then went over to get the broom in the closet to sweep up the mess. A few minutes later, Zack put on his coat, walked into the drawing room, and asked his father if he needed anything.

Pop took Zack's hand, "you did such a nice job helping Mrs. Dupree get dinner on the table. Thank you, son."

Zack reached down and kissed his father on the cheek. "Of course, Pop. I'll be out for a while, then I'll bring Gwen over." Pop asked Zack to pick up some extra eggnog while he was out. Zack briefly looked around the room, and Emily appeared to glare at him as he turned and walked out of the room. He stood outside the door, fiddling with his gloves. He heard Emily speak up but could not make out what she said.

There was a pause, and then Pop said, "leave it alone. Your brother has been through so much. You come home and show pure disdain for him. I see it. Not one of you helped with dinner tonight. Zack's a good boy, trying to do his best, so shut up about him!" Walking to his car, Zack felt a pang of love for his father. Pulling out of the driveway, he felt butterflies for Gwen. As painful as it was at home, Zack felt nothing but unconditional love from and for her.

On Adair Road, the Farrises' stately home was imbued warmly, lit with white lights. After spending a few minutes with Gwen's always-welcoming parents, Zackary and Gwen eventually made their way to the car. The two rode around the Saint streets in the Idle Hour subdivision, looking at the festively lit homes. "Do you mind if we pull over?" he asked.

"No, not at all," she replied.

Once he parked on St. Matthews, Zackary asked, "Can I kiss you?"

Gwen smiled and said, "I was hoping you would ask." The two kissed for several minutes. "I am looking forward to Saturday."

"Me too, sweetheart." Zack sat quietly and told Gwen about the attack by Cam, "I try to get along but despise how he thinks he can order me around. He called me 'faggot' in front of my father. He's a bully."

"He lunged at you last time he was here," she remembered. "Zack, come stay with us."

Zack kissed Gwen. She scooted over, hugged him and ran her hands gently through his hair. "You are so loved. Through all of this, you said, 'God brought us together,' and I believe you. You always have me, you have Jeremiah, and Matt loves you, too."

He leaned in and kissed Gwen passionately, "thank you."

After picking up eggnog, as promised, Zack brought Gwen over for dessert. The two entered the drawing room and Pop jumped up from his lounge chair like a gentleman to greet Gwen. Zack introduced her to his two siblings and Alice, who stood up along with Emily. Mrs. Daniels was passed out on the couch. Cameron rudely remained seated, muttering, "hello." Zack took his date into the kitchen, where they shared a piece of apple pie with ice cream. Pop called Zack to get him sugar cookies and a tumbler of eggnog. He took the dessert to his father, who complained the plate had only three cookies, then returned to the kitchen, sat down and rolled his eyes. Gwen laughed.

"You're the 'daddy' in this house, Zackary," Gwen said. "Did you know that? It's so sweet how you are with him."

"He stresses me out with all his horrible eating habits. This time of year, he really overeats. Then he'll complain he can't feel his feet, and I have to massage them to help regain his circulation. Pop's at high risk for a heart attack. Day after day, his blood sugar readings are high. I have to do something to help him."

"Hon, you do," she rubbed his arm. "But you must know you can't save him."

"Gwen, I know," he tried to explain, "but my father is all the family I have, and I refuse to let God take him from me."

Gwen squeezed his hand, "I know, but Zack, it's so much pressure on you. When are you going to take care of yourself?" Zack paused before telling Gwen he received the rejection letters from his two college applications. "They arrived today?" she asked surprised. "I am so sorry, hon. There are other colleges, don't give up. We should think about this together. Colleges should mail rejections after New Year's. It can ruin a person's holiday." Zack took his hand and pushed Gwen's lovely hair behind her ear, knowing she cared about him.

On the ride back to her house, he realized he wouldn't have made it through the dinner without the reward of seeing her at the end of the evening. Later, standing at the Farrises' front door, the two kissed.

Holding Zack, Gwen muttered, "all I can think of is you. You don't know this, but I used to watch you at school in the hall before we got to know each other. You seemed so sweet. You are so handsome. I could tell you were different than most guys. You've become such a dear person in my life." The two continued to kiss in the cold Christmas air.

When Zack arrived back home, Pop had already gone upstairs to bed. Zack used the downstairs bathroom to change into his pajamas and brush his teeth. He was relieved Pop had said he could sleep with him, avoiding any problems with Cam. Walking into Pop's bedroom, he found his father, as usual, watching television.

"Come on and get in, son."

Zack climbed into the king-sized bed, reached over, and kissed his father, "good night, Daddy." Zack rolled over and fell asleep.

Chapter Thirty-Two

The next morning, Pop woke Zack up at six. Then he roused the rest of the family for breakfast and to open Christmas presents. Zack went downstairs and started the coffee. A few minutes later, while taking Pop's sugar reading, Cam walked into the kitchen.

"Daddy," Zack began, marking the reading in his log, "I know you don't want to hear this, but the numbers are too high."

Cam asked Pop what Zack was doing, "he's taking care of me. Your brother does this every day."

Zack injected the syringe, "okay, hold still…" After the injection, he wiped alcohol and put a Band-Aid on his father's arm. He then got his father a mug of coffee and kissed him on the forehead, "you're all good, Daddy." After disposing of the used syringe, he went out the front door to fetch Pop's newspaper. On his return to the kitchen, he heard Cam and Emily laughing and saying their brother could become a nurse.

"He likes doing female jobs," Cam said, making faces. "He has that fancy typewriter in his room, he could become a secretary. We have a few male secretaries at the bank."

Walking back into the kitchen, Zack placed the *Lexington Herald* on the kitchen table.

"Stop all your nonsense, Zack's going to be an accountant," Pop told them.

"No way, he could never. Accounting is hard," Emily sharply added.

Realizing they were still ignoring his presence, Zack asked, "Pop, should I set the table?" His father nodded.

After breakfast, the family decamped to the living room and opened gifts. Zack gave his father a sterling silver Cross pen-and-pencil set with his name inscribed, along with a new bottle of Old Spice. Zack opened the large box from his father and inside was a Bosca black leather briefcase with his initials in gold. "Son, these are some of the finest bags made in the U.S. You can use this when you become a CPA."

Zackary was overwhelmed. To him, the gift conveyed Pop's confidence in him and his plan to become an accountant. Emily scornfully examined the briefcase. Zack got up, went over, hugged his father, and kissed him, "thank you, Daddy. Thank you so much."

"All this hugging and kissing," Cam commented with a disgusted look on his face, "good God!" Alice whispered for him to be quiet.

Later that afternoon, Zack was in his suit, happily sitting in the Farrises' parlor for Christmas dinner. Dr. Farris was engrossed in telling him a story about fishing in Maine when he interrupted himself, "Zack, I never thanked you properly, but Jenny and I are so grateful to you for standing up and protecting Gwen from Ed and those boys. I'm so sorry you got injured."

Zack sipped his ginger ale, "Sir, I didn't do anything heroic, but I wasn't going to let them touch her."

Gwen's father reached his hand out to shake Zack's,

"I appreciate you being there for her. We know Gwyneth adores you, and you have been such a good friend." Then Dr. Farris looked around to ensure the two had privacy, before leaning forward in his chair. "I don't want to get too personal, but Gwen has shared with her mother and me that you're a homosexual." Zack became uncomfortable, taking in a deep breath. "You're welcome in our home anytime. Gwen is so taken by your kindness. She tells us you have had difficulty with this. Jenny and I think you're a fine boy."

Zack nodded. He knew this was probably not a comfortable topic for Dr. Farris to talk about. "Thank you, sir. That means a lot to me. It's actually been difficult, but your daughter has been beyond supportive. She's become my dearest friend."

After a sumptuous holiday meal, Zack jumped in and insisted on helping with the dishes. Gwen then cleared it with her mother so Zack could go upstairs to her room. She had a festively decorated bedroom with colorful butterfly-print wallpaper and elegant multilayered drapes.

"Take off your jacket, hon," she said. She asked him to come over and sit next to her on the queen-sized bed. As soon as he did, the two began kissing. She eventually pulled back, "mom saw your school picture. She is convinced you are the best-looking boy at Henry Clay."

Zack covered his face, laughing, "oh my God. I feel like your parents might love me as much as you."

Gwen took his hand, "I think you're right." He smiled, looking into her beautiful eyes, "you make me happy." Zack embraced Gwen, and the two fell back on the bed in a kiss. A few minutes later, Zack suggested they open gifts.

Gwen read her card:

My dearest Gwyneth,

No words can ever describe how much you mean to me as my friend. I have no idea what we have going on right now, but I do know I love you more and more each day. My heart has not beat the same since the morning I came up to you in the hallway. While I may not exactly be into girls, I am into you—your beauty, kindness, and willingness to extend your heart to me. God did mean for us to be friends, together—somehow—some way. Let's figure it out together. Merry Christmas.
Love forever, your Zackary

As soon as Gwen got to the second sentence, she was in tears, "no straight guy could write this letter. Zack, you are a gift. Thank you for this!" After an extended kiss, Zack handed Gwen her present. She unwrapped the gift and opened the box. It was a black figurine of Man o' War, one of the greatest American thoroughbred racehorses. It was similar to the one Zack had in his bedroom. "Oh, Zacky, this is beautiful," she said, appearing touched. "It will always remind me of you and your passion for horses!" Gwen hugged and kissed Zack. "I think about that wonderful day you took me to meet the horses. They are more family to you than your siblings," Gwen lovingly relayed, staring at the horse. "This is so nice, honey. Thank you so much!"

Gwen handed Zack his present with a card. "Is this card going to make me cry?" he asked. She smiled as he opened it.

Zackary,

I feel blessed as I get to know you. You constantly surprise me with your love for me. You always show me your tender side—and you trust me. You stood up for me with Ed, and I appreciate you caring for me! I have never experienced this kind of happiness with another person. When you tell me you love me, you often begin to cry and reveal your feelings for me. My heart will never be the same, as it dances with your love. Merry Christmas and Happy New Year!

Love, Gwyneth

Zack had tears falling as he put his hand over his mouth. "This is so sweet," he said, kissing Gwen and hugging her.

"Okay, let's wipe your tears," she replied. They both laughed.

Looking at the present, it was from Tiffany's, "wow, honey, what's this?" he asked.

"We drove to Cincinnati to get it for you."

Opening the hallmark bluish-green wrapping paper, which revealed a similarly colored box, Zack pulled off the lid to reveal a sterling silver picture frame with a photo of Gwen. "Oh my gosh, Gwen, this is so nice. Oh, honey, thank you!" The two kissed. "Don't you look beautiful!"

Gwen also gave Zack two ties from Brooks Brothers, "we got these in Cincinnati as well!" Zack adored the ties and was all smiles. A few minutes later, Gwen turned on some music as Zack lay on her bed. Gwen climbed on top of him as he wrapped his arms around her. He enjoyed putting his hands in her thick hair. She told Zack she could feel his heart beating so fast. The two held hands. Zack told Gwen about the briefcase his father gave him. "Wow. What a really nice statement your pop is making."

"It means so much to me," he said.

Gwen gently brushed a fingertip across one of Zack's thick brown eyebrows, "your father sees your loving heart. You would drop everything to help him, you have been such a good son. I think your brother is jealous, and so is your sister."

Around nine-thirty that evening, Zack arrived home and noticed Cam's Mercedes was not parked in the driveway. He exhaled in relief. It was quiet downstairs and when he reached the top of the second floor, he saw Pop had his bedroom door cracked open slightly. Zack gently knocked, entered, and sat on the edge of the bed.

"Hey, Daddy, how are you? I hope you didn't go overboard with the desserts." Moving his toothpick around, Pop smiled. "Thank you again for the briefcase. It's so nice."

His father reached up and patted him on the back, "I'm proud of you, son. I've never seen a kid who's such a mess like you, but you try so hard. I want to see you get somewhere in the world. That's what I'm banking on."

Chapter Thirty-Three

Around ten a.m., Zackary knocked at Gwen's front door. She peeked through the side window before opening it. The two embraced and fell into a deep kiss. "Gwen, are you okay?" Zack asked.

"I'm so nervous," She exhaled. "I wasn't expecting this." Zack took her hand and told her they didn't have to do anything if she was not ready. She was. She reached up and assured him with a kiss on the cheek. "I guess I needed to hear that. I still want to do this. I'm nervous. Sorry for being so weird."

"It's okay, I am too," Zack said as Gwen took a deep breath and walked into his arms. "Please know I am here for you, and I love you. It's okay to be nervous. If we do this, you can stop at any time. I don't want it to be overwhelming. You don't have to take your clothes off unless you're ready."

"Why are you nervous, Zack?"

"Asking anyone to take off their clothes and touch their body... I don't mind with you… it excites me, but I am shy about my body too."

Gwen went into the kitchen to retrieve a few soft drinks. When she returned, she handed him a soda, took his hand, and the two walked upstairs.

"I'm going to take my clothes off," Zack said. He sat next to her on the edge of the bed and pulled off his shoes, socks, shirt, and pants. Wearing only his boxer shorts, he stood up. Zack stood facing her. Gwen reached up and touched Zack's hairy chest. She wrapped her arms around his waist, and he asked her if she wanted him to remove his boxer shorts. She nodded slowly, pulled back, and Zack removed his boxers, revealing himself completely. He looked away, shy.

"You're so nice, Zack," she said. "You are so much more muscular than I ever knew."

He sniffled, "I'm scrawny."

"You're gorgeous," Gwen felt around Zack's body, rubbing her hand slowly over his stomach. Then she gently put one hand around Zack's penis, while her other hand felt his testicles. Her fingers were cold. She asked Zack to turn around, "oh wow, I love your butt. It's so hairy, so sexy." Gwen stood up and kissed the back of Zack's neck while rubbing her hands all over his rear. "I can see why Jeremiah loves your ass," she said.

Zack laughed nervously, "thank you." The two began kissing.

She reached down and put her hand around the base of his penis. Next, she pulled Zack onto the bed, and he lay on his back. Gwen studied Zack's body as if it were her human anatomy class. She stretched out next to him, running her fingers through his chest hair, "you have an amazing manly chest. Why do you wear such baggy clothes?"

Zack looked away, "I guess I'm trying to hide myself inside my clothes. I want to look nice, but I also don't want people to notice me."

Gwen squeezed his right hand, "you don't have to hide anything from me. There's nothing to worry about here." Zack became quiet. Gwen slowly understood, "is it because those men hurt you?"

Zack nodded, sitting up, "yeah."

"You're safe with me," she said, holding Zack in her arms. He moved his mouth down to her neck, slowly kissing and licking, smelling the lovely fragrance she used. "Oh my God… oh, that feels so good." Gwen reached down and again placed her hand on Zack's penis, then moved down to his testicles and ran her fingers further down into his taint region. Zack moaned. "You like it when I do this?" Gwen removed her hand and unexpectedly removed her tee shirt, revealing her tan bra. She took Zack's left hand and placed it on her well-proportioned breast. "Would you remove it?" He leaned up and reached behind, trying to unsnap the bra to no avail. "Don't worry, let me do it."

Zack touched them, "you're beautiful, honey."

The look on her face became serious, and her breath quickened. Gwen stood up, took off her navy-blue shorts, keeping her underpants on, and sat on her knees. Zack scooted up and turned to his side, holding his hand out. Gwen took his hand and leaned forward, putting it down into her panties. He felt her pubic hair. She took his fingers with her hand, guiding him to a wet area and rubbing his fingers around her clitoris. She used her other hand to pull the skin up, giving him access. "Move your fingers back and forth here. Oh, yeah, like that, but slowly." Gwen began to move her hips forward and backward. "What does it feel like?" she asked.

"It's wonderful," Zack replied in a low voice.

Gwen asked, "didn't you say Matt likes to tongue Colleen while in the shower?"

"Do you want me to do it to you?" he asked.

"Oh, God, would you?"

He grinned. "You have to show me what to do."

She loved to be his teacher. She stood up, took Zack's hand, and the two walked into the bathroom, turning on the shower. They explored each other's bodies. It was the first time Zack experienced performing oral sex on a woman.

222

Chapter Thirty-Four

The next day, after assisting his father with insulin and helping put the breakfast prepared by Mrs. Dupree on the dining room table, Zack noticed Cam, Alice, and Emily were all glaring at him. His father asked them why they were all quiet. "We need to speak with you privately, Pop," Cam muttered, looking directly at his younger brother. Zack felt the tension in the dining room, something was clearly up. "After breakfast" was all Pop said.

A few minutes later, Zack began clearing the table. Unwilling to look at him, his brother did not hand him his plate. "Do you want me to wash it or not?" Zack bluntly asked. "Then hand it to me!" Zack turned around and walked into the kitchen. While cleaning up, he exhaled in frustration, but felt blessed he could spend so much of his time with Gwen over the holidays while his family was there. After wiping down the countertop, Zack took the trash bags out to the garage. When he returned inside, there was shouting. "Pop, we always knew he was!" he could hear Cam say. "He's disgusting."

Zack couldn't make out anything else when they started whispering. He moved closer to the dining room door and heard Pop erupt, "I want you to be nice to your brother. I don't want to hear anymore." Anxious, Zack went upstairs to get cleaned up and meet Gwen. While he was in the shower, Zack realized his siblings may have found his stash of magazines and the book even though he hid them well. *Why would they go through my things? Was that what they were talking about just now?*

That afternoon, he and Gwen walked through a department store at Fayette Mall. Looking over necklaces, she asked, "so, what do you think they were talking about?"

"I don't know. They see me being sweet to Pop. I think they're jealous."

Gwen interjected, "I always wanted a brother or sister but seeing what yours are like, it makes me feel lucky I don't have siblings. I can't believe how cruel they can be."

As they meandered over to men's clothing, Zack looked at dress shirts on sale, "they've been terrible to me since I can remember. Part of it's our age difference. But they also just believe they are so much better than everyone. I don't know why. It must be an insecurity."

She put her arm behind Zack and hugged up against him, "I don't like how this upsets you." He thanked her with a kiss.

In the car driving to his home for dinner, Gwen asked Zack how he was feeling, knowing Jeremiah had left for New York earlier in the day. "I am trying not to think about it," he said. "I can't control any of this. I really miss him, but I feel blessed to be here with you. That's what I think about."

At the stoplight, Gwen put her hand on Zack's leg, "I look forward to being with you again."

"I do too. I love getting you off."

She squeezed his leg, "oh, I'm still feeling great down there."

"That makes me very happy!" he smiled.

Walking into the kitchen, Zack was greeted by Mrs. Dupree and the delicious smell of her roast chicken. He introduced her to Gwen, but then she began to speak in a whisper. "Honey, I didn't want to say anything. When I arrived earlier to fix lunch and prepare dinner, I overheard a lot of fighting between your papa and your brother and sister. It got so bad, they both packed up and left. Zack, it was about you. I don't know what it was about, but they went at it, then I heard your papa scream. God, it was like a bomb went off! I want to finish and go home. Honey, you know I think you're such a nice boy. I will always think that."

He looked down, "thank you, ma'am. I'm so sorry you had to witness that."

"Zackary, your father is not in good health," she said frantically, "and to be upset like this? His heart, oh my God! I feared he would have an attack."

He helped Mrs. Dupree with her coat and walked her to the car. Back in the house, Zack wondered what had transpired while he was out. It worried him that his sister and brother might have found something revealing his secret. He felt his stomach drop. During dinner, there was no conversation between Zack and his father. Zack and Gwen quietly spoke, even occasionally laughed. Pop ate without saying a word and didn't look at Zack once. He noticed Pop was staring at the drawing of a blue jay hanging on the dining room's far end. The pained expression reminded Zack of when Pop committed his mother to the hospital many years ago.

As Zack cleared plates and Gwen walked into the kitchen, Pop put a toothpick in his mouth, "Son, when the holidays are over, I need to have a long talk with you. Cam, Alice, and Emily left. I threw them out. None of you know how to get along."

Zack reached over to touch his father, who knocked

his hand away, "go do the dishes," he said curtly. Zack instantly had a chill go through him. *He knows. They fucking told him.*

Over the next few days, things with Pop became increasingly awkward. He was silent to Zack, leaving money for him to get dinner on his own. When he did speak to him, he screamed over nothing. In the mornings, he turned away when Zack tried to kiss him after dealing with his medication. At night, when Pop entered his room, he closed the door behind him and locked it. One evening, Zack knocked to see if his father needed anything. Pop screamed a litany of obscenities at him through the door, telling him to go away.

Chapter Thirty-Five

January 1982

It was New Year's Day, and Pop watched the bowl games in the drawing room with Pat Daniels. Mrs. Dupree came over midafternoon to prepare his "Hot Brown" for an early dinner. She blended turkey with country ham and melted cheddar cheese over thick toast on the plate. Pop ate this dish every New Year's as a tradition. It was too rich for Zack, who dined with the Farrises'. He had been spending a lot of time at their house with her family and regularly alone with Gwen.

Later that day, Zack took Gwen to the Kentucky Theatre to see *Cabaret*, on its ten-year anniversary release. After the movie ended, Gwen went to the restroom, and Zack walked over to speak to Fred Mills about the possibility of any job openings. "You know, I don't right now," Fred said. "But I may have something in a few weeks. Give me a call or drop by, and we'll see then." Fred then asked Zack about "that hot guy" he was with at the Bar.

"He's studying in New York for a few months. He wants to be the best with his instrument," Zack replied.

"Well, I bet you enjoyed 'studying his instrument,'" Fred replied with a huge grin. Zack's mouth dropped. "I'm teasing you. Keep in touch with me. Hopefully, something will open up soon." Laughing, Zack shook Fred's hand and thought he wasn't unlike the "Emcee" character in *Cabaret*, just in Lexington and not Berlin.

Taking Gwen home, Zack discussed how tension with Pop being so distant drove him crazy. He pulled into her driveway, "I think he knows about me. I think they told him. I'm scared, Gwen. When he gets mad at me, he usually stays mad briefly, and then it goes away. It's been almost a week. This time it seems different."

"His anger with your brother and sister might've spilled onto you," Gwen remarked wisely. "Give it time." Zack walked her to the door and gave her a long good-night kiss.

The next morning, Zack came downstairs early, smelling coffee brewing. "Good morning, Daddy." Pop said nothing, glaring at his son. Zack sat down and took his father's blood sugar, which was the highest reading ever, "Pop, it's really high."

"Shut up! Stop judging me. Who do you think you are, boy?" As Zack wrote the reading down, he nervously looked up and his father glared at him, "GET IT OVER WITH!"

Zack gave him his insulin. After removing the needle, as he reached over with a cotton ball of alcohol, his father pulled his arm away, got up, and walked into the foyer to retrieve his hat and coat. Zack teared up. His father reentered the kitchen and went to the back door, "I don't want to see all those branches and leaves in the yard. And stop crying like a girl. You need to become a man!" He slammed the kitchen door behind him. Zack spent the morning in the freezing cold yard, raking leaves and clearing up small branches.

Pop arrived home, pulling into the driveway as Zack was putting all the brush into the garbage. "You didn't even bother neatening up the edges on the street," his dad said, getting out of the car. "Finish the work!"

Later, after cleaning himself up, Zack came out of his room, and his father sharply yelled, "I want to know where you are going at all times. You write it down on the notepad on the kitchen table. Everywhere you are going!" Zack turned and walked down the steps. He took the spiral notepad in the kitchen and jotted down, *Gone to Gwen's. May go for a drive with her.*

Mr. and Mrs. Farris were off to visit friends for the day. Zack and Gwen took the chance to make love in her bed. They were both getting more used to each other's bodies. Zack spent a lot of time slowly using his tongue on Gwen, enjoying sending her into orbit. As he slowly pleasured her, he tightly held her left hand, loving how he could make her feel so good. Gwen later got the nerve to try to perform oral sex on Zackary. She told him how comforting it was to be with a man who understood her fears and was patient with her, she wanted to try since he was so willing to please her.

The next day, Sunday, Pop again refused to speak with Zack during his insulin reading and shot. After pouring his father a cup of coffee, Zack returned to bed to avoid the tension. Upon leaving to go out to breakfast, Pop left Zack a harsh note indicating that from now on, he would have to wash his own clothes, change his sheets, vacuum, and clean his bathroom, no longer allowing Mrs. Dupree to enter his bedroom. A few hours later, in the basement, while he was folding clothes from the dryer, he could see Pop pulling into the driveway through the basement window. Suddenly he heard his father scream out. "Zack!"

"I'm in the basement, Pop."

Zack's father stood at the top of the steps, "did you read my note on the table?"

"Yes, sir. I'm doing my laundry now."

"When Mrs. Dupree is cleaning, she is not to enter your room. YOU will clean for yourself." There was a long silence. He sounded like he had steam coming out of his ears. Zackary refused to engage with his father, afraid he would discover the truth about him, but Pop let loose, "you're a worthless kid. You're shit, you always have been. There's no other way to think of you! An utter goddamned disappointment and disgrace. Your brother's right, you are a 'loser'! I regret we ever had you!" He slammed the basement door shut. Zack fell to his hands and knees on the floor, dropping the clothes he was holding. He felt his heart break further.

A few minutes later, Zack calmed himself, finished folding clothes and went upstairs to his bedroom. As he was about to put his pajamas away, Zack opened his bottom drawer and saw his magazines had been pulled out of his pajamas, along with the book Matt had given him. *They went through my things. Cam and Emily must've shown them to Pop. Dear God, they are trying to ruin me. He has seen all these pictures in these magazines. Now he knows, he knows...* Zack slowly sat on the edge of his bed, feeling the world closing in on him, overwrought with shame, shaking as tears fell down his face. *Everyone hates me now. What am I going to do?* He couldn't think, feeling overwhelmed, alone and scared.

Zack slowly picked up his phone and dialed Gwen, "can I come over?" He explained what had happened. She told Zack to get in his car immediately. Walking into the upstairs hallway, Zack suddenly heard a woman talking rather loudly downstairs. He listened closer and recognized Pat Daniels's voice, "it's deviant behavior. Zack is having homosexual sex. And he may have brought homosexuals into this house. Dave, I would never allow that in my house. You should put him away. He's sick in the head, I tell you. At the hospital, we isolate queers from the others on the ward. You should not have to put up with this. This is disgusting."

His father quietly muttered, "he's still my son, Pat. I can't do that to him."

Zack tiptoed down the steps, snuck past the drawing room, through the kitchen, and out the back door, into the cold January air with no coat.

Once he arrived at the Farrises' house, Gwen ran outside to meet him. Her mother was standing at the door. Gwen embraced Zack who was engulfed in tears, unable to speak. She helped him walk to the front door. "Zack, come sit in the parlor," Mrs. Farris said, helping Gwen guide him. He was crying so hard he could barely breathe or speak. Jenny instructed Gwen to remove his shoes and for him to lie down on the couch with two pillows under his head. "I'm getting a cold washcloth."

Zack's face was red, he was traumatized by what he heard Pat Daniels say, "Pat said Papa should put me away in a hospital. I'm so scared. My father hates me now."

Mrs. Farris returned and placed a cold cloth over Zack's forehead. Gwen held his hand, "you have us. We love you."

"Zack, honey, you are welcome here anytime," Mrs. Farris said. "We have a guest bedroom if you ever need it. Try to breathe deeply, close your eyes, and relax. You are safe here."

As kind and loving as Gwen and her mother were, Zack felt his life served no purpose. Feelings from his horrific last summer returned. He felt pure emptiness and shame. Zackary didn't know how he could live with this convergence of pain. He thought of one of the notes shoved in his locker, which read, "I hope you die, you fucking fag! DIE!" Distraught, he dozed off.

"Zacky, sweetheart, wake up," Gwen said. "That was a long nap. You hibernated like a bear. I held your hand the entire time." Zack felt dizzy as he slowly sat up. Mrs. Farris handed him a glass of water. Zack couldn't look at

Gwen. Dark thoughts crept back into his mind, causing him to stare at the floor, breathing deeply. "Do you want to stay for dinner?"

Zack eventually shook his head, "I better get home." He thanked Mrs. Farris.

Gwen walked him outside, "I'm so worried about you. You look terrible."

Zack quickly hugged Gwen and got into his car, "thank you. I love you."

A few minutes later, walking into the kitchen door, Zack saw take-out bags from Long John Silver's on the counter with several empty beer cans in the sink. He heard the television on in the drawing room. "GET IN HERE!" Pop shouted. Zack reluctantly walked up and stood at the drawing room door, refusing to look at his father.

"You didn't write down where you were going," he snapped. "DON'T YOU DEFY ME, EVER!"

Zack looked down, "yes, sir." Then tears fell down his face.

"STOP YOUR FUCKING CRYING. WHAT IS WRONG WITH YOU, BOY?" Pop got up from his chair and walked up to Zack, screaming as Zack put his hand over his face. "WHAT'S WRONG WITH YOU?"

Mumbling through his tears, Zack said, "please, Daddy, you're scaring me. Why are you so mad at me?"

"YOU'RE DISGUSTING," his father spat. "I want you to finish school and leave this house, out of my life! STOP CRYING!"

Zack turned and ran up to his room. He undressed, put on his pajamas, and climbed into bed. It was after 5:00 PM. Lying in bed with tears falling down his face, Zack wanted it all to end. *He hates me. They all want me gone. I'll give them 'gone.'* With his head on his pillow, Zack stared out his bedroom window. The sun had vanished, and all he saw was darkness.

Chapter Thirty-Six

"No newspaper?" David Kingdon asked.

Zack walked outside to get the paper at the end of the driveway. He reached down to pick it up and noticed cigarette butts clustered in the same place he'd found them before. Zack's heart sank. *Oh, my God… They're watching me again.* He went inside and performed the daily medical routine with his father who stared at the paper, not muttering a word. Zack smiled gently, "I took down all the Christmas decorations. How are you feeling today, Daddy?" Zack asked, trying to see if his father would let up on him.

Pop looked up, "what? What are you asking?"

"I asked how you're feeling."

"I'd feel a lot better if you weren't here! I don't even like having you at this table. Take your breakfast into the dining room. I don't want you around me."

Zack looked at him, pressed his lips together and did not tear up, instead, he simply smiled at his father. While having cereal and coffee in the dining room, the various items around Zackary, the chair he sat on, the salt and pepper shakers in front of him, the spoon he was holding, suddenly felt like foreign objects. They belonged to the Kingdon family, which he was no longer a part of. The letter he'd received yesterday from his mother added to his searing pain. One of his siblings had told her about the magazines they found, and she wrote, *"You have utterly disgraced this family—and disgraced me. I brought you into this world, and now you are shaming me by choosing to be a filthy homosexual and risk going to Hell for it. This is your choice. You will never be loved if you continue this horrible life."*

The pain inside was debilitating. While forcing the last spoonful of cereal into his mouth, he began to have visions of jumping off the Clay's Ferry Bridge over the Kentucky River. He thought of doing it in the middle of the night. *I won't be able to see the ground below, so I can get it over with quickly,* he rationalized. Zack then had ideas of pills and even using a box cutter but settled on the bridge. *They all hate me. This is what they want. They won't even talk to me.* After a few minutes, he walked back into the kitchen, washed his dishes, and prepared his lunch.

"You're not crying, are you?"

Zack turned around, smiling, "no, sir. Not at all." He surmised his not crying irritated his father, who was determined to make him miserable. After putting on his coat and grabbing his book bag, Zack briefly turned before walking out the kitchen door. "I love you, Daddy!" He then gently closed the door behind him.

Zack had five minutes till the bell rang, but he did not want to see Gwen, as he felt so low. In fact, he did not want to speak to anyone. Later that morning, he walked into psychology class and saw Gwen sitting with Rebecca and Keith, laughing about something. Zack took his seat.

"How are you, hon?" she asked. "I got worried when I didn't see you."

"I'm fine," Zack glanced at her with a neutral, unresponsive look, then stared down. He continued thinking of driving to the bridge that night. *I am going after dark.* The more he thought about the bridge, the more relieved he felt. Zack stopped obsessing about his father's horrible treatment, his mother's letter, the hate from his siblings, and hatred from those who wrote the locker notes. To Zack, they all had their lives. Nobody was making them feel inhuman, like they were somehow a freak. No one was tormenting those people for the way God made them. It was the loneliest Zack had felt in his life. Darkness set in his mind. *I will write a note and leave it in my book bag.* Gwen reached over and offered her hand, which he took. Zack stared straight ahead, body and mind numb. After class, he avoided eye contact with Gwen, who did most of the talking.

"Hon, are you all right? You are so quiet, so distant. I am here for you. Please tell me what you are thinking."

Zack slowly looked up, gazed at her, then went in for a deep, long, sustained kiss. When he pulled away, he smiled, "I love you so much. I'll see you later." He turned and ran up the steps to his trig class. Zack paid attention to Mr. Moss's math problems on the board, writing down the solutions in his notebook. After the lecture, the teacher allowed students to work on their homework assignments. Staring out the window for a few seconds, Zack turned the page in his notebook, put his pencil back in his book bag, pulled out an ink pen, and began drafting a letter to his father.

1/6/82

Daddy,

I wanted to write and let you know I could not live another day feeling the rejection over who I am as a person. You need to know two men almost killed me, nearly suffocated me, raping me on June 17, 1981. I am also attacked and harassed continuously at Henry Clay, one of the incidents, which you are

aware of. My own family has made it clear how much hostility and hatred they feel toward me. You said on Sunday you believed I am shit and wished you and Mommy had not had me. And Mommy's letter arrived in the mail a few days ago, condemning me to Hell. Mommy claimed it was my "choice" to be this way. Given all of this, the real choice I have is to end my pain. Always understand, I am one of God's Children and I came into the world this way. I cannot help who I am, being gay is who I am. No person would ever "choose" to have their life destroyed and be condemned for being this way. I want to be at Peace in a place where I am accepted for who I am. I no longer want to be the "worst disappointment of your life." I dearly love you, Daddy. I do hope God will forgive me, so I can watch over you from afar.
Love forever,
Zacky

Mr. Moss walked up and down the aisles, looking at students' calculations. Zack pulled out his pencil and began his homework. He was starting to shut down mentally. Walking into yearbook class, after lunch, Zack's inbox piled up with requests for caption writing. He went into Mr. Pillsbury's office to ask if he could be excused.

"What's wrong, Kingdon? Why do you need to leave?"

"I'm not feeling well, sir," Zackary replied.

One of the infidels lying on the couch whispered "faggot." Mr. Pillsbury stopped, turned in his chair, and yelled, "You FUCKHEAD. Shut your FUCKING mouth, NOW! Go ahead, Zack." Mr. Pillsbury handed him an early dismissal form.

Zack went to his locker, got his coat and left the building. He pulled into an empty driveway, went upstairs, closed the door to his bedroom, removed his school clothes, put on his pajamas, and got into bed. Feeling tired, he fell asleep.

A little after 9:00 PM, Zack abruptly awoke from his sleep. Staring up at the dark ceiling, he knew it was time. He initially searched for his clothes in the dark, then turned on the bed lamp and dressed. Walking into his bathroom, Zack took one of the ties Gwen gave him for Christmas and put it on. Right before opening his bedroom door, Zack took the briefcase his father had given him and placed it on his desk. He looked around his bedroom and turned off the light. As he walked into the hallway, Zack saw Pop's bedroom door was closed and heard the television blaring. He stared at the light emanating from the bottom of the door, then went downstairs in the pitch dark and turned on the light in the foyer. As he put his dress coat and scarf on, he took one last look around his home. By a narrow slat of light from the foyer, Zack could see his kindergarten picture sitting on Pop's desk in the drawing room, with his high school portrait directly beside it. He smiled for a moment, then turned around, walked to the kitchen, and went quietly out the back door. It was bitterly cold.

Pulling his Toyota out of the driveway, Zack made his way down Richmond Road past Jacobson Park to the entrance of I-75 South towards Richmond. On his way to the bridge, Zack did not turn on the radio. The drive seemed long. As the interstate was so dark, he could not tell he was on the Clay's Ferry Bridge until he was driving over it. There were several trucks passing, causing his car to jolt. He slowed down about halfway across the bridge while looking through each of his rearview mirrors. He came to a complete stop and turned on his hazard lights. Zack considered what he was about to do, then ceased thinking. Two vehicles and a truck were approaching from behind. Once they passed, shaking his car, he took a deep breath. *God, please forgive me.*

Zack stepped out into the cold air and slammed the car door closed. He walked in front of the car with the headlights on bright, over to the thick concrete railing, placing both hands on it. He did not look over and instead stared straight out, pausing for a few seconds. He felt an intense, freezing-cold gust, which was sobering. Suddenly, Zack realized how the two tremendous people who had entered his life in the past months were gifts to him. Perhaps gifts from God. Within months, he'd begun to fall in love with Jeremiah and discovered a profound and passionate friendship with Gwen. Zack stood still. *I can't leave them… I can't do this to Gwen. Dear God, she adores me, and I love her, and I love Jeremiah.* Zack began to cry. Suddenly, he heard a truck approach and slow down.

Chapter Thirty-Seven

The next morning, Zack woke up to his alarm clock. Sitting on the edge of the bed, his body ached with a pressure he hadn't felt since fighting for his life during the rape the previous summer. He stared at his feet and the carpet, then went into the bathroom. Standing in the shower, Zack felt a bit dizzy. He hadn't eaten since lunch the day before. After walking downstairs, he saw Pop was waiting for his paper.

"Are you gonna…" Without responding, Zack walked behind him to the back door and outside to retrieve the paper. Back inside, coming out of the chilly morning air, he placed the paper on the table and started going through the insulin ritual. When he had a syringe in his hand, Pop pulled back, "be careful. You look angry."

Zack looked up at Pop, frustrated, "do you want me to do this? Then sit still. I would never deliberately hurt you."

Minutes later, while heating up his oatmeal, Zack stood at the stove, refusing to sit down. He could see his father glaring at him from the corner of his eye. When it was ready, he silently took his bowl and coffee into the dining room, closing the door behind him.

Before first period, Gwen waited at their locker, "honey, you don't look good."

He put his arms around her tightly, "hold me," he asked. When they released their hug, he was crying.

"What is it, honey? Are you okay?"

He nodded. "I'm good right now because you're here. Gwen, you have no idea how much you mean to me, and I feel blessed."

Gwen had a concerned look, "oh, honey, I hate seeing you hurting."

Zack smiled, wiping the tears falling, "let's get to class." He put away two books and grabbed another from the locker.

She reached in and kissed his head, gently saying, "hey, I love you so much."

Zack smiled, nodding. He turned towards his economics class. As he walked, the thought of surrendering his life terrified him. He knew he had to fight the darkness when it crept into his head. *If I have anything to live for, it's Gwen and Jeremiah. I especially can't do this to her. I can't.*

After school, Zack arrived home, laid down, and dozed off. A few minutes later, he heard, "Zack, Davy, anybody home?" It said 3:42 on his clock. Zack got out of bed and looked out his side window to the driveway. It was Aunt Norma's Oldsmobile. He dressed immediately, opened his bedroom door, and called out to his aunt, "Hello, Aunt Norma! I'll be down in a minute." He went down the stairs, and his aunt emerged from the kitchen, stirring a glass of instant iced tea.

"Hello, Zackary, come give me a hug, sweetheart," she said warmly. The two embraced tightly. "How are you, darling? Let's sit here in the living room and visit." Zack got her a coaster, and she thanked him. "Where's your daddy? Is he still at work?"

"Yes, ma'am, I guess. I was so tired and not feeling well."

"Sweetheart, what's wrong? You look a bit stressed. I

wanted to get over so I could meet you after school," Norma said sweetly, holding Zack's hand.

"I'm having a difficult time right now. Things have gotten really tense at home…"

"What's going on, honey?"

Tears in his eyes, Zack explained that his father was not speaking to him, "Cam and Emily went through my belongings, my drawers, and found, um, some things. Then they showed them to Pop. Now he won't talk to me. He's acting like he hates me."

Aunt Norma shook her head and didn't even ask what it was they had found, "well, honey, I believe everyone is entitled to some privacy, don't you agree?"

Zack smiled, "yes, ma'am."

She took Zack's hand, offering a warm smile, and began, "Sweetheart, I want you to know I love you and always will." Straightening his cowlick, she added, "that's all that matters at the end of the day." Then she hugged Zack, who wiped the tears from his eyes, "and your daddy's still giving you a hard time?"

"He said terrible things and now won't speak to me. He wants me out of the house. We no longer eat dinner together. He bought a bunch of soup for me to eat."

"Ah, it explains all those cans on the kitchen counter," she shook her head as Zack continued to cry. "Honey, I'm so sorry about this. There's not a thing wrong with you, only good things. And I know he loves you dearly. You're a fine boy, about to go to college, prom, graduation, all such good things here." Suddenly, they heard Pop pulling into the driveway. "Sounds like your daddy's home. Why don't you go upstairs and let me speak to him? I need to make it home before it gets dark soon. But you call me if you need anything, or if you want to talk. I'm here for you, anytime. If you need to stay with us, just come on over, sweetheart."

She gave him a hug and a kiss, and then, as Pop entered the living room, Zack went upstairs.

He lay on his bed with the door open to hear the two talking. It wasn't easy since both were speaking in low tones and whispers. "Davy, all I know is Zack is your son, your boy, your responsibility," his Aunt Norma said kindly but firmly. "He has no one to rely on but you. And he loves you so much. That's all that matters."

Pop complained about Zack, "being the way he is… is not normal. Pat Daniels says he's a deviant…"

Norma cut him off, "there is nothing wrong with Zackary. Davy, he's been through so much and has turned out quite well." Norma went on passionately in her Southern accent, "there is no need for all of this. He's a perfectly fine boy. George and I care about him as we always have, and I know you do too."

Pop whispered that Pat Daniels believed Zack was "mentally ill."

Norma stopped him again, "David, I am not a doctor… and neither is she. The boy needs his father. You should not project on Zack what you did with Virginia. There is no need for all this labeling. He's still a growing boy, and he's still a child. He needs lots of love and patience."

After a few more words Zack couldn't hear, Pop walked Norma out to her car. In his mind, Aunt Norma had just filed a "stay" in the "court of life" for him. Lying back on his bed, Zack thought about how much he admired her, then began breathing frantically and ran into the bathroom to throw up. After his aunt drove away, Pop got back into his car and pulled out of the driveway. Zack took off his clothes and climbed back into bed. He was exhausted but felt a strange sense of renewal. Zack prayed to God for forgiveness for even thinking about taking his life. He then glanced over at his desk and saw the briefcase sitting on it before drifting off.

The next morning, after giving his father his medication, he looked at him and smiled. He then got up and poured his father coffee. After taking a long sip, Pop said, "Son, I have decided to take a trip down to the condominium in Florida with Pat. We're leaving Friday and will be there through most of February. I'm going to have Mrs. Isaac come over and stay here. She can cook your meals for you." Zack nodded, simply saying, "yes, sir." As he walked out the door, Zack told his father he loved him, but there was no response. Driving to school, Zack felt relieved Pop was leaving for a while.

At school, as Zack approached their locker, Gwen turned around, looked at him a second, and started beaming at him, "hey, look at you. I like your smile today."

He reached in and kissed her, "I like yours, too. You look so pretty today."

"Just today?" She joked. Zack told her his father was leaving for a nearly two-month vacation. "But you're still coming over on Friday after school, right?"

Zack nodded, then whispered in her ear, "I can't wait to be with you again."

Gwen looked down, then back up, "Zacky, you make me feel so good. You know what I mean."

"No, I had no idea," he smiled, as his heart began to race. He reached in for a kiss, then headed on to first period. "Love, you," he said, walking away.

Chapter Thirty-Eight

On the morning David Kingdon left for Florida, he woke his son early. It was five-thirty, the lights were all on in the hallway and Pop stood with his two suitcases indicating he needed help loading the car. "Daddy, are you sure you should drive all this way?" Zack sleepily asked. "It's a long stretch."

"We'll take turns driving," he said curtly, not looking up at Zack who carried each bag down the stairway separately and placed them in the trunk of the Cadillac. "Now, Mrs. Isaac will be here when you get home from school. Listen, here's three hundred dollars. I don't want any goddamn problems from you." Pop bit down on his toothpick, glaring at the boy.

"Yes, sir. I always mind Mrs. Isaac."

"You'd better," the elder Kingdon warned. "Remember, she's originally from Brooklyn!" The two stood next to the car in the frigid cold and stared at each other. Pop took his hat off, turned, and walked around to the driver's door without hugging his son. Zack didn't attempt to kiss or hug his father either. "Okay," Pop said, climbing in the car. "Take care, son."

He waved, but his father didn't look back after pulling out of the driveway. Zack stared down at the driveway for a moment wondering if life with his father would ever return to what it had been. Then he walked back into the house.

Later at school, Zack and Gwen held hands in psychology class. After the bell rang in the hallway, Zack mentioned how he was looking forward to their alone time. She reached over and touched his arm and whispered, "I think I'm ready to go further with you." He smiled, unsure what she meant. Looking gently into his eyes, she smiled back, "you know…"

"Oh," he nodded before assuring her he too was nervous, and she should never do anything she didn't want to. In turn, Gwen assured him that he allowed her to feel completely in control and then went on to say he was a great comfort to her. Zack thought to himself she was just that to him… even to the point of saving his life.

"Hello," he gently called out back home, so as not to frighten Mrs. Isaac.

She was watching television in the drawing room. "Come in here, sweetheart," she yelled. When Zack entered the drawing room, Mrs. Isaac jumped up and hugged Zackary. "How are you?"

"Good, ma'am. I have missed you!" Mrs. Isaac had been Zack's au pair since he was a baby, watching him when his parents traveled. The house smelled so good from the roast she had in the oven. The two caught up with each other, then walked into the kitchen. Mrs. Isaac took a package of Martha White flour and began to prepare biscuits, Zackary's favorite food.

"Can I help?" he asked.

"No, darling. I looked in the icebox and found a lot of beer. Are you drinking that piss?" she carped. Zack attempted to give an accurate picture of Mrs. Daniels. "Dear God, your daddy doesn't need some boozy lush," she said bluntly. "Your mother, God help her, is a troubled woman. Your daddy told me what her husband did. Let me tell you something, the fucking bastard would have the imprint of my knuckles on his broken jaw if he ever raised his hand to me. I wouldn't just fuck him up good. I'd fuck him up forever!" she shouted as she aggressively kneaded the dough, then took the rolling pin, pressing it out for biscuits. Zack was in awe of how Mrs. Isaac could go from being the gentlest woman to a raging beast in a flash. "Your momma's going to learn at her age, there are no worthwhile men… they don't exist! My husband, Andrew, may he rest in peace, was a wonderful husband. Don't think he didn't cause me troubles occasionally, though. If the son of a bitch who hurt your mother lived here, I'd get my gun and blow his fucking kneecaps off! That's what you do in Brooklyn!" Mrs. Isaac sprinkled her commentary with Yiddish as she sprinkled a smidge of salt over the dough.

After she used a glass tumbler to cut the biscuit shapes and place them on a cooking sheet, she put the tray in the oven and took Zack's hand, "Dearest, tell me about what's going on with you. Mrs. Isaac knows. Mrs. Isaac always knew," she said, pulling Zack to sit at the kitchen table.

He had a strange look, "what do you mean, ma'am?"

"My boy, your daddy called to ask me to stay with you and told me you were a 'bad' kid! He said your family showed him some magazines." Zack panicked, humiliated. She squeezed his hands, "Zack, Zackary, sweetheart. I KNOW, it's okay. I love you, no matter what."

He began crying, looking away in embarrassment. "I'm so afraid Pop hates me now, Bubby," Zack said through tears. "He won't speak to me."

Mrs. Isaac pulled Zack up close and hugged him, "Honey. I've known this about you since you were a little thing. You're a sweet, loving, gentle boy. God made you this way, and God loves you this way. Do you think Mrs. Isaac doesn't know? Who are you fooling? I'm from New York!" she sweetly said, kissing Zack on the cheek.

"It's been so hard," Zack confessed. "I don't know how to relate to people. And I've been attacked at school…"

The bell went off for the biscuits, and Mrs. Isaac rose to go to the oven. "I have known several homosexuals, many who are Jewish and some whose families turned them away. They are wonderful people… loving, kind, and generous, and no different than anyone else," she remarked, taking the biscuits out of the oven. Zack viewed Mrs. Isaac like a momma bear.

"How could you tell I was gay?" Zack said, wiping his tears.

Sitting back down at the table, Mrs. Isaac looked at Zack and smiled, "you are such a good boy. You always mind me. You sit and talk with me so respectfully. You love your parents and have such a nice, gentle sweetness about you that other boys often don't have. You kiss me when you come home, have a beautiful heart, clean fingernails, and smell good." Zack began laughing. "Honey, your father doesn't know what to do with you. I told him, 'Davy, there is nothing wrong with your boy. You should thank God you have such a loving boy. He is a gift. He is your last son.'" Zack smiled through tears. "In the call, I told your daddy that not speaking to you, distancing you, rejecting you is hateful and wrong. I told your papa to stop it! He argued with me that Pat claimed it was a mental condition. I told him if he didn't goddamn stop with his bullshit, I would give him a mental condition!"

Tears continued to fall down his cheek, "thank you for saying all this and talking to Daddy. I can't imagine not having him in my life. It hurts so much."

"Sweetheart, you did nothing wrong. Your daddy told me for years how he was so angry you didn't play football, that you were such a disappointment to him. I told him you were meant for greater things in life than throwing a stupid ball around. God has plans for you. Your daddy didn't always agree with me, and believe me, I lost no sleep over it. He's afraid he may have done something to cause this. I told him to go on his vacation and think about 'how much you love this beautiful boy' and to stop all this mishegoss. There's nothing wrong with boys loving other boys. I reminded him how lucky he was to have a kind, loving son like you in his life who cares so much for him. What more of a blessing from God could you hope for?" Mrs. Isaac held Zack's hand and kissed his cheek, "you go up and lay down. I'll finish getting dinner ready. Mrs. Isaac doesn't like to cook past five."

"Thank you," Zack embraced her. "I appreciate all that you said. I have always loved you."

"Me too, sweetheart," Mrs. Isaac said, then pushed Zack upstairs for a short nap. "Blow your nose and wash your face. Honey, your father is a stubborn man. Like God hasn't given me the honor of dealing with a few of those types in my life? Gee whiz. He and I don't always agree, politics especially, but he and I agree on this, you are a fine boy!"

"Thank you, ma'am," Zack smiled, rushing upstairs.

Mrs. Isaac made a perfect dinner, followed by a picture-perfect double-chocolate cake for dessert, frosting it with icing made from scratch. Zack was ravenous for a good meal.

"Honey, tell me, are you seeing any nice boys?" she asked. "It will be between us. Are you in love with someone?"

Zack finished his cake and put the remainder of the dishes in the sink. He was not prepared to discuss Jeremiah with her. "I have some friends who I deeply care about, but I have a strong friendship love for a girl right now. Her name is Gwyneth, and she knows I am gay, but we have become really close friends."

Mrs. Isaac listened intently, "she must really be special to be with you, knowing you're gay. In the long run, she'll have her own man, and you will have yours. If anything, it's really positive-sounding and loving. There are too many ugly things in the world. I mean, goddamn Reagan is ruining the world…" Mrs. Isaac continued ranting about the president while Zackary washed the dishes.

On Saturday afternoon, Zack went to see the movie *Ragtime* with Gwen at the Kentucky Theatre. She excused herself to the restroom as he walked up to the concession area, happy to see Fred was behind the stand. "How are you, Mr. Mills?"

"Zack, I'm glad you're here. Remember how you mentioned in the past wanting a job here? I actually have an usher position opening next week. I know you're still in school, so I won't work you too late. Are you still interested?"

Zack smiled widely, "yes, sir!"

Sitting in the theater with his arm wrapped around Gwen, Zack was overjoyed. He was finally getting a job at the Kentucky.

Chapter Thirty-Nine

Wednesday evening was Zack's first shift at the Kentucky. He wore a navy sport coat, grey flannel pants, cuffed, a white oxford shirt, a dark blue striped tie with black polished wingtip shoes. Opening the large, thick single glass door, he made his way into the beautiful theatre, which had opened in 1922. The outer lobby, with its walls painted dark red, had dimly lit Tiffany wall sconces and a massive crystal chandelier. Huge, original mirrors hung on the walls, and there was a grand marble floor. Fred came from around the concession counter, where the smell of fresh popcorn dominated. "There he is. Welcome to the theater!"

Fred instructed Zack to work alongside Caroleen at the concession stand, as customers began coming through. After the first feature began, Fred asked Zack to accompany him to the office. The Kentucky was adjacent to the Cinema, which was a separate theater that showed pornographic films, which Fred also managed. Walking into his office, Zack could hear moaning coming through the narrow red door leading to the Cinema. "Uh… Oh… Uh… Ohhhh… Uh… Ohhhh." The sounds of people having intercourse made it difficult to pay full attention to his new boss. Zack couldn't help himself and started giggling.

"What's so funny?" Fred asked.

"I'm… I… I'm so sorry, sir. Those sounds," Zack replied convulsing in laughter.

Fred smiled, "oh, the fucking. Yeah, that's what happens over at the 'Porn Palace,' as we like to call it."

Caroleen then popped in through the red door. The moans suddenly became louder, and Zack continued laughing. The phone rang. She quickly reached over and grabbed it, "Kentucky Theatre, how may I help you? Uh, huh? Uh, huh? I'll find out. Please hold, sir. Fred, when's *Last Tango in Paris* playing?"

He looked at the schedule. "Next Tuesday at 1:30 and at 9:30."

Caroleen gave the information to the caller and then continued listening into the phone. "What do you mean, sir?" she replied with a serious tone, dangling a Kool cigarette from her lips. "Well, I heard Brando gets butter-fucked by his concubine."

"Here, here. Language, Miss Thang, language!" Fred admonished with a devilish grin.

Zack was laughing so hard he had to cover his mouth.

Caroleen hung up the phone, looking at Zack. "Now, honey, what's so funny? You're a cutie," she said, laughing. "I really like him, Fred." She walked back over to the Cinema.

Zack still couldn't control himself and Fred asked if he was alright. "Sir, I haven't laughed this hard in forever. Thank you!"

The following Friday, after school, Zack and Gwen went to her home and made love. She'd already told him she was ready to go to the next level. Being a novice, Zackary suggested he try entering her with both of them lying on their sides. After putting on protection first, he gently used his tongue to pleasure the area, then slowly inserted his index finger, and finally got into position by lifting her right leg and prepared to insert himself. *I don't know what the fuck I'm doing.* Gwen reached down and put some lubricant on him first. When he started to push inside her, Gwen seemed in great pain. Zack clutched her left hand.

"Honey. I don't want to hurt you. Let me know if this is okay or if you want me to stop."

"No, it's going to hurt. I want to keep going…"

Zack continued pushing, holding in place, then pushing further inside her, but Gwen still seemed like she was in agony. "Are you alright, baby? I'm so afraid I'm hurting you."

She kept taking deep breaths, "It's fine. Go slowly, then go further, I like what you're doing."

"You know, Gwen, I love you." A few minutes later, Zack was completely inside her. He slowly moved back and forth as Gwen moaned. He could not tell if she was still in pain or if she was beginning to enjoy the sensation. The warm feeling of being inside her greatly stimulated him. "How is it? Are you all right?" Gwen turned her head and asked him to kiss her, which he strained to reach her, but met her lips. Zack held her hand throughout. Over the next several minutes, Zack moved more rapidly, as she reached down and held her hand over her vagina. Zackary later repositioned himself on top, with one of her legs in the air, and slowly reinserted himself. Zack was better able to lean forward and kiss Gwen while he was making love to her. He muttered, "This is so amazing. I hope you are enjoying this."

"I am," she took a deep breath. "I have wanted to do this with you."

Several minutes later, Zack was nearing orgasm,

feeling the same build-up he had with Jeremiah. When he climaxed, he screamed, his body shaking with intense pleasure, and he pushed himself completely inside her. He began kissing Gwen, as tears came down his face. "I never thought I could ever make a girl happy. This felt amazing. I hope this was good for you." The two passionately kissed.

"I'll never forget this. I love you, Zackary," she replied.

Chapter Forty

Working at the Kentucky, weeks passed quickly for Zack. It not only helped relieve his sadness from the absence of Jeremiah, who sent him postcards signed with the initials JAP, but, not surprisingly, it was an enjoyable place to work. On a Saturday, the day before Valentine's Day, Zack went with Mrs. Isaac to Farmer's Jewelers to find something for the love who was there for him, Gwen. Mrs. Isaac helped him. He'd originally wanted to get a gold heart on a chain, but Mrs. Isaac dissuaded him from that choice, steering him to an emerald and gold horseshoe necklace. "You could give this girl a wrong message. I know you love her, but this charm is about luck, and your special friendship is based on love and kindness and the chance that God brought you together. And the horseshoe sits over her heart." Zack appreciated the thought, but he kept eyeing the heart necklace. "This girl, Gwen, is all right that you are into boys?"

"She is ma'am," he assured her. "She still loves me. We're tremendously close friends."

"I see," she nodded but warned, "if you give her a heart necklace, girls will see her with it, and then the questions come. You may not realize this, you are still so young and naïve, but girls are nosy, especially the yentas. They want to know everything about another girl, particularly if they think she is involved with a man. They come in packs!"

Later that night, after Zack arrived home, he helped Mrs. Isaac up the stairs. "You love this Gwen. Are you and she having sex?"

Zack, with a red face, meekly replied, "now that's a bit personal, ma'am." Mrs. Isaac was no pushover. Once at the top of the stairway, she stopped and looked suspiciously at Zack. "Okay, yes, ma'am, we are," he reluctantly said.

"I knew it," she said. "So, you make love to this girl, did you use protection?"

"Yes, yes, ma'am," Zack admitted.

"Your secret is good with me," she muttered. "Listen, when two people love each other, these things happen, clothes come off. You're a good boy. You can tell Mrs. Isaac anything."

"I hope you don't think less of me."

"Never. My boy, you do know this girl will end up with another boy. I don't want to see you get hurt." Zack looked down and nodded. "By the way, I have some mail for you. Here you go. Good night!" Mrs. Isaac said, handing him a small stack from her purse.

Zack kissed her good night and looked at the mail. There was a letter from Jeremiah. He ran into his bedroom and quickly opened the envelope.

My dearest Zackary,

I hope this letter finds you happy and healthy! I truly miss you and think of you each day and every night! Did you get my postcards? The work is so intense up here, but it is exhilarating. I wish you were up here with me, I miss your sweet face and hearing your beautiful voice. Above all, I need your affection! To be honest, I have had some enjoyable times with a few men. One of the guys I was with had a hairy body, reminding me of you—missing your body! None was

as lovely as you, and I really need to see you when I am home next month. I am coming home in early March and look forward to seeing you then. I cannot wait to hold you, kiss you, and make love to you! So happy Valentine's Day, my dear love! This upcoming week will be full days of rehearsals, then concerts the following week. All exciting, but exhausting! I will write again soon! Can't wait to see you!
Miss you and dearly love you,
Jeremiah

As glad as he was to get the letter from Jeremiah, Zack was still unsure how he felt about him sleeping with other guys, but he was being honest about it. Jeremiah's writing "miss you and dearly love you" kindled a happy flame inside him. On Valentine's Day, Sunday, Zack picked up Gwen at noon, handing her a rose, and then took her down to Hall's on the River in Boonesboro for lunch. Getting out of the car, it was freezing cold, and the two embraced, kissed, and held hands. At the table, Gwen gave Zack a light blue sweater, which he liked, and a card, which he liked even more.

Dearest Zackary,
Your heart is tremendous! I have not felt I mattered to a boy until I met you. You are more than special, you treat me with respect. You care about my thoughts, my dreams, and my feelings. You show me your love and make me feel so amazing! Having you as a friend is a constant that is rare. I know you are a gift that is priceless to me. Thank you for being my loving friend for life. You have changed me forever! I sleep well at night knowing you are there for me, my sweetest man! Happy Valentine's Day!
All my love,
Gwyneth

Zack cried, but they were happy tears for once. He pulled a small card out of his vest pocket. Zack thought she had the most beautiful glow as she opened the envelope.

Dear Gwyneth,

You have held my heart since we met. You know all my deepest thoughts and secrets, and you have been so kind to me. I have never loved any person like you. I wrote this poem to thank you for your warmth and kindness—and express my gratitude for all your affection for me. Now I want to tell you how much I love you.

Zackary

Awakening My Heart

By Zackary Benjamin Kingdon

We were merely two parallel lines
Barely noticeably apart
So anxious to meet, so close
So needing to feel, to touch
When we did meet (finally)
Your gentle sweetness flooded my heart
Re-awakening my soul
Giving me a reason to feel
Love was no longer dormant
You give me a reason to trust my feelings
To laugh, to smile, to cry
To have irrational happiness

You awoke my spirit
I waited for you, and you came
Each week our love and bond grows
Your sweet, lovely face is so sunny

It all happened so quickly
As the intersection of our lines has met
Regretfully, not sooner
You have a friend (always)
You are not alone
You are loved
You are so special
And you did a wonderful thing . . .
You awakened my heart

Gwen put her hand over her mouth.

"I know it has no rhyme scheme," Zack said, "and the stanzas don't necessarily have consistency, but I wanted to give you something from my heart."

Gwen was awash in tears, joy, smiles and rendered speechless. "You keep surprising me," she said finally, wiping her tears. "That was beautiful. Who made you so sweet?" Zack smiled, reached over, and kissed her hand.

After a huge meal and dessert, Zack drove Gwen to Gratz Park, and the two walked over to the fountain, which was turned off and drained, now full of wet leaves, some partly frozen. They sat on the cold concrete bench, looking at the remaining snow patches. "This is where you introduced me to 'mezzanine love' and your heart. Gwen, happy Valentine's Day," Zack handed her the gift.

She removed the red paper and took off the top of the box, before inhaling with excitement when she saw the horseshoe necklace. "Oh, my God! I LOVE IT! Zack, this is beautiful!" she hugged him enthusiastically.

"You wear this horseshoe over your heart," he said, helping her put the necklace on. "It matches the horseshoe belt you gave me for my birthday," he muttered between kisses. "Mrs. Isaac said you are my bashert, which is Hebrew for soulmate."

With tears falling, Gwen said, "You are mine as well. You will be in my heart forever, Zacky." The two embraced on the cold bench as a breeze began to blow.

Chapter Forty-One

It was nearing the end of February, which brought the close of the winter trimester. Beginning the following week, Zack would have four classes with school finishing before noon. At breakfast on a Wednesday morning, he was eating the hot breakfast Mrs. Isaac had prepared for him when she told him that his father was driving home and would arrive early Saturday afternoon. He smiled, "I will miss you. I enjoy having you here." She reached over and pinched his cheek. Zack jumped up, "I insist on doing these dishes, ma'am."

"Put the dishes down. That is my job. Your job is to get to school and learn." After putting his coat and scarf on, Zack went over and hugged Mrs. Isaac, who handed him his lunch. "You are the sweetest boy."

"I'll see you later," he smiled and kissed her goodbye.

At school, Gwen looked concerned, but Zack happily approached her, "hey, how are you?" She was holding a note. "Another something from my fan club?" Zack took the piece of paper and took a quick look before folding it.

"Zack, I didn't want to tell you, but one of the notes said you are 'pussy whipped' by me and you didn't 'have the guts to be the queer you are.'"

He was incredibly annoyed, "nobody's going to define my love for you. It's nobody's business. I don't give a fuck anymore." Zack looked down at his shoes for a moment. "Sorry for the language. I was taught not to curse in front of a lady."

Before he could continue, she pulled him into a hug. "I know, I know. This all really hurts you. But remember, you are strong."

Zack wanted to linger in her arms, but the bell rang. "I've got less than a minute to get down to Economics," he kissed her quickly before pulling away.

"These are so fucking delicious," Matt chewed animatedly in the art studio. "Mrs. Isaac is a kick-ass baker. I have never had a better oatmeal cookie!" Zack quietly finished his peanut butter sandwich. "Zack, believe me, your dad will be so happy to see you on Saturday. You wait and see." Matt began cleaning his brush with turpentine. Despite his cheerleading, Zack noticed his friend seemed down today. "Listen, I wanted to tell you something," Matt said with a strained voice.

Zack poured the last of the tea into his friend's cup. "What is it?"

"So, Colleen said she no longer wants to be exclusive." Matt looked away and began to tear up.

"Oh, no, why would she do that?"

"She says she wants to 'experience dating other guys.'" Zack's lips tightened, "she met some preppy, frat-guy at Transy. Fuck! I can't believe she is doing this! Discarding me."

"I'm so sorry, I really am," Zack stood up, went over, and put his arms around Matt, pulling him tight. "This is awful, man." After embracing, Matt was still in tears. Reaching into his pocket, Zack handed Matt a handkerchief.

"I'm turning into a crying baby like you," Matt began

eating another cookie. "This fucking guy she sees looks like a Green Hall-type jerk who drives a BMW. He dresses in expensive dress pants, oxford shirts, and fancy sweaters." Zack looked at his own outfit, which Matt happened to be describing almost exactly. "She hates elitist shit. Now she prefers him over me! His name is, get this, Rupert."

Zack slowly nodded, grimacing while listening. He felt so bad for Matt. Colleen was his first girlfriend. And it was the first time he had seen his friend rejected and devastated.

The following Friday, after another late afternoon in bed together, Zack and Gwen were in her shower. "I feel bad for Matt," Zackary told Gwen. "He's really hurt. I called him last night, and he was a mess."

Washing Zack's back, Gwen paused, then said, "I seem to remember Matt claiming he 'felt so bad for Amy' and shoving her new relationship in your face. You know I am not fond of him. He comes across as so full of himself."

A few minutes later, after the two cleaned up and got dressed, Zack sat on the bed. She sat sideways on his lap as he wrapped both arms around her, "you're so beautiful."

Gwen appeared distant and quietly questioned, "so, Jeremiah is arriving next week? I know you need to be with him, but are we still meeting next Friday after school?"

Zack nodded, "of course. I wouldn't miss our date. Does it bother you that he's coming home? You can be honest."

She looked away, "I'm not, but I understand. Honestly, I can't compete with a man. I will say this, even without knowing him, I don't think he can love you as deeply as I do."

Zack smiled, gently putting his hands through her hair, "I won't argue with you. You've been here for me all this time. There's nobody like you." They looked into each other's eyes, then kissed.

A few minutes later, she said, "Zackary, you know that

interview I had in December with the alumna from Bryn Mawr?" Gwen lit up with excitement, "well, she called my mom yesterday. It's unofficial, but it looks like I got in!"

"Congratulations, hon. That's what you wanted. I'm happy for you," he said with forced enthusiasm. They hugged, but Zack immediately thought of himself as the guy left behind in Lexington while Gwen was going off to Bryn Mawr.

The next day, Zack brought Mrs. Isaac's bags downstairs and placed them into her car. He put on his coat and raked up any twigs, leaves, and other debris, making sure the yard looked perfect for his father. The green of spring was teasing, and an orchestra of flowers and plants was about ready to emerge in the next few weeks. Later that morning, mail arrived. Zack retrieved the stack of envelopes in the entrance hall. There was one addressed to him from his mother. He stood momentarily and looked at it, thinking about her letter from January. Zack put it in his desk drawer, refusing to open it.

Around one-forty-five, Pop's Cadillac pulled into the driveway. From his bathroom window, Zack could see Pat Daniels was not in the car. Mrs. Isaac came out of the kitchen door and greeted Mr. Kingdon. Zack slowly came downstairs and walked outside. He could hear Mrs. Isaac sternly say, "Davy, your son Zackary is the finest child you have. So, stop this ridiculous cold-shoulder treatment. The boy loves you, and I know you love him. You're his father and all he has." The two walked into the house. Zack went to the car, retrieving the bags. When he walked into the house, Zack looked right at his father's eyes to see if he could capture a glimpse of his mood. *Does he still hate me after weeks away? Did he miss me?* But Pop actually smiled.

"Hi, Daddy, how was your trip? I missed you," Zack said in a quiet voice.

"Good, son. How have you been holding up?"

"Good. I hope you had a nice time. I hope the weather was pleasant," Zack continued with small talk.

Mrs. Isaac stood and watched, seeming ready to jump in if things took a wrong turn. The smell of roast turkey mingled with that of cinnamon from a cooling apple pie. A few minutes later, Zack walked Mrs. Isaac to her car. The two hugged tightly.

"The fact you still tear up when I leave is remarkable," she said, kissing him. "You will always be a little boy inside. So sweet."

"I always miss you. Thank you for, well, everything." He stood in the driveway, waving and as she pulled her Cadillac out. She blew a kiss. Zack started inside, holding a box of grapefruit and oranges, which he deposited in the kitchen, and then carried his father's bags up to his bedroom. Pop seemed tired from the drive but was in his washroom, changing and freshening up.

Through the partly open door, Zack hesitated before asking, "Pop, do you want some food now, or do you want to wait? Is Mrs. Daniels coming over?"

Pop turned around and switched off the light behind him as he walked out, "Pat won't be coming by anymore," Pop said sternly. "I want you to throw out all the beer."

Zack suddenly felt a load fall off him. He wondered, had Pop finally seen Pat Daniels for who she was? "I'm so sorry, Pop."

"Son, go and put the food out. Let's eat now."

"Yes, sir," Zack replied. "I am really glad you're home." Pop looked sad but nodded his head, putting on a gentle smile. Walking into the hall and down the stairs, Zack was ecstatic to hear Pat Daniels would no longer appear in their house. As he quickly reheated the potatoes, asparagus, and cooked carrots, Pop arrived in the kitchen. Walking by, he put his hand on the back of Zack's head, patting him, rubbing up and down like he had done when Zack was a child. He then sat at the table and began glancing at the paper. Zack stood still at the counter and immediately began crying.

"What is it, son?" Pop asked.

Zack turned to face him with tears falling down his cheeks. His lips trembled, "Daddy, I, I know you don't approve of me. I know you wish I were different. I can't help who I am, I can't change what I am, and I can't take losing you. I love you so much. Please, Daddy, don't hate me." Zack held onto the counter with one hand and covered his face with the other.

Pop got up from the table, walked over to Zack, and embraced him, "come here, I love you, son." The two stood hugging for a few moments as Zack cried. Pop then helped Zack over to a chair to sit down. He got him some napkins. The release was intense, as Zack shook and sweated all over. Pop got up and took the vegetables off the stove while Zack sat at the table, trying to pull himself together. Then Zack got up and helped his father with the plates. After putting them down in their proper places, he hugged his father tightly.

"Pop, I've missed you so much."

"Come on, son, let's eat."

The two sat quietly, enjoying their meal together. After the dishes had been washed and put away, it started to rain. It became dark outside. Pop retired to his bed and watched the UK-Vanderbilt basketball game. Zack walked up the stairs, and his father's bedroom door was open. He walked over and saw Pop was sound asleep. He stood for a few seconds, grateful his father was safely home. *God, thank you for bringing him back to me.*

Chapter Forty-Two

The next morning, Pop's blood sugar was high. It was the first time Zack had given his father insulin since early January. "Thank you, son," Pop said sweetly. After putting on the usual Band-Aid, Zack smiled but did not kiss his dad. There was still some pain.

Pop wanted to go to the Cracker Barrel for Sunday breakfast. On the drive over, he asked Zack about school and his grades since the trimester had ended. Zack had gotten all As and one B. He told his father about his job at the theater, "with school now done by eleven-thirty, I can go to work earlier at the theater."

Pop moved his toothpick from left to right, which meant he was in deep thought, "all right but try to avoid working late at night during the week."

During breakfast, Pop talked about how Pat would sleep all day, then got up and drank, "I am afraid she has a real drinking problem. When I confronted her with this, she got red-hot mad at me, like your momma used to."

"I'm sorry it didn't work out," Zack said diplomatically.

"Son, you didn't goddamn like her. Truth is, she wasn't nice to you. I would never have considered marrying her.

Pat had problems with you. Therefore, she has problems with me."

That night, Zack was in bed reading about Ole Miss, looking through the course catalog and other materials. Keith had been accepted to Ole Miss and was going to major in premed. He had strongly encouraged Zack to apply. It was after eight in the evening, and the phone rang. He thought it was Gwen, so he quickly answered.

"Hello?"

"Zackary?"

"Jeremiah, how are you? It's so good to hear your voice." Zack feared Pop would pick up the phone and listen, but he knew his secret was out.

"It's wonderful hearing yours. Your sweet Southern accent is music to my ears! Zackary, how have you been, I've missed you so much?"

"Fine. How's New York?"

Jeremiah spent the next few minutes talking about his journey to Stockholm and the few days he toured London. He then discussed his time in New York. "I hope I didn't upset you with my reporting on the sex I've had. You know you are the one I love, Zackary. You are who I care about."

There was a pause, "I know, hon. I know."

"Zackary, I am looking at your picture now. I keep it next to my bed. God, I miss you! And those lips of yours."

Zack laughed, "I've missed your gorgeous face."

Jeremiah mentioned how he would be arriving late Monday night at Bluegrass Field and Zack explained how he got out of school early now, "I can probably come over by one-thirty on Tuesday."

"Fantastic! I know we need to spend some time in bed. I desperately want to hold and kiss you, my gorgeous young man!"

"Oh, I agree," Zack replied as his pajama bottoms started to tent. "You have no idea."

An hour or so later, Zack walked in, checked on his father, and sat on the bed. Pop began to rub Zack's back. "You're a good boy," he said.

Zack put his left hand on his father's chest, "you're a good daddy."

"Son, can you get your daddy some ice cream?"

Zack turned with a glare on his face. "No. You had a huge slice of chocolate cake after dinner, and I know you ate another piece of apple pie earlier. I washed the plate. And I found the empty package of pinwheels in the trash."

Pop's toothpick pointed up to his nose, "get me the goddamned ice cream. Two scoops! That's an order."

Zack stood up and yelled, "Mashugana." Mrs. Isaac had rubbed off on him but not enough to say no to his father. He walked down the stairs to do his dad's bidding.

Monday morning, Zack had two classes with Gwen, Advanced Psychology in first period, then a course in Contemporary Music during third period. He noticed she was wearing tighter, more form-fitting clothing than usual. After first period, he whispered how he could not take his eyes off her butt, admiring how sexy she looked. She threw him a coy look in return. But after their music class, Zack told Gwen he was meeting Jeremiah the next afternoon. She seemed distant. "Honey, is my seeing him a problem for us? Be honest with me."

She looked down, then back up at Zack, "I am not threatened. I know he can satisfy needs that I can't. And I know you really care about him. But I don't want us to drift apart. Leave some love for me."

Zack smiled, "Sweetheart, of course, I will always love you! Gwen, you satisfy needs that he can't." He kissed her. "Gwen, I'm here forever."

"I know, and I understand you need his affection."

"Thank you for understanding." The two hugged, and Zack headed to the art studio to see Matt. As he walked, conflict within him began to surface from his conversation with Gwen. He was in love with Gwen and in love with Jeremiah, attempting to justify each relationship differently. *I do love them both dearly.* He had his special love with Gwen, which evolved into something romantic. Zack began to realize he was walking a dangerous line, for himself, Jeremiah, and Gwen. *This could blow up in my face.*

"It's nice to be done with trig and computer science. Pillsbury's letting me do yearbook class as an independent study this term," Zack pointed out while eating his sandwich.

Matt shook his head in frustration at the easel, putting his brush down to open his lunch. "I can't paint, I can't sleep, I am miserable. I love this girl so much," He began crying out of control. Zack jumped up and put his arms around his friend and then pulled up a chair next to him and sat down.

"I'm so sorry, Matthew. I'm here for you. I feel terrible," he took his monogrammed handkerchief out of his pocket and handed it to Matt, who wiped his face. "Go ahead, blow your nose. You can keep it."

"Fuck! How could she do this to me? We were so good together," tears fell down his face. "You know Amy says she was still in love with you after you broke up with her."

Zack kept quiet, not wanting to get into all of that with his friend. *She left me for her boyfriend. Why does she still have feelings for me?*

Chapter Forty-Three

After school, Zack ran home for a quick lunch and shower, then headed to Jeremiah's. His heart raced as he walked to Jeremiah's apartment door, hearing opera blaring. Zack looked at the bottom of the adjacent window and the blinds were down and drawn as usual, but as he could see lights on, and through a gap, spied a stack of sheet music secured by a treble clef paperweight. The door opened, and a bearded Jeremiah stood beaming. Zack ran into his arms. The two embraced tightly. After closing the door, they kissed. Zack liked Jeremiah's new facial hair, making him even more handsome. "I have missed you so much," Zack muttered between kisses.

"I love you, Zackary," Jeremiah pulled Zack's peacoat up, and he began to reach his hands down his pants and underwear, putting them on his butt. "I have missed this too." For the next few hours, the two men engaged in an intense lovemaking session, starting in the shower and then in bed. Zack began moaning out of control as Jeremiah's soft beard felt amazing when he pleasured him. He was in such a state that his hips began to gyrate, his heartbeat fast. Zack got the same reaction when he pleasured Jeremiah, and enjoyed feeling in control, making his partner go crazy. It all culminated with Zack penetrating Jeremiah and holding both of his hands while he made love to him. Zack's intense climax was building as he moved himself back and forth. Then he released, feeling his entire body tense up and then melt. Jeremiah kissed him and slowly got up, pulling Zack with him to the shower. As Zack followed, he stared at Jeremiah's tall frame from behind, trying to memorize the details of his body. Turning on the water spray, Zack thought how he loved soaping Jeremiah from head-to-toe.

"Zackary, I thought I was going to lose my mind when you ate me. You've been pleasuring Gwen, haven't you? I can tell. Man, you're good with your tongue!" Zack turned red, nodding. "Do you know what I love about you?" Jeremiah asked.

"I get a feeling you're going to say, my butt," Zack replied, laughing as he stepped back into the hot water spray as Jeremiah began washing him.

"Yes, of course," The two kissed. "But I love that you're an innocent boy trapped inside a man's body. I touch and kiss this hairy, gorgeous grown-up body, but inside, you have such a loving, tender heart. You give your complete self to me. I have so missed you." Jeremiah continued washing him while telling Zack about his frustration with bathhouse sex. "When I gently bite a man's nipple, they don't react. When I do it to you, you convulse."

"Well, you are the first person I have ever made love to. I'm sure those men are much more experienced," Zack said, enjoying feeling his partner soaping his body.

After drying off, returning to bed, and pulling up the covers, Jeremiah played with Zack's chest hair. "Experience doesn't always make you a better lover. Up in New York, not one man had their head in it. It was so mechanical.

Okay, I still enjoyed it, but when I was in the heat of the moment, as I was cumming, I closed my eyes and thought of you, and my love for you. I… I've never had that before, Zackary."

Zack covered his mouth and his eyes starting watering, "thank you, that's sweet. It's difficult when you're away, my heart hurts."

Jeremiah wiped his tears, then brushed Zack's cowlick back, "my heart missed you too. I dearly love you." Jeremiah then wanted to hear about Zack's sexual experiences with Gwen.

"It was great. I mean I asked her to show me what to do, and I think I make her feel wonderful."

"Zackary, I am no expert on women, but I know this, a woman feels loved by a tongue on her clitoris, not a dick. Straight men don't get it. They think it's an obligation to satisfy a woman orally. It's mandatory if you care for her. Same when I am with a man. We get it."

Zack felt embarrassed and shy, amazed at Jeremiah's intuitiveness, "I wanted to show you I love you."

Jeremiah kissed his nose, "I know you do, sweetheart. You have cared for me more than any man has. Gwen must be a lucky girl to have you, and I have you in my own way. I really want to meet her sometime."

"Gwen is so beautiful. I know you would like her."

Jeremiah pulled Zack up to lie on top of him, reaching down and feeling his butt, "she must be, to be with you." Zack was all smiles, feeling butterflies in his stomach. *God, I adore this man.* He moved closer to Jeremiah, the two cuddled together and fell asleep.

The rest of the week, Zack worked at the Kentucky on Wednesday and went over to Jeremiah's on Thursday. They never seemed to tire of each other's bodies. That Friday afternoon, Zack and Gwen had one of their most enjoyable lovemaking encounters. Lying in bed at home that night after having one of the most passionate climaxes with her, Zack realized he had had sex three times in four days. *Early dismissal at school arrived at a perfect time,* he laughed to himself. Zack thought how he was feeling more like a man than a boy. He thought how months ago he was so unskilled in the bedroom, so afraid to be sexual, to be himself. Then, he met these two wonderful people who helped him find his heart. After doing so, he found a way to show what was inside him.

Zack picked Jeremiah up for breakfast on Saturday morning before catching a matinee. When he approached the apartment, he heard beautiful violin music. Jeremiah greeted him with his coat and scarf already on but pulled Zack inside for a kiss. "Hey, how are you?" Jeremiah said looking great in tight jeans and a thick, short coat. "I adore your face and eyes." After getting into the Toyota, Jeremiah ran his hands through Zack's cowlick and glanced at his lap, "Oh, you are as stiff as a telephone pole."

"I know. And I have to drive this car and not crash, so don't tempt me," Zack laughed.

Pulling into Jerry's Restaurant, Zack parked, turned to Jeremiah, and asked, "do you ever see us together as a long-term couple?"

Jeremiah smiled, "Zack, like I've told you, I've never had a long-term relationship. But I do feel differently with you. We're both in transitory places in our lives. I'm going back and forth from Lexington to New York and other destinations, but I feel something deep and special with you. You make this home for me. I love you, my gentle darling. Yes, I do see us together," he said gently, squeezing Zack's right hand.

"Thank you for that. I find you wonderful. I feel something real with you," Zack replied with a tear falling.

The two shared a passionate kiss as Jeremiah wiped away Zack's tears. He understood that there was a four-year difference between the two. Jeremiah was a fully developed man, and Zackary was still impressionable and young but trying hard to become a man.

"Let's go get some pancakes, cutie," Jeremiah said.

After breakfast, Zack and Jeremiah held hands in the narrow movie theater, which only had a handful of patrons. The movie, *Making Love*, was about a married man who leaves his wife to be with a man. Once the end credits rolled, Jeremiah wanted to talk about the film, saying he thought it implied gay lives were not substantive. "There was an overt lack of hope, lots of self-doubt, the critics panned the film." As the two walked up the aisle, Jeremiah excused himself to go to the washroom. Zack stood in the lobby and stared at "Coming Soon" film posters.

A voice came from the concession counter. "Zacky, Zacky." Zackary shook his head and glanced over. It was Matt with Leanne, one of the angry girls, with a container of popcorn and beverages.

"Oh, I thought I heard someone," Zack replied, completely caught off guard. "Hi. How are you both? Are you seeing this?"

"No, we're seeing *Rollover*," Matt replied. "So, are you here by yourself, or are you with Gwen?"

Suddenly, Jeremiah emerged from the washroom and walked over, standing next to Zack. "No, I am here with my friend Jeremiah. Matt, Leanne, this is Jeremiah Pruett. Jeremiah, this is Matt Adler and Leanne Van Zandt. We all go to Henry Clay."

"Nice to meet you," Jeremiah said, shaking their hands.

Matt smirked and asked condescendingly, "so what are you two up to now?"

Zack fumed, noticing how the two stared Jeremiah over,

trying to suppress their laughter. Leanne asked Jeremiah if he was in college.

"I graduated from UK," Jeremiah politely responded. "I play in the string section in the Lexington Philharmonic and I am currently in a music study group in New York City."

"Well, we have to go. Good to see you all. Enjoy your movie," Zack said.

He and Jeremiah were walking away when Matt yelled, "nice to meet you, Jeremy. How's Gwen doing, Zacky?" Incensed, Zack kept going. As he and Jeremiah got to the theater exit, Zack heard them laughing. *Fucking jerks!*

Once on the street, Zack thought about how he'd had romantic feelings for Matt at one time. But his resentment deepened for his friend after being humiliated just now. Zack knew Jeremiah could tell he was angry but just said, "that was weird."

Frustrated, Zack stopped walking and turned to him, "I'm so sorry. Matt's my best friend, well, supposedly, and Leanne is one of his gossipy friends who told people at school that I am gay."

"They're children," Jeremiah smiled warmly. "They laughed because they're seeing you with a man, Zack."

"It's cruel how they're behaving."

"If anyone should feel awkward right now, it's the two of them. Let's get home and get into the shower and bed."

"Jeremiah, you make such perfect sense. God, I adore you!" Zack replied, smiling.

Once in the car, Zack leaned over to Jeremiah, gently kissing him, "I'm in control of the bar of soap this time!" They both giggled. Jeremiah's eyebrows went up and down.

After hours of blissful lovemaking and lying in bed, Zack's face was pressed up against Jeremiah's chest when the musician asked, "I am wondering if someday we could have an apartment together in New York?" Zack moaned, conveying he was listening, squeezing his partner's hand. Jeremiah ran his other hand through Zack's thick brown hair. "When you walk out onto the streets, there's an energy unlike any place."

"Jeremiah, I want to be with you," he answered softly. "I have to get my education first." Suddenly, it was Jeremiah who was crying. Zack leaned up on his right shoulder, "what's wrong, darling?"

"I know, I know our lives are not easily compatible. No one's life is compatible with mine. But I badly want you in it."

Squeezing Jeremiah's hand, Zack kissed his forehead. "I'm here. I'm not going anywhere. You have to know that." They held each other.

Jeremiah was returning to New York the following week, so they spent several afternoons together. Their last time at his apartment, Zack broke down in tears while drying off after a shower, "I'm going to miss you. It's been wonderful having you at home. When will I see you again?"

Jeremiah hugged him tightly, "Zackary, I am hoping June, but I've been wanting to tell you something… I may have to stay in New York longer than I anticipated. I'll let you know as soon as I know more."

Zack glanced up, "longer? These nine weeks have been so long. That's nearly four months from now." He put on his shoes and socks. "I'm sorry. I have a hard time with you leaving. You make me so happy. I love you so much. I'll miss you."

Jeremiah held Zack tightly as tears fell from both of their cheeks, "Zackary, you give me such reason to come home. I have so enjoyed our time together these past few days. I promise to write you."

Zack released the hug, taking Jeremiah's hands, "I wish I knew how to get in touch with you. I am always thinking about you. Please be safe and take care of yourself. I want you back soon. I love you so much."

Jeremiah told Zackary not to be sad, he would be home soon and they would be together. He insured his love he would miss him every day and night during his travels. The two embraced and kissed passionately. Jeremiah was overcome by emotion as Zack opened the door and quickly walked to his car.

After making it through two stoplights, Zack started to calm down. *If this man is going to be part of my life, I will have to get used to him leaving Lexington quite a bit. It's not fair, but I love him.*

Chapter Forty-Four

Arriving home from work at the Kentucky Theatre one night, Zack found a note to call Gwen. He soon discovered she'd received her expected acceptance letter to Bryn Mawr. She was ecstatic, but he mostly felt anxiety. First, Jeremiah left, now Gwen was leaving, too. He barely slept that night.

Walking into school the next morning, Zack noticed Gwen at the locker in a tense conversation with Rebecca.

"Hey, how are you?" Zack asked. "Congratulations again, darling!" He reached in and kissed her. "Hi, Rebecca, how are you?"

"Good, Zack," Rebecca said meekly, looking at him, then at Gwen, who nodded at her. "So, Zack, um, I went midnight bowling on Saturday at Southland Lanes with my youth group from church. We were in a lane right next to Matt Adler, Amy, and the group of girls he's friends with. I overheard Leanne telling everyone that she and Matt saw you at the movies with a guy. She said his name is 'Jeremy.' Matt told Amy he didn't know who this guy was. That you, Zack, must have been seeing him in secret. Then Amy began crying and yelled, 'Zack is a f-ing faggot!' They all consoled her, including Matt, who got on his knees and said, 'we didn't mean to upset you,'" Rebecca sighed. "I thought you should know." Then added, "I heard someone in the group ask, 'Does Gwen know?'"

Zack became visibly angry and turned to Gwen, who said, "Zack, this was in our locker this morning." She handed him a note. *Gwen, Did you know your 'boyfriend' Zack has a boyfriend? Did you know your 'boyfriend' is a FAGGOT! Zack Kingdon has lots of surprises the longer you are with him. You deserve each other!*

Zack looked up at the two, "this is Amy's handwriting. Gwen, I am so sorry you saw this. Did you know I was gay?" The three strained to laugh. The first period warning bell rang, and they began walking to psychology class. Zack was fuming.

"Hey," Matt said, opening the studio door.

"Hey, how are you?" Zack asked.

"Good, I guess," Matt resumed painting.

As he walked into the studio, he felt the tension, "I'm not here for lunch."

"So why are you here, Zack? I didn't know you were fucking a guy. Oh, 'Matt, I'm a virgin.'"

Zack stayed calm, knowing Matt would soon throw more grease on the pan, "he's a guy I've been seeing."

"Fucking, you mean," Matt said.

"Matt, you're not the only person here who has the right to date people or be in love. I thought you'd be happy for me. I guess not, now that Colleen's left you."

After glaring at Zack, Matt got down on one knee and concentrated on his work, "no, you must have been fucking 'Jerome' and didn't think that I needed to know. I tell you about my life, every detail, and you kept this from me? It was so embarrassing to run into you with some stranger. Zacky, I thought I knew all about you." Then Matt revealed he had gone to a midnight movie at the Kentucky a few weekends ago with his friends and Amy, then went for food at the Parkette drive-in afterward. "And you and Gwen Farris came up in conversation . . ." Zack shrugged his shoulders. "I knew you two were friends, but Amy, Leanne, and Alex said you and Gwen act like a couple in the hallway. That you kiss, hold hands and share a locker. It was all news to me."

"Why do you care?" Zack asked his old friend. "Gwen's one of the nicest people I've ever known. She had a rough breakup with Ed. Lay off her."

Putting down his paintbrush, Matt walked towards Zack and aggressively shouted, "so, you're fucking Gwen Farris too?"

Zack's lips tightened, "stop it! I love her more than any girl I've ever known. And she loves me. She knows I'm gay and she still loves me! She doesn't condemn me!"

Matt crossed his arms, fuming, "you're fucking her, then you go and let Jerome fuck you in your butt. Wow!"

Zack lost his temper, "STOP IT, MATT! I MEAN IT! His name is Jeremiah. We love each other. He's a tremendous guy. You know it's been so difficult for me to allow myself to meet and experience what it's like to be with a caring, loving, and trusting man. I live in constant fear of being harassed and beaten, and you're angry I didn't tell you?" Tears fell from his face, "I would have eventually. He's hardly in town."

"How long have you known him? How long?"

"Since November. I met him at the Philharmonic."

"So, the two of you have fucked since November?"

Zack became visibly angry, "stop saying fuck!"

"All right, he puts his cock in your butt. Do you now eat Gwen's pussy as well?"

Zack's tears worsened, "I can't believe you would talk to me like this. You really don't care about me. You're like those angry girls. In your mind, only you can have sex, only you can be happy, only you can have love in your life. You never thought it would happen to me, did you? That maybe… maybe I deserved to be loved. But apparently, it's somehow a clown show to you, it can't be real, that I deserve less than others because I'm gay? Well, FUCK YOU." Matt resumed painting. "And fuck you for telling Amy about Jeremiah. You sure felt wonderful for her when she started dating Rick. You never once had my back. I can see why Colleen left you. You're heartless and mean, like the group of poser idiots you hang around with. When you're jealous of others, you throw tantrums and skewer them, make fun of them. Like you did to me on Saturday. You hate the rich kids at Henry Clay. Deep down, I think you hate me, too. I always thought you were there for me when those kids picked on me at Morton because of the way I couldn't get my words out or finish my sentences. Now I think you were laughing with them behind my back."

Matt turned red in the face, threw his brush down, then walked over and pushed Zack against the wall, "YOU FUCKING PATHETIC ASSHOLE! WHO THE FUCK DO YOU THINK YOU ARE? YOU ARROGANT SHIT! I was there for you, and you say this to me? Nobody cared about you more than me!"

"Then why did you make fun of me to your friends?" Zack screamed. "Amy calls me faggot and you comfort her?! Why did you do this to me?! You have hurt me the last time." Matt punched Zack in the face, then the ribs and stomach. "Stop!" Zack yelled, covering his face.

Matt punched him two more times in the face, hitting his hands, yelling, "Fucking hit me back! Hit me back!" The two had never fought before and Zack's nose bled. "Why won't you hit me? If I'm this 'terrible guy,' why won't you hit me?" Matt yelled.

A stunned Zack pushed Matt off him, turned and picked up his book bag, and ran out the door. Tears falling down his face, Zack opened his book bag and pulled out the note, which had been shoved into his and Gwen's locker. Walking up to Amy's locker, he crammed the note into the vent then walked out to the parking lot. Minutes later, once he was in his car, Zack cried uncontrollably.

285

Chapter Forty-Five

April came and Spring break was around the corner. This time of year made him especially aroused, the warming air, the flowers' scent, and the birds' early morning sounds. It had been a month since Jeremiah returned to New York, and Zack had not received a letter or a postcard. He opened the back kitchen door to let in the sunlight and step outside to fetch the newspaper. Walking towards the outer side of the garage against which the concrete birdbath pan was leaning, he gently picked it up and carried it into the backyard, placing it on its thick concrete stand. Once secure, he screwed on the water hose and filled the bath with water. Zack and Pop had always enjoyed seeing the birds visit the backyard.

After retrieving the paper, he returned to where his father was waiting, "good morning, Daddy. Did you sleep okay?" Pop nodded as he took the rubber band off the paper, chomping on his toothpick. As Zack was taking his father's blood sugar reading, he turned to reach for his notebook and saw something. He stood up and quickly went to the window above the sink. There was a cardinal swimming in the birdbath.

"Pop, Pop, come quick, it's beautiful."

"Wow, that's a gorgeous sight, son," he said, leaning in next to Zack. "When did you put up the bath?"

"This morning, sir."

It had thick, jungle-red feathers with a burnt black color over its face and around the beak. The bird fluttered its wings around the bath, jumped up on the edge, and then flew away. Zack smiled, patted his father's arm and the two sat back down. After giving his father his medication, he poured their coffee and began digging into his bowl of Life cereal.

"Now, listen," Pop said. "I told you not to work this Sunday. It's Easter, we have to go over to Danville to see your aunt and uncle. And we're all having lunch at the Beaumont Inn."

Later that afternoon, lying naked together in bed, Gwen seemed so happy. Zack thought it was her relief from receiving her college admission, or maybe it was just because school was winding down and spring break was around the corner. "You seem so content," he said, kissing her neck as she lay with one arm around him while fondling the horseshoe necklace in her other hand.

"I am," she sat up. "But you know what would make me even happier? Going to prom with you."

"Of course, I'll take you," Zack assured her. "I'd do anything for you, but I worry I'll be walking into a room with a firing squad."

She laughed, "Zacky, you are overreacting, sweetie. I know people have been cruel, but you'll be with my friends, and they all like you."

"You're not getting it," Zack said uncomfortably. "Just because it's prom doesn't mean those assholes who hate me won't yell 'faggot' at me all night."

"I won't let anyone hurt you," she said. "Don't be scared, honey, I'll be there with you the whole time. I am going to prom with the handsomest man at Henry Clay!"

He smiled gently and kissed her, "I'll go for you. You're my special girl."

Spring break started with Pop driving Zack and Gwen to Danville to spend Easter Sunday with Zack's aunt and uncle. The rest of the vacation, Zack was either with Gwen or ushering at the Kentucky at night. Every morning, he worked in the yard, spending a great deal of time with mulch and peat moss to plant a variety of flower bulbs they had picked up at Hillenmeyer. One day, amidst blooming daffodils, peonies, and azaleas, Zack planted other seeds expected to bloom later in the spring. When his father pulled into the driveway, he yelled, "Make sure the flowers are at least two inches apart, goddammit! You plant them too close to each other!" Zack shot an annoyed eye.

With his failing health and weight, Pop could no longer bend down or sit on his knees, so he spent a lot of time in his lawn chair, screaming his head off. Zack wore his Cincinnati Reds cap to avoid the sun and avoid looking directly at his ranting father. "You never follow my instructions correctly," he complained. "I told you to cut a circular hole, no bigger than an inch! Don't drown it with soil." Zack came to the realization that his father felt he served no purpose if he wasn't screaming at him, trying to toughen him up. "An inch, son, a goddamned inch!"

Zack turned, "Oh, for God's sake, I heard you the first time."

"Don't you smart talk your daddy!" he yelled, chomping his toothpick.

While Zack worked, his father sat in a chair and watched him, grousing cantankerously, barely under his breath how he was incompetent, and didn't listen, was unreliable and lacked talent. Zack continued working, rolling his eyes and holding his tongue. He glanced at his father feed nuts to a squirrel, which had perched itself on the armrest of his lounge chair. Pop always kept a small bag of nuts in his pocket in case his blood sugar fell. "He'll eat the whole damn bag if I let him," Pop muttered, sweetly putting cashews on his hand and watching the squirrel pick them up.

Zack smiled, "that's so sweet. I believe he lives up in the oak tree." *At least we both love nature and animals*, he thought. Once he completed work in the flowerbed, Zack watered the soil.

Pop put the few remaining nuts on the armrest for the squirrel and got up, "great work, son! It's beautiful. Supposed to get cold this weekend, possible frost. Frank Faulkner, on the weather, said 'blackberry winter' might set in." The yard was David Kingdon's passion, a blank canvas eventually populated by nature's loving colors and life. Tending to the grounds gave Zack great joy, even with all of his father's barking, complaining, and apparent dissatisfaction with his efforts.

In the kitchen after work, Zack saw mail sitting on the counter. He grabbed a letter addressed to him with Jeremiah's initials, JAP, on the top. There was no return address. The postmark was "New York, New York, 10017." Zack quickly opened the letter and sat down.

> *My Dearest Zackary,*
>
> *I have been so busy that I collapse into bed late at night. I am sorry to take so long to write you. I miss you terribly and think of you daily. You were completely on my mind when I "pleasured myself" late last night. I feel quite alone up here and wish I could see you and have you in my arms. I look forward to that soon, sometime this summer. I will let you know. The work is intense, and we work long hours. I had to re-bow my violin twice in one week! Imagine that? However, it is exhilarating on many levels. Some discussion of a Juilliard audition by my*

new coach. I don't know, and I'm unsure if I'm good enough, but others seem to believe I have the ability to compete at an even higher level. Throughout all of this, I think of you—how much I miss you and dearly love you. I think of your beautiful brown eyes, face, eyebrows, lips, and gorgeous nose. And I go to sleep wishing I had my hands all over your furry butt! I know how hard this must be for you. Please be patient with me. I will be home, probably late June or early July. I will try to write more soon. I love you dearly, Zackary Benjamin Kingdon! (Your name so excites me!)

Love,

  Jeremiah

I miss you too, my sweet love. Thank God, he wrote me! His thoughts were interrupted by a sudden yelling from upstairs. He took the letter, folded it, and put it in his pants pocket. "Papa, what is it? Are you all right?"

"I'm fine," he said. "I want some ice cream."

As he scooped Pop's ice cream, Zack smiled. *Jeremiah loves me and thinks about me. I love him, too.*

Chapter Forty-Six

Saturday, May 1st was Derby Day in Kentucky. It was also prom and David Kingdon lovingly bought Zackary an expensive tuxedo and a white dinner jacket. Zack and Gwen had reserved a room at the Hyatt where the event was held, but Zack would have to get up early Sunday morning to go and give his father his medicine.

The day of the prom, Zack arrived at Gwen's just before five in the afternoon. Dr. Farris answered the door and ushered him in to the living room. The two sat and watched the Derby while Gwen was still getting ready. Zack watched the horses line up for the race, but his mind was full of concern about rumors of being nominated for prom king. Images of people glaring at him, calling him 'faggot,' whispering things and looking away, raced through his head. Zack had become somewhat numb to this as the year progressed, but today it caused him great anxiety and frightened him. Minutes later, as Gato Del Sol pulled across the finish line at Churchill Downs, Jenny Farris called out that Gwen was at the top of the stairs. Walking into the foyer, Zack could not believe what he saw. Gwen looked like an elegant princess, wearing a three-layered light blue dress with subtly stitched flowers in one layer. "You look beautiful. Oh my Gosh!" he said, tearing up.

As she slowly walked down the steps, Dr. Farris took pictures. Zack reached up and helped her down the steps. "You're crying," Gwen said. "Mom… he's crying. Zack, you're incredible!"

Zack wiped his tears, "I'm overwhelmed right now… you're so gorgeous." Once he calmed down, he helped Gwen put on a pink rose corsage, which contrasted perfectly with her dress.

"It's beautiful," she said.

"You're beautiful," Zack replied.

Mrs. Farris helped him secure the corsage, she then helped Zack with his light blue boutonniere. Dr. Farris took several pictures of the two. Zack grabbed a bag and gown case, carried them to the car, and returned to the house. As Zack and Gwen made their way to the Cadillac, Jenny hugged Zack tight, "Zackary, you're wonderful to her," she said out of Gwen's earshot. "She loves you so much. We love you. Now, you two go and have fun!"

"Thank you, Jenny." Dr. Farris came around and hugged Zack. "Oh, thank you, that's so sweet," Zack said before running around to help Gwen into the front seat and reaching over for a kiss. As they drove away, everyone waved. Gwen clasped Zack's hand. He loved this family, particularly their warmth and acceptance.

When they arrived for dinner at the Lexington Country Club, the two felt like everyone was staring at them. "Gosh look at you," Gwen gushed. "Nothing makes a man more handsome than a tux. You look like Gatsby," she laughed.

"You are the most beautiful woman ever, like royalty. That is a stunningly gorgeous dress!"

"Mom took me to Cincinnati to get it. She's dreamt of the moment I walked down the steps in a prom dress. She kept saying while I was getting dressed that you are the kindest boy to ever come into my life, and you are." The two laughed about his breaking into tears when she appeared at the top of the steps. "Zacky, Southern women dream of walking down a long staircase wearing a beautiful long dress… to a gorgeous man."

"Yeah, to a crying man," he chuckled.

She leaned in, "Honey, your being overwhelmed by my dress as a gay man is the best compliment I could ever imagine receiving."

Once they arrived at the ballroom at the bottom of Rupp Arena, Zack noticed loads of gorgeously dressed "Greenies" populating the hall. As the couple made their way through the ballroom, he noticed other couples stopping and smiling at them, particularly girls. While the entire ordeal made him uncomfortable, he sucked it up, putting on a huge smile. Several girls surrounded Gwen, whose dress caught much attention. Gwen hugged Rebecca and several of her friends.

"Look at you! Zacky!" Rebecca yelled before taking him aside. "Zacky, I want you to know my girl thinks you are the greatest man in the world. I love how you two have found such a loving place. She suffered so much with Ed and she looks so happy, and you do too. I think you're an amazing guy," Rebecca finished with a hug.

"Awe, thank you. That's sweet," he replied.

Suddenly, the music began to get loud, and Gwen squeezed Zack's hand, his cue to take her to the dance floor. The two started dancing around friendly people. Keith danced with his date, along with Rebecca and her boyfriend. There was no sign of Matt Adler. Zack kept guard in case he saw Amy. The band played Jackson Browne songs. Peering around, he saw people smile. Suddenly, he spotted Amy staring at him. She was with a guy, presumably Rick, who was quite tall and not particularly striking. Her mascara was smudged, she looked stiff and miserable. Zack looked away, reaching for another kiss from his date, casting Amy out of his mind.

A few minutes later, after getting them punch, Keith sat next to Zack at a large round table. "Hey, Zack, you should still try to get your application into Ole Miss. You might still be able to get in if it's not too late." Keith had been accepted into Ole Miss's pre-med program. "Gwen is probably the most stunning person here tonight," he whispered. "Her dress is elegant. Was it a designer dress?"

"Halston, I believe. Thanks, it is lovely. I call her 'Gwen O', like 'Jackie O'. I still have my application for Ole Miss sitting on my desk. I'll definitely think about it."

Then, out of nowhere, two guys walked behind Zack and yelled, "FAGGOT!" Zack forced a laugh, then rolled his eyes. He looked at Gwen and kissed her. Everyone at the table stared at him.

"Yeah, maybe so, but I still got the prettiest date tonight!" Zack thought about what Fred Mills had told him, that the anti-gay bullying at school was about to be over. College was a reset, allowing him to meet new people who know nothing about him. Fred said it was his chance to be whomever he wanted to be and reveal only what he wanted in a safer environment. He turned and looked at Gwen, "are you having fun, honey?"

She nodded, "I sure am."

As the hour became late, Zack and Gwen continued dancing, surrounded by friends. For just a moment, Zack looked at Gwen and saw a young woman who was someone who could become his wife someday. Deep down, he sadly knew he could not be that man for her. It hurt him, but Zack compartmentalized his feelings. While she would always be a loving part of his life, the fact that he was gay was like walking on a pier that only went so far when it came to Gwen. For that night, he chose to believe she was his love. *Gwen is a woman to love. She will make another man happy someday. No matter what, I will always love her deeply.* When the song ended, the student body president walked up to the stage to announce the prom king and queen. Gwen and Zack walked back to their seats. Keith had gotten another round of punch refills. She squeezed his hand.

"Look at me… You'll be fine. You probably won't win. The funny part about you, Zackary, is that you have no clue how many people find you so handsome. That's a big reason why you got nominated."

Zack looked down, embarrassed. When another name was announced as prom king, Zack hugged Gwen in relief. "Thank you, God!"

After the prom queen was announced, everyone stood, and many couples walked to the floor to slowly dance to "Could I Have This Dance" by Anne Murray. Filled with a sense of relief, Zack looked into Gwen's eyes as the lyrics touched him. He reached in and kissed her. As he pulled back, tears fell down his face, "I'm sorry, I get so emotional…"

She squeezed his hand, "the fact you cry makes me know you love me. And that matters so much!"

Around eleven-forty-five, the two snuck out of the ballroom and returned to the connecting hotel and their room. Zack had fresh flowers on the table for Gwen. The two stared out the window at the view of downtown Lexington at night. They collapsed on the couch, drinking soft drinks in glasses and eating snacks he bought.

"I sure want to see you out of that tux tonight," Gwen said.

"Don't worry, you will!"

A few minutes later, the two were undressed and taking a hot shower. Zack took his time orally pleasing Gwen under the water spray. Once they were in bed, Gwen took charge, pleasuring Zackary, performing oral sex on him slowly, causing him to feel like he was convulsing. She was much more comfortable the past several months. Zack later got on the floor, kneeling, and pulled Gwen's body up to the edge, lifting her right leg and putting it over his shoulder as he kissed her stomach and began moving down to her public region, "I love you," he said, putting his tongue on her, gently and slowly pleasuring her. After several minutes, Gwen began to cry, her mouth and body shaking, squeezing Zackary's hand as she concentrated on the insatiable pleasure. She clenched her teeth when she climaxed, moaning loudly. Zack climbed back on the bed, and the two embraced and kissed.

"You are the most romantic man a woman could dream of…" Zack put his lips on her mouth and held the kiss.

"You're my princess." Zack then stood up and pulled Gwen back to the apex edge of the bed, which had become one of his preferred penetrating positions. He put on a condom and entered Gwen. After a few minutes of thrusting back and forth, as Zack got close to ejaculating, he leaned forward and reached in, kissed Gwen, then climaxed. He felt it was one of the most romantic moments ever. She kept passionately kissing Zack, sharply pushing her pelvis back against his penis, which was still inserted.

"I love you, Zackary. God, I love you," she muttered.

"Oh, I love you, too."

After showering, Zack helped Gwen into one of the hotel robes. He walked around the room naked. "I brought my pajamas, but I'm going to try to sleep naked with you. Is that okay?" Gwen, who wore a tee shirt and underwear, said she preferred he sleep without pajamas. As they climbed under the covers, the two lay next each other face-to-face. It was their first time sleeping overnight together.

"You know, honey, I have a five-thirty wake-up call in the morning. I have to go give Pop his medication. He thinks I'm staying in this room with Matt. You can stay in bed, I will come back, and we can have breakfast. How's that sound?" She nodded, smiling. Zack kissed Gwen, and the two fell asleep against each other.

Chapter Forty-Seven

He picked up the pace running down Fontaine Road and hit the point where he was breathing rhythmically, and Zack felt a sense of freedom in his movement. He had become a more determined runner. Zack thought about how beautiful Gwen looked at the prom the previous weekend. School was about to end, which was a tremendous relief. During the days, the temperature had been in the mid-eighties and humid, but it cooled off at night. Zack often ran two miles at a time, five times a week. It allowed him to clear his head and take in the greenness of the neighborhood. Approaching eight in the evening, as he was running on the sidewalk, nearing home, thinking of how much he missed Jeremiah, he heard a car slowly driving behind him. He heard a sudden honk, turned and saw Matt. Slowing down and out of breath, Zack stopped next to the car.

"What have you been up to lately, stranger?" Matt meekly asked through his open window.

"Nothing."

"Are you ever going to talk to me again?"

With sweat saturating his running clothes and rivulets falling down his face, Zack glared at Matt, looked around, caught his breath, and said, "to be honest, no."

"What? We're no longer friends?" Matt put the car in park. "Your father told me you were out running, so I started driving around to find you. I don't want it to be like this."

Zack looked around, feeling awkward, then stared back at Matt, "you hit me, man."

"I shouldn't have done that, Zacky. I feel bad…" Not knowing what to say, Zack listened. "We've been so close for so long. It hurt that you didn't tell me you had a boyfriend or were all smitten with Gwen." Zack stared at him, rolled his eyes and started to jog away. "Stop!" Matt screamed. "Get in the car. Let me drive you home."

Reluctantly, Zack got into the car, "I'm completely covered in sweat."

"That's fine…"

Matt was parked in the Kingdon driveway before Zack shared his true feelings. "The things you said to me were unforgivable. You say I 'betrayed' you somehow? Matt, when Colleen left you, I was there for you. I hurt for you. Yeah, when you first began dating Colleen, I was a bit standoffish, but I grew to really like her. I care about your feelings, and I was happy for you both. But you see me having love in my life as a betrayal to you? Are you sure you don't have a thing for me after all?"

"YOU ARE MY BEST FRIEND. You kept all this from me for months! Zacky, we never kept secrets."

"I did for a reason," Zack said shaking his head. "You ran and told Amy about Jeremiah. You judged me, Matthew. You hurt me. Then you fucking attacked me when I confronted you."

"Where do we go from here?" It was clear Matt would never apologize for his behavior.

Zack stared at him, "you and your hateful friends judged me. I was called 'faggot' by Amy, and you consoled her, then you're trying to 'marginalize' me and my choices." Matt rolled his eyes, grimacing. Zack held his stare, "Matt, we've been best friends for a long time, but I'm not sure I can get past this. You've changed, man. You're so bitter about everything. You always used to be on my side…"

Frustrated, Matt stared back at his friend, "you deceived everyone, Zack."

"How? For having new people in my life who bring me kindness, joy, and love? If I told you, you would have spilled it to everyone, just like you didn't hold back at the beginning of the year, telling Amy and those angry girls you hang around that I was gay."

"You think it's all about you. You are such a narcissist…" Matt said again,

Zack looked to the sky, away, "I'm the 'narcissist'? You should read some of the notes shoved into this 'narcissist's' locker. You can't be happy for me, or respect who I love, can you? You're not fine with me being gay. You were fine with it because you think of me as lesser than you. Well, I'm not."

"That is so fucking not true!" he said angrily.

"Matt, I've loved you since I met you… adored you! Then you judged me."

The two sat silently for nearly a minute before Zack finished the conversation, "I've gotta go. Thanks for the ride."

Back in his bedroom, Zack typed his application for the University of Mississippi while the rain poured outside his window. There was one more week of school, then graduation on May twenty-eighth. Gwen encouraged him to go away for school, and Ole Miss had a strong accounting program. The thought of leaving his father behind, though, conflicted him. He wanted a clean start, a chance to go away and develop his own identity and independence. At the same time, he felt obligated to his father to remain in Lexington. *What will I do, stay here and take care of Pop?* But the lingering humiliation from the cruel things his family had said and written sparked Zack's determination to leave. He remembered what Fred Mills had told him, "To Hell with anyone who isn't going to love you for who you are. You need your own life, have your own friends, become your own man. You can't live your life for other people, especially those who judge you." After completing the Ole Miss application, Zack drove to the post office and dropped it in the mail.

That last week, large trash cans lined the halls as students emptied their lockers for the year. Zack was at his and Gwen's by himself early before her arrival. As he began to clean out his things, a folded-up note with spiral-shredded edges fell out of the locker. Examining it closer, he found a cluster of other hateful notes shoved inside one of Gwen's sneakers. There must have been a dozen of them. *She kept these from me. Bless her.* He ripped them up and pitched them into the trash. Moments later, Gwen showed up, and the two gently hugged. After picking up their caps and gowns for graduation, they walked to the registrar's office and filled out requests for their final transcripts. Zack had one mailed to Ole Miss. They walked together, holding hands, out of Henry Clay for the last time.

Once in the car, they kissed. After arriving at Zack's home, the two went upstairs, took off their clothes, and quickly made love to each other in the shower. At the kitchen table, an hour later, neither said anything while they ate lunch, just smiled, gazing at each other. Suddenly, Zack heard the mail being inserted in the box on the front porch. He got up and walked to the front door.

"Nothing!" he said, going through the letters and bills. "Jeremiah hasn't written me in six weeks. He left in March, and I've heard from him only once. I miss him so much. Gwen, it's starting to get to me." Zack noticed a sad look on her face, "what is it?"

"Nothing. I wish you loved me the same way. Funny, I had dreams wishing I could become 'Mrs. Zackary Kingdon' someday. I know it's silly, but I know I can never fulfill all your needs."

"Gwen, honey…"

She unzipped her book bag, opened a spiral notebook, and showed it to Zack. On several pages, front and back, she had scribbled *Mrs. Zackary Benjamin Kingdon.* Zack sat stunned. "That's how much I love you," she said.

Zack continued staring at the many pages of signatures. He went around and hugged her tightly, "I love you back. We'll always have each other, somehow, somewhere."

She squeezed back hard, "A Lexington girl can dream."

That afternoon, after taking Gwen home, it started raining. Pop arrived shortly before four.

"Son, get ready to go to dinner," David Kingdon said. "That goddamned momma of yours is coming to your graduation."

"NO, Pop, I don't want to see her," Zack pleaded.

"I don't either," said his father. "But she's your mother and has a right to be there. This was negotiated in the divorce settlement. I don't like it any more than you. I hope she's not drunk…" Pop moved his toothpick from left to right. "At least your Aunt Norma will be there."

Later that night, Zack came into Pop's bedroom. He sat down on the edge of the bed and his father began rubbing his back. "I've gotten you through high school. We did this together, son, with no help from your goddamn momma."

"We did. You've been a great father and mother to me since I can remember." Pop asked Zack for a few pinwheel cookies and a glass of milk. "Oh, here we go. For God's sake, sometimes I think you say all these sweet things, so I'll go fetch you sweet things." Zack dutifully went downstairs to get his father cookies.

Chapter Forty-Eight

Aunt Norma and Pop took pictures of Zack in his blue cap and gown in the front yard. After posing, Zack left to pick up Gwen. The Farrises were coming to the ceremony from work. Driving to Rupp Arena, the two held hands, realizing the next chapter in life was before them. After Zack parked, he and Gwen continued to hold on to each other as they walked into the venue. Once inside, he walked her over to the area where she was meant to assemble, not far from where he had to line up. Gwen hugged him. "I'll call you when I get home later. Love you!" he said.

After the two kissed and Gwen walked away, Zack turned around. Matt was standing there, staring at him. "Hey," he said, extending his hand, which Zack warmly took hold of with both hands. "Lookin' handsome, Kingdon." Zack smiled, giggling on the outside, still hurt on the inside. "So Zacky," Matt said, fidgeting with his cap, which kept falling off, "it appears you're in love with Gwen."

"She means so much to me," Zack confessed, "and I dearly love her."

"So you love Gwen, and you love Jeremiah?"

"And I still love you," he nodded. "Matt, I'm done

explaining this to you. I have affection for them both, somewhat similarly, and differently."

Matt had a confused look on his face, but he seemed to want to discuss further. Zack tried to change the subject, "congratulations on your awards." Matt's academic honors were received at the end-of-year convocation.

"Thanks! Congratulations to you on yours. The *Carousel* number you sang was great. During the ceremony, we saw you sitting and holding Gwen's hand."

Zack smiled, but he was becoming tired of his personal life being scrutinized by his old friend. "Listen, Matthew, you and I go way back. I want you to know how much I appreciate your friendship, particularly in those early years. You knew I struggled and was hurting, and you were there for me. I will always be grateful and love you for it." Zack embraced Matt in a tight hug, then said, "congratulations, I gotta get in the line." He released the hug and walked away. A somber feeling overtook Zackary as he searched for his lineup position, disappointed that Matt, the friend he came out to and once had romantic feelings for, had steered his loyalty away, judging him so harshly, not unlike his family.

As Zack made his way to the "Ks" section and got in line, he saw Amy walk by. She had the usual frown on her face. *After today, I hope I never see her again.* The Henry Clay orchestra began playing "Pomp and Circumstance," as each line of students entered the arena. The ceremony felt long, but it was going well. When the principal called for "Zackary Benjamin Kingdon," he walked across the stage and shook Mr. Hunt's hand. He heard a few claps, but no one yelled "faggot," which he had been afraid of. After the ceremony ended, it was chaos getting through the auditorium to meet up with his family at the restaurant. Pop had made a reservation at the Hyatt Glass Garden, adjacent to Rupp Arena.

With his graduation regalia still on, Zack walked towards the table where everyone was seated in a large semicircular booth. He heard his mom loudly announce to everyone, "you're a son of a bitch, Davy!" Ignoring her outburst, he just greeted her with "Mommy." Wearing a beautiful pink dress and holding a cigarette, Zack's mother saw Zack and stood up.

"Hello, baby. Come give your mother a hug!" Zack obliged. "My gosh, you've grown since last summer. You're a man now!"

"So, how've you been?" he asked, gently smiling, releasing her embrace, going around to hug Aunt Norma. Pop sat in the middle. Zack reached in and squeezed his father's hands. He noticed he appeared extremely uncomfortable, sweat dripping down his face. Norma handed Zack a card and there was a check enclosed. "Thank you so much, ma'am. That is so sweet of you."

Pop handed Zack a card with a deposit slip for one thousand dollars, "this is from your mother and me. I opened you a checking account at First Security." Overwhelmed with gratitude, Zack thanked them both.

Once they ordered dinner, Zack's mother requested a Manhattan as she was finishing her first… or maybe second. "My God, Zackary, you look so much like your daddy. So handsome, both of you are heartbreakers." Zack sipped his iced tea, awkwardly smiling. She asked him to come sit by her, which he did. "You are growing up so nicely."

"Did you get my senior picture I mailed you?" he asked. "You didn't mention it in your letters."

"Oh yes, it was so nice. Your grandparents send their best. They would like to have come, but it wasn't written up in the divorce decree!" Zack's mother blurted out.

"I had it drawn up to protect my boy," Pop curtly replied.

"Oh yeah, 'your boy'… um huh, son of a bitch," Virginia

grunted, crushing her cigarette into the ashtray, glaring at Zack's father.

"Mommy, no…" Zack smiled sweetly, holding her hand just like he did when fights emerged when he was a young child trying to referee. "Let's have a nice dinner, okay?" She nodded and kissed him. Her drink arrived, along with the salads. Zack got up and sat back down next to his aunt.

"Did you get your admission letter from UK?" Norma asked.

"No," Pop remarked with a testy tone. "They won't admit him until they have proof he graduated. Zack's not bright enough to get regular admissions." Zack quietly ate his salad.

"Well, Davy, that's not a nice thing to say about our Zackary," Aunt Norma replied. Zack was livid but smiled at his aunt. She winked back. Zack's parents resumed their ongoing feud while Zack and Aunt Norma tried to buffer themselves with a conversation about his graduation and her family, and then she asked about Amy. "How is she? I know you said you all are not dating, but are you all at least still friends?"

The food arrived, and Zack's filet mignon was before him, "no, ma'am. Amy's not speaking to me anymore. It got complicated, unfortunately."

Zack's mother chimed in, holding her cigarette up, "Amy was the girlfriend? Well, she figured things out, didn't she?"

Zack glanced over at her, chewing his food, then covering his mouth, he said, "excuse me, Mommy?"

"Virginia, goddammit, leave the boy alone," Pop interrupted.

"Listen, all I'm saying is the girl figured things out and moved on. Amy had to take care of herself. What choice did she have?"

Zack was extremely uncomfortable but remembered

his father taught him that gentlemen never make scenes in public. Plus, the audience for the family grew larger as the restaurant kept getting busier. His parents continued bickering, only pausing for another drink to be served to Virginia. Zack and his aunt continued to make pleasant conversation. Pop told his ex-wife she was "sick in the head" for going back to her abusive husband last year.

"You can't say anything," she snapped back. "You don't even have a dick that works. You never knew how to satisfy a woman!"

Zack panicked, "Mommy, please don't say those things!" Adrenaline shot through his system, angry his mother would speak so disrespectfully in public to his father.

"Why, you're a disgrace," David Kingdon angrily countered. "You drink too much, Virginia."

"I should have raised Zack," she yelled. "You ruined him. You made our son a queer!" The table was still as patrons at adjacent tables turned and stared. His aunt put down her fork and grabbed Zack's wrist. Zack stared straight ahead, chewing his steak. He looked at his mother, thinking how he spent a good portion of his life worrying about her, fearing she would harm herself. When he was in third grade Zack would get off the school bus on his way home and head down the narrow hill towards the Lakewood home. During that walk, he wondered if he would find his mother still in bed or if she was dead. He never knew if he would find her sitting in the living room drinking instant iced tea with vodka or gone with no note explaining why or in the hospital. Every day, Zack didn't know what to expect. He felt he came home to an empty house with a mother who wasn't present. He became highly protective of her, deeply terrified he would lose her. This fear probably made him love his mother more.

"Goddammit, Virginia!" Pop replied.

Zack gently placed his knife and fork on his plate in a four o'clock position, slowly wiped his mouth with his napkin, and then stood up from the booth, "I have to go. Aunt Norma, thank you for coming and for the gift. Give my love to Uncle George, Ann, and Kenny. Have a safe drive home. Pop and I will come visit real soon." Zack reached in and hugged and kissed her. He walked over and begrudgingly hugged his mother tightly, whispering, "I love you, Mommy!" He kissed her on the cheek then reached over and squeezed his father's left hand. "Thank you for coming, Daddy. I'll see you later tonight. I love you all!"

"Son, come on now, finish your dinner," Pop said.

Upset but unwilling to show it, Zack forced a smile and walked out of the restaurant. Only in the parking lot did he let the tears fall down his face.

Chapter Forty-Nine

In the weeks after graduation, Zack worked at the Kentucky and spent much of his free time with Gwen, playing tennis, swimming at the country club, taking long walks, and enjoying their time in bed. He still missed Jeremiah and hadn't heard from him since his last letter in April. One late June morning, Gwen rang, needing to talk in person. Zack picked her up and the two went over to the estate of home of Henry Clay where they walked through the garden holding hands. The sun was high and no one else was around. To cool themselves, they sat down on a bench in a shady area near the goldfish pond.

"What did you want to talk to me about?" Zack asked, smiling.

Gwen had a difficult time looking directly at him, "Honey, this is going to be hard for me to say, so just let me say it." Zack got nervous as Gwen took both of his hands and tears appeared in her eyes. "Zackary, my dearest friend. I have never loved anyone like I have you. You've brought such a sense of unbridled happiness to my life. You made me feel safe. Being with you has given me such faith in men, confidence, and the ability to experience pleasure I never knew I could as a woman. When we made love, you were wonderful to me. You took the time to show me how much you loved me, and it's been so meaningful and intense. You're what I have always dreamed of in a man. But…"

Zack suddenly felt his heart stop as tears fell from Gwen's eyes. "Honey, you need to be with a man," she continued. "That's who you are. Both of us know this. It's time we both face this reality. It will hurt not to be romantic with you anymore, but I want you to be happy, whether it's with Jeremiah or another man. I will always be here for you. Zackary, you are the greatest friend I could ever hope to have, and I want you to be in my life forever! If we continue this romantically, I'm afraid we will both get hurt, and I don't want to risk it. I don't want to be jealous of you being with someone else." Zack began crying, putting a hand over his face, feeling pain in his heart. "My sweetheart, more than anything. I want you to know, I felt it. I felt your love for me when you pleasured me. I will always love you forever."

Zack, engulfed in tears, wiped his eyes with his handkerchief. "Gwen, I thought what we had was so special. I could love you like we have…"

"Honey, no," Gwen said seriously. "I'll miss being intimate with you but you need to show it to a man…" He put his handkerchief over his face, leaning forward, sobbing. Gwen hugged him. "You've made me the happiest girl ever. Zackary, you made this woman feel so loved. Oh my God, you will make Jeremiah so happy. You've been such a gift in my life. Think how wonderful this has been for us. Let's enjoy our friendship together."

Zack nodded, tears falling, "it's not fair, is it? I… I love kissing you, kissing your body, making you feel so good, holding you and loving you. But you're breaking up with me."

She gave Zack a long, passionate kiss, then whispered, "no, never with you, my darling. Never with you. You are my irreplaceable love."

Over the next few days, Zack walked through his life feeling utterly depleted and sometimes cried himself to sleep but he was aware Gwen needed to separate herself from him romantically. After dinner with Pop, Zack drove to the Kentucky. The line for the 7:00 showing of *Reds* had formed at 6:00 as Zack arrived for his shift. He was adept at quickly counting change and rapidly moving patrons through the box office and into the theater. This was the only film of the evening, given its three-hour and twenty-five-minute running time. Fred came out and knocked on the box office door.

"Zack, you moved people through the line so efficiently, we could sell just about everybody concessions. When you're in the box office, we sell more popcorn, candy, and soda. I'd like to keep you here if you don't mind," Fred smiled. "So, have you gotten a letter from your man?"

"Not since the one in April, sir."

"He must really be busy up in New York," Fred said, placing his hand on Zack's back. "It's hard. Zack, I hate seeing you down. We adore you here."

"I appreciate all you all have done for me," Zack told him sincerely.

All he could think about on the way home was how having to pull back from Gwen was only making him miss Jeremiah more. At home, he went to the sink and filled a glass of water. As he was drinking, he saw the mail on the kitchen table. There it was a letter from Jeremiah. Weirdly, it was postmarked in Lexington. Sitting down, Zack tore it open and began reading.

My Dearest Zackary,

I have missed you so much! I recently traveled to

Italy and Spain with a brief stopover in London. I sent you a postcard. Did you receive it? We played in some amazing venues. It was the most inspiring time ever! First, I want to tell you I miss you and love you, but you are not going to like what I am going to say next. I have been accepted to a graduate program at Juilliard, a dream of mine. I am moving out of my Lexington apartment and relocating permanently to New York. I am deeply saddened to tell you that I don't think we can be together anymore. That does not mean I don't love you, I do. I so wish we could continue to be a couple. Our time together, albeit brief, was the best time I ever had in my life. I regret writing this letter because I deeply love you, Zackary. We met when my musical career was taking off. I think about you constantly. Your face, smile, gorgeous body, kindness, and loving heart. I stare at your beautiful picture. I would have called when I arrived in Lexington, but the grant was extended through August, and school begins in September. I had to move out in less than 48 hours and get back to New York. I literally flew in and packed up. I am writing this letter before I leave in the morning. I am going back to Europe in July, this time to Vienna. Zack, I know you will be upset and hurt. I hate that I am breaking your beautiful heart. I want you to know there is no man as wonderful as you. I still feel your heart, and always will. I've never been intimate with a man more giving than you! When you go to bed at night, think of me—and I will be thinking of you, my dearest. Do remarkable things, young Zackary. Maybe we will run into each other someday. (I pray we do!) You have been a blessing in my life!
Love to you forever,
  Jeremiah

With tears falling down his face and hitting the paper, Zack put the letter on the table. *No, no, no...* wiping his face, he began to shake. There was no return address given. *Why did he leave me? Why couldn't he still keep this going?* Zack put his head on the kitchen table, sobbing. *I'll never see him again.* First Gwen and now Jeremiah. His life was unraveling again. Once in bed, staring at his bedroom ceiling, Zack wrapped up in his blankets. *How could Jeremiah just end this? We could have remained in a long-distance relationship. He didn't even see me to say goodbye. I thought I was the one he loved. I love him. Did I dream the whole thing? Everyone is leaving me.*

Chapter Fifty

Zack awoke after having cried himself to sleep. It wasn't quite five-thirty, and bright sun filled his room. He pulled back the blankets and sat on the edge of the bed, feeling achy and sluggish, but his mind raced. Tears fell as he realized he would never have his arms wrapped around Jeremiah again, see his gorgeous face, hold his hands, feel his breath on his neck, feel the love from his kisses. Zack continued to cry, shaking his head. It was forecasted to rain later in the day, so he got up to start his yard work. The day before, Pop had picked up some flowers for him to put in the beds. After slowly dressing, he went downstairs to turn on the coffee machine.

When he went outside for the newspaper it felt good. The air was humid, warm and the early sun shone down on his face through tree limbs. He went over to the hose, turned on the spigot, and filled the birdbath with fresh water. Going back into the kitchen, Zack discovered his father waiting. "Good morning, son. You never came in to say good night last night."

Zack began taking his father's sugar levels reading. "I'm sorry," he sweetly replied, his eyes welling up, "how are you this morning, Daddy?"

"Good. Are you not feeling well?"

"I don't know."

Pop continued reading his newspaper but said under his breath, "you know, Pat used to say you seemed moody all the time."

"She did?" Zack replied while writing down Pop's sugar reading. "Did she notice this after I brought her the eighth beer?"

"That's not nice…" his father said.

"It wasn't meant to be nice. Now hold still." Zack made an injection in his father's left arm.

A few minutes later, he went out to plant the new bulbs in the flowerbed in front of the house. Pop walked around from the back sipping his coffee, "Son, you seem upset about something. What is it? You can tell your daddy."

Zack dug into the soil, "oh, it's probably lingering growing pains."

"Do you want to come to Tommy's with me?"

"No, sir. Thank you, though." Zack got up, walked over and kissed his father on the cheek, "I forgot to do that this morning."

Pop bit down on his toothpick, "all right, what's on your agenda today?"

Zack got back on his knees and resumed work, hoping any tears were mistaken for sweat on his face. "I am going to go for a run later, then go to dinner with you, then go to work."

Pop stood there. Zack could tell he was watching him, "I'm going to get going. I'll be in the office later if you need me, son."

Zack turned around, smiling, "I love you. Have a good day."

Reluctant to call Gwen to tell her about the letter, Zack needed to spend time with some of his other friends. He drove to Winn-Dixie and picked up some apples and carrots, then over to Lakewood to see the horses. Walking up to the fence, Zack made his smooching noises with his lips. "Where are y'all? Come over and say hello. I have treats," he said aloud. Three horses immediately appeared, with the mule trailing at a distance. "Let me give you some carrots, sweetheart," Zack said, petting and showing affection to each horse. "You're a new baby," Zack said to a light brown horse he did not recognize. "You're a gorgeous sweetheart, aren't you? I'm Zackary, your friend." Tears fell down his face while handling the horses. *You all love me. Many of you are still here.* After the horses took their treats and received their affection from Zack, they slowly moved on. The mule stubbornly stood away but began moving towards him. Feeding carrots and an apple to the mule, Zack looked around. "There you go, darling. You're so sweet. You need your loving too," Zack said, wiping tears. *I strangely thought I would somehow end up with Jeremiah. We would have a life together. What was I thinking? I'm such a fool. I love him so much. He was so kind and loving to me. What do I have here now? Gwen's leaving for school. I adore this place, but there's nothing here for me besides Pop.* Zack finished giving love to the mule and took a bite of one of the apples.

Driving home, Zack dropped by Jeremiah's old apartment complex. Walking up to his door, he saw the blinds drawn as usual. Zack peeped through the window, looking down he saw the sheet music stacked next to the door was gone, and the floor was bare. He walked by the mailboxes and noticed "Pruett" had been scratched off. He sat down on the step, exhaling in frustration. He thought about Jeremiah's handsome face and tall frame, his sensuous lips and his kisses, their lovemaking, the feel of Jeremiah's hands on his body, the sound of his heartbeat, and their urgent embraces. *My head fit perfectly on his shoulder.* Zack sat to cry before he stood up, wiped his face, and climbed back into his car. *I had to see it to believe it. He's gone.*

It was early afternoon and hot when he arrived home. He put on his jogging shorts and went out running. Zack thought about how he had never experienced so much love in his life, but the sadness in his heart only intensified. Gwen and Jeremiah helped him realize he could feel again that he was worthy of love, particularly after the rape. But they were gone now. After his shower, Zack sat on his bedroom floor listening to music. He played "Since I Fell for You," sung by Barbra Streisand, which he thought was one of her most passionate songs, causing him to cry. "I'll always love him," Zack said aloud through his tears. "Why did you leave me? Was I not worth it? I was patiently waiting for you. Like you asked me to do. I would have kept you in my life, even from a distance. That's how much I loved you." Zack sat drowning in emotion.

Chapter Fifty-One

Hearing a car door shut, Zack glanced up and saw Gwen walking down the driveway as her mother pulled away. He had just finished working in the yard. It was the first time he had seen her since she broke up with him. "How are you?" she asked, coming towards him.

Still, in his sweaty work clothes, holding a rake, he muttered, "I'm good, you?" The two did not kiss. In his mind, Zack thought he would have invited her to his bedroom to join him in the shower, but everything was different now. They silently walked through the yard and into the kitchen. "God, it's hot. I made some lemonade, want some?"

"That'd be nice," Gwen said as she sat down at the kitchen table. Zack poured two glasses, handing her one. Parched, he quickly downed his glass, then poured himself a second helping.

"Gwen, would you mind if I quickly showered and changed? Here's today's newspaper."

A few minutes later, Zack reentered the kitchen, clean and freshly dressed. He handed Jeremiah's letter to her. "This came for me in the mail."

Gwen began reading. She put a hand over her mouth, "Oh, honey… I am so sorry. Zacky, you must be devastated. When did this arrive?"

"A couple of days ago." Zack told her he was tired of thinking about Jeremiah. He felt he had already cried a river of tears. "Gwen, you're my greatest friend, and I deeply love you. I loved him too, but he's gone."

She leaned forward, took his hand and said, "you'll always have those memories. Jeremiah was a tremendous person in your life. I saw what he did for you. His love helped you so much."

"I think so," Zack nodded, wiping a tear away. "So did yours."

Gwen reached over, and they embraced. "You know I love you, sweetheart," she whispered.

"I do. I love you, too." Zack stood up and prepared sandwiches for the two of them. While they were eating, the mail arrived. He excused himself from the table and returned holding up a letter from the University of Kentucky Admissions. He opened it, "I got in. I am going to college."

"That's great! Any word from Ole Miss?" Gwen asked.

"I received a postcard that they received my transcript. I think I applied too late."

A few days later, Zack didn't get home from his shift at the theater that night until close to ten-thirty. He immediately went in to check on his father, "hey, Daddy, how are you doing?" Untying his necktie, Zack sat on the bed next to him.

"Did you see the letter?" Pop muttered.

"No, sir. What letter?"

"There's a letter from Ole Miss on the kitchen table."

Zack immediately felt nervous, realizing he had not told his father he'd applied. He looked at Pop, who had a grimace on his face and was biting down hard on his toothpick. "Well,

I'd better go read it. Good night, Pop. I love you," Zack said, kissing his father on his forehead.

"Good night, Zackary."

He never calls me Zackary. Zack walked downstairs to the kitchen. He took a deep breath, afraid to open the letter. If it was an acceptance, Zack had his ticket to leave. If it weren't, he would be raking leaves and reading sugar levels for the foreseeable future. He opened the thick envelope.

Dear Zackary Benjamin Kingdon,

   It is a pleasure to offer you admission as a freshman to the University of Mississippi as part of the Class of 1986! Your major is classified as Accountancy, and your course of study will be advised from the School of Accountancy.

He did it. He'd gotten in. Zack's heart was beating so fast as he read through the many information pages in the envelope. He saw another letter from the housing office. He sat at the kitchen table. Taking it all in was overwhelming. *What will Pop think? He's going to blow up!* Zack picked up the phone and dialed Gwen. "Hey, hon. I hope I didn't wake you. I got into Ole Miss!"

He heard her scream, "Zack, that's fantastic! Are you going to go? Yes, right?"

There was a pause.

"I don't know," he replied suddenly torn. "I'd have to leave Pop. He was somewhat distant when I checked in on him. He didn't know I applied. But, yes, I am so excited. I think I'd like to do this. I'm torn right now. I have to send in the tuition and housing deposits by the fifteenth."

"Honey, you have to do what's right for you, but I hope you go. You need this. I am so happy for you."

The next morning, Zack noticed Pop was already downstairs. He could smell the scent of Old Spice as he walked down the stairs and into the kitchen. He sensed he was angry as he performed his father's sugar reading.

"So, you got in," his father said. "You didn't even tell me you applied. Why?"

Zack quietly wrote down the reading, then injected his insulin, "I… I guess I forgot, sir. I bought a money order and mailed in the application before graduation. Honestly, Pop, I didn't even think I'd get in at this late date."

After pouring their coffee and sitting down, Zack reached for his cereal, avoiding eye contact. Pop read over his *Lexington Herald*, holding his toothpick steady. Sipping his coffee, Zack noticed his father wasn't really reading the paper but gazing elsewhere, maybe at the birdbath in the backyard. Zack stood up to see and saw a bluebird with its newborns splashing in the water.

"Pop, they are so beautiful, aren't they?"

Pop pulled his paper back up to read, "pretty soon, those little babies will be flying on their own." Zack quietly ate his cereal. "I want to know why you think I should pay for you to go to Ole Miss. You don't handle academic pressure well, son. You're not strong in the head." Pop flipped to the sports page, "you know it, everyone knows it. I'm fine if you go to UK, but honestly, you can't handle college, period. I correctly predicted you were a failure. That guidance counselor at Henry Clay told me when you failed those classes that you were not college material. I think he's right. Now, I know you don't want to hear that."

Zack was fuming and dropped his spoon into the bowl. "Excuse me, sir. So, you have no problems with me going to UK, but now that I was accepted to Ole Miss, I'm somehow 'not college material.' Are you kidding me? I got As in most of my classes this year, except for Bs in trig and the grade I received in the Novelists class. Okay, I messed up during my junior year, but I worked my tail off to improve my grades. I didn't apply to Yale, Daddy. Ole Miss is a good school, you said so yourself. They have one of the best accounting programs in the country. Why can't I go? I want to experience what it's like to go away to school. You had no problems when I applied to Miami and Indiana."

"That's because I knew you would be rejected, son. You don't see what I see. You have minimal potential in life using your brain. You're so weak. We all saw this when you were a little boy. You're a good boy, but you really are quite limited. Frankly, you've been the biggest disappointment of my life. I had high expectations, but you never wanted to play football!"

"What's football got to do with anything? SERIOUSLY! How can you say all this to me? I take care of you. I get up every day at the crack of dawn to give you your medicine. I do it because I love you! And I try to get you to stop stuffing your face with cookies and pie and ice cream, but I'm 'worthless' and the 'biggest disappointment' of your life? Then why did you give me the briefcase for Christmas? I honestly felt bad for you, how awful Mommy was to you. I defended you! Pop, all I have ever done in my life is do the best I can. I know I am not that good of a student, but I try so hard! For you to say these things to me," Zack eyed his father sharply, "you're cruel."

Pop's face was red. "You and your bullshit! You don't do a goddamned thing right. You never listened to me. You never have. You disappoint. You're worthless!"

Zack had tears, but they were angry tears, "So, I'm your 'worthless' son? Seriously? Pop, you are my daddy, and I love you, but you don't even get to decide this. You're talking to me like I'm some worthless, pathetic person? But I'm your son. I'm your last child. Don't you want me to turn out well in life? You break my heart."

Pop put the paper down on the table. "I know you'll never be able to compete in this world with all your deficits. That is when your heart will really be broken. It's better you hear it from me than others!"

The chair screeched as Zack quickly pushed away from the table and got up, staring down his father, "If you won't let me go to Ole Miss, fine. But to call me 'worthless' over and over. You can't take those things back… I now understand why Mommy left you. I also see clearly why Cam and Emily fled this place. You taught them to be so hateful."

Zack's father pounded the table, coffee spilling everywhere, "Don't you dare speak down to me! YOU ARE OWED NOTHING, BOY!"

Zack angrily stared at his father, picked up his cereal bowl and threw it into the sink, then yelled, "FUCK YOU!"

As Zack walked upstairs, his father yelled for him to return, "Get in here!"

"I SAID FUCK YOU!" Zack yelled, punching the wall in the foyer at the stairwell entrance, breaking a hole in the drywall.

Zack fled home and drove to Lakewood by his childhood house and the Engel farm. He wanted to see his equine friends. Feeding the horses with apples, Zack noticed a tree stump on the opposite side of the fence. Zack slowly climbed over the fence and stepped up on the cut trunk next to a beautiful, brown mare. He gently rubbed the horse, assuring her he would be loving and gentle. "You're gorgeous, honey," Zack reached up and lifted his right leg over the mare, mounting her. Once secured, he reached up and carefully reassured her that he was going to be gentle. "It's okay, sweetheart. I would never hurt you." Her soft coat was velvety smooth, and her back was hot from the sun. The horse turned to the right and began slowly walking. Keeping his hands to his side, Zack sat upright as the horse walked forward, then stopped to graze. Zack hoped no one saw him, knowing he was taking a big risk. The view down to the reservoir was stunning. "You love your grass, don't you?" The horse resumed walking. On the short horseback ride, Zack heard a snort blow from the horse a few times. "I feel the same way, baby," he muttered.

Later that morning, after cleaning up, Zack drove over to Gwen's house to give her a hug and talk with her. When she opened the front door, they embraced. "I'm so happy for you," Gwen said.

Zack had a sad face, "let's go inside and talk." In the Farrises' living room, he told Gwen about the exchange with Pop in the morning, which infuriated her.

"How can he say this? Zacky, he's wrong."

Zack sat fuming, then exhaled, "but what should I do? I mean, I was so excited when I got the letter last night, but…"

Gwen interrupted him, "Hon, you mail in the deposit. If you don't go, you lose the deposit, but for now, at least, hold your place. You're going to have to work on your father. Didn't your aunt say you needed to go away to college? Call Norma. Get her to speak to your father. You want this. This is not over, sweetheart, but there's not much time."

Zack suddenly had a wide smile on his face. "Thank you," he replied, nodding. She reached down and took his hand, and then the two kissed for the first time in over a month. It started thundering in the background.

"Zack, now you're possibly leaving Lexington, too. With Jeremiah gone, you do need to go away to school. We're moving on with our lives, aren't we?"

"I know. If I go away, though, I'll feel like I'm abandoning Pop."

Gwen put her head on Zack's shoulder. "Hon, you're not abandoning him. You're becoming a man, seeking and finding your way. He wants what's best for you. He doesn't know how to show it, perhaps he's threatened by this, doesn't want to let you go . . . but your daddy loves you so much. Give it time. But get that deposit in the mail!" Gwen squeezed Zack's hand. "I love you. I miss our intimate time." She reached in, and the two kissed for several minutes.

"I do, too," he told her.

It was pouring rain outside when Zack got home. He walked up the stairs and Pop's door was closed, but his television was on. Zack stood there, concerned his father was angry and shutting him out, not unlike after his brother and sister had outed him. He went into his bedroom, took his Bosca briefcase, placed it in the hallway, then closed the door.

The next morning, Zack pricked his father's finger. "You're going to pay for the damage you did to the wall in the foyer," Pop said.

Zack cut him off, "just tell me how much it costs, and I will pay you back."

Pop glared at Zack, "I ought to punch you into tomorrow for using that language on me."

He gently pinched Pop's arm and inserted the needle.

"What's your briefcase doing in the hall?"

Zack quickly scowled at his father, "doesn't belong to me anymore." After disposing of the syringe, he poured Pop's coffee and returned to his bedroom.

A few days passed, Zack and his father barely spoke, interacting only during the morning insulin injections. Clearly, Pop had been ruminating and nursing his anger. He could not contain it any further. "When I talk about your deficits," he barked, "I know what I see. We all know what you are. Who do you think you're fooling thinking you can ever become a professional like a CPA? Nobody will ever hire you the way you are. So why would I spend my money to see you fail in life?"

After recording the sugar reading, Zack put the pen down and crossed his arms. "Sir, what are you talking about?"

"You know, son. We all know about you."

"Oh, that. Um huh! You are making me so goddamned mad, Pop!" Zack scooted his chair back and stood up.

"Watch that mouth! Aren't you gonna give me my insulin?"

"I don't know, do you want your 'faggot' son to give you insulin?" He stared directly into Pop's eyes. Sitting back down, he took an alcohol swab, rubbed his dad's arm, and injected the medicine. As he was putting on a Band-Aid, "there, I won't kiss you since I disgust you."

"You have to hide it, son. You'll never be accepted in this world, ever. You will have a hard life. I never wanted this for you. Pat says people like you are deviants."

Zack took the used syringe and threw it across the room. "STOP IT! STOP IT! DO YOU HAVE ANY IDEA YOU CAUSED ME TO NEARLY KILL MYSELF LAST JANUARY? You always call me 'worthless,' well, you made me FEEL worthless! I am not a 'deviant,' I am your son. I don't care if you don't love me anymore. The cruelest people in my life are my family, including you! You considered me a 'freak' as a child, an 'utter disappointment,' the 'slow kid,' and you reminded me every day about my so-called 'deficits.' All I ever did was love you and be kind to you, all these years. It's been only you and me. We became a new family together. You're my daddy. Now this. Well, go ahead and reject me too. YOU CAN BE SUCH A CRUEL MAN. I want to get away from your cruelty," Zack stormed out of the kitchen. "You break my heart, Pop."

Chapter Fifty-Two

Days passed while Zack and his father lived in silence. One night, as Zack arrived home from the Kentucky, he noticed two checks from Pop sitting on the kitchen table. Each was made out to the University of Mississippi for the deposits. Zack stood in place, stunned. The following morning, Pop was quiet as Zack injected this insulin, "Daddy, I greatly appreciate your allowing me to go to Ole Miss. I promise to do well."

His father moved his toothpick, mumbling, "you'd better. You get one chance, that's it!"

Zack placed a Band-Aid on his father's arm, "I will, I promise."

David Kingdon drank his coffee and stared at his son pouring milk on his cereal. "Son, I don't know how I'll handle you not being in this house. You've been with me since you were such a little baby. I don't know." He stopped talking and gazed out the window at the birdbath.

"Pop, I know it will be hard. You might find life is good with me gone. You always tell me I'm a handful."

Pop repositioned his toothpick, "you are, and then some! You've always been nothing but a pain in the ass to me!"

"And you mine," Zack smiled, glancing out the window as he got up to rinse his bowl. He turned and put a hand on his father's shoulder, "I'm going to miss you, Daddy." Pop offered nothing in return. Zack picked up the checks and walked up the stairs to bathe. He felt a sense of excitement, picturing what it would be like to be away at school. *Thank you, God. Thank you.*

It was well into August, and Zack's last days in Lexington were slipping away. He spent much time with Gwen, going to the movies and shopping at Mr. Wiggs for dorm room necessities. Perusing various bedspreads, Gwen asked Zack if he planned to write her. "Of course," he said. "Definitely twice a week." She appeared to be contemplating a blanket with a pastel flower pattern. "Gwen, I called Keith and told him I'm coming to Ole Miss. His dorm is close to mine. It'll be good to know someone down there from Kentucky." Zack noticed Gwen was hiding her eyes, crying. "Honey, what is it?"

"I'm leaving in a few days, so are you," she cried. "I feel so afraid of leaving you, Zacky. I love everything about you, every detail. I stare at you all the time because I want to memorize your face, your body, even your smell."

Zack also teared up, "my smell?" he giggled, touching her arm. "You know, sweetheart, we had a great year. I have enjoyed being with you, making love to you. I'll always feel something for you. Our friendship is forever. I will always have you in my heart, all the way from Oxford or wherever I am." The two kissed, then hugged.

"Zacky, this is so tough. My heart hurts more each day."

"Mine too, mine too," Zack kissed her on the cheek. "I'm going to miss the smell of your beautiful hair."

Pop laid a map from Lexington to Oxford over the kitchen table, showing Zack where to get on the Bluegrass Parkway from Versailles Road, past the airport. Zack poured milk over his Life cereal and sat down. It was his last full day in Lexington with his father. It all became overwhelming as he prepared to drive over to see Gwen off. "Why's it so hard to leave, Daddy?" Zack asked, moving the cereal around in his bowl.

Pop moved his toothpick, glancing up from his paper, "Son, you're leaving your home. The people you know, your family, me, and all your memories. This is the only place you know. It'll always be here for you."

"I have to get over and see Gwen off. This is going to be so difficult."

Pop smiled, "she's a lovely girl, son. She's been a great friend to you."

A few minutes later, Zack parked at the edge of the Farrises' circular driveway. Gwen's father was doing some final packing in the station wagon they rented to haul her belongings to school.

"Good morning, sir," Zack smiled.

"Zackary. How are you? Gwen's inside."

Zack walked into the house and overheard Gwen, who was sitting on the couch with her mother, sobbing, "I can't leave Zack. He's the greatest friend I've ever had."

He slowly stepped into the living room, "I'm always going to be here for you." She turned and looked at him. He walked to her and knelt down, handing her a small box. "I always wanted to give you this, so you will always know that I love you, that I was your first true love, and that you meant something to me."

Gwen opened the box. It was the heart necklace he'd seen when he bought her the horseshoe charm for Valentine's Day. "OH MY GOD! It's beautiful!" She reached over and hugged Zack, kissing him all over his face.

"You have this as a daily reminder of us. Look closely." Zack had GF + ZK inscribed on the back of the heart.

"I will wear this every day, along with my horseshoe necklace. This means so much to me."

As they made their way to the car, she turned to him and said, "Honey, listen, I wanted to give you this." She handed Zack a sealed card. "You can't open it until you are out of Lexington, on your way to school. I wanted to say a few things to you. It's in here."

Dr. Farris locked the front door behind him, ready to start their trip north. He hugged Zack, "good luck at Ole Miss!"

"Thank you, Dr. Farris."

Then Jenny embraced Zack, "we're so proud of you."

"I'll miss you, Jenny!" Zack said.

Gwen's parents got into the car and Zack stepped over while he and Gwen placed their foreheads together, both in tears. "Remember, the hurt is our love, our deep affection for each other," he said, pulling her in tightly.

"I love you, my dear friend," she said. The two allowed themselves one last long kiss.

Zack put his hand up to her face, brushing her hair aside, "I so love you, Gwen Farris." He helped her into the back seat and closed the door. "You do well at Bryn Mawr! Fly away, my little cardinal!" He turned and walked away as the station wagon pulled out of the driveway. Zack watched it disappear at the end of the street, climbed into his car and placed the card on the dashboard. *God, please protect her. She's so precious.* Zack then realized Gwen was really gone now, but he felt her heart was still with him.

Later in the morning, Zackary went through several undershirts that Mrs. Dupree had folded and placed on his bed. He noticed several were size XXL. "These are Daddy's." Zack walked across the hall to his father's bedroom. He opened the top drawer of his dresser, which contained underwear, another drawer was full of socks. Zack opened the bottom drawer, seeing his father's undershirts neatly folded. Zack began putting the shirts into the drawer, but it was tight. He moved items to try to make more room and saw a pair of pajamas at the bottom of the drawer, which covered up some magazines. Zack pulled one out and suddenly could not breathe. Covering his mouth, Zack saw that it was one of five or six magazines filled with photos of naked men having sex. They had not come from Zack's drawer. After flipping through a few magazines, he gazed up at a picture of his dad on the wall. He was feeling shocked but also sadness and love for his father. He stayed there kneeling on the carpeting for several minutes, trying to process it all, then placed the magazine back exactly as he'd found it, carefully buttoning the camouflaging pajamas. He looked back up at his father's picture with tears falling. *Oh my God, he's like me… or I'm like him… He's been trying to protect me.* Zack closed the drawer, took the stack of undershirts, and neatly placed them on his father's bed, then walked back to his room.

Chapter Fifty-Three

Zack was filling up his car with boxes and suitcases when the Cadillac pulled up. Pop got out of his car, repositioning his toothpick, "how's the packing going, son?"

"All good, Pop," he smiled gently, staring at his father. Pop came up beside him and put his arm around him. Zack leaned in and hugged him tightly, "I love you so much!"

He hugged Zackary back, "I love you, too, son. Now go up and get ready for dinner. And put on a tie."

It was only a few minutes past four and the two Kingdons were the only ones in the restaurant. Pop stared at Zack, appearing sad. "Are you all right, Pop?"

He nodded, taking a sip of his iced tea, "now, you call your daddy once you arrive in Oxford. You call me if you ever need me. But call me every Sunday." Zack smiled, reached his hand across the table to his father, who squeezed his hand tightly. "I'm proud of you, son. You're such a good boy."

Zack thought about when he was about five, and his mother was in the hospital, and Pop took him to the dentist. Pop was not used to tending to the needs of a young child. He and his father were standing at a corner in downtown Lexington waiting for the pedestrian light to change. He held his hand out, but his father did not take it, so Zack just reached up and clutched his father's fingers. "What the hell are you doing, son?" Pop had asked.

"Mommy always holds my hand when we cross the street. Daddy, I need you to hold my hand, too." Pop began holding Zack's hand from that point on.

Zack kept smiling at his father with great affection and empathy as he ate his dinner that afternoon. *He's had to hide who he is his entire life from himself, Mommy, and me. God, he must be in pain. I will always love him.*

After he got home from dinner, Zack went and met up with Fred Mills and some of his other Kentucky Theatre friends and went to the Bar for a goodbye send-off. Zack spent several minutes laughing and dancing with Caroleen, Bryan, and Fred, who loved to dance.

"Listen, I can't stay too much longer. I get too emotional knowing you're leaving," Fred said.

"Fred, I want to thank you for all you've done for me. I can't wait to see you when I get home for Christmas." Suddenly, "I Love the Nightlife" began playing.

"This is my song," Fred yelled. "Come on, you two." He pulled Zack and Bryan onto the floor as it filled up. Zack laughed, trying to disco dance, remembering when he and Matt boogied in junior high to the soundtrack from *Saturday Night Fever*. As Zack was dancing, he suddenly felt such a sense of relief. After all the pain he had endured the past year, his body allowed him to feel a sense of euphoria, breathing in a free and easy way. He was beginning his own identity as a young man. Fred reached in and hugged Zack at the end of the song, crying. "I have to go. Good luck to you. I love you, Zackary," he said, kissing Zack on the lips. "You're a special man!"

Zack hugged him, "thank you for everything, Fred. I will miss you. I promise to write."

While the rest of the group stood and talked, Zack noticed a tall, familiar-looking man at the other end of the bar with a few others, and he was staring at him while smoking a cigarette. Zack froze, holding his gaze. They started leaving, and he began walking towards where Zack was standing. Given the darkness and strobing lights, Zack initially had difficulty making out the man's face. Then just as he passed, Zack was suddenly motionless. *Oh my God. It's him. I don't think he recognized me.* In that brief minute, Zack stood slightly stunned, aware that Tom, one of his rapists, was walking right past him. But Zack wasn't scared. He was furious, thinking how he and that other monster had destroyed his innocence, nearly killing him. *But I'm leaving Lexington. He'll just always be a little man in the background of some small, dark dive bar.*

Zack tried to shrug off his anger. This was his night. As he turned around, the three of them went and danced to one more song. As it ended, they made their way outside, where Caroleen kissed Zack, then he and Bryan hugged. "Stay in touch, honey. We'll miss you!" she said.

Once he was home, Zack went upstairs, showered, and put on his pajamas. He walked into Pop's room and quietly sat on the floor beside the bed. His father reached down and began rubbing the back of his head. Zack held his father's hand tight while staring ahead at the television. Tears fell down Zack's face as he glanced over at the dresser, imagining the pain his father had endured.

Chapter Fifty-Four

Hearing a knock at his door, Zack opened his eyes to the ceiling he'd woken up to and stared at for the past six years. He turned to his clock. It was six-oh-seven. "I'm coming, Daddy," called out thinking about how much his life was about to change. He wondered how Gwen was doing. Then Jeremiah came into his head. Both images brought him bittersweet feelings. Zack pushed the covers back and the chill of the perpetually cold house propelled him into a hot shower. After he got dressed, Zack looked in the corner and saw his briefcase on the floor next to his desk. *The briefcase will be here for me to use when I graduate.* He stared back at his bedroom, then took his duffle bag with him down the steps.

"I got the paper, son. Guess I have to do that myself now."

"Good morning, Pop," Zack muttered, pouring coffee. After he tested his blood sugar, Zack wrote down the results.

"Son, that book is filled with pages of detailed notes and numbers. You're a born accountant."

Zack glanced at his father, smiling, "I sure hope so, sir."

As he injected the insulin, he viewed his father completely differently.

"I deposited all your money in your First Security account."

After applying the Band-Aid, Zack kissed his father on the forehead and then wrapped his arms around him, "thank you, I love you. I'm going to miss you."

Pop hugged Zack back, "come on, son, get your breakfast. You have a long drive." Zack let go of his dad. The two then sat quietly as Pop went through the paper. "I hired a landscaper to take care of the yard. The place will probably start looking nice for a change."

Zack laughed, "You didn't just say that." Pop smiled, his toothpick pointed towards the ceiling. "I'm going to miss this place," Zack said.

Pop put the paper down and stared out the kitchen window, "son, you are about to meet a lot of interesting people in college. At the end of the day, you will realize, as I did, there is no place in the world as beautiful as the place you're from. Your home. Kentucky is the most beautiful place, and I bet you never realized this, did you?" Zack smiled and shook his head. "Your home never leaves you. Kentucky will always be here for you," Pop said. "'Miss-sippi is full of kudzu vines."

"What's that, Pop?" Zack asked, finishing his coffee.

"Oh, you'll see when you get down there."

Zack got up from the table and washed his dish, took the hot water off the stove, and made his hot tea for the drive, "I guess it's time, Daddy."

Pop opened the kitchen door for Zack, who stepped out and walked over to his car, shoving the duffle bag into an already crowded trunk. Pop just stood there with an incredibly sad face. Zack walked up to his dad and hugged him tightly, crying, "thank you for being such a good father, for protecting me, for loving me."

"You call me the moment you get there. I'm going to be by the phone. You know you'll be an hour behind Kentucky time. Now you drive safely. Keep out of those truck lanes. Pull over at a rest stop if you get tired." Zack kissed his father on the cheek. "Your daddy loves you."

"Now, Pop, watch the sweets."

His father stood in place as he got into his car and started the engine. "Son, you do well in school!"

Zack poked his head out of the window, "I will, sir. I promise!"

Once he pulled out, Zack stared down the driveway. His father had a handkerchief covering his face. Zack then began to roll away, waving at his father, who began walking to the front of the house. *Take care of him, God. I love him so much.* After composing himself, Zack realized he had never seen his father cry. As he looked at all of Lexington's familiar homes and streets, Zack imagined that the world he was about to enter would be very unfamiliar. Making his way onto Versailles Road, Zack glanced to his right, seeing the gorgeous horses on the rolling hills of Calumet Farm, which still had deep green grass, even for August. He passed the airport to his left and Keeneland horse racing track to his right. Minutes later, he saw a sign for the Bluegrass Parkway a few miles down the road.

Driving onto the "Bluegrass Turnpike," as Pop called it, Zack noticed there wasn't much traffic. He kept the music off and briefly opened his window to breathe in the fresh air. It wouldn't last long, as another hot, humid Kentucky summer day began to cook. He rolled his window back up and turned on the air conditioning. Zackary had so many different thoughts running through his head. After driving for over an hour, signs appeared for a tollbooth about two miles away. This was where Zack would get on I-65 South to Nashville. Suddenly, rain began hitting the windshield, and the drops quickly turned larger, hitting faster and becoming a blinding downpour. Zack slowed down and stopped the car on the side of the road. Parked, he could barely see anything as water pummeled the windows. He glanced at the map on the passenger seat and then noticed Gwen's card sitting next to it. He picked it up. *I'm out of Lexington, so I can read it now.* The storm worsened. A loud crack of thunder sounded in the distance. Zack opened the envelope and inside was a card with a picture of a beautiful sunflower on it.

My Dearest Zackary,

You are now outside of our hometown, standing in front of the wilderness of your life. I picked this card out for you. You love flowers—and sunflowers represent sun, happiness, and joy—all things you represent. I pray all the best comes your way in Mississippi, and I will write you weekly (and you had better write back!). I cannot wait to see you at Christmas. Zacky, you made me believe in myself, helped me become a woman, and made me feel so loved, as you have been the kindest person I have ever known. Remember, we will always have Kentucky! That's where we will always be in my mind. Zackary, you have many special gifts—now use them.

Always know—you are my mezzanine love.

Love forever, Your Gwyneth

"God, I love her," he said, bursting into tears. Zack took his handkerchief and wiped his face as the rain began to taper off. *I'm going to be fine. I can do this.* As the sun reappeared, he turned his wipers off. He could see the tollbooth down the highway in front of him, which was the end of the turnpike. Zack put the card down, placed the car into drive, and began moving forward. Fumbling with change, Zack paused long enough at the tollbooth to toss the coins into the basket and put on his right blinker. Looking in the rearview mirror, Zack quickly straightened his cowlick, then noticed a beautiful rainbow appearing behind him. He veered to the right and exited the Bluegrass Turnpike onto Interstate 65 South.

Acknowledgments

The process of marinating the concept of Exiting the Bluegrass Turnpike took several years—just to conceptualize the narrative. One of my dearest friends, my nutritionist, Sheryl Moller, helped me realize that I needed to tell this story through the eyes of "Zackary Kingdon." I have learned so much from you and appreciate your love and kindness. Sheryl introduced me to David Cassion and Virginia King of Kevin Anderson Writing & Associates. A former book editor with a big five house, David helped me organize the story, strengthen the narrative, and coached me while I wrote this book; he is a tough and honest editor, for which I am grateful. And then I met Erin Chandler at Rabbit House Press in Versailles, Kentucky. Erin and her amazing team, Brooke Lee (amazing cover art), Emily Wilhoit, and Kristen Minter, have given this book the extra help it needed, and I am forever grateful. I want to mention Michael Goldstein, who introduced me to Carolyn Schurr Levin, my intellectual property attorney who assisted me. Thank you both. Several beta readers gave me tremendous feedback and support, including Lori Seto, Rosanne Sonatore, Ann Young, Teresa Danile, Bryan Taulbee, Niall Hegarty, Jon Corcoran, Mark Daniel Compton, Victoria Shoaf, Michael Roggow, Susan McCall, Lina Cajiao-Quiroz, Stacie Musser, Jeri Musserstam, Elda Tsou, Gerald Cusack, Joe Cucci, Fred Mills, Jeff Raby, Ramon Silvestre, Sylvia Clark, Bryan Marsee, Liz Carey, Fran Guastello, Father Patrick Flanagan… I am so thankful to each of you for helping me make this a better book. In addition, I want to especially thank Ken Howard, LCSW, CST of Los Angeles for your professional guidance on this book, particularly in helping me in coping with and properly describing the effects of being a trauma survivor through Zackary's eyes. Also, I could never have attempted this had I not had Frank Hernandez, my loving husband, in my life. Frank's love since we first met in March 2000, has changed me as a person. Like "Gwen Farris," you are my bashert. In my life,

I have had the privilege of working in some fine organizations, and now at St. John's University. I want to especially thank my colleagues who supported me while I was working on this book. However, in my long career, the most enjoyable and fulfilling job I ever had was working for Fred Mills at the Kentucky Theatre. When I was eighteen year old, Fred lovingly helped me become less afraid and to find inner acceptance of myself as a gay kid. To this day, he is someone who will always be a special part of my family. And to the woman for whom the "Gwen Farris" character is based, you know—and I know—how much I dearly and deeply love you, my true "mezzanine love."